HIDDEN
Affections

Books by

Delia Parr

Hearts Awakening
Love's First Bloom
Hidden Affections

HIDDEN
Affections

DELIA PARR

BETHANY HOUSE PUBLISHERS
Minneapolis, Minnesota

Published by Bethany House Publishers
11400 Hampshire Avenue South
Bloomington, Minnesota 55438

Bethany House Publishers is a division of
Baker Publishing Group, Grand Rapids, Michigan.

Printed in the United States of America

Library of Congress Cataloging-in-Publication Data

Parr, Delia.
    Hidden affections / Delia Parr.
        p.   cm.
    ISBN 978-0-7642-0672-6 (pbk.) 1. Divorced women—Fiction. 2. Forced marriage—Fiction. 3. Philadelphia (Pa.)—History—19th century—Fiction. I. Title.
    PS3566.A7527H53   2011
    813'.54—dc22

                                                                    2011002920

Dedicated to

my three beautiful grandbabies.
You fill the world around you
with faith, hope, and love.

Chapter One

❄

Annabelle Tyler may have hoped she would marry again someday, but she never dreamed she would be wearing handcuffs during the ceremony when she did.

Scarcely thirty-six hours after leaving Hanover, Pennsylvania, to forge a respectable future for herself, she barely listened to the man next to her as he grumbled his vows. She was still struggling to make sense of the frightening turn of events that had led her here, to this nondescript minister's cottage in a small rural hamlet where she knew absolutely no one.

Despite the sheriff's coat around her shoulders and the hearty fire burning in the small parlor, Annabelle shivered with cold that had penetrated every bone in her body. She glanced up at the man by her side. Harrison Graymoor had been a complete stranger to her until only yesterday, but the ordeal they had endured together had taken its toll.

His finely tailored vest and cambric shirt were badly soiled with the same dirt and grime that stained her travel gown, and exhaustion had painted dark circles beneath his ebony eyes. His determined fight to prevent this marriage had now been replaced by a resignation that surprised her, since he had far more at stake by marrying than she did. The grim reality that he was being forced into this marriage, however, had erased his rakish smile and the surprisingly deep dimples in his cheeks, but he held his head high when he finally gritted, "I do."

She swayed a bit, locked her knees, and dropped her gaze. She had not eaten since the day before yesterday, and she used every last bit of her waning strength to keep standing on her own two feet, if only to maintain a modicum of dignity in front of the four men who were witnessing this mockery of a ceremony. When she adjusted the heavy coat about her shoulders, she inadvertently yanked the short chain on the metal cuff on her right wrist that kept her linked to Harrison.

She froze instinctively, and his hiss of pain distracted her from the minister's monotone recitation of the vows she was supposed to pledge. When she looked down, she saw a fresh trickle of blood ooze down the back of his hand from beneath the too-small cuff that dug deep into his swollen left wrist. She quickly averted her gaze, but not before she got a glimpse of the end of the rifle barrel nudged against his back. "I didn't mean to hurt you again," she whispered. "I-I'm sorry."

"The proper response is 'I will' or 'I do,' " Reverend Wood admonished, as if she had been speaking to him.

When she turned her attention back to the minister, she wondered if he could see anything more than a few inches in front of his face, since his eyes were so clouded by age.

"I'm still waiting for you to recite your vows and acknowledge them," he demanded, clearly annoyed that he had been dragged from his bed shortly before dawn to marry them.

One of the two men standing directly to her left edged closer in an unspoken warning to cooperate, reinforced as the two men on Harrison's side nudged him closer to her. Determined not to utter any words that would seal her union to Mr. Graymoor, she took a deep breath to gather up the last of her rapidly fading strength. Now that it appeared she had no other choice, she swallowed her pride and decided she had to admit she was not the maiden they believed her to be. "Please. Just let me explain. There's no need to force this man to marry me."

The minister's voice hardened with impatience. "Do you or do you not recognize the scandalous nature of your situation and the attempt we're all making on your behalf to salvage your reputation?" he snapped.

"I'm a God-fearing woman of faith, and I'm telling you that nothing improper happened," she insisted, repeating the claim she had made to the four men when they had rescued her, as well as Harrison, less than an hour ago. "I give you my word."

Harrison cleared his throat. "I'm afraid it's not your word and your character that are in question. It's mine."

She looked up at him and frowned. "That may be, but my future's at stake, too," she quipped before turning her attention back to the minister again and softening her voice. "The men who stopped our stage robbed us, handcuffed us together, and left us tied to the stagecoach while they escaped with the driver and all of our possessions. It's not Mr. Graymoor's fault or mine that it took a full day and night to find us. Mr. Graymoor was a complete gentleman and quite concerned for my well-being the entire time," she insisted, remaining silent about his attempts to flirt with her when they first boarded the stage or the fact that the robbers would never have robbed the stage if he had not been aboard in the first place.

The sheriff snorted. "Harrison Graymoor may be exceedingly wealthy, but he's also a cad and a libertine who needs to be held accountable for his outrageous behavior, particularly with women. His reputation, I assure you, is well-known far beyond Philadelphia, where he resides."

"We're far from Philadelphia, and we should all avoid gossip that no one here can confirm," she argued, but she was also relieved they were a far cry from Four Corners, the small town where she had become equally infamous.

The minister nodded. "I'm retired from active ministry now, but I'm not a hermit. I recognize the family name, as well as this man's reputation," he informed them and looked directly at Annabelle. "The sheriff told me he found you lying in this man's arms after spending the night with him alone. Are you now disputing that fact, or is it true?"

She blushed, although she could not remember exactly how or when she had ended up cuddled against his side during the night. "Yes, it's true," she admitted, "but the weather had turned exceedingly cold again and the thieves had stolen my cloak as well as his coat. Mr. Graymoor eventually freed us from the ropes they used to bind us to the stagecoach, but there was nothing he could do to remove the handcuffs," she explained, still ridden with guilt for injuring Harrison when she tried to do just that. "We tried walking to find help, but a thunderstorm forced us back to the stagecoach for shelter. By then, we were both drenched and—"

"And this wretched man used this poor woman's distress to his sinful advantage." The man directly to her left squared his shoulders and took a step forward. "My name is James Jenkins. One of Graymoor's country estates is near my home in Chad's Landing. My wife, Camille, went to work there when he showed up four months ago, and this man . . . this man . . . seduced her," he murmured, repeating the charges he had made to the sheriff earlier.

"I did no such thing," Harrison argued in a low voice that was just as authoritative as it had been earlier when he'd tried to reason with Jenkins and the sheriff. "I did not seduce Mrs. Jenkins, and I did not seduce Miss Tyler."

"He gave this to my wife," Jenkins charged, pulling an intricate gold bracelet from his pocket and dangling it in front of the minister, who leaned his face so far forward to see it that Annabelle wondered how he kept his balance. "What sort of man gives a *married* woman an expensive gift like this unless he's seduced her?"

The minister pulled back and pursed his lips. "Mr. Graymoor?"

Harrison shrugged. "It was a parting trinket to thank her for her work as a temporary member of my staff. Nothing more."

Jenkins shoved the bracelet back into his pocket. "You gave it to her to assuage your conscience, although I'm surprised you have one," he charged and drew in deep breaths of air as his cheeks reddened with the shame of his wife's betrayal.

"I did not seduce your wife, and she did not betray you. Not with me," Harrison argued.

Sheriff Taylor shook his head and addressed the minister. "I'm afraid Mr. Graymoor's reputation as a womanizer makes it difficult, if not impossible, to take him at his word. Not where women are concerned."

The minister cleared his throat, effectively ending the discussion. "Perhaps if Mr. Graymoor were to be married to a 'God-fearing woman of faith,' " he said firmly, using Annabelle's own words against them both, "she might inspire him to lead a life of honor befitting the name he carries. More importantly, Miss Tyler should not bear the burden of having her reputation or her name sullied—"

"There is no burden," Annabelle argued, tilting up her chin. Although she was weakened by fatigue as well as frustration, she could not overlook the absurdity of the predicament she was in

DELIA PARR

or the fact she was actually handcuffed to the man she was being forced to marry. Handcuffed!

"Even the appearance of impropriety demands that you be protected. If you were a married woman, that would be a matter for Sheriff Taylor to address. You are, however, a single woman, and it is a matter for me to remedy," he insisted and turned to Harrison. "Are you prepared to fulfill the vows you have already pledged or do you rescind them?"

Harrison sighed. "No. I do not rescind them," he murmured and arched his back as if the barrel of the rifle had been pressed harder.

"And you, Miss Tyler, will you accept this man as your lawful husband and be faithful to the vows I've already recited for you?"

She swallowed hard. She was only twenty-four years old. She could hardly believe that all the hopes she had had for the future would be gone once she married this stranger, but she was too disillusioned and too exhausted to argue anymore. Holding tight to her faith in God, if only to give strength to her belief that He was totally in charge of the new path her life was taking, she let out a long sigh and finally uttered the words the minister wanted her to say. "I . . . I will."

"Then as a minister of the Word, I now declare that you are man and wife. Go in peace, together, to serve Him in this world in order to rejoice with Him for all of eternity. Now then, would you like to kiss your bride, Mr. Graymoor?"

Harrison held up the handcuffs that still bound them together. "I believe my wife and I would like these handcuffs removed before I consider anything else," he countered.

When she nodded her agreement, the minister smiled for the first time that morning. "There's a blacksmith not more than a few miles from the inn, which is about five miles farther away," he offered. "Sheriff, I trust you'll deliver Mr. and Mrs. Graymoor there? They're obviously both in need of nourishment as well as rest before they continue their journey."

"I will indeed."

"Then once the marriage certificate is duly signed, you can all be on your way." He walked over to a small table in the corner of the room and signed the paper lying there. One of the men who had helped Sheriff Taylor rescue them signed right after the sheriff, who ordered all three of his companions to go outside to ready the horses.

In turn, the minister motioned Annabelle and Harrison to come to the table. "While you two sign this marriage certificate, I've got to record the marriage in my book, which I've left in the other room. Sheriff, perhaps you could ask one of your men to saddle up my horse for Mr. and Mrs. Graymoor to ride. Joshua Lawrence, down at the inn, will see that it's returned," he said before taking his leave.

As Annabelle and Harrison slowly made their way to the table, she took great care to make certain she did not pull on the chain that bound them together. Under the sheriff's watchful gaze, they each signed the document, and she noted the crooked scrawl the minister had managed to write.

"Wait here. I'll be back to get you both as soon as we have your horse ready," the sheriff ordered before he left them alone for the first time since they had been rescued.

Once the ink dried, she folded the certificate, planning to add it to the few things she had been able to hide from the thieves by storing them in a cotton pouch she had pinned to her chemise. She also pressed her arm to her side to make certain the knitting stick she had convinced the thieves to let her keep was still at her waist. "There was no need for you to be saddled with me as your wife. Why didn't you argue with those men more?" she whispered.

"I seem to recall having the barrel of a rifle planted in the small of my back, in case you didn't notice," he replied. But there was just a hint of that twinkle back in his eyes as he snatched the certificate out of her hand and stored it beneath his vest.

"But we didn't do anything wrong. I mean . . . you didn't . . . we didn't . . ." Unable to put such a delicate matter into words, she dropped her gaze and hoped her cheeks were not as red as she feared they were.

"No, we didn't. Your virtue is intact, which is another reason why I didn't need to waste precious time arguing with men who weren't prepared to listen to anything either one of us had to say. Once we get these handcuffs removed, get something to eat and some well-deserved rest, we'll travel straight to Philadelphia, where I can have this marriage annulled."

"You're certain we should arrive within a day or two?"

He nodded. "You won't miss that appointment of yours," he promised, and she was pleased that he recognized how important it was for her to arrive before the deadline. "When I meet with my lawyer to get the annulment proceedings started, I'll also have him draw up a settlement for you."

Annabelle shook her head. "That won't be necessary."

"I rather think it is," he argued. "At the very least, you'll need to replace what the thieves stole from you, which I assure you I can easily afford to do." He smiled when she nodded reluctantly.

"Are you absolutely certain there won't be a problem obtaining a quick annulment?"

He shrugged. "Since our marriage never has and never will be consummated, I should expect it will be rather easy to obtain within a month or so," he said, using an authoritative tone that invited no argument from her. "Granted, it may be a bit awkward for both of us for a while, but the annulment should be granted so quickly, no one need ever learn we were married at all."

"There are more than a few people who already know we're married, and Reverend Wood is recording it in his book as we speak," she reminded him, worried that he was either overconfident or merely accustomed to getting what he wanted because of his immense wealth that everyone else had mentioned.

"We'll never see any of these people again. Even if their gossip spreads to the city, I've learned that rumors quickly disappear when no proof emerges," he countered. "Don't worry. I'm absolutely certain I can have our marriage annulled. When I do, it will be as if it never existed at all, legally speaking," he said as he led her closer to the fire to share one last bit of warmth before they ventured outside again into the freezing cold that had blanketed the area for most of November. "If all else fails, of course, I can always petition for a divorce, which will be a first for anyone in my family."

A chill raced up the length of her spine, and she trembled. "I'm afraid it won't be the first time. Not for me," she whispered so softly she barely heard her own words.

At least this time she knew the man she had married was a womanizer before they were wed.

Chapter Two

❄

For half a heartbeat, Annabelle feared that the young blacksmith would refuse to remove the handcuffs, even though Sheriff Taylor had given his assurances that there was no legal reason the newly married couple had been handcuffed together in the first place.

Once the sheriff left to make arrangements for them to stay at the inn, Matthew Owens reluctantly started to perform the task, but only after she had added a plea of her own. Holding a chisel in one hand and a mallet of some sort in the other, he looked directly at Harrison. "Are you quite certain you want these handcuffs removed, sir? Might be a good way to keep an eye on this new wife of yours. I'd be willing to bet my finest horse that your missus will be quite a looker. Once she's cleaned up, that is," he teased.

Annabelle blew away a wisp of blond hair that had fallen across her face, along with the man's audacious compliment, and glared at him, hoping Harrison would say something to the impudent young man to defend her honor. With her wavy hair in disarray and her travel gown carrying enough dirt and grime to double its weight, she did not need anyone to remind her how bad she looked at the moment. In point of fact, she could scarcely imagine that a full month of hot baths would even thaw out her bones, let alone get her clean again.

Much to her relief, Harrison snorted his displeasure. "Your cavalier comment about my wife is both unwarranted and unwelcome," he said firmly.

"I-I'm sorry, ma'am. I . . . I meant no disrespect, sir," Owens stammered.

Harrison lifted up his left wrist, forcing her to lift her arm as well, and laid the chain links in the center of the anvil that stood between them and the blacksmith. He tugged back the cuff on his shirt to reveal the narrow U-shaped metal band, held in place by a metal pin with a lock at one end, that was far too small for his wrist. "I should hope that if common sense does not dictate your full cooperation, this nasty wound will be reason enough to comply with our very simple request. Now unless the sheriff made a mistake in thinking you'd be willing to help us, I suggest you break these cuffs apart and remove them. Immediately," he ordered.

"Y-yes sir. Right away. I'm not quite certain if I can remove them, but I can separate the links in the chain easily enough," he said as he carefully arranged and rearranged the three links lying on the anvil. When he was apparently satisfied, he looked up at both of them. "Just . . . just hold very still. And keep the chain lax," he urged, forcing Annabelle and Harrison to step closer together before he started working on breaking one of the links in the chain.

Annabelle turned her head to avoid seeing what would happen if he missed his mark and flinched when he struck each blow to the links. Although it was merely uncomfortable for her to feel the vibrations absorbed by the metal cuff around her wrist, she could only imagine how painful it must have been for Harrison.

"There. You're separated, once and for all," he announced,

placing his tools back onto a small table he had moved next to the anvil.

"Hardly," Annabelle quipped as she flexed her wrist. She had no idea exactly how long it would take before an annulment legally freed her from the man whose name she reluctantly carried, but she held on to his promise that it would only be a matter of a month or two. Satisfied that the narrow band of metal around her wrist had done nothing more than chafe at her flesh a bit, she felt a pang of true regret when she saw Harrison step away from her and cradle his wrist in the palm of his other hand.

The young blacksmith looked directly at Harrison. "The cuffs themselves are next. Ladies first?"

When Harrison nodded, Owens wiped the anvil with the tip of his apron. "If you could rest your wrist here, ma'am, I'd like to take a look at the lock before I try to bust it."

She complied and watched closely as he turned the U-shaped band until the pin was perpendicular to the anvil and the lock itself was facing up toward the beams in the ceiling.

Her optimism faded when he shook his head. "Are you absolutely certain that neither one of you has the key?"

She glared at him.

So did Harrison.

"Hold the lock exactly where it is," he suggested before walking off.

"Wait! Where are you going? You can't leave now!" she cried, tempted to stomp her foot in frustration.

He waved back at her over his shoulder. "I'll be back in a minute."

Harrison sighed. "While he's gone, perhaps you can help me do something," he murmured, his voice as husky and deep as when they had first met aboard the stage.

Was the man actually flirting with her? Again? She dropped her gaze. "What do you want me to do?" she grumbled.

Still cradling his wrist, he moved beside her and nodded toward his chest. "There's a handkerchief in my vest pocket. I'd be obliged if you'd remove it for me. Once Owens removes the cuff from my wrist, I'll need it to wrap the wound to stem the bleeding."

Harrison was not an uncommonly tall man, but compared to her own small stature, he seemed very tall indeed. Avoiding his gaze, Annabelle reached into the very same pocket where he had kept the pocket watch the thieves had stolen. When her fingertips brushed against his chest, her heartbeat quickened, but she dismissed her reaction to him as merely a consequence of her utter fatigue.

After tugging the monogrammed linen handkerchief free, she took a step back and handed it out to him. "It looks clean enough, I suppose."

He looked down at his injured wrist and shook his head. "Since I don't have a free hand at the moment, perhaps you should keep that handkerchief for me until I need it."

Moistening her lips, she tucked the handkerchief beneath the wooden knitting stick still safely secured to the narrow band of fabric at her waist. Although all of the knitting needles she usually kept stored in the sheath were now gone, including the one she had bent trying to pick at the lock on the handcuffs, she could one day replace them.

The knitting stick itself, however, was priceless, if only to her. With the tip of her fingers, she traced each of the letters of her mother's name that her father had carved into the sheath of wood when he made this courtship gift for her. Annabelle was deeply grateful she had been able to convince the thieves to let her keep it.

When Owens abruptly returned to the shop a solid five minutes after he had left, reality quickly consumed the memory of her late parents. She dropped her hand away, placed her wrist back onto the anvil, and made certain the lock was back in place exactly where it had been when the blacksmith left.

"Ready?" Owens asked as he placed several tools onto the table next to the broken chain.

She rolled her eyes.

While holding the pin steady with one hand, he lifted her wrist until there was a small gap between the U-shaped metal band and her flesh. "Hold it right there," he murmured and slid a narrow wad of muslin between the metal and her wrist. "That should help absorb some of the blows I have to make to break the lock, but I'm afraid—"

"Just get the cuff off," she insisted and used her other hand to hold her arm steady. She closed her eyes and braced herself. If he was going to end up smashing her wrist, she had no desire to watch him. To her surprise, Harrison stepped closer to her, as if offering his presence as support.

"Seems a shame to ruin a fine pair of Darby cuffs. I've only seen one other pair. They're rather rare," he explained as he started tapping at the lock.

Harrison huffed. "Apparently not rare enough if common thieves can acquire them and use them for nefarious purposes."

"The thieves were hardly common. Not if they deliberately chose to target you," she quipped, still annoyed that he had chosen to ride the very stage on which she had also been a passenger after his private coach had broken an axle.

"How kind of you to remind me. Then again, you seem to have a penchant for reminding me rather often that this whole affair is my fault," he retorted. "If the thieves were that smart, they would have brought along a pair of handcuffs that would have actually fit me properly."

"Actually, Darby cuffs are made in four or five sizes," Owens interjected. "But if they'd used one to fit you, sir, your wife could have slipped her wrist right through. Then again, the cuffs are rare enough that they probably only used what they could get their hands on."

Harrison scowled at him.

"You would have fared better if you hadn't fought the thieves when they tried to put them on or made such a vigorous attempt to remove them later, which only made your wrist swell even more," she offered.

He frowned at her.

"Actually, it's nearly impossible to remove these cuffs without a key. Or some good tools like mine," Owens added proudly.

"Just do your best to remove the cuff. Quickly," she urged before Harrison could remind her that she had been foolish to think she could have used one of her knitting needles to force the lock to open.

Many long, nerve-racking taps later, she heard the lock at the end of the pin pop free and she opened her eyes. Amazed by how efficiently he had completed his task, she watched as the blacksmith slid the pin free before he eased the metal band away from her wrist. "Thank you," she murmured as she rubbed at the skin that had been chafed by the metal.

He grinned at her before giving Harrison a nod.

Annabelle forced herself to watch as her companion placed his cuffed wrist onto the anvil and cringed. The flesh around the metal band was scarlet now and even more badly swollen. Apparently, the simple process of removing the chain holding both cuffs together had reopened the wound and fresh blood trickled down onto the metal anvil.

Owens studied the cuff for a moment and shook his head. Swallowing hard, he paled. "I . . . I don't think I can cushion the blows at all for you, sir, but if you could just turn your wrist—"

"Just do what you have to do," Harrison gritted.

"Wait. Just a moment," Annabelle insisted and stepped around him to snatch the muslin that Owens had used earlier to cushion her wrist from the table where he had tossed it. "Have you any more muslin I could use to make a bandage?"

"I might be able to find more in the house. Might take a few minutes to find it."

"Make do with what you have," Harrison demanded.

"Perhaps for now we could," she replied, knowing how badly he wanted to be free from the restraint. As she returned to her place, she slipped his handkerchief free, ready to use both the muslin and the handkerchief as a makeshift bandage, if necessary.

Instead of watching Owens or closing her eyes this time, she kept her gaze squarely on Harrison's face. With each tap on the lock, he paled and tightened his jaw, but he stared directly down at the anvil and made no effort to halt what must have been an exceedingly painful process. His eyes flashed with relief when the lock finally popped free, but he quickly shuttered his gaze and reached forward.

She tensed and watched in horrified fascination as he pulled the metal band free from his swollen flesh. Without hesitation, she pressed the muslin against his wrist and quickly bound it against the wound with his handkerchief. "Is there a doctor nearby?" she asked the blacksmith.

"Doc Marley is—"

"The inn. How far is the inn?" Harrison asked, using the authoritative voice that told Annabelle not to interfere.

Owens looked from Annabelle to Harrison. "About five miles. Straight down the road, sir, but Doc Marley is—"

"How much for your services?" Harrison asked as he scooped up the pieces of the handcuffs and shoved them into his trousers pocket.

"Since you were robbed, and I really don't expect—"

"How much for your services?"

"If I could keep the handcuffs, I'd be willing to call it even," he replied sheepishly.

Harrison cocked a brow. "Need I repeat myself yet again?"

Owens blushed. "Fifty cents."

Harrison bent down, undid the strap lying across his boot, and secured a coin from a hidden pouch before fastening the strap again.

When he put the coin on the table, Owens's eyes widened. "That's ten times what you owe me. I haven't got enough coin to give you change."

"You've earned every cent. Thank you," he murmured, then placed his hand at Annabelle's back and urged her to the door.

Flabbergasted that he had any coin at all, she leaned toward him. "I thought the robbers took everything," she whispered, painfully aware the thieves had taken every coin she had hidden in the bottom of her knitting bag, which they had also stolen.

He managed half a grin. "Not everything. I travel frequently, and I'm always prepared for the unexpected."

"This whole sorry affair qualifies as a bit more than 'the unexpected,' " she offered. "Why didn't you just let the man have those horrid handcuffs and save your coin to pay for lodging at the inn?"

He paused and glanced down at the knitting stick she wore at her waist. "I have more coin. Besides, you have your little treasure. Would you deny me mine?"

She covered the wooden heirloom with her fingertips and sniffed. "I hardly think those handcuffs should be considered a treasure, especially now that they've been reduced to nothing more than pieces of metal. I don't suppose you'd care to tell me why you want them, would you?"

His eyes sparkled. "Not unless you'll tell me why that rather ordinary hunk of wood you fought so hard to keep from the thieves is so important to you."

She shook her head, convinced a man of his wealth and reputation would never understand the sentiments her father's courtship gift to her mother represented.

He cocked a brow. "In that case, I'll just let my reasons remain secret."

"Fine. You keep your secret and I'll keep mine," she retorted, determined to keep a far more important secret to herself, as well.

Chapter Three

❄

Even though the handcuffs had been removed, traveling five miles by horseback with only a thin cambric shirt to protect Harrison from the rapidly falling temperature would have been challenge enough. Riding on a single horse with a brand-new wife he had no intention of keeping, however, made the journey the most difficult test of endurance he had ever encountered in all of his twenty-nine years.

Or so he thought. Convincing this obstinate innkeeper he needed separate accommodations instead of a single room was proving to be an even greater challenge. He had little patience left to waste arguing.

He ignored Annabelle, who stood next to him, shivering from the cold that had taken up permanent residence in his own bones, and spoke directly to the innkeeper with a softer tone of voice. "Perhaps I didn't make myself clear, Mr. Lawrence," he said and dropped the last of his coins into the man's fleshy palm—money enough to pay for a month's stay. "I need a room with a hot fire, a hot bath, and a hot meal for myself. I need another room with a hot fire, a hot bath, and a hot meal for this young lady. Two rooms. That's all I need."

The balding man dropped the coins into his apron pocket and shrugged. "I'd like to accommodate you, but the common room upstairs that most travelers find quite comfortable has no hearth to provide any heat at all. Even if it did, during last week's storm, the roof leaked pretty bad, and I haven't been up to fixing it yet."

"But surely you can—"

"Like I said before, I've only got one room available for you, and it's on the first floor, right next to the kitchen. I promised Sheriff Taylor I'd have that room ready for you and your new bride, Mr. Graymoor, and I do." Leaning closer, he lowered his voice to a whisper. "My wife ain't as young as she used to be, and she can't climb steps so good anymore either, so it's probably best if you stay close to the kitchen so she can help see to your needs."

Annabelle glanced at Harrison and frowned. "It appears you'll have to add another name or two to that list of people who know about our marriage. Please do something about securing a separate room for me. Anything. Please," she urged, apparently as anxious as he was to avoid sharing the same room.

He bristled. Although it was a toss-up as to whether he was more aggravated by the fact that the innkeeper knew his name or that Sheriff Taylor had also told the man about Harrison and Annabelle's marriage, he decided he was most annoyed with this woman for reminding him, yet again, that keeping their marriage secret might not be as easy as he had originally thought.

Sleeping in the common room without any heat was starting to sound rather appealing, but he determined he'd try one last time to convince Lawrence there had to be a way to provide him with a room he did not have to share with his new wife.

Wife. Harrison shook his head. He had trouble accepting the idea he had a wife at all, so contrary was the very word to his confirmed stance against marriage. But he calmed his agitation with the realization that she would not be his wife for very long.

Just then a rotund woman hobbled her way over to them, drying her hands on her soiled apron as she approached. "You must be the Graymoors. Just look at you, poor dear thing," she crooned, putting her arm around Annabelle's shoulders. She turned her toward the large dining area, which was nearly deserted at mid-morning, except for three elderly women sitting at a table near the fire blazing in the hearth.

"You're such a tiny thing it's a wonder you didn't freeze to death, riding around in this cold without a proper cape to keep you warm. Come along," she insisted. "I've got a good fire going in your room, and I'll have hot water for your bath right quick."

As the woman ushered her away, Annabelle looked back at him over her shoulder, a look of pure panic etched in her features. She mouthed, *Do something*.

Obviously, she was just as unhappy about sharing a room, so Harrison made one final effort to secure separate rooms for them. "I don't mean to be indelicate, but after the ordeal that my wife has experienced, she needs—"

"What that poor woman needs is a man who will stand by and protect her reputation," Lawrence said as his gaze hardened. "The sheriff told me how you took advantage of that sweet, lovely woman, so don't bother denying it. I'd have no objection if you took a seat over there by the fire, as I expect your wife would like a bit of time alone before you join her. I'll bring you something hot to eat and drink while you're waiting." He turned and walked away.

Harrison tightened his jaw. He was sorely tempted to turn around himself, get out of this inn, and ride straight back to Philadelphia, leaving that "sweet, lovely woman" right here. Unfortunately, the horse they had borrowed from Reverend Wood was so old, he doubted the animal would even make it back to its owner without a full day of rest first.

He shifted his weight to take the pressure off the wound in his thigh he had gotten as a result of Annabelle's attempt to force the lock on the handcuffs—but winced when he flexed his left wrist. In his current state, he doubted he could manage to ride that far even if he had a strong horse. The way the temperature was continuing to drop, he would likely freeze to death along the way.

Resigned yet again to circumstances well beyond his control, he glanced beyond the three women still chatting together to the table sitting directly in front of the fire. Exhaustion, cold, and hunger overruled caution, and he limped his way past the trio, offering only a smile and a quick nod to acknowledge them. Judging by their country style of dress and their conversation, he had no fear they were women traveling to or from Philadelphia, at least not in the same social circle he enjoyed.

He eased down on a bench positioned near the fire and rested his bandaged wrist on his lap, grateful for the opportunity to rest. While he avoided putting any pressure on the wound that encircled his wrist, he slid his knees beneath the planked table to hide the bloodstains on his trousers.

The fire quickly did its job of thawing him out. Unfortunately, the warmer he became, the more exhausted he felt and the more his wounds throbbed. But the warmth also helped him to think beyond mere survival, which was a greater blessing.

"Blessing," he murmured and shook his head. There was not a single blessing to be found in this whole wretched affair, but he was not surprised. He could not recall a single instance in the past twenty-odd years when God had shown that He really cared about him—which made it quite easy to rely on his own wits, instead of the faith he had been raised to claim.

e~

Two hours later Harrison had a full stomach, but he was barely able to follow Mrs. Lawrence and limp into his room for want of sleep—deep, healing sleep that would give him some respite from the constant pain in his wrist and thigh. Once he was inside the room, he was relieved to see that Annabelle was already slumbering, but he gave up any hope that the innkeeper's wife would quickly take her leave when she closed the door behind them and pressed a finger to her lips.

"I've got fresh hot water in the tub for you, and I set some bandages out right next to the towels, just like your wife asked me to do. Just be very, very quiet. And don't you dare wake your wife. You've done quite enough to her already," she admonished.

The accusatory look in her eyes and the tone of her voice made it perfectly clear that she expected him to refrain from exercising his husbandly rights, even before she hobbled her way to the door, turned, and shook her finger at him. "That poor thing needs her rest," she added before easing the door closed behind her, completely unaware that he had no intention of sharing the marriage bed with the woman sleeping just a few feet away from him. Or any other woman, for that matter.

As he tiptoed several steps to the tub, which was on the floor on the far side of the small room between the bed and the fire blazing in the hearth, he studied the only woman who would ever carry his name. The matted blond hair that had framed her face now lay in shimmering waves on the pillow. Beneath her closed eyes, which he remembered as being a pale shade of green, dark shadows testified to her total exhaustion. Her cheeks were chafed pink from being exposed to the harsh winter elements for too long and marred the porcelain complexion he recalled as flawless when he had first met her upon boarding the stage in Hanover.

A huge mound of blankets and quilts concealed her lean, diminutive form, but he had already been surprised by the womanly curves he had inadvertently discovered last night when she had turned to him in her sleep and he had held her close to his side to keep them both warm.

"Sad to say, that wasn't the first mistake I made during this regrettable trip," he muttered, but blamed the subtle scent of summer roses she had worn for distracting him from using his common sense. He closed his mind before he replayed the entire fiasco that had begun by his paying far too much attention to Camille Jenkins while staying at his country estate.

In all truth, when it came to women, he did not discriminate. Short or tall, raven-haired or blond, single or married, he found them all equally fascinating and enjoyed flirting with them. When pressed, however, he did have to admit to a particular fondness for dark-haired, voluptuous women—women exactly like Camille.

Vowing to confine his interests to single women in the future, he eased out of his vest and shirt. He tossed them both to the floor in disgust. The only person he could rightfully blame for ending up in this mess was himself. If he had not fallen asleep holding Annabelle, placing them both in a very compromising position, he would have heard the sheriff and his band of rescuers ride up. There was nothing he could have done, at least at that point, to keep Camille's husband from pressing the sheriff to do something to avenge his wife's honor, but he never expected the sheriff to force him into a marriage he clearly did not want.

Stooping down, he tugged the marriage certificate he had commandeered from Annabelle out of his vest pocket, took the pieces of the handcuffs out of his trousers pocket, and placed everything next to the towels stacked on a small table by the tub. Once he had pulled off his boots, which was no easy task one-handed, he tucked the treasures inside of one of his boots.

"Treasures indeed," he murmured. They were far too important to his plans for an annulment to leave them lying about in full view, and he had no intention of revealing the reason he had kept the handcuffs, either.

The other women he had known who were as young, petite, and fair as Annabelle had been nearly devoid of any intellect, let alone common sense. Annabelle, however, was surprisingly different. She was clearly very bright, and if she gave it any thought, she should be able to figure out the reason he wanted to keep the handcuffs.

He could not prove he had had a rifle pressed at his back at Reverend Wood's, but the handcuffs were hard evidence that they had both been coerced into marriage, even if the scar he knew he would carry on his wrist did not suffice.

Since Annabelle had been as opposed to the marriage as he had been, he had no fear she might be attracted by his wealth and tempt him to consummate the union. He had successfully eluded women far more determined to marry him than this one to avoid the heartache and grief that marriage eventually would bring into his life. He was equally confident that his very competent, very expensive lawyer would be able to arrange for a quiet annulment before anyone in Philadelphia heard the faintest bit of gossip that might reach the city.

Satisfied he had regained control of his life, he turned and studied Annabelle for several long minutes. When he was absolutely certain she was in a deep sleep, he attempted to remove his trousers but stopped almost immediately. The blood caked on them had dried so stiffly that he knew he would rip open the hole she had punched into his thigh with one of those knitting needles of hers if he forced off his trousers. Instead, he eased into the tub while still wearing them to let the warm water work through the dried blood first.

He had to sit rather awkwardly and bend his knees to fit into the tub. Once he got as comfortable as he was going to be, he grabbed one of the towels from the table, folded it into a makeshift pillow, leaned back, and closed his eyes. He'd remain just until the warm water did its job on his trousers and eased out every last bit of cold in his bones, as well. Then he'd fully undress and wash himself clean, make a bed on the floor out of some of those quilts, and get a well-deserved night's sleep.

Chapter Four

❄

The first thing Annabelle saw when she opened her eyes was the figure of a man bathed in a soft glow of light coming from the dying embers of the fire. To her horror, he was lounging in the metal tub next to the bed, with a bandaged wrist dangling over the side. It took several moments before she could remember where she was and why she was there and that the man in the tub was no stranger.

He was her husband.

With her heart still pounding, she slammed her eyes shut again. Fortunately, Harrison's face was turned toward the dying embers in the hearth, which meant he had no idea she was even awake. In the weak light, all she had actually been able to see was the outline of his broad shoulders, just a hint of dark wavy hair that spread across his muscled chest, and his bent knees. But her cheeks burned nevertheless.

With her senses reeling, her mind grappled with the very aggravating reality that she had actually gotten married again and wondered what Harrison would say if he knew he had married a divorced woman instead of a single maiden. Memories of the scandal that erupted when news of her divorce spread through the small community she had called home for all of her life were still so raw, anguishing pain tore through her very soul and stole her breath away. She would never forget the harsh comments and cold rejection she suffered from people who had been her friends and neighbors, and it had taken many long months of prayer to forgive them.

Determined never to experience that sort of rejection from anyone again, she held on to Harrison's promise that their marriage would simply be annulled and regarded as if it never existed. With a glance his way, she tugged, as quietly as she could, at the oversized flannel nightgown Mrs. Lawrence had lent to her that had risen up to her knees.

She did not know how long he had been in the tub, but she was certain she did not want to disturb him, either. Not this man. He was far too comfortable in his own skin to care that she might see him while he was still bathing.

Minute after anxious minute, she held absolutely still, too afraid to move a single muscle and half afraid to breathe while she waited to hear him resume his bath. When her muscles started to ache and she still had not detected any sound, other than that of his heavy breathing, she wondered if he had actually fallen asleep. She herself had drifted off while bathing on occasion, but nonetheless she found it hard to believe he might have done the same thing. Hopeful that he must simply be resting a bit or thinking, she forced herself to wait him out and stay awake in the process.

Eventually, however, curiosity overwhelmed her common sense, which told her he was far too tall to extend his legs, slide under the water, and drown. She risked another peek from beneath the quilt, but the air in the room was so chilly, she quickly slid back under the covers again.

Confounded man. He had not moved at all. Either he had

heard her wake up and was feigning sleep in some twisted attempt
to embarrass her, or he had actually dozed off.

When he began to snore, however, she knew the latter was
true and faced a difficult dilemma. If she let him continue to sleep
in a tub filled with water that must be chilled by now, in front
of a fire that had been reduced to embers, he could end up with
lung fever. Added to the injuries he had suffered—one of which
she was partly responsible for—he could very well become so
ill that he would not be able to travel for a good week or more.

On the other hand, if she woke him up, she would be within
arm's reach of a naked man, and there was no telling what he
might do, particularly since he was legally her husband.

Since she had to be in Philadelphia in a matter of days or lose
her one opportunity to make a new life for herself, she knew her
situation was desperate. She sighed in frustration, turned her face
in the opposite direction, and snapped the quilt down from her
face again. "Mr. Graymoor! Wake up!" she whispered and waited
to hear the water slosh to let her know he had heard her.

Drat! Not a sound.

She cleared her throat and tried again, raising her voice as
loud as she dared without startling him overmuch.

Still no response, except for footsteps just outside the door.

Moments later, a thin ribbon of light appeared beneath the
bedroom door, and she heard someone she assumed to be Mrs.
Lawrence clang some pots together. Within moments, the tantalizing smells of frying bacon wafted into the room, and Annabelle groaned. The innkeeper's wife was making breakfast, which
meant Annabelle must have slept clear through the night to the
next morning.

The only question that remained to be answered was whether
or not Harrison had spent the entire night in that tub.

Frustrated when he continued to snore, apparently oblivious
to the increasing noise in the kitchen and tantalizing aromas that

made her stomach growl, she scooted up into a sitting position. She worked as quietly as she could to fashion the top half of the quilt into a cape of sorts, letting the tip of the quilt fall forward, much like a deep hood would have done. Satisfied she was as properly dressed as she could be, considering Mrs. Lawrence had taken all of her clothes away to be freshened up, she narrowed her gaze and glanced around the room looking for something to toss at him to wake him up.

She opted for one of the pillows, caught her breath, and tossed it in Harrison's direction. When it fell short and landed on top of his boots, she grabbed the other pillow and aimed for his knees again. Instead, it landed squarely on top of his head.

Cringing, she saw his arms flail. Water sloshed over the rim of the tub, and before she could avert her gaze, he scrambled to his feet, slipped, and fell sideways. Her heart nearly leaped right out of her chest when his torso landed on the bed. In his frantic attempt to break his fall, he yanked at the bedclothes and pulled her makeshift cape right off of her, along with the rest of the blankets and even the sheet as he struggled back to his feet.

Yelping, she scurried to reclaim the sheet and cover herself. "Stop! Right now! Stop!"

He groaned as he untangled himself from the bedclothes and tossed them back onto the bed. "W-why is it so c-cold in here?"

"The fire is nearly out, although I rather think that the fact you fell asleep in the tub has something to do with it," she replied, trying to push the wet blankets away without looking directly at him.

"It's been a rather trying two days, in case you've forgotten," he snapped.

"Unfortunately, I doubt I'll forget the past two days if I live to be ninety." She sniffed her displeasure as she felt the mattress give way, and she assumed he had sat down on the bed. But she didn't dare look his direction. "What are you doing now? I . . . I thought you were making arrangements with Mr. Lawrence for a separate room for yourself."

He huffed. "I failed, which shouldn't surprise you, since I've been nothing but inept for the past two days. And if you must know, I'm removing my dripping wet trousers, then I'm going to crawl into this bed—which, sad to say, is the only bed available—and try to get warm."

She scooted to the far side of the bed. "Is it customary for men from Philadelphia to wear trousers when they bathe, or is that just one of your many odd personal habits—in addition to toying with the affections of married women like Camille Jenkins?" She was horrified to think that she was mere moments away from having a naked man in her bed, even if he was her husband. She'd only shared the marriage bed once during her previous weeklong marriage.

"Are you deliberately trying to be difficult, or is that simply part of your nature?" he grumbled. "Never mind. I spent enough time handcuffed to you to know it's an annoying combination of both."

"Actually, it's neither. I'm merely curious." She started shivering and yanked a dry blanket free from the tangled mess of damp ones to try to get warm again.

He sighed. "First, I didn't toy with Camille's affections. I merely listened to her and made her feel important, which is something her husband should have a mind to do once in a while. Second, I didn't remove my trousers before I got into the tub for a very simple reason. The blood was so caked around the hole you poked into my thigh with those knitting needles of yours that I thought it might be better all around to let the hot water soak the blood free first before I tried to remove my trousers."

"You wouldn't have had that problem if you'd listened to me and stopped to see Dr. Marley. We practically passed his home on our way here. And that wound in your thigh isn't entirely my fault. You wouldn't have been hurt in the first place if you'd held still while I tried to fiddle with the lock on those handcuffs to see if I could force it open," she argued, determined not to let him add another layer to the guilt she already felt for injuring him.

Coughing, he eased into the bed and covered himself with the blankets and quilts, which sent her scooting to the very edge of the mattress. "I don't need a doctor. All I need is a good warm bed and an equally good night's sleep. I'm too cold and too tired to argue, so I'd appreciate it if you'd leave me to suffer in peace."

She slipped out of bed, horrified to think he was lying there naked, mere inches away from her, and kept the blanket wrapped tightly around her. He was shivering so hard now that he actually shook the mattress. "In point of fact, it's morning, which means you've already missed out on a good night's sleep, and unless I get that fire going strong again, those blankets aren't going to be enough to warm you up. Not after spending most of the night in that tub," she suggested.

"I'll take care of the fire. I just need a minute to—"

"Don't move. I'll do it," she insisted and she worked her way around to the foot of the bed.

"Are you sure you know what you're doing?"

She sniffed, tripped over one of his boots, and barely caught herself before she pitched forward onto her knees. "I grew up on a farm and had plenty of chores to do. Tending the fire was one of them," she explained and carefully loaded more wood onto the fire from the large stack of wood stored next to the fireplace.

Satisfied with her work, she made her way around the tub and back to her side of the mattress. She was reluctant to get back into the bed when he was lying there, even though it appeared he had already fallen asleep, but she had no desire to spend the next few hours standing around wearing a blanket, either.

In all truth, she really wanted to get a bit more sleep, which she could not do when he was in the bed, too. Desperate, she suddenly remembered something her mother had once told her about the days when Annabelle's father came courting, and she knew exactly how to solve her problem. She made several more trips back to the stack of wood, choosing the straightest logs she could find, and started lining them up in a row that ran from the head to the foot, right down the middle of the mattress.

He roused, took one look at what she was doing, and bolted up into a sitting position. "W-what are you doing? Planning to set the bed on fire?"

She covered the logs with a blanket and slipped back into bed. "If you must know, I'm making a bundling board of sorts. It was common practice years ago when couples who were courting lived miles apart and—"

"I know what a bundling board is, but we're not courting. We're married," he argued. Shivering hard, he slipped back down under the covers.

"Only temporarily," she countered.

He coughed again. "Finally."

"Finally?"

"We actually agree on something," he managed before he sneezed.

"Get some sleep. I'll keep the fire going to keep the room warm," she promised.

He sneezed again. "Your kindness is appreciated."

"I'm not being kind," she insisted. "Merely pragmatic. When the stage for Philadelphia stops here tomorrow, I want to make certain we're both on it. I'm prepared to do everything and anything I have to do to make that happen, even if it means waiting on you like a servant."

Chapter Five

❄

The stage came and went twice over the course of the next several days, but Annabelle and Harrison were not on board. Dr. Marley visited frequently, but Harrison refused to let the doctor get close enough to treat him, sending him away every single time.

Whether it was lung fever or an infection from his wounds that ravaged his body mattered little to Annabelle. Reducing his fever, tending to the wound on his wrist, and getting her stubborn patient to take some nourishment proved to be all-consuming tasks that had drained her stamina, as well as her patience. Fortunately, the wound in his thigh was healing quite well, which saved her the embarrassment of having to apply poultices to that part of his body.

Six days after their arrival, she awoke at dawn after getting her first full night of sleep. She glanced up from the cot Mr. Lawrence had put next to the sickbed for her, eyes widening the instant she found Harrison was leaning up on one elbow and staring down at her. "Y-you're awake," she murmured, surprised to see that the sparkle was already back in his eyes, since his fever had only broken yesterday afternoon.

"Quite so," he murmured, grinning when she clutched at her blanket and held it just below her chin. "I'm feeling much better now, so I should warn you that I'm well prepared to defend myself if you make any further attempts to torture me," he said with a shudder, although he never lost that twinkle in his eyes.

"It was my pleasure to torture you," she retorted. "I just can't decide which I enjoyed more: packing towels with the snow that fell over the past few days and using them to help bring down your fever, or using that awful-smelling ointment from Dr. Marley on my hands, which ended up being chafed from handling all that snow."

"Wrapping me in towels filled with snow was particularly barbarous treatment. There must have been another way to bring down my fever," he argued.

"I tried. Nothing else seemed to be working," she countered, noting how easily he dismissed her own discomfort and focused on his own. "I might argue that changing the poultice Dr. Marley recommended for the infection in your wrist was rather barbarous from my point of view, considering I ended up with a blackened eye for all my efforts," she quipped.

"I've never hit a woman. Not ever!" he exclaimed. He got back up on his elbows again, leaned forward, and studied her face. His voice grew husky. "Are you quite certain I actually hit you hard enough to blacken your eye?"

"It wasn't really your fault," she assured him, regretting her quick words. Annabelle turned her face so he would not see the bruise encircling her eye, even though it had already faded from deep purple to a pale but garish yellow. "You were fevered, and you reacted instinctively when you tried to yank your arm away while I was cleaning the wound you got from those horrid handcuffs. I just didn't get out of the way fast enough. I did every time after that, though," she added, trying to keep her tone light so she would not appear to be whining.

"I'm sorry. Truly, truly sorry for hurting you. And for complaining, as well. Instead of being ungrateful and dwelling on my own discomforts, I should be thanking you for taking care of me all this time." He lowered himself down and rested his head back on his pillow.

"Everyone helped. Besides Dr. Marley, who was very kind and very interested in your welfare despite the fact that you dismissed him every time he tried to come near you, Mrs. Lawrence was very kind to us both. She prepared all our meals, including the broth you had to be cajoled into swallowing in order to rebuild your strength. She helped me change the bedclothes as well and tidy up the room," she gushed, feeling guilty for taunting him a bit when he really could not be held responsible for his behavior. He had been a very sick man. In point of fact, when he was not sleeping, he had rarely been strong enough to talk to her, except to ask what day it was.

"Where did you get that cot you're resting on?"

"I have Mr. Lawrence to thank for that. He also filled buckets with the snow so I wouldn't have to go outside, and he made sure we had enough wood to keep the fire going. He . . . he said you spoke with him once or twice while I was in the kitchen with Mrs. Lawrence taking a meal," she prompted, hoping he would tell her what they had been talking about, since Mr. Lawrence had been so closemouthed about their conversations.

"As a matter of fact, I did," he admitted, without offering her anything more. "Today's date. Do you know it?"

"It's Thursday, which means it's the first of December," she whispered, unable to keep the disappointment out of her voice.

"You missed your appointment."

She cleared her throat and batted back tears of disappointment. "It was yesterday. Mr. Saddler has surely offered the position to someone else by now." She stared up at the ceiling. Although she would have been satisfied working in Mr. Saddler's candy shop, she was still deeply disappointed she would never be able to teach again. Since divorced women were not permitted to teach, her first husband had taken that right away from her when he divorced her to marry someone else. "I'm hopeful there will be other opportunities. In a city the size of Philadelphia, there must be more than one shopkeeper who needs to hire someone."

"I promised you a settlement once our marriage is annulled, which should allow you to live comfortably for the rest of your life without worrying about finding a position," he said firmly, although his voice sounded much weaker than it had only moments ago. "In the meantime, I can hardly abandon you to your own resources when I have more than enough to share with you."

Although she had agreed to let him replace what she had lost during the robbery, she had no intention of relying on this man who had so reluctantly been saddled with her as his wife—regardless of how he felt about it. "For a man who prides himself on being able to really listen to women, you certainly haven't listened to me, even though I've tried several times to make myself very clear. I'm not interested in a settlement from you of any kind. Just an annulment, thank you. And the opportunity to live independently through my own labor," she added.

"And I've tried to make it equally clear that you have no say in the matter. In the first place, I was the one the thieves targeted when they decided to rob the stage. In the second, if I hadn't taken ill, you would have arrived in Philadelphia in time for your appointment. That makes it my obligation to see that you're taken care of until we're both freed from this marriage of ours."

"Then consider yourself relieved of any responsibility for me at all," she argued. "But since I'm completely unfamiliar with the city, I would appreciate it if you could help me find a suitable place to live."

He let out a long sigh. "I can't risk inviting questions by having you stay at my home, even for a short period of time. I'll make arrangements for you to live quietly, using your own name, in a respectable boardinghouse. Other than having to wait until my lawyer has the marriage annulled and trying to convince you I truly do have your best interests at heart, I can't foresee any problems that might arise. Do you?"

She shook her head, fully confident the only possible problem that could arise would be her former husband, Eric Bradley, though he would have no reason to suspect she was anywhere other than in Four Corners, where he had abandoned her. Even if he did, he had told her himself he was well-established with his new wife in New York City, eliminating any fear she might have had that she would encounter him in Philadelphia. "No, I suppose I don't, but—"

"Good. Now get some sleep. I'd like to leave after breakfast, and we're not going to stop until we're in the city again, which I suspect will be sometime tomorrow afternoon."

"We can't leave today. The stage isn't due to stop here again until tomorrow," she offered and wondered whether he was getting fevered again or was simply anxious to be rid of her company.

"We're not taking the stage. We're—"

"Well, we certainly aren't going to ride that far. I've been astride quite enough lately, and you're definitely in no condition to ride. Like it or not, you'll have to be content to wait for the stage. . . ."

"Do you always leap to conclusions, or do you simply enjoy arguing for the sake of arguing?"

She huffed. "I didn't leap to any conclusion, and I'm not trying to argue with you. I'm simply trying to point out that we don't have any logical way to travel to Philadelphia other than by stage."

"I never said we were taking the stage. By now my private coach and two of my drivers should be parked somewhere in the vicinity of the inn's stable, waiting for us. I promised Mr.

Lawrence a handsome reward some days ago to send word to my staff in Philadelphia that I needed both. Unless I was dreaming last night when I spoke to the innkeeper, which I most definitely was not, he assured me that all would be ready for us to leave this morning after breakfast."

"He never said a word!"

A chuckle. "I told him not to tell you."

"You might pray that the drivers you sent for are close-mouthed. Otherwise, you can add yet two more names to the list of people who know about our marriage."

Harrison snorted. "I don't need to rely on prayer. I pay my staff extremely well to be discreet."

"Given your reputation, I shouldn't be surprised," she snapped.

"Go to sleep. And stop sounding like a . . . like a wife."

She pursed her lips and wondered if this man prayed for much of anything at all.

e

There was indeed a private coach nearby, ready to take them both back to Philadelphia.

By ten o'clock, Harrison had dressed in the clean clothes his drivers had brought for him. While he ate a solid meal for the first time in many days, Annabelle slipped back into the room they had shared. Grateful for the privacy she needed to dress and get ready to leave, she was surprised to see that her travel gown, which Mrs. Lawrence had freshened and pressed, was lying on the bed next to a hunter green cape.

When she picked up the soft woolen garment, she grinned when she saw that it had a full hood and deep pockets that held a pair of leather gloves dyed to match the cape. She was so happy she would have something to keep her warm during their journey, she wasted little thought on his extravagant gift or how he had managed to secure it for her on such short notice.

Instead, she dressed quickly, making sure the certificate for her first marriage and divorce decree, along with her first wedding ring, were safely tucked away inside a thin cotton pouch she pinned to her chemise. Her knitting stick was secured at her waist.

After brushing her hair with her fingers, she twisted the long, wavy tresses into a thick braid she let fall down her back, donned the cape, and met him back in the kitchen with her gloves in her hands. "I'd like to say it wasn't necessary for you to provide me with such a fine cape to wear, but that wouldn't be altogether true. I appreciate that you thought of my comfort, and I . . . I thank you," she murmured.

When he smiled, his dimples deepened and his eyes glimmered with satisfaction. "The color becomes you. I'm glad you're pleased."

His gaze was so intense, she felt her cheeks warm, and she looked beyond him to see Mrs. Lawrence standing next to the table holding a pair of wooden baskets. She was wearing a grin so wide it nearly reached her ears.

"Mr. Lawrence is out at the coach with your drivers setting in those warmed bricks you asked for, and I've got enough victuals packed up in here for everyone to last the entire trip, just like you wanted," she offered, handing over both of the baskets.

Harrison grasped them, and when he looked down and smiled at her, the innkeeper's wife actually blushed. "You're a good, good woman. Thank you," he said and pressed a kiss to her forehead.

As Harrison exchanged a few words with Mrs. Lawrence, Annabelle was fascinated by the transformation that had taken place in their relationship. When they had first arrived at the inn, the woman had made it perfectly clear that she thought he was the worst kind of scoundrel. That he had been able to charm the woman into changing her opinion of him, only hours after emerging from their room, merely added more credence to the claims about this man's reputation she had heard from both Sheriff Taylor and Mr. Jenkins. If Harrison could charm this elderly woman, Annabelle had no doubt he would have an even greater effect on women his own age.

"All the more reason to leave and make my own way in this world," she whispered, determined not to be swayed by a sweet-talking womanizer. Not again. Not even if he did come from the wealthiest and most prestigious family in Philadelphia.

Chapter Six

❊

When the coach stopped in front of his Philadelphia home the following evening, Harrison ranked his decision to spend some time on his country estate in western Pennsylvania as the greatest mistake of his life—quite an accomplishment considering the many mistakes he had made over the course of the past several years.

If any one of his friends had told him four months ago when he left that he was going to return with a wife, he would have called them an addled fool and laughed. He was most definitely not laughing now, and only the thought that he would soon be single again gave him the strength to tolerate this very temporary marriage and keep his hidden heartache and pain at bay.

Although still feeling weak and travel-weary, he helped Annabelle down from the coach a good half day after he had expected to arrive. He watched with amusement as she looked about to get her very first glimpse of the property his family had occupied for nearly a hundred years. Massive stone walls, with narrow doors to provide access from the street, started at the sides of the house and continued around the perimeter of the property that swallowed up nearly half a city block.

The walls guaranteed privacy for him, as well as his guests, to enjoy spacious gardens in fair weather. In addition, the narrow doors allowed him to slip in or out of the house without alerting the staff or any of the neighbors.

The mansion itself was constructed of red brick, like most houses in the city, but the entranceway was by far one of the most ostentatious. Tall marble columns supported an intricately decorated gable roof over the massive front door, which was surrounded by more marble and small glass windows that allowed the light from a crystal chandelier in the foyer to illuminate two wide marble steps outside and spill out to the walkway.

Heavy wool curtains covering the windows on the second and third floors blocked out the unusual cold but also kept any houselights from shining out. Since he had not been in residence for some time, Harrison did not expect the rooms to be lit, since the staff lived in quarters behind the kitchen at the rear of the house.

Annabelle dropped her hood, in spite of the frigid wind whipping at her cape, and gripped his arm to maintain her balance on the icy walkway in front of the house. With her cheeks brushed pink by the cold and her pale green eyes wide with wonder and disbelief, she looked up at him. "This is where you live?"

"Only for the past eight years," he admitted. After he waved off the drivers, he ushered her toward the house, but he kept their pace slow and deliberate in order to avoid slipping. He was anxious to get her inside before anyone noticed he had not returned home alone, but he was twice as anxious to crawl into his own bed. Tomorrow would be a long day, and he would need a good night's rest if he planned to meet with his lawyer and make all the necessary arrangements to place this woman in a proper boardinghouse by tomorrow night at the latest.

She tilted her head back to get a full view of the three-storied mansion. "The house looks quite grand, even at night. I can only imagine what it must look like in the full light of day," she murmured.

He chuckled. "I've heard that some people actually refer to it as Graymoor Castle," he said, unwilling to admit that he had only moved into this massive house out of a sense of duty to family tradition—one of the few family traditions he had chosen to follow when he became the sole remaining heir to the family name and fortune.

She dropped her gaze. "Those high walls on either side do make it look like a fortress of sorts," she offered as they approached the entranceway.

"They're only there to protect the rather extensive gardens, which I fear may not survive this brutal winter." He was surprised when she stopped, forcing him to do the same.

She pointed to the narrow door within the wall, nearly hidden by night shadows. "Since neither one of us would like to make our presence known, wouldn't it be better to slip inside one of those side doors instead of using the main entrance? It's so well lit, I suspect someone will notice us."

"We'll be inside well before we're noticed," he countered and ushered her up the two marble steps to the landing at the main entry. Before he even had a chance to knock, however, the door swung open. Pleased that the staff had been alerted to his return by the instructions he had forwarded through the innkeeper, he greeted the staid housekeeper, Mrs. Faye, with a smile.

She acknowledged them both with a prim nod of her head but spoke directly to him. "Good evening, sir. Welcome home," she murmured as she stepped back to allow them entrance. "Your rooms are ready, just as you instructed," she informed him as she closed the door behind them.

"It's a relief to be back," he replied. Once he had Annabelle safely inside, he helped her out of her cape. After he had removed his own heavy cloak and hat, he bent down to kiss the house-keeper's cheek before handing her all the garments.

Flustered as usual by his informal manners, she swiped at her cheek before carrying the garments to a narrow bench at the far end of the hallway and leaving them there.

While he waited for her to return before introducing Anna-belle as the young woman he had described in his instructions, he caught the sound of laughter and conversation coming from the second floor, which was reserved for entertaining, saw the light spilling down the staircase, and froze.

"Mr. Philip is in residence, and he's entertaining tonight," the housekeeper explained when she rejoined them. "Before anyone comes downstairs, please allow me to extend to you best wishes from the entire staff, sir."

"Best wishes?" Harrison managed and dismissed the notion that he should have taken Annabelle's suggestion not to enter the house through the front door. Instead, he tried to wrap his mind around the fact that they were not alone in the house, as well as the highly improbable notion that news of his marriage had somehow reached the city.

"On your recent marriage, of course. We're all delighted." She walked over to the narrow rosewood side table next to the staircase and handed him a copy of *The Philadelphia Inquirer*.

He heard Annabelle gasp slightly, but he was far more inter-ested in reading the announcement printed above the fold on the first page, fully aware that she had leaned closer and was also silently reading it:

> *Readers will be delighted to learn that the city's most eligible bachelor, Harrison Graymoor, has wed, although many of this city's maidens are bound to be disappointed. He is expected to return to the city with his bride very soon, at which time we will*

*be providing the details surrounding this most newsworthy event,
which may well be the highlight of this year's social news.*

Shocked, Harrison struggled to maintain control and grimly
handed the newspaper back to the housekeeper. Gauging his
sour mood, she quickly disappeared, leaving him standing in
the foyer alone, with Annabelle at his side. He looked down at
the trembling woman by his side and saw the same disbelief and
distress he felt etched into her pale features.

"H-how could you let this happen?" she whispered.

"Obviously, I didn't 'let this happen.' I didn't want anyone
here to learn of our marriage any more than you did." He raked
his hand through his hair.

"What are you going to do now?"

"Obviously our plans to keep this marriage secret, as well as
the eventual annulment, are no longer viable." Frustration made
his words short and clipped. His mind raced to formulate another
plan of action before anyone ventured downstairs.

"But what are you going to do about it?" she asked, taking
a step back, as if she were prepared to rush right back out the
door and disappear if she did not like the answer he gave her.

"I don't know," he murmured. "But for now, I suggest we take
the servants' staircase in the back of the house to the third floor
before anyone else knows we're here." He was unwilling to even
think about the many notables his cousin had likely gathered
together on the second floor for one of his fund-raising events.

But he was too late.

They had barely taken two steps when he heard the door
at the top of the stairs open and someone rush down the steps.
"Cousin! You're back!"

Harrison recognized Philip's voice and fought the urge to run
straight back to him and strangle him. Literally.

Instead, he stopped and turned around, urging Annabelle to

do the same, but kept her standing slightly behind him. "Don't say a word. Just follow my lead," he whispered before he glared at the man who approached them wearing a grin on his face that Harrison could only describe as indescribably silly for a man who was only a few years shy of forty.

"Cousin!" he exclaimed, using the familial term again instead of Harrison's given name, which was his most annoying custom. "Mrs. Faye informed me that your coach had pulled up. I'm sorry for rushing down so quickly, but I simply could not wait any longer to welcome you back and meet your new wife," he said and extended his hand.

Begrudgingly, Harrison accepted his cousin's handshake. "Philip. You seem to appear and disappear—"

"At the most inconvenient of times, I know. But this time, let me be quick to apologize. If I'd known you were returning tonight with your bride, I would have changed my plans. By the time we received word you were coming home, it was too late to cancel my dinner party. Besides, the shortage of firewood in the city is so severe, forcing the price beyond the means of far too many souls, that I simply had to help raise funds to provide them with some relief one last time before I left the city." He leaned around Harrison to get a better look at Annabelle.

"She's lovely. Quite lovely indeed. Now hurry and introduce us before everyone else pours downstairs to get a glimpse of her," he insisted before he addressed Annabelle. "I really must get you to tell me how you managed to get this cousin of mine to slip a ring on your finger."

Harrison fumed. Now he needed to buy a ring, if only to keep up appearances, and he scowled. Although he was an inch or two below six feet, he was still taller and carried more muscle than his slimly built older cousin. Stretching to his full height, he stared down at him. "I'll introduce you, of course, but I'd also ask you to consider that my wife and I are quite fatigued from travel. Neither one of us is prepared to visit with you or anyone else tonight," he explained.

When Annabelle shyly stepped forward, he quickly introduced her to Philip, who kissed the back of her hand and offered her a smile of approval. "You look remarkably beautiful, in spite of your travel," he murmured. "I'm looking forward to getting to know you a bit before I leave for Boston. I'd almost given up hope that Harrison would ever settle down."

Harrison dismissed the odd twinge of jealousy that coursed through his body as nothing more than the direct result of his fatigue, rather than any concern that Philip was being overly attentive to Annabelle. Placing his hand gently at her back, he nodded to Philip. "If you'll excuse us, my wife and I would both like to retire, and I'd appreciate it if you would not mention anything about our arrival to your many guests." He then urged a quiet and totally amenable Annabelle toward the back of the foyer.

"Harrison Graymoor! If you think you can bring home a bride and fail to introduce us, you're quite mistaken, young man."

He stopped abruptly, recognizing the voice immediately. Glancing at Annabelle, he noted his own disappointment and frustration mirrored in her wide eyes. There were many people he could dismiss, by virtue of his standing in this community, or disarm with a smile.

Unfortunately, Mrs. John Wilshire III was not one of them.

As one of the city's social elites, the elderly matron prided herself on her ability to spread as much gossip as possible, but she was also one of Philip's major contributors to the many charitable causes he had taken up.

When Harrison turned around to reply to her, he was even more dismayed to see that she was not alone. Many, if not all, of his cousin's guests were filing down the staircase to join Mrs. Wilshire in the foyer. He would be hard pressed to escape without providing them with at least some of the details surrounding his marriage, and he drew in a long, deep breath of air to try to clear his head.

As easy as it was for him to fully engage and entertain most people—especially an attractive woman he found even mildly interesting—it was hard for him to think of a way to satisfy everyone in the crowd of men and women before him. At least in a way that would make his ultimate decision to end his marriage seem reasonable.

Swallowing hard, he took Annabelle's trembling hand in his own and saw her tuck her other hand within the folds of her skirt, no doubt hiding the fact that she had no wedding ring on her finger. He plastered a smile on his face, and he was pleased when Annabelle did the same.

"What are you going to tell them all?" she whispered as she stepped a bit closer to him.

He forced himself to smile. "As little as possible," he murmured. "I suggest you simply agree with whatever I say or do."

"That's worked well for both of us so far tonight, hasn't it?" she quipped.

"You really don't know how to hold your tongue, do you?" he countered, unaccustomed to having anyone, especially an attractive young woman, criticize him. Before she could give him an equally unwelcome retort, he walked her back to greet Mrs. Wilshire and made one general introduction by announcing Annabelle's first name and the fact that they were married a little over a week ago after a whirlwind courtship. "I know you'll all forgive me if I wait until another time to introduce each of you individually to my wife. We've been traveling practically nonstop since yesterday. She has a rather delicate constitution and needs her rest."

Mrs. Wilshire narrowed her gaze, and she studied Annabelle as intently as she would inspect an exquisite, extremely valuable painting to determine if it was authentic or merely a counterfeit.

"Is that the hint of a bruise around your eye?" she asked, inviting the others to lean forward for a better look.

Harrison froze the moment he looked down at her face. While the bruise was barely detectable by daylight, he realized, too late, that it was quite noticeable under the glaring light of the chandelier, and he wondered how Philip could have missed it.

Before he could come up with a reasonable explanation for her bruise, Annabelle smiled sweetly. "I'm afraid it is," she said softly and gripped his hand even harder, silently warning him to hold his own tongue. "We were riding last week when we were accosted by thieves who were total brutes. Harrison was gallant enough to risk his own life to save me from being truly injured," she explained, continuing to weave an incredible tale that twisted the actual facts into a story that had the entire audience of guests mesmerized into believing he had been quite a hero, even at the cost of suffering injuries to himself in order to protect her.

Mrs. Wilshire dabbed at her eyes with her handkerchief as she apparently embraced the fairy tale Annabelle had created, which Harrison knew would lead the other guests to accept it, as well. She looked up at him and smiled. "I always knew you would make your parents proud someday, and now you've proved yourself to be a true hero who rescued a beautiful maiden in distress. And she stole your heart away, didn't she?"

Annabelle's smile grew. "I believe he stole mine first," she murmured as if she really meant it and smiled up at him, too.

"Do let me see your wedding ring," the elderly woman insisted.

"I haven't purchased a ring yet," Harrison said quickly. "I was waiting until we returned to the city so I could choose something as extraordinary as my wife." He offered the woman a smile that left her blushing.

Annabelle looked up at him with a grateful smile before turning to face Philip and his guests again. "I hope you all won't be dreadfully disappointed, but my husband still isn't completely recovered from his injuries and needs to rest. If you'll excuse us for now, I'm hopeful that we'll be able to spend time with each of you very soon."

Mrs. Wilshire clucked her approval, no doubt giving them her permission, which no one among the assembled guests would dare protest. Harrison led his new bride away and limped slightly to give the impression that the injury to his thigh had not healed, even though it had.

When they were still within sight, but out of earshot, he leaned toward Annabelle. Although he was completely surprised at how quickly she had been able to spin a tale that stretched and reworked the truth, he could not imagine why she had chosen to make him out as a hero. "Wherever did you learn to invent a story like that so quickly and easily?"

"I had a teacher once who was a master storyteller," she murmured.

He pondered why her voice sounded rather sad as he followed her up the stairs. He also wondered what he could do come morning to get them beyond the reach of the city's gossipmongers. Fast. Before Annabelle met anyone else and embellished the tale she had told that would truly paint him an unredeemable cad when he had their marriage annulled and set her aside.

And before Philip could complicate his life any more than he already had before he returned to Boston to spend the Christmas season with his sister and her family.

Harrison paused as he joined her on the landing of the second floor, inspired by an idea. The muted sounds of gaiety, if not gossip, just on the other side of the wall convinced him that moving out to Graymoor Gardens, his country estate just west of the city, was not merely brilliant or convenient. It was absolutely necessary.

He placed his hand at her elbow and guided her down a narrow expanse toward the second set of steps leading up to the sleeping rooms on the third floor. At this point, he himself barely had the energy to walk, and he was not surprised that she was now leaning on his arm for support. "We're both exhausted, but there's much to be done tomorrow morning. I'll be leaving at first light to see my lawyer, as I've promised, but I expect you to keep several early-morning appointments that I've arranged, as well," he informed her.

She stopped abruptly and looked up at him. "Appointments for me? Tomorrow? Why?" she whispered as her voice cracked. Her features were etched with exhaustion, but he had never seen her eyes well with tears before, not once during the entire fiasco of their enforced marriage.

"I'm sorry. I know how difficult this must be for you, but after tomorrow, I promise you'll feel much better about this whole situation."

She sighed and swiped at her tears. "I don't think I can face another night like this one."

He smiled. "You won't have to. If all goes as planned, we'll be leaving tomorrow, right after dinner," he promised. He was confident that Graymoor Gardens was exactly the right place to keep her isolated from society, yet still be able to monitor her every move. Living there would also give him the privacy he needed for himself, and he made a mental note to tell Graham, one of his drivers, that he would also be moving there temporarily so Harrison would have a private coach at his disposal.

The only negative aspect of his plan, however, was a big one, but he needed a good night's rest before he tackled the worst problem he would find waiting for him at Graymoor Gardens: Irene, the well-intentioned but troublesome woman who was the head housekeeper there.

Chapter Seven

❄

By ten o'clock the following morning, Annabelle had bathed, dressed, and met with three different women, each with a unique talent with the needle who had come to the residence at Harrison's request. In quick succession, a number of other tradespeople came and went, ending with the middle-aged woman standing behind her who had come to trim and style her hair.

Annabelle stared into the mirror hanging just above the rosewood dressing table and blinked hard when she ventured a first look at the woman's handiwork. Her hair had been parted in the middle, as usual, but instead of fashioning a thick braid or winding it into a bun at the nape of her neck, which was her wont, Mrs. Lynch had smoothed her hair over her ears and arranged her long blond hair into a sculptured mass of curls that fell to the middle of her back.

Annabelle shook her head and met Mrs. Lynch's gaze. "I appreciate what you've done, but I'm afraid this is far too fancy for everyday."

The woman's cheeks blushed deep pink. "Mr. Harrison sent

instructions that I should teach you how to do it. It shouldn't take but a few days of practice—"

"Men should know better than to tell a woman what to do when it comes to her hair," Annabelle murmured. She was still annoyed that he had also been quick to give his own instructions to all the other tradespeople he had sent to her this morning. But she had been equally assertive and adjusted his requests to better suit her, and she was fully prepared to defend her decisions if and when he offered any objection.

"Surely there must be a simpler way to fix my hair to meet my husband's expectations as well as my own," she prompted.

Mrs. Lynch nodded, her eyes bright. "There may be something," she said, sorting through the valise containing her tools of the trade. Eventually she pulled out a ball of tan netting, which she smoothed before placing one edge at the top of Annabelle's head. Working quickly, she started tucking all the blond curls into the netting. "Snoods aren't exactly all the rage here, but they're still quite popular in Europe where women have worn them, off and on, for centuries. I just carry this one to show my clients what they're like," she explained. "My daughter has made a fair number of them out of lace and such for evening wear. She doesn't have many clients yet, but most of them are younger women, like yourself, although I'm not certain the gentlemen like them, as well."

Annabelle grinned. "I should like to order one or two from your daughter, I think. Actually, this particular snood would serve rather well for everyday, and it seems simple enough to use."

Mrs. Lynch eased the snood away from Annabelle's hair and handed it to her. "Here. Try putting it on yourself before you decide," she prompted and watched carefully as Annabelle attempted to put the snood back in place. "I do believe men can get used to most anything a woman wants to do—especially a woman as beautiful as you are, if you'll forgive me for saying so."

Annabelle dismissed the woman's compliment as nothing more than an attempt to please her and concentrated on replacing the snood precisely where Mrs. Lynch had put it. On her second attempt, she had it perfectly in place and smiled.

"Well done!" the woman murmured.

Pleased to think how much time she could save by tucking her hair into a snood instead of fashioning it into a braid or a bun, Annabelle smiled. "I think we've found the perfect solution. I'd like to keep this one, if I may."

Mrs. Lynch moistened her lips. "I have others at my shop which are closer in color to your hair. I can send one right out to you this afternoon, if you like. I can also make a list of others you could order from my daughter, or I can send her here—"

"Let's make a list," Annabelle suggested, returning the snood, and then quickly fashioning her hair into a long braid.

Half an hour later, Mrs. Lynch left with an order for two snoods for day wear and three snoods Annabelle would use for evening, which would go well with the day dresses and gowns she had reluctantly ordered. They amounted to less than half of what Harrison had instructed her to do.

Exhausted by her busy morning, Annabelle lay down on the bed, too tired to think why she should need any gowns at all, since she and Harrison were supposed to be leaving right after dinner. "Not that I have a single clue about where we're going," she grumbled. She crossed her arms over her chest and glanced around the elegantly appointed bedroom. Surrounded by a single room of furniture that would have taken her father two lifetimes or more to afford, and lying on bedclothes made of silk and trimmed with lace so delicate it must have been imported from Europe, she had never felt more uncomfortable in her life.

Until she thought about the fortune it must be costing Harrison to supply her with a completely new wardrobe, which went far beyond replacing the meager one that had been stolen.

It seemed a terrible waste of money, considering she would only be here for a matter of weeks, or a month at the most.

Dismayed, she closed her eyes and folded her hands together. "Father, I don't know why you've brought me into this man's life and here to this place, but I trust you. I know that my life will unfold according to your plan, but right now, I don't understand what that plan might be. You know, above all others, that I have simple needs and that I long for nothing more than to please you. Help me, Father, to accept your will and to use whatever talents you have given me to serve you. Amen," she whispered.

She was just dozing off to sleep when there was a sharp rap at her door. Sighing, she climbed off the bed and tightened the rose silk robe about her waist that she had found lying across the bed when she arrived last night. "Come in."

The young servant girl, Lotte, who had brought her breakfast several hours ago, walked into the room carrying a tray. "Mrs. Faye thought you might like some refreshment," she offered and placed the tray upon a table set near the fireplace.

Annabelle got one whiff and smiled as she walked over to the table. "Is that hot chocolate?" she asked, glancing at the steam coming from the silver pot in the center of the tray.

"Yes, ma'am, it is. There's an assortment of sweet confections, as well, but if you'd prefer something else, I can get it for you."

"No, thank you. This is perfectly wonderful," she said, popping a tiny caramelized treat into her mouth. She savored the sweet, buttery flavor while Lotte poured hot chocolate into a petite silver mug for her. Convinced there were enough sweets stacked on the large oval platter to feed four or five people, she took her seat. "There are far too many sweets here for me. Please, have some," she insisted.

Lotte backed away from the table. "Oh, I couldn't do that, Mrs. Graymoor. Not at all."

"And why not?" Annabelle tried to take a sip of the hot chocolate but quickly set it down to cool a bit.

"Why, it wouldn't be proper, ma'am. I couldn't possibly take any. They're for you, and Mrs. Faye wouldn't like it at all if I took some."

"All of this is only for me?"

"Yes, ma'am. Just like Mr. Graymoor instructed."

Taking a napkin, she wrapped up most of the sweet treats, rose, and handed them to Lotte. "Then consider these a gift, from me to you, and you're welcome to share them with any of the other members of the staff, if you like. And you don't need to worry about Mr. Graymoor or Mrs. Faye. If they ask, which is highly unlikely, since they both have far more important things to occupy them, I'll explain that it was all my idea," she murmured.

Lotte dropped her gaze. "Yes, ma'am. Thank you." She bobbed a curtsy and quickly left when Annabelle assured her there was nothing more she needed.

Moments later, Mrs. Faye arrived.

Annabelle suspected she might have come to reprimand her and braced herself.

Instead, the woman stood just inside the door, took one glance at the near-empty plate of treats, and quickly erased the look of surprise that flashed through her eyes. "I came to see if you are finding the refreshment to your liking."

"I am indeed," Annabelle replied and stifled a grin.

"Now that your appointments for the morning are finished, Mr. Graymoor instructed me to also ask if there's anything more you'd like that he hasn't already taken care of for you."

Overwhelmed by his interest in pleasing her, she dismissed his attentiveness as nothing more than his attempt to keep up appearances, even with his staff. She was inclined to send the woman away without asking for anything more, until she thought of several things that had been stolen from her and one she had destroyed before leaving Four Corners that she wanted to replace. "Actually, I do have a number of items I'd like to have," she replied and quickly dictated a list.

"I'll have them delivered to you," the housekeeper replied, without giving a hint of what she thought of the rather ordinary items on Annabelle's list. "Mr. Graymoor has sent word that he's been unavoidably detained and that you're to leave immediately. He'll be joining you later, perhaps in time for dinner."

"Did Mr. Graymoor tell you where we're going this afternoon?" she asked, reluctant to travel about in a city that was completely unfamiliar to her.

Mrs. Faye tilted up her chin. "He didn't share that information with me, but even if he had, I wouldn't be able to tell you. It's not my place." She left the room, leaving Annabelle still uncertain about her destination.

᠅

"No annulment?"

Incredulous, Harrison leaned forward and stared at his lawyer, who was leaning back in his chair on the opposite side of the desk that separated them. "Why not?"

George Marshall rested his gnarled hands on his well-rounded stomach and sighed. "Plainly speaking, there isn't a single man in the legislature in Harrisburg dealing with these matters who would be tempted for more than a second to consider that you spent an entire week sleeping with this young woman without consummating the marriage. Not with your reputation—which I daresay I've warned you about many, many times."

"My reputation shouldn't matter, particularly since my reputation is nothing more than sheer gossip and innuendo," he spat. "What about the courts? Didn't you just say we could apply there instead of petitioning the legislature?"

Marshall sat up straight and squared his shoulders. "The men sitting on the Court of Appeals are no different than the legislators. You can't sweep your reputation aside quite that easily, even with your uncommon wealth."

Harrison pointed to the pieces of the handcuffs he had salvaged, which were lying next to a sheaf of papers full of notes his lawyer had taken when Harrison first arrived. "What about those handcuffs or this?" he asked before he pulled up the cuff of his shirt to reveal the angry scar that was forming around his wrist—a scar he would carry for the rest of his life. "Even if someone were tempted to dismiss the handcuffs as evidence, surely this scar should prove I was coerced into marrying this woman."

"The scar proves nothing more than the fact you wore a handcuff that was too small for you. Unless you can bring forward some witness who would be willing to testify on your behalf—"

"Forget it." Harrison snorted and leaned against the hard back of the chair. "Jenkins wouldn't testify on my behalf under any circumstances."

"Perhaps rightly so, since you were so unduly attentive to his wife," the lawyer admonished. "What about the sheriff or the other two men you say were with him?"

Harrison shook his head.

Marshall shifted through the papers stacked in front of him. "Is there any chance Reverend Wood would step forward to corroborate your claims?"

"Hardly," he retorted. "I don't think he could see well enough to even notice the barrel of the rifle shoved against my back."

Instead of offering any other ideas, Marshall turned to study the notes he had taken while Harrison gave an account of the past week. "By my count, there are half a dozen other people who knew about the marriage, including the innkeeper and his wife. Were any of them present during the actual ceremony?"

"No, but couldn't Annabelle sign some sort of affidavit to verify my testimony? I'm quite certain that she'd be agreeable."

Harrison's words finally brought a smile to the lawyer's face. "Are you really that certain?"

"Of course I am. She is just as opposed to the marriage as I am."

His lawyer shrugged. "Even if you're right, she's the aggrieved party here, and I highly doubt her word would be taken as fact, at least not until the proper number of months have passed. Once the possibility that she might be with child has been eliminated, I could take her statement and try to persuade—"

Harrison's heart pounded in his chest. "Wait nine months? Never. It's out of the question. I need this matter resolved much more quickly. In fact, I want this marriage ended by the end of January, at the latest. If that means I have to settle for divorcing her, then so be it."

"Remember what I told you," his lawyer cautioned. "Legislative issues and court decisions are a matter of public record and reported in the press on a daily basis and draw particular attention when they involve someone as well-known as you are. It's one thing to request an annulment, but it's quite another to ask for and be granted a divorce. You'd find yourself shunned by most everyone who is important in this city and shame the very name you carry. The stigma of divorce would also guarantee that you'd never find a suitable young woman to marry one day."

"I'm not interested in being married. Not now. Not ever," Harrison said firmly, surprised that his lawyer would bring up such a sensitive topic when he knew full well that Harrison had good reason for remaining a bachelor. "Are you quite certain there's no other possible recourse?" he asked, hinting at the possibility that a few well-placed bribes might be the best approach.

Marshall frowned. "None that are legal, although there may be something I could suggest, since you seem so determined to get a quick resolution," he mumbled, then turned and opened a drawer on the side of the desk. He set several papers on top of the desk and read them before meeting Harrison's gaze. "I have several reports here that indicate you might easily be granted a divorce elsewhere."

Harrison's heart pounded with hope. "Go on."

"Apparently, Indiana is emerging as a state intent on attracting new settlers. There's even a circuit court in each county with the power to grant divorces rather quickly."

Harrison's hope quickly evaporated, and he snorted. "That's all well and good, but I don't live in Indiana."

"You can purchase property to qualify. A lawyer representing your interests could also petition for a divorce on your behalf, but I have no indication in these reports that they consider annulments at all, which means you'll have to settle for a divorce. At most, considering the travel involved, I should think it might take a matter of a month or two, perhaps less, which would certainly meet your expectations to have your marriage legally ended by the end of January. I couldn't possibly travel that far, mind you, but I have a young lawyer in mind who might be interested."

Harrison let out a long breath of air. "Do it. Hire whomever you want and do whatever you think is necessary to make this divorce happen, and be certain that the settlement you prepare for Annabelle is substantial enough to allow her to live comfortably," he said firmly, satisfied but not wholly pleased that there seemed to be a way out of the mess he had created for himself. "Just be discreet."

"As always," the lawyer replied. "I'll talk to Blair Fennimore about representing you for the divorce and have him get in touch with you."

"I'd rather meet with him right away," Harrison countered, even though it meant he would have to delay leaving the city for another hour or two. "I've arranged to send Annabelle ahead to Graymoor Gardens without me, just in case the snowstorm that's threatening makes travel by coach difficult," he explained. "I'd rather not get stranded here in the city while she's alone with

Irene for more than a few hours, but I'm not leaving the city without the documents I need Annabelle to sign."

His lawyer chuckled. "Knowing Irene, you probably should have waited to take Annabelle there with you. In any event, I'll send a messenger to Fennimore and tell him that you need to see him here immediately." He quickly wrote a brief note and sent one of the two clerks in the office to deliver it. "Have you given any thought to what you're going to do about Vienna Biddle? I understand her father is rather piqued that you married someone other than his daughter."

Harrison drew in a long breath of air. "Not really," he admitted.

They continued to discuss a number of financial matters while they waited for Fennimore to arrive. When Harrison finally left his lawyer's office, he had signed all the necessary papers, received Fennimore's promise that he would leave at first light for Indiana, and lined the man's pockets with more than enough coins to assure his loyalty as well as his discretion.

Anxious to exit the city, he hurried to complete one last task, one he never, ever believed he would be doing: He had to buy a wedding ring.

Chapter Eight

❄

Once an outcast in her hometown after being divorced, Annabelle was again being forced into exile.

She parted the curtain on the private coach carrying her westward to a country estate she had never seen and caught one last glimpse of the city. A thick glob of clouds overhead completely obscured a weak winter sun, and the still-frigid air was ripe with the promise of a snowstorm.

Graham, the driver who was also moving out to the country estate while she and Harrison resided there, drove the coach down Market Street. Traffic was extremely light, and she was able to note the orderly grid design of the intersecting streets that were set at right angles from one another. Nothing looked familiar to her, however, since they had arrived last night well after dark.

Sighing, she dropped the curtain back into place and leaned into the thick velvet cushion at her back. Feeling as if she had been lost in a maze where she was finding one disappointment after another, she removed one of her gloves to reach inside her cape. She wrapped her fingers around the knitting stick once again secured at her waist and closed her eyes.

With the rocking motion of the coach soothing her tangled nerves, she held on tight to memories of home and the parents who had loved her and raised her, by example, in the faith that was the only constant in her life. With another sigh, she surrendered her dreams of a life as a wife and hopefully a mother someday. Oh, to have had them snatched away from her for the second time.

Annabelle did not know the exact legal steps Harrison's lawyer would have to take to get their marriage annulled, but she contented herself with the knowledge that her husband had both the desire and the wealth to guarantee the annulment would be granted as quickly as possible. All she had to do was find a way to survive until then.

Less than forty minutes after leaving the Graymoor mansion, the coach stopped and the driver opened the door. Without saying a word he helped her to disembark, nodded, and returned to his seat. A gentle but steady snow with infinitely small flakes brushed at her face as she watched the coach travel back along the circular drive before heading back to the city proper to bring Harrison here.

Once the coach was out of view, she turned around to face the house she would now call home. It sat atop a high knoll that was surrounded by massive barren trees with thick limbs that reached out to catch the falling snow. The square building was covered with white stucco, and was much smaller and simpler in design than the formal mansion she had just left.

She did not have to worry about neighbors here, since the closest home they had passed was a good several miles away. On the eastern side of the house, the outline of what appeared to be a small wall surrounded a portico that overlooked a heavily wooded landscape ending at the banks of the Schuylkill River. Shivering, she caught a glimpse of drifting blocks of ice floating by before starting for the front door.

As she walked she saw several outbuildings on the western side of the house, including a stable and what appeared to be a small cottage where smoke billowed from the chimney. She tugged her cape a bit tighter, prayed that she would be able to quickly warm up again, and proceeded up the short walkway to the rather plain wooden front door, where deep blue shutters hugged the windows on either side of the door, as well as the two windows on the second floor. Heavy woolen drapes, however, blocked any view of the interior.

Annabelle approached the front door, mindful of the stiff formality of the staff she had left behind in the city. She'd found it disconcerting, and she was surprised when here she had to use the brass knocker on the door not once, but twice. She was about to knock a third time when the door swung open, revealing a woman with gray-streaked hair wearing a thick woolen sweater with the most ample bosom Annabelle had ever seen on such a slender woman.

Standing just inside the doorway, the woman hurriedly finished wiping her hands and shoved a well-soiled cloth into her apron pocket. "Come in, come in, although I can't promise you'll be completely out of the cold," she urged, promptly closing the door once Annabelle was inside.

Within a heartbeat, Annabelle found herself being hugged as hard as if she were a long-lost friend, and the hood on her cape slipped back.

"You must be Miss Annabelle. Welcome! I'm Widow Cannon. I'm the head housekeeper here at Graymoor Gardens. We didn't expect you till close to suppertime. I hope I didn't keep you waiting. As luck would have it, I was just wiping down the balustrade; otherwise, I never would have heard you knocking," she gushed.

She had barely paused long enough to take a breath before she set Annabelle back and studied her from head to toe, clucking her approval. "Even with that bruise you got from those horrid men who robbed the stage, you're just a picture of goodness itself, just like I heard. You're not a city girl, are you?"

Still reeling from this most unexpected welcome and surprised that news had spread this far, Annabelle twisted at the folds of her cape. "No. I grew up in Four Corners, about a two days' ride from Hanover in the western region of the state. How could you possibly know—"

"Just instinct," Widow Cannon stated as she helped Annabelle remove her cape. "I've been waiting for you for years, not that I'll ever admit that to your husband. He knows well and good how I feel about the life he's been leading, but that's all behind him now that he's finally gotten married."

Taken aback, Annabelle furrowed her brow. "You've been waiting years? But I only arrived last night and just left the city—"

"And just in time to save that young rake from himself." The housekeeper urged Annabelle not to remove her gloves or cape. "We're nearly out of firewood, so there wasn't enough to set a good fire down in the main house today or anywhere else, except for the kitchen. Now that Harrison is coming back, I'm expecting someone to deliver more before long." She took Annabelle's hand and patted it. "Just call me Irene like everybody else does. We don't hold with being as formal out here as they do in the city. I hope you don't mind."

"Actually, I'm a bit relieved," Annabelle admitted, grateful for this first ray of normalcy since she had arrived.

Irene smiled and held on to her hand as they walked down the narrow hall that served as a foyer. "I've been praying every night that Harrison would settle down with a good woman like you seem to be. I don't know how you did it, since he's managed to evade the grasp of most of the eligible young women in the city. But I'm happy he had the good sense to bring you here instead of that museum he calls home now. "

Annabelle swallowed hard. Although she was thrilled to find the housekeeper so friendly, she was reluctant to disappoint her by telling her that in truth she was Harrison's wife in name only and that her stay here was merely temporary. To her profound dismay, Annabelle's stomach growled loud enough to elicit a chuckle from Irene, who pointed to the staircase. Its wrought-iron balustrade seemed far too ostentatious when set against plain whitewashed walls nearly devoid of decoration except for oil-lit sconces providing light.

"Unless you're curious or just needing a rest, I can show you the sleeping rooms and the library upstairs later. For now, I'm thinking you'd like to warm up and maybe have some dinner."

Annabelle grinned sheepishly. "Thank you. I think I'd like that," she murmured and tried not to think about sharing a sleeping room with Harrison again.

Stopping abruptly when they were halfway down the foyer, Irene lifted the edge of a heavy baize curtain and pulled it back. Annabelle looked upon an expansive room that contained a dining area with a table large enough to seat six people, a matching sideboard, and a wooden chandelier as simple in design as the furniture. The light from the hallway also revealed an area beyond the dining room where a large parlor stretched across the east side of the house. More woolen drapes along the entire outer wall suggested a full expanse of windows. Irene confirmed her suspicions, explaining it was a glass wall with French doors that led out to the portico Annabelle had seen earlier.

"It's a real pretty view from the parlor any time of the year, but with the severe winter we're having, the drapes are in place to try to stave off some of the cold. Once that firewood gets here, I'll see that there's a good fire going and those drapes get taken down."

When Annabelle shivered with a sudden chill, Irene frowned. "There's a good fire in the kitchen, which is about the only room we've been heating for nearly a week. If you don't mind taking your dinner with the rest of us, I can set a place for you quickly enough, or I can make up a tray—"

"No, I don't mind at all," Annabelle replied with a smile that came straight out of her heart. This temporary home was going to be a blessing.

Irene grinned. "I was hoping you wouldn't." She dropped the baize curtain back in place before leading Annabelle to a small door in the far western corner of the foyer.

"We've got a bit of a walk ahead of us, but don't worry. You won't have to go outside in the elements again."

Curious as well as confused, Annabelle followed Irene down a set of stairs that led to the basement. Several oil lamps on the thick walls lit their way to yet another door, which Irene tugged open to reveal a narrow walkway as well lit as the basement. Annabelle's eyes widened. "It's a tunnel!"

Irene chuckled. "The tunnel leads from this basement to the one beneath the cottage. If you need any one of us, just ring that bell," she explained and pointed to an impressive bell hanging at the entrance.

"You'll be able to hear it?"

"We're paid to hear it," Irene replied and led Annabelle into the brick-lined tunnel, securing the door behind them. "Isaac Graymoor, your husband's great-grandfather, had this country estate built to escape the hot, humid summers in the city long before I was born," she began as they started walking down the tunnel, which was surprisingly warmer than the house they had just left. "As I heard the tale, he was rather eccentric. He also had a very sensitive nose and couldn't tolerate cooking smells beyond mealtimes. He had a real penchant for privacy, too, which explains why he had a cottage built forty feet away from the house—where he put the kitchen as well as rooms for the staff. There's a second tunnel leading from the cottage basement down to the river, so the family wouldn't be bothered by supplies being delivered, either."

Annabelle shook her head. "You have to walk through a tunnel that's forty feet long each and every time you need to enter the house to do your work?"

"Keeps the figure trim and the legs from seizing up with old age," Irene teased. "The bricks keep the temperature in the tunnel cooler in summer and warmer in winter than either the cottage or the house, so I'm not complaining. Oh, I should probably tell you that these oil lamps along the way are only lit until sunset or so, so you shouldn't try to use the tunnel at night."

Annabelle shook her head again, surprised at Irene's openness and positive outlook. When she caught the aroma of food, her stomach growled again, even louder this time.

Irene paused and cocked her head. "How long has it been since you've eaten?" she asked, as if she was prepared to reprimand Harrison when he arrived for not being attentive to his bride's needs.

"Just a few hours. I'm not shy when it comes to mealtime," she admitted.

Irene hooked her arm with Annabelle's. "I knew I liked you the moment I laid eyes on you." She smiled and quickly ushered Annabelle through a final door that opened into the cottage basement.

Annabelle followed the housekeeper up the staircase and into the kitchen. Greeted by a warm blast of air and mouthwatering aromas, she was surprised to see only two other servants, a middle-aged man and woman, seated at the large round table in the center of the room.

Irene quickly introduced her to Alan, who had a shock of startling red hair on his head and immediately rose to his feet. His reed-thin wife, Peggy, stood up next to her much-shorter husband. "Please. Don't let me interrupt your meal," Annabelle urged, but they both looked to Irene for permission.

"Go ahead. Do as Miss Annabelle asked."

Both of them returned to their seats, but wore a look of total surprise when Irene took Annabelle's cape and gloves, pulled out a chair, and Annabelle joined them at the table. "Miss Annabelle is hungry. You can't expect her to take her meal at the main house in an unheated dining room," she admonished.

Alan's cheeks flushed bright red. "I'm sorry, Miss Annabelle. I'll see to setting the fires on the first floor right quick, just as soon as that firewood gets delivered."

"I suppose I'll need to help," Peggy murmured reluctantly.

Irene cast a hard glance at the woman. "We all have to do what we can now that Mr. Harrison and Miss Annabelle will be in residence." She set a napkin, a plate of thick pottery, and utensils in front of Annabelle and smiled before spinning the raised center of the table to give Annabelle a full view of the food prepared for dinner. "If there's nothing here that suits you, I'll fix something else."

Annabelle bypassed the platter of thickly sliced ham and ladled a spoonful of steaming chicken topped with featherlight dumplings onto her plate. "This is my favorite dish in all the world," she murmured. Troubled by Peggy's comment, however, she paused before taking a bite and addressed Irene, who was clearly in charge of the staff. "I don't mean to burden any of you by arriving unexpectedly."

Irene sat down next to her and filled her plate. "It's no burden at all. We're just short a pair of hands at the moment."

Peggy frowned. "We wouldn't be shorthanded if that silly goose, Jane, hadn't run off to marry that nitwit who convinced her to travel west with him."

Irene took the knife she was using to butter her dumplings and pointed it at the woman. "There's no need to bother Miss

Annabelle with such gossip. Or Mr. Harrison when he first arrives, either. Other than spending a weekend or two here occasionally, he hasn't been back here to live for eight years, and I won't have you or Alan start complaining. There's time enough to tell him tomorrow, which I plan to do myself," she said, taking firm command.

Annabelle was tempted to ask what had prompted Harrison to abandon this home to live in the city, but she was far too intimidated by the look on Irene's face to say a word, even though the housekeeper was directing her glare at her staff. Instead, she polished off her entire plate, took a second helping, and finished that, too. She'd asked Mrs. Faye to purchase a diary for her to replace the one she had burned before leaving home, and she planned to add this scrumptious meal to the list of treasures she'd record for today.

Hopeful that the other items she had requested would also arrive soon, she nearly gasped when Irene took her plate and replaced it with a smaller plate filled with dessert. "I couldn't possibly eat that piece of pie. It's enormous!"

"Of course you can," Irene countered. "Besides, it's the only thing I know how to bake that tastes any good."

Annabelle took one bite of the cinnamon-laced confection and sighed. "It's heavenly. I highly doubt that anyone who can make a pie this good wouldn't be able to bake anything to perfection."

Alan chuckled. "Actually, Irene's right. She can't bake much of anything else. Not that I'm complaining," he said before helping himself to a healthy serving of the pie.

Before he had a chance to take a single bite, the sound of a wagon pulling up in the outside yard had him leaping to his feet. He took one look out of the kitchen window and grinned. "Firewood's finally here," he explained and charged out of the kitchen, donning his coat as he hurried off.

He had no sooner closed the door when the sound of a distant bell echoed up the basement staircase. Irene answered Annabelle's unspoken question with a smile. "That would be supplies coming from town. The bell they ring to let us know they've arrived has a different pitch," she offered. "Peggy and I will need to take care of this. We'll be a while, so if you get tired of waiting after you finish your pie, you might want to walk around the house and take stock of your new home. If you need me for any reason, I'll be in that tunnel I showed you. The one that leads down to the river." Then she followed Peggy down the steps to the basement.

After Annabelle finished her pie, she was so full she could barely move. Although she was curious about the second floor of the house, she did not feel comfortable wandering about and felt guilty that everyone else was busy while she had virtually nothing important to do. She took one glance around the kitchen, took note of the dirty dishes on the table and the pots and pans on the cookstove that had been set into the old walk-in hearth, and smiled.

She removed the clean apron hanging from a peg next to the water pump and put it on before she set a pot of water on the cookstove to heat and started tidying up. She was scraping the last platter clean when she heard footsteps coming up the basement staircase. "I thought you said it would take you a while. I hope you don't mind, but I was feeling rather useless, so I thought I'd help by cleaning up from dinner. I'm not certain what you do with the scraps—"

"Annabelle, just exactly what do you think you're doing?"

The sound of Harrison's voice, though not stern, startled her so badly she dropped the platter, which broke into several pieces on the floor at her feet. "Harrison! I thought you weren't going to arrive until much later."

He shook his head. "I finished up my errands much faster than I expected, although I must admit to hurrying so I could make it out here before the worst of the snowstorm hit," he explained as he stepped toward her. "Obviously, my unexpected arrival has proven to be more fortuitous than I thought it would be."

"Oh?" she managed, surprised at how her pulse began to race when he approached her, his hair glistening with several snowflakes that had yet to melt.

"Apparently you and I need to have a talk." His eyes sparkled with more humor than disapproval.

She swallowed hard. "A talk?" She dropped her gaze. "What about?"

"As my wife, I have certain expectations, certain wants and needs that I need to discuss with you. Privately, before my staff finds their way back here," he added gently before retrieving her cape and handing it to her.

Her heart thudded in her chest, and she moistened her lips as she slipped into the cape. She did not know why or how he might possibly have had a change of heart about having their marriage annulled after meeting with his lawyer. But if he did and if he had any expectations that she might be interested in being anything other than his wife in name only, she was going to set him straight. Right here and right now.

Just as soon as she found her voice, which seemed to be just beyond her reach at the moment.

Experience, however, had taught Annabelle that a handsome, charming man, more often than not, led to one thing and one thing only: heartbreak.

And she was never, ever going to let that happen again.

Chapter Nine

❋

Harrison had been pleased that Annabelle had not balked when he pressed her to keep their marriage a secret and to live quietly in a boardinghouse while he pursued an annulment. With that plan now eliminated, convincing her to play the role of a loving, dutiful wife both at home and at several social events they would be expected to attend offered an even greater challenge.

He could ill afford to antagonize her for fear she would simply walk right out of this house and disappear. He needed her, and her cooperation, at least until she signed the documents young Fennimore had drafted as well as the settlement agreement his usual attorney had prepared.

Pleased that his calming words had eased the uncertainty from her gaze while they traveled through the tunnel back to the main house, he led her up the curving staircase to the second floor and into the library. The room was as cold as all the others in the main house, and he made a mental note to talk to Irene and ask her why she had waited so long to order more firewood.

He closed the door to assure their privacy, and he was confident that he had the arsenal of weapons he needed to get her to do as he asked: money, jewels, and a charm that most women found irresistible.

He watched her as she moved directly past the desk in the center of the room, where a pair of gas lamps provided light. She stopped in front of one of the three walls lined with shelves of books that stretched from floor to ceiling. "When Irene mentioned the library, I had no idea there would be so many books here."

"Do you like to read?" he asked as she worked her way down the length of the wall, studying the collection his grandfather had gathered here.

She nodded, then suddenly stopped and pointed to a thick book bound in rich, well-worn leather that stirred no memories for him. "Would I be able to take this one and keep it in my room, or must I read it here?"

He didn't bother to check which book she had chosen and merely shrugged. "Whichever pleases you more."

She took the book from the shelf and tucked it under her arm. "I think I'll take it with me, since there isn't a fireplace or warming stove in here, let alone any windows," she noted and cocked her head. "I thought I saw several upstairs windows when I first arrived."

"You did, but the library was built squarely in the center of the second floor for a reason. My grandfather designed the room as his refuge that was sacrosanct. When he was in residence, no one, not even the staff, was permitted into the room without his express permission, which is a tradition that remains in place today."

"Did he like to read, or are all these books just for display?"

"I've been told he was well-read, but he also used the library to maintain extensive correspondence that demanded strict privacy. He slept here occasionally, as well." He pulled a curtain aside to reveal a narrow bed tucked within the alcove before dropping it back into place.

"Have you read any of these books?"

"I have," he replied, "but rather than analyze my taste in literature, we have much more important things to discuss."

Her chin tilted up just a tad.

He pulled the chair out from the desk. "If you'll take a seat, I have two legal documents for you to sign." He walked around to the other side of the desk where he had placed the documents earlier and flashed her a reassuring smile.

"Are they part of your 'expectations,' " she quipped, although she took her seat and placed the book she had selected on her lap.

"I suspect they're yours, as well," he murmured, then selected the most important of the two documents and opened it. "This is simply a recounting of the coercion used to force both of us to marry against our will. This may or may not be necessary in the end, but my lawyer agrees that it's best to be overprepared."

"I agree," she said. "Did your lawyer give you any indication of how long it will take to obtain the annulment?"

He swallowed hard. He did not correct her assumption that it would be an annulment rather than a divorce; instead, he eased the concern in her gaze with the one truth he was prepared to share with her. "By the end of January, if not sooner."

She offered him a tenuous smile of gratitude before she drew a deep breath, read the entire document carefully, and finally signed her name.

Pleased that she offered no argument, he set the document aside. He was prepared for quite a different reaction this time and used the same low, persuasive voice that usually convinced even the most hesitant young woman to trust him. "I truly hope you'll sign this document," he said and opened the second one, which provided a substantial sum to be paid to her annually on the anniversary of the yet-to-be determined date their marriage legally ended. His lawyer had cleverly worded it without using the term divorce.

While she skimmed the one-page document, a band of guilt wrapped around his conscience and squeezed hard. He could not explain exactly why he did not want to tell her that an annulment would be virtually impossible to obtain because of his reputation. Harrison recalled how upset she had been when he had first uttered the word *divorce*, and he realized now that he had been overconfident, if not arrogant, when he had promised her an annulment.

Only slightly assuaged, his conscience demanded he face the uncomfortable truth that he actually wanted to see her able to live out the rest of her life in comfort. In spite of the fact she spoke her mind far too often and chose to defy him when it suited her, he sensed she possessed an inner goodness that made her extremely vulnerable. He dismissed the notion he could protect her from troubles and heartbreak. Experience had been a cruel taskmaster in that regard, and he refused to let a woman like Annabelle tempt him to believe otherwise.

She stopped reading before she had finished the entire document and shook her head. "As you must recall, I told you that I don't want a settlement."

He nodded. "I do, but if you'd trouble yourself to read just a bit further, you'll find that you retain the right to reject the annual stipend at any given time."

She cocked her head. "Even before the first payment?"

He pointed to the final paragraph, turned his head to be able to read it, and read it aloud. " 'Any and all payments can be terminated anytime by the recipient by providing written notification to Mr. Harrison Graymoor or his designated legal representative.' "

Her eyes lit with hope. After reading the entire document, she signed it. "Is that all you wanted to discuss?"

He smiled before he walked around the desk to open a side drawer. He removed a narrow case he had stored there before traipsing out to the cottage to find her and set it on top of the desk. "As far as anyone is concerned, which includes Irene and the rest of the staff here as well as in the city, we're legally married and intend to stay that way, which makes it very important for you to wear a wedding ring. Mrs. Wilshire may have been the first to ask about it, but she won't be the last," he cautioned and opened the case.

She gaped at the contents and clapped one hand to her heart, which was precisely the reaction he had hoped she would have. "Mercy! How . . . how many rings did you buy?"

He chuckled. "A dozen, but I didn't buy them. Once you've made your selection, the rest will be returned. Since you weren't with me, I couldn't be certain of the size, so there's an assortment of sizes, too. If there's a ring you like that's too large for your finger, I can have it resized." He felt a bit awkward about the whole process, since he had never planned to buy a wedding ring for any woman. Not ever.

He glanced down at the sparkling precious jewels embedded in most of the rings, which paled when set against the amazement that lit her features. He was curious to see which ring she would pick, but he was not surprised when she selected a delicate braided band of gold and platinum and slid it onto her finger.

"It fits perfectly," she whispered in a voice cracked with emotion. He assumed it was due to the fact that the ring was a visible reminder of the vows they had exchanged so unwillingly.

"You can remove the ring anytime you're all alone in your room, if you prefer. Otherwise, I'll expect you to wear it."

She dropped her gaze and her hand slipped to her lap to rest on top of her book. "Of course."

"I need you to select a second one. I'm afraid the ring you selected isn't quite appropriate for a number of important social events we'll be attending."

She looked up at him, her eyes wide with surprise. "We will?

But I thought you wanted to keep me out of sight. Isn't that why you moved me all the way out here?"

He moistened his lips. "That was before we encountered Philip and his guests."

"If you expect me to accompany you to these affairs, wouldn't it be easier if we lived in the city? I don't understand why you think it's better to live here."

He let out a long breath. "The women of Philadelphia will be most anxious to meet you and will be sending invitations to visit. Living out here will make it easier for you to decline. Graymoor Gardens is just far enough west of the city to make traveling back and forth very inconvenient, although the snow that's falling will be helpful in that regard."

She wrapped her hands around the book on her lap. "Won't those women expect to be invited here?"

He chuckled. "Proper etiquette dictates that no one would dare call on Mrs. Harrison Graymoor without being invited first, regardless of where she's living."

She cocked her head. "Are you that important?"

"Sadly, yes. Now, as I was saying, the social events we'll be attending are rather formal affairs, which means you'll need to wear a ring that is more in keeping with your status as my wife," he cautioned gently.

She hesitated for a moment and shrugged. "Which one would you prefer I wear?" She slid off the ring she had chosen and laid it on top of the desk.

He selected the ring he favored most, a unique combination of opals and diamonds set into a slim band of gold, and slipped it onto her finger. The diamonds reflected the green tint in the center of the opals that also matched the color of her eyes, but he was disappointed to see that the ring was too large for her. "I prefer this one, but if you dislike it and want another, or you hold with the new idea that opals bring bad luck, I have no objection if you want to choose another. Otherwise, I can have this ring remade to fit you properly."

"No, if you like it, then it's fine. Besides, anyone foolish enough to believe that luck determines life's fate rather than God's grace also believes that opals are only bad luck when they're not the wearer's birthstone. My birthday is in October, which means the opal is my birthstone," she said. She placed the ring back into the case before slipping the original one she had chosen back onto her finger.

Smiling, he closed the case. "Then it's settled," he suggested. Pleased that he had been able to charm her into doing exactly what he wanted so far, he hoped she would be just as agreeable to the rest of what he had to say. "As my wife, I also have other expectations, which will make life easier for both of us if we're going to convince everyone that we take our vows seriously," he began.

She rose to her feet and tucked the book back under her arm, but he was so much taller than she was, her obvious attempt to create the illusion they were equal failed miserably. "Since we don't love each other, which will obviously be more difficult for me to feign than it will be for you, given your experience misleading women in matters of the heart, I can only reasonably conclude that you expect me to both honor and obey you."

He smiled, although he already knew that outmaneuvering this quick-witted, intelligent woman would require his constant attention, along with a fair bit of patience to tolerate her barbs. "I'd be satisfied if you'd simply honor my requests and not challenge me in front of anyone else, since you've already proven you're quite open to doing precisely that while we're alone. If I order something for you, such as a suitable wardrobe, you can't countermand my instructions and reduce the wardrobe by more than half."

Her eyes flashed with surprise that he already knew how her morning had transpired, but she held her tongue.

Emboldened, he continued. "I also don't expect nor can I allow you to perform chores such as washing dishes. Or to take your meals with the staff."

"What exactly would you like me to do with myself all day?" she asked, as if the prospect of having the day to spend as she pleased was distressing.

"You can read. Or you can knit, although I'd rather not be in your presence again when you have such sharp weapons in your hands." He focused his gaze on the knitting stick at her waist that seemed to be part of her regular wardrobe.

Blushing, she waved off his suggestions. "But surely it wouldn't hurt to do some sort of work. Although this house is half the size of the one in the city, it takes a great deal of work to keep it in order."

"It's not your place, and you'll only confuse the staff if you do any of the work that's been assigned to them. Whether we're in the city proper or here, you also can't treat members of my staff or any other as if they're your friends. You can't share gossip with them, you can't trust them to keep a secret, and you can't reassure them that you have any authority over them because you don't. There's a strict hierarchy among the staff, with either Mrs. Faye or Irene at the top, just below me. We have the final word on any matters concerning the staff."

Her cheeks flushed bright pink. "You're talking about Lotte, aren't you!"

"You shouldn't have offered the sweets to her, and she should have known better than to take them," he said firmly.

"She's been reprimanded?" she whispered, clearly distressed.

"Mrs. Faye fired her."

"That isn't fair! She can't do that."

"Yes, she can, and I won't override her decision where the

staff is concerned or any decision Irene makes, either. Not without making either of them appear weak in front of the employees they oversee. Otherwise, they'll all run to me—or you will on their behalf—every time there's a silly squabble. And I have no desire to waste my time settling matters that are of no real consequence."

She blinked hard, visibly struggling for control. "Well said for a man with such incredible wealth that he's willing to squander it foolishly by giving it to a woman who doesn't want it. I'm sorry if I broke one of the many rules you seem to live by in this city, but Lotte is just a very young woman. She shouldn't be punished for my mistake," she whispered.

When he tried to speak, she held up her hand. "You've made it very clear that I have no say in the matter, so I'll just agree that I'll try to remember all your rules and follow them. For appearances' sake, I'll also honor and obey you. I just won't like it, and I most assuredly won't be tempted to like you very much, either." She walked over to put the book she had selected back onto the shelf and left the room.

Harrison stared at the door she had eased closed for a good long time. Oddly troubled that he had brought her close to tears, he was even more surprised that he actually cared what she thought of him. He raked his fingers through his hair. She was a very troublesome woman, the likes of which he had never had to handle before.

He immediately dismissed the thought when Irene charged into the room and shut the door behind her. With hands on her hips, she glared at him. "Whatever did you say to that sweet wife of yours? She was trembling so badly when I passed her in the hall that I took her right to your room and promised I'd bring her a cup of hot tea to help calm her down."

He drew in a long, deep breath. Moving out to Graymoor Gardens had also put him back in the same house with another troublesome woman he could not control, even if he tried. For half a second he seriously considered returning to the city mansion, until he remembered that Philip was living there. "I was only trying to explain that—"

"I don't need to know what you were explaining. Just try harder to do it better, and I know more than anyone else that you're capable of doing that. Or have you lost every bit of common sense and decency you possess to the ills of that city you called home for the past eight years?" She used the same no-nonsense tone he had heard for years, then turned and marched back out of the room.

Harrison threw his hands up in the air. If he had any sense at all, which Irene seemed to think he did, he would go straight back to his home in the city, where not a single member of the staff would dare challenge him. Even though he would have to tolerate having Philip living there until he left for Boston, he found the idea appealing.

And he had no idea how soon he would have any interest in venturing back to Graymoor Gardens, if indeed he would ever return at all.

Chapter Ten

❄

Keeping her promise to obey her husband had already stretched the limits of Annabelle's endurance, in spite of the fact that he had left Graymoor Gardens last night right after supper to return to the city.

She rose just before dawn the next morning and said her morning prayers. Although she was grateful to have this sleeping room to herself until he returned, she had the sense he would not come back to live here at all if he had any choice in the matter.

In point of fact, she much preferred the homey sleeping room here over the very lavish one in the city, although she was not accustomed to having such a large room—even larger than the parlor in her family home. The painted walls suggested just a blush of pink, but the heirloom quilt on the bed was made with fabrics of shades ranging from the deepest rose to a pink so pale it appeared to be white at first glance. The furniture was sturdy enough, but there were enough scars and nicks in the wood to suggest it had been here a very long time.

She pulled back the heavy night curtain that covered the window overlooking the front of the estate, but she had to narrow her gaze to see much of anything in the dim gray light. Once she realized that the snowstorm that had started yesterday had dumped much more than a foot of snow, she dropped the curtain back into place. Undeterred, she dressed as quickly as she could in the dark, slid her cape around her shoulders, and carried her gloves with her as she slipped out of the room.

At this hour, she doubted she would see either Alan or Peggy, but she wanted to avoid Irene most of all as she tiptoed down the hallway. Annabelle knew the woman was concerned about her, in spite of her efforts to convince the woman otherwise.

As she worked her way down the staircase, she held tight to the banister. Torn between keeping her promise to treat Irene as merely a member of the staff and not the friend she suspected Irene could be, she went directly to the front door and left the house.

Outside, the air was frigid. The sun had not struggled past the gray horizon yet, leaving the world bathed in dim, hazy light, but she could hear the sound of the icy river that flowed through the city. Anxious to dispel the cabin fever, she pulled up her hood and donned her gloves.

After taking a deep breath of fresh, cold air, she started down the circular driveway that Alan had shoveled clear after supper last night. She had no intention of trudging through the snow-covered landscape but simply planned to walk back and forth, from one end of the drive to the other, until she drove out every last vestige of her pent-up energy.

She walked as briskly as she dared without losing her footing and was grateful to be living out here in the country, where life was more familiar and she had much more freedom than she would ever have had in the city. When she reached the end of the drive and turned to retrace her steps, she noticed a series of footsteps in the snow that wound from somewhere behind the house and disappeared down the gently sloping ground into the woods.

Her spirit soared. She did not know who had been walking outside last night, but she was excited that their footsteps had packed down the snow so she could follow. Looking closer, she saw that the path actually appeared to start from the side door of the cottage where smoke was rising from the kitchen chimney. Apparently Irene was already up and preparing to cook breakfast, but there were no telltale aromas that would make Annabelle's stomach growl. Anxious to leave before Irene spotted her, she followed the footsteps that led her through a thick stand of barren trees.

Without any foliage to block her view while she walked, she could easily see the eastern sky and the wildlife that struggled to survive the harsh winter. Close by, an owl hooted a good-bye to the night. A black cloud of crows flapped directly over her head, while two other flocks hugged the branches of adjoining trees. Overall, the landscape was a stark winter portrait, painted in nature's unforgiving tones of black and white without a hint of color. It reminded her that Harrison's rules left no room for exceptions.

"Don't do this. Don't do that," she grumbled and kicked at a clump of snow. "What he really meant was don't *think*. Not beyond the rules I must follow."

Hopeful that she would not have to wait long to escape the strict boundaries he had imposed, she was still annoyed with herself for not being able to control her temper when he had imposed his rigid expectations of her. If she had remained calm, she might have been able to reason with him, at least to the point that he might have agreed to reconsider what had happened to poor Lotte and perhaps even rehired her.

She dropped her gaze and kicked at the footprints in the snow as she walked, imagining that she was kicking away her promise to blindly obey him—a promise that had left her afraid to say anything to the staff that might encourage conversation. "I'm not some mindless puppet he can manipulate," she cried, surprised that she had spoken loud enough to hear her words echo through the woods.

"I should hope not."

Startled, she stopped so abruptly she nearly lost her footing. Annabelle looked around and saw Irene sitting on a bench just a few yards away facing the horizon.

Irene smiled at her. "There's enough room for two, if you'd care to join us. You'll need to walk very slowly so you don't scare my little friend here and make him run off before he finishes his breakfast."

Curious, Annabelle took a few deliberate steps toward the bench until she was able to see a black squirrel sitting on top of the snow just a few feet in front of Irene. It was nibbling at a nut of some kind. She stopped immediately, more afraid of engaging in conversation with Irene than she was of getting close to the wild animal. "I had no idea anyone was out here. I shouldn't intrude."

"You're not intruding. Not unless you're still too annoyed with me to bother talking to me. Sit down for a bit so I can introduce you to Jonah," she suggested and tossed another nut to the ground, which the animal quickly snatched up.

Annabelle's heart skipped a beat. "I'm not annoyed with you. Not at all. I've . . . I've just had a lot on my mind." She kept her gaze on the squirrel as she made her way to the bench and sat down. Up close, she could see that the poor creature looked as if it had gone up against a bully and lost. One of its ears was missing, along with half of its tail, and his body was a maze of bright pink scars. "What happened to Jonah?"

Irene shrugged. "I'm not certain, but I suspect he got himself snatched up by a hawk and somehow managed to escape. He survived, but he must have been pretty scared at the time."

With visions of what she might be like when she was finally able to escape the life she had been forced into, Annabelle swallowed the lump in her throat. "I know the feeling."

"Of being caught or escaping?" Irene asked and her gaze gentled. "It's not uncommon, you know, for a newly married young woman to find married life a bit confusing, especially when she hasn't got any family close by to help her. I was married for ten years before God called Harry home, and I'm a good listener, in case you ever want to talk about how you're feeling. It might help."

Annabelle was sorely tempted to pour out her troubles to the woman, but Harrison's list of commandments she had to follow flashed before her mind's eye. "I-I'm sorry. I . . . I can't . . . that is, Harrison said I shouldn't . . ." she stammered, unable to finish, and moved to get to her feet.

The housekeeper caught Annabelle's arm and held her back. "Harrison said you mustn't do what?"

When she did not reply, Irene seemed to be satisfied that Annabelle was still sitting there and simply continued to feed the squirrel until the silence between them snapped Annabelle's willingness to keep her promise.

Mindful of the absolute need to hide the true circumstances of their marriage, Annabelle slowly and carefully explained the rules Harrison expected her to follow regarding the staff, as well as the mistake she had made with Lotte.

Irene listened and nodded occasionally but never offered a comment until Annabelle finished. "To be fair, Harrison's not entirely wrong. There are certain things you need to avoid when you're the mistress of the house. Gossip is surely one. Considering every member of the staff as your friend could be a problem, too, but he should have explained it better to you instead of upsetting you the way he did."

"But it's not his fault. Not entirely," Annabelle admitted. "I've always done my own chores, and I've never lived anywhere that everyone didn't do their share, even when I was teaching at Mrs. Poore's Academy. It's just that I've never had a staff to wait on me before."

"Here, give Jonah this last nut and tell me about this Lotte you're so worried about," Irene prompted and placed a nut in Annabelle's hand, which she promptly tossed to the ground.

"I don't know much about her at all, except that she was very pleasant and very anxious to do a good job," she offered and furrowed her brow. "As I recall, I think I overheard her say something about finding her position through a Mrs. Cooper."

Irene nodded. "Eliza Cooper. I know of her. She operates an establishment in the city that most of the well-to-do turn to when they need to hire another member of their staff."

Annabelle's heartbeat quickened. "Then she'll be able to help Lotte find another position!"

"Not likely," Irene said as she brushed her heavy coat free of several broken shells. "Without references, which Mrs. Faye surely refused to give her, the poor girl will be hard pressed to find work." She got to her feet as Jonah raced off with his last handout. "I'd best be getting back to cook up some breakfast before Alan and Peggy have something else to complain about. Do you want to stay here for a while or walk back with me?"

Annabelle shivered, in spite of the fact that the sun was just beginning to break through the clouds. "I'll walk with you."

Hooking their arms together, Irene walked alongside of her. "You know, we do need to replace Jane. I can't promise I'll be successful, but I can try to see if there's some way for me to get in touch with Lotte through Eliza Cooper. And don't worry about what Harrison might say about the matter. I've always had free rein to hire the staff at Graymoor Gardens. He knows that."

"You'd do that? You'd actually consider hiring her to work here? You'd take my word that—"

"If you've been a teacher, then I have to assume you've got

a good head on your shoulders and know what people are like and what they're not."

Annabelle swallowed hard and wondered what this woman would say about her ability to judge other people if she knew Annabelle had wrongly married not one man, but two. "I always thought I could."

"Then trust yourself to know which people can be a friend and which people are likely to betray the trust you place in them. You're much too good and too smart to be anyone's puppet. Pull your own strings," she urged.

Annabelle grinned. She knew without any doubt that this woman was someone she could trust as a friend. She just did not know if she would have the opportunity to prove to Harrison that she was intelligent enough to pull her own strings. As she walked back to the cottage with Irene, Annabelle prayed he would return to Graymoor Gardens soon so they could discuss the matter.

Just as they arrived back at the cottage, a coach drove past and headed for the carriage house next to the stable. "Harrison must be back," Irene announced and hustled Annabelle into the kitchen, where Alan and Peggy were so busy arguing about what to ask Irene to make for breakfast that they never noticed they were no longer alone.

"Hurry through the tunnel, get back to your room, and get yourself freshened up for your husband," Irene whispered as she guided her down the basement steps.

When Annabelle frowned, Irene chuckled. "Never underestimate the power you have over him. It's a power he's never relinquished to any other woman before you."

"What power?" Annabelle asked.

"Permission to love him," Irene said quietly. "I can see it in his eyes every time he looks at you. And if you're the woman I think you are, you'll use that power to help him become the man I've always known he can be. Now go!"

Annabelle swallowed hard and rushed to the tunnel, hoping she could get back into her room before he discovered she had been in the kitchen. Unlike Irene, she had no false illusions, but she had little time to think about what Irene had said because the sound of footsteps echoing in the tunnel far ahead of her captured her every thought.

Chapter Eleven

❄

The footsteps Annabelle had heard did not come from Harrison after all, but she did not know if she was relieved or disappointed when she realized who was coming through the tunnel.

She recognized the man who approached her as a member of the staff from the city mansion and wondered if Harrison had indeed returned but was waiting for her in the main house.

When he stopped a few deferential feet in front of her, she could see that his ears and nose and cheeks were deep red from the cold he had endured during his journey. "Good morning, ma'am. Mr. Graymoor sent me ahead to deliver your packages, and he asked me to tell you that he expects to return home later today. I carried all the packages to the upstairs hallway, but I was coming to ask Irene if she would see that they were put away properly."

"Thank you, but I'll see to that myself. Was there anything else?"

"No, ma'am. Now that I've made my delivery and spoken to you, I need to return to the city."

"Before you leave, you should see Irene and have her fix you something to warm you up again," she suggested before dismissing him.

Anxious to see what had arrived, she hurried ahead to the main house, but she stopped to hang up her damp cape in the foyer before she mounted the servants' staircase to reach the second floor. There were so many packages lined up in the upstairs hallway, however, that she decided she had better ask Irene to send Peggy up to help her put everything away.

Judging by the sheer number of packages, she did not have to open any of them to know Harrison had to have ordered some additional things for her. It must have taken a bevy of women working into the night, all night, as well as a handsome sum of money, to create this extensive wardrobe in a matter of days. She wondered if it was a peace offering of some kind or simply another opportunity for her husband to show her his authority over her.

She was more interested in the articles from the list she had given to Mrs. Faye, so she searched for the smallest package she could find and peeked inside to make certain she had found the right one. Grinning, she carried it straight to the room she would be sharing with Harrison if he ever decided to spend the night. Rather than think about how awkward it would be to be sleeping in the same room with him again, she set the package on top of the lady's writing desk just opposite the window. She untied the string and peeled back the brown wrapping paper to find three items lying inside.

She carefully untied the string around the first item, pulled back the brown paper, and practically squealed with delight. Instead of the one set of knitting needles she had requested, she found two. One set was made of metal, like the ones she had lost during the robbery, and the other was made of bone.

Thrilled, she tore the largest package open to reveal a handsome brocade knitting bag filled with enough skeins of wool to make several ladies' reticules like the ones she and her mother used to make. After her father died, she had temporarily given up her teaching position to stay at home to care for her elderly mother, and they had spent all of their free time knitting reticules they sold to support themselves.

Precious memories of both her parents, who had given up hope they would ever be blessed with a child before she was born, washed over her, and she blinked back tears while she slipped both sets of the knitting needles into the knitting bag. She reached down to retrieve her knitting stick out of the drawer where she had stored it to keep it safe and added it to the bag before she set it on the floor at her feet.

She opened the smallest package last, expecting to find a simple diary like the one she'd had before—the one she had burned, along with all the letters she had received from her first husband, Eric. Instead, she ran her fingers across an exquisitely pale leather cover before untying the attached leather thong that wrapped around the diary to keep it closed. She was so excited to have a diary again, she did not even care that the cover of the diary had been monogrammed in gold with what appeared to be the Graymoor family crest.

Only time would tell if she would end up burning this diary one day, too, but the one way she had always been able to strengthen her prayer life and to steady her faith was to make an accounting each night of God's many blessings that day and treasure them for what they were: His gifts to her.

Smiling, she stored away the diary. There was no doubt in her mind that tonight Irene's name would be the first she would write in her diary . . . which prompted her to think of a way to thank the woman for her many kindnesses.

⁓

Annabelle retrieved the Bible she had left behind yesterday in the library after arguing with Harrison. She spent some time in her room reading a few of her favorite passages and reflecting on them to find the peace her faith never failed to provide. Although she had many questions about the family history she had found in the Bible, she decided to wait to ask Harrison about it at some point and spent an hour making something special for Irene.

She waited until she was certain that the kitchen had been cleaned up and that Alan and Peggy were both working in the main house, however, before venturing back out to the cottage to see Irene. Armed with the gift she had made, she entered the kitchen to find Irene busy at the table rolling out the crust for one of the apple pies she was making for supper.

"You can't be hungry again already. Not after what you just ate for dinner."

"No, not quite yet," she replied, then walked over to a bowl of sliced apples Irene had already filled and snatched a slice for herself. "I thought maybe we could visit for a spell."

Irene nodded, but she never lost her rhythm as she continued to stretch the dough thin. "Sit yourself down. Just don't get too close to all this flour dusting the table. Otherwise, you'll end up spoiling that pretty new gown you're wearing."

"I'll be careful," Annabelle promised, took a seat across from Irene, and urged the chair a little closer to the table to protect more of her pale lavender skirts. She had never owned a gown this color before, simply because she had never had the luxury of not doing anything that might soil it. "I've brought you a gift," she said and placed it on the table, close enough for Irene to see it, but far enough away to keep the papers she had placed there from being dusted with flour.

Irene glanced at the papers, abruptly lost her rhythm, and fumbled for a moment before she found it again. "What's all that?"

"Recipes," Annabelle replied. "I wrote down some of the recipes for things my mother taught me to bake."

Irene's cheeks flushed pink. "If you're not happy with the

meals I make for you, which seems mighty odd, since you never finish a meal without taking a second helping of something, I'll try to make—"

"Not make. Bake," Annabelle gushed, appalled that she had hurt Irene's feelings again, even unintentionally. "Yesterday you said the only dessert you knew how to bake well was apple pie. I thought perhaps, if you had recipes to follow, you'd see how easy it was to bake some molasses cookies or a strudel. Once you're good at baking those, I can write out some more dessert recipes for you."

Irene's cheeks deepened to scarlet, she set down the rolling pin, and reached over to retrieve a tin pie plate sitting on the table just within her reach. "I thank you for your gifts, but . . . but I can't accept them."

Annabelle's heart dropped. "Why not? Is there some rule Harrison didn't tell me about that makes it inappropriate for me to give you a gift as simple as a few recipes? And even if there is, I thought you'd appreciate the fact that I'm pulling my own strings and doing something I want to do for someone else."

Irene set the tin plate down on top of the pie crust and gazed at her. "I doubt Harrison would care one way or the other that you gave me those recipes. Even if he did, I've got my own reasons for not accepting them."

When Annabelle cocked a brow, Irene moistened her lips and rested her hands on the table. "I can't read."

"You can't read?"

"Not a word. Never learned. Never needed to learn, although I've often wished I could read the Good Book for myself when bad weather makes it impossible to attend services on Sunday, like it does today."

Annabelle's eyes widened. "Today is Sunday?" she asked and wondered if she would ever again be settled enough in one place to keep track of the days.

Irene chuckled. "All day. At the rate this winter is going, I doubt there will be more than a few Sundays we'll actually be able to get to the church."

Disappointed to think she would not be able to attend services regularly each week, Annabelle tried to make the best of a situation she could not control and focused on one she could. "I can teach you to read."

Irene waved away her offer and chuckled. "At my age? I'm sixty-seven years old. I doubt I have enough years left in me to learn how to read, and I sincerely doubt that Harrison would be very happy when he finds out you've turned this kitchen into a schoolroom. Not that I'm worried about what he thinks of me, mind you, because he can't fire me even if he wants to. I'm more concerned about what he'll say to you."

Annabelle furrowed her brow. "Why can't he fire you?"

Irene grabbed the pie plate, set it before her, and started lifting the crust to set it within. "His late father, Thomas, rest his soul, gave me the right to stay at Graymoor Gardens for the rest of my life. At least that's what the lawyer said who read part of the will to me."

Annabelle recognized the name she had seen in the Bible, but rather than ask Irene the reasons he had had to give her that right, she pressed the woman to focus on accepting her offer. "Please. At least consider my idea."

"Even if I wanted to learn how to read, I don't have the time. I have more than enough work to do all day to keep my hands busy."

Annabelle refused to accept the woman's excuse. "Then we'll work together at night. After supper's been cleared away. You're finished with your chores by then, aren't you?"

Chuckling, Irene shook her head. "By the time the sun is well set, I'm so tired I take to my bed. Otherwise, I'd never have the energy to get up in the morning."

"You're up early enough to take a walk before breakfast and spend time with Jonah. If you can make time for that, you can make time to learn to read in the morning, too. Since I prefer to get up before the sun like you do, I can meet you here in the kitchen. We'll take a walk together first, then start on your lessons. And in case you're still too stubborn to say yes, then consider this a formal request from the mistress of the house, who very much wants her new friend to learn how to read." She looked around the kitchen. "Is there a clean apron I can use?"

"Whatever for?"

Pleased that the housekeeper had given up arguing, she grinned. "I'm going to show you how to take that crust and use those apples, plus a few other goodies, to bake a strudel that will make you want to cry because it's just that scrumptious. All I need for you to find for me are some walnuts, raisins, and any berries you might have dried from last summer's bounty."

This time Irene did not offer a word in protest, but instead handed Annabelle a clean apron she retrieved from a corner cupboard. She gathered up the requested ingredients, which included some dried plums, and once she had set them onto the table, she cocked a brow. "If I can really make all this into something that tastes as good as you say it is, I have a mind to make another one for Christmas dinner. I've only got three weeks to practice, though."

Annabelle eased her hold on the apron strings she was tying into place. "Christmas. I can't believe I've forgotten all about it."

Irene smiled. "It will be a blessed Christmas indeed to have you and Harrison here this year. Now show me what to do."

They spent the next few hours laughing and chatting together, and before long, the kitchen was filled with the aroma of the strudel baking in the oven. Peggy returned to the kitchen, but Annabelle held a finger to her lips to encourage Irene to keep the new dessert a secret.

Peggy, however, had news of her own. "I came to tell you that Mr. Philip has come to call. He's waiting for you in the parlor, Miss Annabelle."

Chapter Twelve

❄

Harrison knew there could be any number of surprises waiting for him when he returned home to Graymoor Gardens late Sunday afternoon. But he was bringing back news of his own that may not exactly please Annabelle or Irene.

Surprised to see much deeper snow here in the countryside, he instructed Graham to bypass the approach to the main house altogether. He dismissed him when they reached the shortcut to the cottage he had used many, many times as a youth to return from one escapade or another. He entered the kitchen, hoping to speak to Irene before he saw Annabelle, and frowned. Irene was nowhere in sight, and the only evidence that supper was going to be served tonight was a rather tempting-looking strudel left to cool on the table.

Well aware of Irene's limitations when it came to desserts other than apple pie, he dismissed any thought of slicing off a piece of the strudel. "Appearances can be rather misleading," he murmured.

Anxious to find his housekeeper, he went straight to the basement tunnel and met her when he was halfway to the main house. "I'm rather hungry. Are you serving anything for supper tonight other than strudel?" he teased after planting a kiss on her forehead.

Clearly flustered, she swatted at his arm. "You should save your kisses for your wife, although I've a mind to give you a bit of advice on how to help that young woman adjust to married life. You should try spending the night here at home instead of going back to the city, too."

Harrison ignored her reprimand, but cringed at the thought that his wife had spent the past day or so sulking.

"And don't tell me how to run my kitchen," she added. "I've got a very hearty supper planned, although I'm serving it a bit later than usual, since we have a guest."

"What guest?" he asked, surprised that any of the city's matrons would have broken with custom and decided to call on the new Mrs. Graymoor without being invited.

"Mr. Philip arrived several hours ago."

His hands clenched into fists. He had not seen Philip at all back at the mansion yesterday afternoon. Last night he had spent the entire evening getting reacquainted with a few old friends who were equally inclined to enjoy some of the more pleasurable pursuits the area had to offer. He met them on Petty's Island, a small bit of land located close to the New Jersey coastline that was also well beyond the scrutiny of the prim and proper city elites.

Today he had slept until midmorning and left to complete a few necessary errands in the afternoon, assuming that his cousin must have already left for Boston, as planned.

More anxious than ever to reach Annabelle now that he knew Philip had not left the area at all, he quickly told Irene about the surprise he had for her. "I've hired a replacement for Jane," he informed her. Before her frown ended with a reminder that he should have consulted her first, he held up his hand. "She's already been told that you have the right to decide whether or not she's the right person to add to the staff. She's been promised a week to prove herself. Nothing more."

Irene sighed. "When is this woman supposed to arrive?"

"In a few days."

"One week, you said?"

When he nodded, she merely shrugged. "I'll have Peggy get Jane's room tidied up first thing tomorrow."

He kissed her forehead again and grinned. "Good. Now if you'll excuse me, I should get to the house to see Annabelle and Philip."

"Take your time. They're not back yet."

He clenched his jaw. "Back from where?" he asked, holding a tight rein on his temper.

"If you must know, Mr. Philip took her for a sleigh ride, but don't blame him. I suggested it. And before anyone else tells you, I didn't make the strudel you mentioned by myself. Annabelle helped me, so you might want to try a slice, although I did add a few plums you seem to detest so much," she quipped and walked past him to get back to the cottage.

೧

After pacing back and forth in the parlor for a very long hour while his imagination flashed all sorts of troubling images of Philip and Annabelle in his mind's eye, Harrison finally heard the muted sound of horses' hooves drawing the sleigh up the circular drive.

He parted the delicate curtain that had replaced the heavy woolen drapes on the windows and doors, including the ones that led out to the portico overlooking the river, but he was careful to only pull back enough of the fabric to get a clear view of the outside without being noticed. He took one glance at the couple seated next to each other with a thick blanket lying across their laps to keep them warm and instantly dropped the curtain back into place. But the image had already been indelibly etched in his mind.

With her cheeks flushed pink and her lips forming a smile, Annabelle's features had been lit with total joy. He had never seen her look this happy or this . . . "Radiant," he whispered and clenched his fist. He fought against a surge of jealousy that was almost as instinctive as it was annoying, especially when he considered Philip was the one who was responsible for her transformation. He also found it odd to be jealous when his relationship to Annabelle was based on sheer circumstance, rather than anything as dangerous as affection.

Fortunately, Philip was scheduled to leave any day now to return to Boston. As for his own feelings where Annabelle was concerned . . . he knew it was too great a risk to have any feelings for her at all if he wanted to avoid the inevitable heartache she represented as his wife.

He turned and set a chair before the fire so he could warm himself and still see both of them the moment they entered the room. When he noted the knitting bag sitting on the seat, he paused to look inside, and smiled. She had not started to knit anything yet, but she had stored her knitting stick and needles in the bag—which meant he was relatively safe as long as he kept that bag out of her reach.

After placing it out of sight in the far corner, he sat down and waited. He tensed when he heard the front door open, but quickly relaxed when he heard Philip drive away with the sleigh. Relieved that he would have a few moments alone with Annabelle while Philip took the sleigh back to the cottage and turned it over to Alan, he was also determined to surprise Annabelle by being more understanding of the difficult position she was in.

He listened to her footsteps as she walked down the long, narrow foyer, stopping only long enough to store away her winter outerwear.

She was smiling and humming softly when she lifted the baize cloth covering the doorway and entered the dining area. She lost her smile, as well as her voice, when she spied him, just as he was getting to his feet. "I knew you were planning to return this afternoon, but I . . . I didn't expect you'd arrive this early." She tilted up her chin just a tad and joined him in the parlor. After taking a seat on the winged sitting bench across from him, she folded her hands demurely on her lap.

Surprised by her graceful movements, he had trouble gathering his own wits. Unlike her baggy, poorly fitting travel gown, the lavender day gown she was wearing fit her to perfection and hinted at her tempting womanly curves. Instead of the long braid or tight bun, her blond hair was gathered up into a shimmering net held in place at the crown of her head. Indeed, her grace and beauty rivaled that of the city's most beautiful women, a most unexpected turn of events, considering she was born and bred in the rural part of the state.

Pleased to see she was wearing her wedding ring, he smiled. "I didn't expect to find you gone or my cousin here visiting. I'm glad you're back," he said, keeping all hint of displeasure out of his voice. "You appear to have survived the snowstorm rather well."

She blushed, adding even more color to her cheeks. "I've found ways to keep busy," she replied and glanced around the room.

"Your knitting bag is over there," he said, pointing to the far corner of the room. "Other than reading, if you went back to the library to get that book you left behind, or getting your knitting bag in order or teaching Irene how to bake something other than apple pie . . . what else have you done to keep yourself occupied?"

She raised one brow. "You don't mind that I've been teaching Irene how to bake—"

"Anything you can teach her in that regard is more than fine with me, although I'd rather not have anything with plums in it."

"Then that would include teaching her how to read so she can use the recipes I've written out for her or any others she might find, too, wouldn't it?" she asked, her lips once again shaping a smile.

He swallowed hard, unable to fathom an argument that might undermine her logic. He also found himself unwilling to take away even this limited opportunity for her to resume her role as a teacher—a role she would lose forever once her name was tainted by their eventual divorce. "No objection at all. In fact, I can see some real advantage, since she'll be better able to verify that the charges for supplies I've ordered are valid instead of relying on the deliveryman's word," he admitted. Harrison rose to place a small box on her lap before he retook his seat. "I had the opal ring resized, and I'd like you to wear it Thursday night."

Growing pale, she did not make any effort to open the box. "*This* Thursday? That's only four days from now. Isn't that a bit soon for us to be going—"

"There's an annual ball this Thursday that's too important for us not to attend. I was hoping we could spend some time together talking about what you might expect from a social event that is probably much more formal than what you're accustomed to." He offered her a reassuring smile, although in truth, he would feel much more comfortable about attending himself if he knew Vienna Biddle was not going to be there.

"I appreciate your concern, but there's no need." She dropped her gaze for a moment before looking back at him again. "While I was raised in a very small town, which you already know, I was fortunate to be able to attend Hamilton Female Academy, which prepared me for much more than the teaching position I obtained with Mrs. Peale."

"Go on," he prompted when she seemed reluctant to continue.

She drew in a long breath, but her gaze was steady when she met his own. "At Hamilton, I learned when to talk and when to hold silent when attending formal or informal events. I know what topics to choose for polite conversation and which to avoid and . . . and I even learned how to dance, although I'm not very good at it. I haven't had the opportunity to practice much of what I learned, but I'll do my best not to embarrass you."

Held captive by her pale green eyes, which glistened with hope and earnestness, he dropped his guard. In the space of a single breath, she nearly slipped past all the defenses he had built up to protect his heart, something other women with far more experience had never been able to do. But he raised his guard just in time to avoid sure disaster and drew another very long, very deep breath. "Perhaps I could simply tell you about some of the people you're likely to meet at the ball," he suggested.

"Cousin! Welcome back. Did I hear you say something about the Sullivans' ball this week? I assume you'll both be attending," Philip said as he entered the room.

Once Harrison rose and exchanged handshakes, Philip sat down right next to Annabelle.

Harrison shrugged. "Is there anyone of any importance in the city who won't be attending?" he asked, growing annoyed that his cousin was sitting just a little too close to Annabelle to suit him.

Philip laughed, but he looked at Annabelle when he replied, "I hope you'll save a dance for me."

"I thought you were returning to Boston to spend Christmas with your sister and her family," Harrison blurted before she had a chance to respond.

"That was exactly my plan until yesterday, when I got word from my sister that two of her children had taken sick, along with her husband," he replied. "I didn't think you'd mind if I stayed for another week or two, considering that you'll be living out here with your wife now. I contacted Mrs. Sullivan to see if it was possible for me to rescind the decline I'd sent her, and she was gracious enough to assure me that I'd be welcome to attend." He narrowed his gaze. "Unless that interferes somehow with your plans or you mind that I'll be relying on your hospitality a little while longer," he added.

Annoyed that he had betrayed his thoughts by frowning, Harrison forced himself to smile. "Not at all," he assured his cousin, unwilling to tell him that what he minded most of all was the look of pleasure on his wife's face that Philip's extended stay had inspired.

Chapter Thirteen

❄

Within three days, Annabelle developed a fairly satisfying daily routine, though she still hoped to find something to do with her time that was more meaningful.

After dinner she skipped the short nap she had planned and took her knitting to the parlor with her when Philip arrived for a visit for the fourth afternoon in a row. By his suggestion, she continued to work at knitting a pair of socks to be donated to the local almshouse. It would be far more useful than the lady's reticule she had started, and she even had plans to expand her knitting to include mittens and scarves, although she doubted she would be here long enough to finish more than a few of them. "Tell me what you've been able to learn about my idea," she urged Philip, hoping to distract him from asking her for a second time to spend part of the afternoon in the city to visit some of the many landmarks.

Lounging on the winged bench seat, he sighed. "Very well. I checked this morning with Nathan Drummond, who is the director at the Refuge, which provides a temporary home for indigent women and children, and Byron Calder at the Graymoor Home for the Blind and Lame. Both welcomed your offer to volunteer your time, although they were quite surprised, given Harrison's total lack of interest in either institution."

Heartened, she was too excited to be able to concentrate on her knitting and set it on her lap. "They did? Truly?"

He chuckled. "If half the people I approach to support any number of charities were half as enthusiastic as you are, there wouldn't be the great need to encourage them to untie their purse strings. Which means I wouldn't have anything to do with my life," he teased.

Embarrassed, she dropped her gaze. Impressed by this humble man's decision to make his life's work the betterment of others by raising money to help those unable to help themselves, she had already come to think of him as the brother she never had. At thirty-eight, he had no income of his own other than a small inheritance that provided for his limited needs. He also had no family of his own, yet he seemed very content and satisfied working for the benefit of others.

As unfair as it might be, she could not help but compare him to Harrison. Harrison spent much of his massive fortune indulging his own selfish interests, showing little concern about anything or anyone else. She was glad he was spending most of his days and nights back in the city, although she never knew when he was likely to show up for a few hours and leave again.

"Which institution appeals to you more?" he asked.

She glanced up at him. "Truthfully, I'm not quite certain. Perhaps once I've had the opportunity to visit each of them—"

"Why not do that this afternoon? I'll take you myself and have you back in time for a late supper, although I have plans for this evening and would have to send you back in my coach alone."

Sorely tempted, she pressed her lips together and shook her head. "I probably shouldn't. Harrison may come back this afternoon, and I wouldn't want him to worry if I'm not here," she offered, although she really had no idea if he was going to return at all until the night of the ball.

Philip got to his feet. "I saw Harrison myself this morning. As I recall, he mentioned remaining in the city tonight, but said he would be returning to Graymoor Gardens tomorrow to escort you to the ball. I thought you knew."

"No, I didn't," she murmured, embarrassed that she did not know of her husband's plans for tonight. Although he had returned to tell her about the people attending the ball, he still had not finished his description of one last family, and she hoped he would find time to do that.

Without wasting another thought to worry, she stuffed her knitting back into her knitting bag. "I can be ready in ten minutes. No, wait. I need to go out to the cottage to let Irene know to plan for a late supper. Give me fifteen minutes," she said and hurried from the room.

After storing her knitting back in her room, she rushed down the servants' staircase and grabbed her cape and gloves, but she did not put them on until she was in the basement. By the time she entered the tunnel, she could not decide if Harrison had a single redeeming quality, other than his charm and handsome looks, which he most definitely used to his own advantage.

"Selfish, selfish man," she grumbled as she walked. "He doesn't even have the decency to let me know he's not coming home so I can tell Irene, which means more food will go to waste. And I expect this man to be more supportive of the less fortunate? A man who won't even maintain the same level of support to the very charities his own family started? That man?"

Her own words echoed back at her in the tunnel, but when she heard the sound of distant footsteps, she held silent and prayed none of the staff had heard her. She traveled a few more feet before she could see the figures of two women approaching, heard the faint echo of their conversation, and smiled. Irene probably would not have heard Annabelle at all, not with Peggy complaining to her again about something or other.

She hurried her steps but stopped dead when she was close enough to see that the woman walking next to Irene was not Peggy at all. With her heart rejoicing, she held her place until Irene was close enough for Annabelle to give her a hug. "You did it. You found Lotte! Thank you," she whispered.

Grinning, Irene hugged her back. "I'm taking this hug because I don't get too many, but you're mistaken. You need to talk to Lotte and let her tell her tale. That's why I was bringing her to you after she arrived with the rest of the deliveries Tim brought us." Confused, Annabelle glanced at the young woman who was watching them with wide, wide eyes. "I'm so sorry you lost your position in the city," she offered.

Lotte blushed. "It wasn't all your fault, Mrs. Gray . . . Miss Annabelle. I promised Mr. Harrison that I'd tell you that."

"Mr. Harrison?" Annabelle repeated, looking from Lotte to Irene and back again. "You saw Mr. Harrison?"

"Yes, ma'am. I guess he found out where I lived from Mrs. Cooper, and he came to my home and asked me if I wanted a chance to prove myself in a position out here, which I do. I surely do."

"She's got a week to do that," Irene added, sternly enough to let Lotte know that she had to work hard to earn the position and to let Annabelle know that Irene would do her best to help the young woman succeed. "Tim also brought you a message from your husband," Irene added. "He'll be home tonight, but very late, so you shouldn't wait up for him."

Completely ashamed of herself for grumbling that Harrison was a selfish man with no redeeming qualities, Annabelle wondered if Irene might be right. Perhaps those qualities were really there, hidden beneath an armor only she had the power to penetrate if she could find it in her heart to accept and embrace his well-hidden permission to love him.

This was quite a ridiculous notion, given the fact that he had already started proceedings to end their marriage.

She could, however, choose to rely on Harrison to keep her informed about his plans instead of anyone else, including Philip, who had no idea that Harrison had changed his plans for the evening and would be coming home to spend it with her.

Nevertheless, she hurried back to tell Philip they only had a short time to spend in the city because she intended to be here before Harrison returned.

e

For the first time since she had arrived in the city of Philadelphia, Annabelle thought she might be getting a glimmer of the path God had set out before her. The need for volunteers was great at both the institutions she had visited, although she was most drawn to the plight of the women living at the Refuge. But the greatest need seemed to be for firewood, which was incredibly scarce due to the record freeze that had enveloped the city.

Philip had also taken her shopping. After ordering a diary for Harrison identical to the one she had gotten for herself, except with a darker leather cover, Philip had also escorted her to the candy store, where she wanted to purchase a few sweets as Christmas gifts for the staff—gifts Philip confirmed would be appropriate.

She had not been surprised to learn that Harrison had an account there or that the young woman who had assisted her with her purchases had very recently been hired. Annabelle assumed it had been her promised position that had been filled.

Working every day would never have allowed her to volunteer as much time as she would be able to as Harrison's wife, and Annabelle was grateful for the opportunities before her. But accepting a settlement from him, which would give her even more freedom, still did not sit well with her.

Exhausted but exhilarated after a very long but rewarding afternoon, her stomach was growling when she entered the house, and she chuckled. She was definitely going to have second helpings of supper tonight.

She peeked into the parlor to make certain Harrison had not returned yet before she hung up her cape and hurried upstairs to hide the gifts she had purchased. Noting the uncommonly warm temperature in the house, she determined to change into a different gown and freshen up her hair before letting Irene know she had returned. She took two steps into the sleeping room, rocked back on her heels, and tightened her hold on the packages she was carrying. Supper had been put out on a small table that had been set up in front of the fire, and her husband was sitting in one of the two chairs at the table nibbling on a biscuit. "Harrison! Wh-what are you doing?"

"Nothing, other than waiting for you." He got to his feet and waved his hand over the table. "This wasn't my doing. Irene thought it would be a good idea for the two of us to share a quiet supper up here, rather than in the dining room."

"You're the master of the house. Why didn't you tell her no?" Annabelle placed her packages on top of the lady's writing desk before she crossed the room.

He chuckled as he helped her into her seat. "I've tried, but I haven't had much success in that regard. Have you fared any better?"

"No, although when I needed to convince her that she should learn how to read, I did find a way to get around her," she admitted. "In fact, I believe you did the very same thing recently, or so I was told before I left today."

He sat down across from her and cocked a brow. "I did?"

"Lotte told me you sought her out and promised her a position here at Graymoor Gardens if she could prove herself to Irene. I thought you weren't going to interfere," she offered.

He shrugged. "I have a weak moment now and again."

"It wasn't a weak moment at all. It was a very kind thing to do. Thank you. It means a great deal to me that you helped her."

He took a hot biscuit and slathered it with butter. "It's Irene's decision now."

Dreadfully hungry, Annabelle, too, reached for a biscuit and quickly took a few bites. "Irene mentioned that your father had drawn up some sort of agreement that allows her to work here for the rest of her life, so you can't dismiss her. Not for any reason. Is that really true?"

His gaze darkened with a sadness he quickly shuttered from her view, and she saw his hand tremble ever so slightly as he ladled out some thick potato soup into their bowls. "As a matter of fact, he did. It was part of his will, although I doubt he had any idea that the will would be executed as soon as it was. He and my mother were killed in a freak accident when I was only five. My older brother, Peter, was fifteen at the time."

"How awful," she murmured. Although he confirmed the identical dates she had seen recorded in the family Bible next to his parents' names, he also reminded her that she should be very grateful she had been blessed to have her parents as long as she did. "Did you have family to take you and your brother in?" she asked, curious to know more, since Harrison had never even mentioned he had an older brother.

He let out a long breath and added more butter to his biscuit before he polished it off. "My mother's sister, Ana, who was Philip's mother, wanted us to come live with them in Boston. But my father's will dictated that we had to remain in the family mansion, and he appointed his lawyer, Nicholas Etting, as our guardian. He raised us."

"Is he still alive?" Annabelle asked.

Harrison stirred his soup to cool it. "No, he died a number of years back, along with my brother, Peter, and . . ." He locked his gaze on something behind her. "I should tell you about Peter," he said.

Annabelle remembered Irene making a remark referring to his brother as deceased, but she felt hesitant having Harrison discuss so many obviously troubling topics tonight. "Supper is getting cold. Perhaps you can tell me about Peter another time," she suggested.

He blinked hard, as if her words had brought him back from another place, and set down his spoon. "No, we need to talk about my brother and his family now. People who will be attending the ball tomorrow night will expect you to be familiar with my family background."

"Yes, I suppose they will," she said, realizing that the family he wanted to tell her about and had saved for last had been his own. She sat back while she waited for him to continue.

He nudged the bowl of soup away from him. "Peter was . . . he was born to be a Graymoor. He was very smart and very quick, and he loved everything about being the scion of one of the most prominent families in the city, one of the few that can trace its roots back to the days of William Penn. He wasn't the first-born son, though. We had an older brother, William, who died before his fourth birthday. Peter, as the second born, was raised to take my father's place. He continued family traditions, married, and had two sons he was raising in the city. That left me free to live out here at Graymoor Gardens and to do whatever pleased me. Which I did . . . until Peter succumbed to yellow fever eight years ago, along with his wife and my two nephews."

When he paused, obviously struggling against memories that were still very painful, her heart ached for him and trembled with painful memories of her own.

"As the sole surviving heir, I had no choice but to step out of the shadows and into the bright light of family responsibilities, which I accept on a very limited basis, as you well know," he offered in a raspy voice.

When he paused again, she saw his gaze harden, but beneath the protective shell he wore, in the place that gave life to the twinkle in his eyes when he was being totally charming and disarming, she could see the pain of the many losses he had suffered—losses far beyond what she had experienced in the past few years.

"I'm so sorry." She realized she had been so engrossed in the incredibly sad story of his life that she had completely lost her appetite, and Harrison . . . he was so overwhelmed by the pain he had endured by losing his entire family that he had lost all of his hunger for God's love.

He shrugged. "Loss is part of life and the only way to avoid it is to make absolutely certain you don't love anything that will cause you grief when you lose it. Fortunately, the only thing I'm sure I won't lose is the fortune I inherited, because I couldn't possibly spend all of it, no matter how long I might live. I just make absolutely certain there's nothing else as important to me as spending it on as many pleasures as I can—including any number of young women who misconstrue my intentions as a prelude to serious courtship. Or I did, until we got married."

She now understood why he was so opposed to any type of marriage at all. "Is there a specific young woman who will be at the ball who might be upset that you returned to the city as a married man?"

He nodded. "One of the reasons I left last fall was to avoid Vienna Biddle," he admitted. "I'm certain she's rather upset with me, but I told her more than once I was not interested in getting married. I doubt she'll approach you at all, but I'm confident she'll add her disappointment to the rest of the gossip that surrounds my name. But you needn't worry. Most of the people you meet will be too polite to say anything about me to you directly, but you may overhear more than a few whispers that you're married to a complete scoundrel."

Although she was not surprised to learn about Vienna, she was troubled most by his jaded view of life and his apparent determination never to marry anyone in a misguided attempt to avoid the heartache that life often brings to everyone, regardless of whether they are married or single. Or even divorced. She suspected that he had been the subject of gossip for so long he had actually allowed his poor reputation to define him and overshadow his better qualities—qualities she had only begun to recognize herself. She moistened her lips. "Would you . . . that is, do you agree with what they say about you?" she asked, if only to confirm her own thoughts.

He smiled. "I'm afraid I do. I live by one motto: Live a long life, and you'll end up outliving everyone you love. Live a short life instead and simply love living. Does that disappoint you?"

She tried to return his smile, but failed. "I'm afraid it does. Perhaps you should consider changing your motto to something else."

"Such as?"

"My own motto," Annabelle suggested. "If you live a life centered on the love God has for you, He'll always give you the strength to embrace love and the courage and grace to face all the disappointments that life can hurl at you." She looked up at Harrison and there was a moment of poignant silence.

Irene had been wrong. Harrison Graymoor would not become the man of character he could be by giving her or any other woman permission to love him.

Harrison needed to open his heart and his soul to the only One who could: his Creator.

Chapter Fourteen

❄

At dawn the following day, the sun climbed up from the horizon below a band of clouds that wrapped across the sky like a thick gray blanket. A light layer of new snow dusted the landscape, and the world was hushed, as if holding its breath in anticipation of the coming of the holiest season of the year.

Annabelle crossed the cottage basement just after six o'clock in the morning, but she was surprised when she caught a whiff of breakfast foods and heard Irene giving orders to the staff.

"Peggy, you know where the boxes of Christmas ribbons are stored. Take Lotte with you and bring the boxes to the kitchen and unpack them so we can start cleaning them up. They're bound to be covered with eight years of dust. Alan, I need you to bring in more wood for every room in the main house and don't be stingy or you'll be back outside this afternoon for more. Now scoot!"

Fortunately, Annabelle had not started up the steps before Peggy and Lotte rushed down to do Irene's bidding; otherwise, they would have knocked her right over. After quickly acknowledging her, they proceeded to the tunnel, and she joined Irene in the kitchen, just as Alan slipped out the back door. She glanced at Irene, who was at the kitchen table fumbling with one of the wide red ribbons lying there.

Annabelle frowned. "I suppose this means that we're not taking a walk today."

"No time. I've got a house to get ready for Christmas, and you've got a fancy ball to get ready for," Irene replied without bothering to look up.

Annabelle walked over to the table next to the cookstove, swiped a link of cooked sausage, and nibbled at it. "What about your lessons?"

"No time. I've got a house to decorate for Christmas, and you've got a fancy ball to get ready for," Irene repeated and finally looked up at her. "I shouldn't ask you why you left your sleeping husband to be up and about so early with me, so I won't. But since you're here, you may as well help me. I spent half the night undoing some old bows and pressing out the wrinkles in this ribbon. After eight years, I can't seem to put the bows back together again."

Wondering what the housekeeper would say if she discovered that Harrison had spent the night sleeping in the library alcove again, Annabelle polished off the sausage link and wiped her hands on a cloth hanging by the water pump before she stored away her cape. "I'll make the bows if you get your chalk and slate so you can practice some of your letters," she suggested and sat down next to Irene.

"I'm not convinced I'll do any better than yesterday," Irene grumbled, but she handed over the ribbon she was holding and glanced down at her thick-veined hands. "These hands of mine are still able to do most anything I want. Except when it comes to shaping letters."

"It gets easier with practice," Annabelle replied as she turned and twisted the ribbon exactly as her mother had taught her to do.

Irene got up, walked over to the corner cupboard to retrieve the chalk and slate she had found stored away with some of the family's heirlooms, and carried it back with her before retaking her seat. "I don't get much time to practice. Not with Peggy and Alan lurking about, and now Lotte." She awkwardly formed the capital letter *A*.

Annabelle cringed until the woman finished. "Good job. Excellent, in fact," she said. "But try holding the chalk on the side so it won't squeak when you're writing. Yes. That's perfect!" she announced when Irene adjusted her fingers. "Do the lower case *a*."

This time Irene managed to form the letter without making more than a gentle sound as the chalk scraped across the slate. "*A* is for Annabelle."

"And *B* is for bow," Annabelle quipped as she placed a perfectly formed bow onto the table and grinned.

They bantered back and forth as teacher and student for the next twenty minutes, choosing words that began with each letter of the alphabet Irene had learned so far. By the time Irene was ready to learn the first of two new letters planned for the day, Annabelle had also fashioned the last ribbon into a bow. She reached over and cleaned off the slate. "Watch carefully," she urged and formed both the upper and lower case letters for G. "The letter G has both hard and soft sounds, like the letter C, so G is for Graymoor or ginger," she said, pointing to the letters she had written.

Irene's eyes sparkled. "Or G is for God, who blesses us all every day, and . . . and gem, right?"

"That's right," Annabelle confirmed, pleased that Irene was such a quick learner. "Or G could be for gumption you possess, as well as gentle, which also describes you occasionally," she teased.

"Every woman needs to have gumption. You have a good dose of it, too," Irene countered as she traced over the letters Annabelle had made before attempting to chalk them herself.

"Me? I don't think so." If she did, Annabelle would have

followed Eric to New York City and demanded that he return all the money her mother had received when she'd sold nearly all of the land she had inherited as a widow. She'd given the money to them as a wedding present—money Eric was supposed to use to establish himself in his law practice in New York City before sending for Annabelle and her mother.

Instead, her charming, sweet-talking husband had used the money to travel to Indiana for a quick and quiet divorce and to fund a whirlwind courtship with the heiress he eventually wed. Eric returned to Four Corners nineteen months after he left, on the very same day she buried her mother. After the other mourners had left the graveside, he'd handed her a copy of their divorce papers.

It suddenly occurred to Annabelle that she had already spent more time with Harrison than she had spent with Eric, but she doubted their marriage would be legal for more than another month or so.

"How's that look?" Irene asked, bringing Annabelle back from the past to the present.

"Perfect," Annabelle pronounced. "Want to try again or one more new letter—"

"Make the next letter for me, but be quick," Irene said with a chuckle as she cleared the slate. "I need you to show me how to make those molasses cookies you mentioned, and you need your breakfast."

Once Annabelle had written the letters *H* and *h*, she returned the chalk to Irene. "*H* is for Harrison and hungry," she said, choosing the most obvious examples that popped into her head.

Irene traced over the letters. "*H* is also for heart. Harrison's heart, which is so hungry for love, and your heart, which is chock full of love to give him."

Annabelle blinked back tears, quite certain that Irene was wrong again. Most of the love she had or thought she had, in hindsight, she had wasted on the wrong man. And she did not believe she had either the heart or the gumption to give what little she had left to a man who definitely did not want it.

e~

Annabelle knew that getting dressed to attend her first formal event would take hours, but it took even longer because she and Harrison had to take turns using the sleeping room.

For reasons only the two of them understood, she bathed in the morning while he made arrangements with Graham to drive them to the ball later that night. He bathed right after dinner and dressed, while she went over the menu for Christmas dinner that Irene insisted on making, even though the holiday was two weeks away. Finally, while Harrison enjoyed a light supper, she skipped eating altogether and used the time to dress with Lotte's help.

She dismissed the young woman once she was ready to fix her hair. When she caught her reflection in the mirror as she approached the dressing table, she had to blink several times before she could accept the idea that the image before her was not an illusion. The pale green silk gown rustled as she walked and fairly glimmered with a life of its own. The bodice scooped lower than she was accustomed to wearing, leaving the delicate lace trim to lay a few inches below her collarbone. Beneath a wide band of lace just below her breasts, her skirt fell in shimmering waves to the top of her matching slippers, and more lace cuffed the wide sleeves that ended at her wrists.

When she raised her hand to finger the opal pendant hanging from a slender gold chain, which Harrison had lent to her this evening from the collection of jewelry his mother had worn, she caught sight of the braided ring on her finger and quickly replaced it with the ring Harrison had chosen for her to wear when they were going out socially.

Sighing with relief that she had remembered to change rings, she was also anxious not to keep Harrison waiting. After she studied her face to make certain all hint of her bruise had disappeared, she spent the next ten minutes trying to fix her hair into a thick braid she hoped to twist into a crown on the top of her head. But she soon gave up because her sleeves kept getting in the way. "Lotte was right. I should have fixed my hair first," she grumbled.

Annabelle brightened the moment she remembered the fancier snoods that Mrs. Lynch's daughter had made for her. She opened the bottom drawer in the dressing table where she had stored them away and found the snoods easily enough. But her heart began to race as she sorted through them, because she could not remember which gowns she had chosen for them to match. When she reached the very last one, she smiled. Made of fine delicate netting the precise color of her hair, the snood was decorated with tiny pale green sequins that caught the light and sparkled the moment she lifted it out of the drawer.

After refreshing the center part, she brushed her wavy hair and set the brush aside. She concentrated hard to place the snood properly and eased her hair into the delicate netting to avoid tearing it, exactly how Mrs. Lynch had shown her. She was rewarded for her patience on the first try.

Now that she was finished, she studied her image once again, but before she had a chance to consider whether or not she should wear her hair this daringly different to the ball, a knock at the door interrupted her.

"Miss Annabelle? Mr. Harrison said I should tell you to please hurry," Lotte said. "He's waiting for you downstairs. He says it's time to leave."

"That settles the matter of what to do about my hair. Nothing," she whispered and turned to face the door. "Tell Mr. Harrison I'm coming in just a moment." She grabbed a new evening cape trimmed with fur that she had never worn before. Though she was tempted to don the cape and put the hood up, she decided it was not worth taking the risk of disturbing the snood and left the room carrying the cape instead.

As she hurried down the hallway, she hoped Harrison would be pleased with how she looked, but she was more worried about keeping her promise to act properly. Annabelle paused at the top of the staircase to whisper a quick prayer to ask for His help tonight before she took hold of the balustrade and started down the steps.

Harrison paced the length of the narrow foyer and checked the time on his grandfather's pocket watch, which he had taken to using since he had lost his own to those thieves. Concerned that they were going to be more than fashionably late, he slipped it back into his pocket. He reclosed the heavy coat he was wearing over his formal attire and wiped the sweat beaded on his forehead. If Annabelle did not come downstairs soon, he was afraid he would melt into one big puddle that Irene would complain about having to clean up.

He headed straight for the staircase, ready to charge upstairs to get her, but rocked back on his heels the moment he saw her descending. He would have thought she was floating if he had not seen her whitened knuckles as she held on to the balustrade.

Without hesitation, his heart leaped and pounded against the wall of his chest, completely overwhelming his misgivings about possibly seeing Vienna Biddle tonight and his concerns that Annabelle would be able to comport herself as well as the wife of Harrison Graymoor would be expected to do.

Most men would agree that Annabelle was more than easy on the eyes. Some men might even say she was beautiful, but he could only describe her tonight as the most stunning woman he had ever seen.

Unlike the other women he was acquainted with, Annabelle carried her beauty sweetly and demurely. She appeared to be completely unaware that she was a vision of loveliness that any man would be hard pressed to resist, or that she inspired him with an uncommon urge to be her protector.

He did not know what she had done to her hair to make it look as if she had captured miniature snowflakes, bathed them with moonlight, and miraculously kept them from melting, but he found it mesmerizing.

In all truth, Annabelle's innocent beauty far surpassed the elegant gown she wore. Her cheeks were flushed rosy pink, the same shade as her lips, and he could not help staring at her luminous, gorgeous eyes that met his gaze and held him captive until she reached the bottom step and waited for some sign of his approval.

Alarmed by his reaction to her and mindful of his vow to keep his heart safe, he swallowed the lump in his throat. Smiling, he took her hand and raised it to his lips. "You're breathtaking," he whispered, catching just a hint of the scent of summer roses. Rewarded with a blush that deepened the color of her cheeks, he decided he was entitled to one night, just one that he could spend with this woman when he would not have to dwell on the past or dread the future.

He flexed his left wrist and the scar tightened. This night he claimed as the one special night they would share with each other which would erase the difficult circumstances that had brought them together . . . before they faced the coming scandal of their divorce.

Chapter Fifteen

A ballroom that seemed endless. Candles by the hundreds that glittered throughout the ballroom. Freshly cut evergreens decorated with gold and silver bows that scented the air. Orchestra music that gentled the chatter. And people! More people than Annabelle had ever seen assembled indoors all at the same time.

With her senses reeling and her heart barely able to keep a steady rhythm, Annabelle held on to her only lifeline: her husband's arm. She was so intimidated by the ostentatious display of wealth, she was sorely tempted to ask him to take her back to Graymoor Gardens, where she could spend a quiet evening. Since that option was clearly out of the question, she kept a tight hold on the gumption she would need to survive this ball without embarrassing her husband. She also whispered a quick prayer that her empty stomach would not growl and embarrass her, too.

As they approached several couples waiting to speak to their host and hostess, who stood just inside the ballroom entrance to greet the city's elites who had been invited, Harrison bent his head low. "Don't forget. You just have to remember one thing," he whispered.

"I'm trying to remember so many things you told me, I'm afraid you need to be more specific," she whispered back as she tried to sort through all the additional advice he had given her while riding here in the coach.

"Everyone here is anxious to make a good impression on *you.*"

Highly doubtful that Miss Vienna Biddle was one of them, she moistened her lips. She almost wished he had not mentioned the woman he had been so attentive to before leaving several months ago. But he had, which only made her more apprehensive about attending the affair, despite the fact that he had assured her he would not leave her side.

Instinctively, she tightened her hold on his arm, and he glanced down at her with tenderness and gave her a smile that warmed her straight down to her toes. "You're the most intriguing, beautiful woman here," he murmured. "Remember that, too."

His gaze was so intense and his words so seductive that her heart fairly leaped into a fairy tale where Harrison was a handsome prince who was desperately in love with her. No man had ever looked at her the way he did right now or made her believe she was precious and truly treasured. Not even Eric, who in hindsight had paid more attention to her elderly mother than he had to her, for reasons that had only become obvious when it was too late for her to realize he had never loved her at all.

Struggling to breathe, she reminded herself that Harrison had probably spoken those very same words to every woman he singled out to receive his attentions. But her heart refused to listen, and she held on to the notion that just for tonight, she might pretend he had saved them just for her.

The last couple speaking to Edward Anderson and his wife, Martha, stepped away just as Harrison and Annabelle approached, giving Annabelle her first view of the couple. With light gray hair and deeply wrinkled features, they both appeared to be in their seventies. Reed thin, they reminded her of a pair of scarecrows, although she had never seen anyone dressed as elegantly or wearing gaudy jewels like the ones Martha Anderson wore around her neck and both of her wrists.

Harrison formally introduced the couple to her with a look of pride on his face she had never seen before.

"So you're the pretty little lady who finally snatched up this young rake," Mr. Anderson teased.

His wife nudged him with her elbow. "Just how do you expect poor Annabelle to respond to that?" she admonished. "What my husband meant to say is that we've all been waiting a very long time for Harrison to settle down with a wife and start a family. Philadelphia just wouldn't be the same without a Graymoor. Even though others had quite given up on him, I was confident that all he needed to do was to meet the right woman to make him realize he had a responsibility to continue his family line," she stated, broaching a topic Annabelle thought would never be discussed in polite conversation.

With a blush traveling up from the soles of her feet to her cheeks, she glanced at her husband while the woman congratulated him for making such a fine choice, along with the admonishment that now that he was married, he might find more time to spend on the philanthropic ventures his father and grandfather had started instead of being self-indulgent. Although Annabelle knew he could not be pleased by the woman's words, he never lost his smile or the dimples that were planted in the middle of his cheeks.

She waited until they were a good distance away before expressing her concerns. "Will everyone here feel so inclined to express their opinions about such private matters?" she asked.

He chuckled. "No. The Andersons are the exception to the rule."

"You might have warned me," she quipped. "Why are they the exception?"

"Status as the head of the only family in the city who can claim any ties to William Penn himself, or the greatest wealth of any family in the city, or old age. Each one gives them the privilege to say exactly what they think. Take your pick," he teased as he ushered her into the ballroom. There he introduced her to so many people her head was spinning and her cheeks were sore from smiling so much. She also had to answer more than a few questions about the snood she was wearing, although most of them came from young women closer to her own age.

After he got them both some liquid refreshment, he guided her to the edge of the dance floor, which was so crowded, all she could see was a blur of expensive fabrics and exquisite, sparkling jewelry. Her mouth went dry, as if she'd had nothing to drink at all, and she caught her bottom lip. "Are you certain you want to dance?"

He pressed a kiss to the back of her hand. "I most definitely do want to dance and only with you," he whispered and whisked her into his arms and onto the dance floor.

The orchestra, which was hidden from her view by the throng of dancing couples, was playing a slow, sensuous melody. She stumbled a bit at first, but only because the light pressure of his hand on her back sent troubling sensations racing up the length of her spine. But it was his simmering gaze as he looked down at her while they danced that made her heart fairly tremble.

She was grateful that the dance floor was far too crowded for anyone to notice that she was not as light on her feet as she should be, or that she stumbled time and time again.

He let go of her hand for just a moment to tilt up her chin. "Don't look down at your feet. Look at me and feel the music." He captured her gaze and held it.

Mesmerized, his gaze seduced her, even more than the haunting melody that filled the air as they swirled around the dance floor. Finding his gaze too intense, she dropped hers to the middle of his chest, which inspired memories of the night she had spent sleeping in the stagecoach, her head cushioned by his shoulder, the comfort she had found in his arms.

She glanced away quickly and noticed that the other couples who had been dancing had moved off to stand in a circle around them, leaving Harrison and her as the only couple left dancing. She instantly lost the rhythm of the music. "Th-they're all watching us," she whispered, close to panic.

He increased the pressure at her back, tightened his hold on her hand, and effortlessly eased her back into the music. "They're not watching us at all. They're watching you and wondering why such a beautiful woman would choose an unredeemable scoundrel like me to marry when she could have her pick of any man she desired," he countered, just as the music ended.

"Then they would be wrong. They just think you're a scoundrel, and you've let them convince you they're right," she said impulsively before he released her.

Judging by the perpetual smile he never lost, her words had been drowned out by the rush of applause that filled the ballroom. She caught a glimpse of the orchestra and saw the musicians set down their instruments before they left for what she assumed would be a short break.

Without the music or her husband's touch, she quickly stepped from the fairy tale she had been living in and returned to reality. Harrison had only one reason to be so charming and to act as if he had fallen in love with her: to impress the city's elites who were his peers and to avoid any hint that their marriage was only a façade.

When he excused himself to get some refreshments for them, she did not bother to remind him that he had promised to remain by her side the entire night. On second thought, she tried to make her way through the crowd of people to follow him, but she wound up getting nudged in the wrong direction and ended up in a far corner where a few chairs had been set up for guests who became tired.

She had barely turned around, prepared to try to reach him, when a young woman slowly approached her. Other than the fact that she was probably close in age to Annabelle, they had little in common as far as appearances were concerned—with dark hair and eyes and a very full, womanly figure, she stood a good head taller. The hard expression on her face warned Annabelle that she was about to meet someone who did not like her, even though they had never met before.

When the young woman finally stopped a few feet in front of her, Annabelle forced herself to smile. "May I presume that you're Vienna Biddle?" she asked.

"Well, at least you're not as witless as I've heard you were," she countered. "Indeed I am, and I simply couldn't resist the opportunity to speak to you once I saw that you were alone. That's what Harrison does best, you know."

Annabelle tilted up her chin, ever so grateful it was impossible for Vienna to see that her knees were shaking. "Just exactly what is it that you think my husband 'does best'?" she asked. Deep disappointment lay beneath the woman's glare, making it painfully clear Vienna was still in love with Harrison.

"He charms you, he seduces you, and then he abandons you." Vienna narrowed her gaze and shook her head as if she found it distasteful to look at Annabelle at all. "In truth, I can only think of one reason that he might have chosen to marry you instead of me," she said and leaned closer. "Tell me. Is the babe you're carrying due to arrive in May or June?"

Horrified by the woman's assumption that she was pregnant or that she would sleep with a man without the benefit of marriage, Annabelle gasped. She instantly took a step back, hit the seat on one of the chairs, and barely managed to stay on her feet. Her cheeks were so hot she thought she had suddenly grown fevered, and when she balled her hands into fists, her wedding ring bit into the palm of her hand.

Vienna laughed at her. "Poor naïve Annabelle. Did you really think everyone here would simply assume that Harrison met you and married you in the space of a few days, even though he loved me and was going to propose to me as soon as he returned from his holiday? Don't be a fool. And don't expect to be welcomed into polite society when the reason he married you becomes more . . . obvious," she scoffed, then turned and walked away.

Annabelle blinked back tears to clear her vision as she stumbled her way back to where Harrison had left her. She had been humiliated when Eric divorced her and the people who had been her friends and neighbors for years had turned against her. They had not even had the decency to confine their opinion of her to whispers. Like Vienna, many of them had walked right up to her and thrown the scandal of being a divorced woman in her face; Vienna's words had reopened the wounds Annabelle had prayed so hard to seal.

She was trembling so hard, she paused to draw a deep breath and take control of her emotions when she noticed a couple standing just a few feet away from her, who had apparently just arrived and were attracting a good bit of attention. She did not know the barrel-shaped woman dressed in a glaring red gown, but she most definitely recognized the man standing next to her.

"Eric," she whispered before her breath caught in her throat. Her knees gave way, and it took all of her willpower not to fall to the floor in a dead faint. She gulped hard and closed her eyes for a brief moment, hoping he was nothing more than a figment of her imagination, but he was still standing there with a woman she assumed to be his wife when she opened her eyes.

She caught her lower lip and edged sideways to avoid being seen and caught a bit of their conversation as the woman described their infant son, now three months old, who had accompanied them on their journey from New York City to Philadelphia to spend the holidays with her relatives.

Although Annabelle was surprised to learn that Eric now had a child, she was only able to rein in her galloping heartbeat when she reminded herself that she had nothing to fear. Eric would be just as reluctant to let anyone, especially his wife, know that he and Annabelle had once been married as she was to have Harrison find out he had been forced to marry a divorced woman.

Coming face-to-face with her past, however, still left her feeling light-headed, and she swayed on her feet. Her legs would have buckled this time if Harrison had not returned at that precise moment and put his hand to her back.

"I've been searching all over for you. When I couldn't find you, I thought I might get myself introduced to the Bradleys. They seem to have the ballroom abuzz," he said, then looked down at her and frowned. "What's wrong?"

"I-I'm not feeling well," she managed, dreadfully afraid of what he might do if he found out the truth about her past—a past that was standing only a few feet away.

When he studied her face, his gaze grew troubled. "You're uncommonly pale," he noted and wrapped his arm around her shoulders when she leaned into him. "You're obviously weak, as well. Did you eat any of the supper I asked Irene to send up to you while you were dressing?"

She rested her eyes for a moment and sighed, but latched on to the one good excuse she could give him for feeling unwell. "I sent it back. I was too busy dressing and . . . Would you be upset with me if I asked you to take me home?"

He held her close and turned her about. "Not this time," he replied, "but the next time we go out for the evening, we'll have supper together so I can make certain you eat something first."

After they made their apologies for leaving early to their host and hostess, they headed directly back to Graymoor Gardens.

With the city quickly disappearing behind them and Harrison seated alongside of her, holding her hand in the darkness that enveloped them inside the coach, Annabelle finally felt her nerves begin to untangle.

"Did you ever decide if we'll travel back into the city to attend services, too, or can we stay closer to home?" Anxious to keep as far away from the city as she could now that she knew Eric was there, Annabelle needed to know how hard she would have to plead her case to attend the small country church Irene had mentioned.

"I told you. I hadn't really thought about attending services at all, and I haven't given it any thought since you mentioned it the first time," he said and let go of her hand.

Annabelle caught a gasp before it escaped. "But I . . . I just assumed we'd be going to church. In fact, now that we're settled in one place, I was hoping to attend services every week."

When he held silent, she continued to argue her position. "If you don't want to go on Sunday, then just say so. But I'm going to ask Irene if I can join her and the rest of the staff when they leave for services."

He sighed. "In the past, if I were to attend services anywhere, which is not a habit I enjoy except on very rare occasions, I prefer to go into the city to the Church of the Resurrection, where my family has a pew. If I were to go on Sunday, I'd be inclined to do the same."

"Are you so inclined?" she asked and turned her head toward him, but it was too dark to see anything more than a silhouette of his face.

When he shrugged, his shoulders rubbed against her. "The only reason I'd even consider having us come back into the city for services on Sundays would be to get the opportunity to meet the Bradleys."

Her heart skipped a beat before it pounded out one heavy

heartbeat after another. "How can you be so certain they'd be there?"

"Everyone of prominence either belongs to that congregation or attends services there when they're visiting the city."

Desperate to keep him from going anywhere near Eric, most especially with her, she changed the direction of their conversation to the one topic that might be enough to distract him. "Vienna Biddle spoke to me tonight."

He flinched and turned toward her. "When?"

"Right before you found me," she admitted. "She's still very much in love with you, and she's very hurt that—"

"I told you. I made her no promises," he said firmly. He pointed up toward the roof of the carriage and held his finger in front of his lips. "Lower your voice. I don't want Graham to hear us," he cautioned.

Convinced there was practically nowhere that she did not have to guard her words, she lowered her voice to a whisper. "I can't judge whether you made any promises to her or not, but she's very angry."

"She's a spoiled woman. I'm sorry. She should have vented her anger at me instead of you, but I don't think this is a topic we should continue to discuss until we get home," he warned.

Her cheeks burned as her mind replayed her humiliating encounter with Vienna. Blinking back tears, she ignored his warning. "She accused me of tricking you into marrying me because . . . because I'm carrying your child."

He laughed out loud. "That's ridiculous!" he exclaimed, clearly ignoring his own warning.

Shocked that he dismissed her words so easily, she stiffened. "I can assure you that I did not feel ridiculous when she made her claim against me," she whispered. "I was humiliated and embarrassed that she or anyone else might think that—"

"If you let that woman upset you, then you're the one being

ridiculous. You know it isn't true, and time will prove to Vienna and everyone else who listens to her malicious tongue that it isn't true. Rather than dwell on something so petty, we should talk about something else that's more important."

Fuming, she could not believe she had ever seen this man as a prince of any kind, and her anger refueled all her resentments about being forced to marry him. "I'm tired of whispering. Let's talk about attending services each Sunday," she suggested in a normal tone. "I'd like to go with Irene and the rest of the staff, and I would hope you would be inclined to go with us, instead of traveling into the city to attend services so you can meet people who seem to be more important to you than we are. Besides, I think it's important for you to introduce me as your wife to the minister here before you explain to him why I'll be attending services each week without you," she said, as sweetly as she possibly could.

She could not see his glare, but she felt it.

"Fine. I'll go with all of you this Sunday. Will that make you happy?"

"I believe it will," she murmured, but she did not expect to be truly happy again until she set aside her childish dreams of romance and her marriage to this man was annulled.

Chapter Sixteen

�֎

As far as Harrison was concerned, attending services at the rustic country church a few miles west of Graymoor Gardens was a small price to pay for peace within his household.

He tuned out the minister's voice as he droned a final long-winded message and ignored the puffs of clouds his breath created in the freezing air to glance down at Annabelle, who was sitting next to him on a crude bench in the front of the church. He had no idea how she could be so devoted to a God who had obviously abandoned her, too, but he coveted the peace and serenity that had etched her features from the moment the service began. He also resented the fact that had he not agreed to be here today, Irene would have made his life unbearable.

With his cousin coming for dinner today, Harrison was convinced his life was already about as miserable as it could get, considering that his plans for a memorable evening with Annabelle at the Sullivans' ball had ended so abruptly. Spending an hour this morning in this unheated church was even more difficult, since he had struggled to keep warm for the past few nights in his bed in the library alcove. He was shifting his weight from one foot to the other to keep them from permanently freezing to the dirt floor when he caught a change in Reverend Bingham's voice and realized his sermon was finally coming to a much-welcomed end.

"And so to all of you on this blessed Sunday morning, let me end with a challenge: In order to know God's love and see His presence in your lives, you must open your hearts to Him, for it is His love and the grace He gives to each one of us that will nourish us, sustain us, and bring us all home to Glory. Alleluia. Alleluia!"

"Alleluia!" the congregation replied in unison, albeit without Harrison's voice among them as he simply mouthed the response.

While the congregation celebrated the end of the service with a hushed hymn, he looked around at the fifty-odd people who were huddling side by side wearing heavy winter coats and capes in the small log building that had slipped into disrepair. The warming stove was stone cold, which he attributed to the scarcity of firewood that plagued most of the city. Glass windows that he remembered being here had been replaced with oilcloth, which did little more than keep rain or snow from blowing into the church. Overhead, several patches in the roof were clearly visible, but daylight streaming in through a fair number of holes in the roof indicated that more repairs were necessary.

He dropped his gaze, turned, and scanned the crowd. He had not attended services here since he was a boy, so most of the people were strangers. He did, however, recognize a few. Jacob Pugh, nearly eighty now, had lost his wife and two grown sons to the same epidemic that had claimed Harrison's brother and his family. Albertine Murdock, who had been widowed twice before her thirtieth birthday, was almost fifty now and was wearing a black-veiled bonnet, which suggested she was mourning the loss of yet another husband. Alexander Cranshaw was also there, with his wife and three marriageable-age daughters.

Caught up in memories that filled his heart with deep sorrow for all that he had lost, he was amazed that other people who had all suffered from great tragedies would still be so committed to their faith. When he got a sharp poke in the middle of his back, he flinched and realized the final hymn had ended and people were beginning to file out of the church.

He turned and looked over his shoulder at Irene, who was sitting with the rest of the staff on a bench directly behind him, and frowned. "There's a lot to be said for attending services in the city where they have proper pews instead of rickety benches and people can't poke at other people. What is it now?"

"Nothing, unless you'd rather not join your wife," she said and pointed to the left.

When he looked in that direction, he saw Annabelle speaking to Reverend Bingham. Since he had already introduced her to the minister when they first arrived and made a weak promise to return each week with her, he wasted no time in joining them. "I apologize," he said and placed his hand at her back. "I'm afraid I was still thinking about your impressive sermon, and I didn't even realize services were over."

Beaming, the young minister, who was wearing a threadbare overcoat, nudged at the spectacles that had slipped down to the tip of his nose until they were back in place. "Considering it's cold enough in here to keep the snow that drifted inside from melting, that's quite a compliment. Thank you."

Annabelle looked up at him. "Before we left I wanted to make certain that Reverend Bingham had plans for dinner today," she offered a bit sheepishly.

The minister actually blushed. "Everyone takes pity on a lonely bachelor, but as I was just about to tell your wife, I've accepted an invitation to share dinner with the Cranshaws. You know them, of course."

Harrison nodded stiffly. "For some time," he replied, without adding that it had been eight years since he had seen Robert or his family.

"Perhaps you can join us another time," Annabelle suggested and put her hand on Harrison's arm. "Shall we go? Irene is anxious to get back to her kitchen, and Philip should be arriving soon."

"I should go, as well. I'll give your regards to the Cranshaws," the minister suggested. "I'll see you both next Sunday."

Harrison nodded again, although returning to this church again meant that sooner or later he would have to explain to the young minister why he had divorced the woman he had so recently married.

~

Sunday dinner was a veritable feast. Roast venison. A bowl of potatoes, carrots, and turnips. Thick dark gravy to pour on top and rich, sweet butter to melt on hot, golden biscuits. Yorkshire pudding.

Annabelle could not decide which dish to select for a second helping. She solved the problem by taking a little bit of everything and savored every scrumptious bite. She did not realize that both Harrison and Philip were staring at her until she finished and dropped her gaze. "Have I done something wrong?" she murmured and fidgeted with the napkin on her lap.

Harrison chuckled. "Not at all, although I don't believe I've ever seen anyone your size eat quite as much as you do."

"Nor have I," Philip added with a chuckle. "In all truth, most women I know don't eat enough to keep a sparrow breathing, although I suspect it's more a matter of what they perceive to be proper for a young woman to eat than actual hunger."

Annabelle narrowed her gaze and looked from one end of the table to the other to study each man's expression. "It's not proper to eat?"

"Men eat. Ladies nibble at their food, at least in public," Harrison suggested.

Philip nodded in agreement. "I couldn't prove it, but I suspect most ladies enjoy their fair share of food in the privacy of their own homes."

Making a mental note of yet another rule to follow when she was not at home, she grinned. "Then since I'm home, neither one of you should mind if I have one more slice of venison."

"You might change your mind about that once you see my desserts," Irene prompted as she entered the dining area, with Peggy and Lotte following right on her heels.

Annabelle took one glance at the massive tray filled with desserts that Irene was carrying and needed no further encouragement. She noted the surprised looks on Harrison's and Philip's faces as they stared at the tray and indulged in a giggle.

Within minutes, Peggy and Lotte had dinner cleared away and the center of the table was lined with desserts, fresh plates, and utensils before they left. Irene stood next to Harrison with a silly grin on her face. "In case you're wondering, that's my usual apple pie right there in the center, but I also made an apple-plum strudel, which is closest to you, Mr. Philip, since Harrison doesn't enjoy the flavor of plums at all. Harrison, you've got some fancy molasses cookies right here in front of you. Peggy should be here with some warm beverages for all of you shortly, but while you're waiting, you might want to try a bit of each of my desserts." She winked at Annabelle and left the room.

Before Annabelle could even begin to fill the dessert plates, Harrison nudged the plate of molasses cookies closer to him and stared at the cookies for a moment before he laughed. "Is this your doing?" he asked, looking up at Annabelle.

"Yes, I gave Irene the recipe," she replied and her spine stiffened. "I sampled a few yesterday when they came out of the oven and they were delicious. You might want to try one before you dismiss the cookies as some sort of joke."

He sobered immediately and moved the plate closer to her so she could have a better look at the cookies. "Did your recipe also call for this specific type of decoration?"

"There's no decoration," Annabelle argued, but took back her words the instant she saw the letters that Irene must have carved into the cookies while they were still warm. Shaking her head, she laughed, too, which inspired Philip to get out of his seat.

Standing between Annabelle and Harrison, he studied the cookies and chuckled. "I wasn't aware that Irene knew her letters. Did she actually carve each of these cookies with some of the letters of the alphabet?"

"Not all of them. She's only learned half of them so far," she offered.

"Annabelle's teaching Irene how to read and write," Harrison said, and she caught just a hint of pride in his eyes before he looked away.

"Only to help her to be able to read some new recipes. Besides, everyone should be literate."

Harrison snorted. "That may or may not be an advantage where Irene's concerned."

"How so?" Philip asked as he snatched up two of the cookies and returned to his seat.

"Once she's able to read and write, I have no doubt she'll start leaving me lists of complaints instead of simply being so outspoken."

Philip swallowed a bite of cookie and smiled. "If teaching her how to read results in cookies as good as these are, then I would say it's worth the risk. Besides, now that you and Annabelle are married, you have no right to complain about anything at all, not even a housekeeper who doesn't seem to know her place."

Embarrassed by Philip's compliment, Annabelle was relieved

when the two men bantered back and forth debating the merits and disadvantages of living here at Graymoor Gardens, where life was more casual than at the city mansion.

Instead of contributing her own thoughts, she filled each of their plates with a sampling of desserts and finished her plate. She was slicing another small wedge of pie when a woman's scream, followed by a crash of metal and china, came from directly below them, startling Annabelle enough to make her drop the knife she was using and end the men's conversation.

Harrison immediately got to his feet. "That sounds as if Peggy dropped those warm beverages Irene promised. I'd better check on her," he said and rushed out of the room.

With her heart still racing, Annabelle frowned. "I hope she didn't get burned."

"She's probably fine." Philip leaned closer to the table. "You're doing fine, too."

When she raised her brow, he offered her a reassuring smile. "You're exactly the woman Harrison needs as his wife. He chose you above all the other women he's ever known and rightly so. Don't let anyone ever convince you otherwise, especially someone as self-serving as Vienna Biddle."

Horrified by the mere thought that he had become privy to the conversation she'd had with the woman at the ball, Annabelle could barely draw a decent breath of air. If he knew what Vienna said, then others did, too—which meant Vienna had been right to suggest that people were gossiping about her. No doubt she'd added her own tidbit of gossip.

"You know what she said to me . . . what awful claim she made?" Annabelle locked her hands together to keep them from trembling and laid them on her lap.

"I know how very difficult it must be for you to know that people think the very worst of you. I truly do, and I'm so very, very sorry. I only wish there was something more I could do, other than staunchly defend you and set people straight when the opportunity presents itself."

"At least you're willing to do that. Harrison found the whole matter laughable when I told him about it, and he prefers to completely ignore the gossip rather than say anything to stop it."

Philip shook his head. "My cousin is basically a good man, despite what others think of him, but it seems he has a lot to learn about matters of the heart. Give him time, Annabelle. Loving someone and expressing that love is something he has to learn how to do."

Annabelle let out a long, sad sigh. Although she was comforted by his words and concern, which were based on the illusion that Harrison actually loved her, she could not help but compare his sympathy and understanding of her feelings with Harrison's reaction.

Although she also had been comforted by the service today and truly believed God had placed her in Harrison's life for a reason, she was now very confused. In all truth, she was not even certain she had the gumption and the strength to continue to play the role of Harrison's wife—a role that constantly kept her swinging from pretext and lies to reality and truth and back again. After having the ball ruined by Vienna's hurtful accusations and seeing Eric there, she could not imagine what other disasters were waiting for her in the days ahead.

After she thanked Philip for his concern and he promised to return for her in the morning to take her to the city so she could volunteer at the Refuge, she excused herself from the table. Walking quickly, she went directly to the main staircase. As she mounted the steps to return to her room, she had to decide whether she could stay here as Harrison's wife in name only or simply leave this house and never come back.

Faced with a dilemma that was deeply troubling, she slipped into her room and leaned back against the door. She needed time alone to think and pray so that tonight, one way or another, she would be able to tell Harrison what she was going to do.

Chapter Seventeen

Fortified by prayer, Annabelle came up with a compromise to solve her dilemma that would make it easier for her to remain here, although she still had to think of a way to avoid seeing Eric. Convincing Harrison to agree with her idea, however, was the key to making it work. Unless he did so, she needed to figure out a way to leave in the morning.

She had to wait until very late, however, to speak to Harrison alone. Right before Harrison secured the house for the night, she asked him to join her upstairs in her sleeping room as soon as he finished. While she waited for him to arrive, she arranged two chairs in front of the fireplace before she took her seat and started to knit to remain calm. When he knocked once a few minutes later and slipped into the room, she set her work onto her lap.

"You wanted to talk to me?" he offered as he sat down across from her.

She rested one hand on the diary she had ordered for him that was hidden in the folds of her skirt and laid the other on top of her knitting. "I think we have to talk about a number of things."

When he glanced at the knitting needles protruding from

the sock she had been knitting and cocked a brow, she slid her knitting into the bag on the floor at her feet, then drew a deep breath. "I can't keep up this charade any longer. Not as we've been doing. I've truly tried my best, but it's simply too hard and too complicated." She locked her gaze with his. "Can you honestly tell me that *you've* enjoyed this past week and a half? That it's been easy for you?"

He clenched and unclenched his jaw, and his gaze darkened. "Whether or not either one of us has been happy is irrelevant. Establishing and maintaining the illusion that we're happy is a necessity for which you should thank Philip. If he hadn't returned for a visit and chosen the night we returned to host a dinner party, no one would have ever known that—"

"You can't blame Philip," she argued, surprised by the tone of his voice. "Have you forgotten the announcement of our marriage that appeared in the newspaper that was dated the day before we returned?"

He dropped his gaze for a moment before meeting her own. "You're right. I did forget." His gaze softened, then hardened again, as if he were shifting blame from his cousin to whoever had sent the news to *The Inquirer*.

"You still haven't answered my question," she prompted.

He let out a very long breath of air, as if he had been hoping she had not noticed. "Have I been happy misleading everyone other than my lawyer about our marriage?" He shrugged. "In all truth, I can't say that I've found it particularly satisfying, but that doesn't mean I can afford to do anything about it, and neither can you. We're both stuck with the situation, and we need to make the best of it, no matter how hard it gets for either one of us."

She slipped her fingers around the leather diary that was identical in color to her own instead of the darker one she had requested. "I completely agree."

He cocked his head and narrowed his gaze. "If you agree, then I don't understand why you were so insistent that we talk about it."

She smiled. "Because if we make the effort to talk with one another about it, neither one of us will feel so . . . so alone."

He snorted. "I'm quite accustomed to being alone."

"I'm afraid that I'm not," she countered, keeping her voice low and gentle. "When I was growing up, I was able to confide in my parents. Later, when I left home to attend the seminary and began teaching, I always found a friend to talk to about things that bothered me. After my father died and I went home to live with my mother again, she was the one who listened to me when I was upset about something or shared my joy when I was happy." Her heart seized a bit at the memory.

"I buried my mother nine months ago, and I miss her companionship and her friendship every day. Now that she's gone, I have no one left who will accept me without judging me when I have a problem."

He cleared his throat. "I'm sorry. I didn't realize she passed so recently."

"You couldn't have known. Not unless I told you," she reassured him. "But here's what I needed to say to you about our situation," she continued. "I think we're both finding it hard to keep up pretenses, whether we're out in public or here at home. I also think we're both resentful, to some degree, that we were forced into a marriage neither one of us wanted. We can't trust anyone with the truth or speak openly of our situation. You just admitted you have no one to talk to about what's happened to you. Not even your cousin Philip," she said, certain that if Harrison had confided in Philip, his cousin would have told her.

"No, I haven't."

"You told me that you've been spending time with old friends back in the city. Have you told any of them the truth?"

He held up his hand. "Absolutely not!"

"I haven't told anyone, either—not even Irene, who is becoming a good friend. And I feel terribly disloyal for misleading her."

When he opened his mouth to offer a comment, which she suspected would be a reminder not to become friends with any of the staff, she blurted out the rest of what she had to say. "Since neither one of us has told anyone, then neither you nor I have had the opportunity to share how incredibly hard and . . . and nerve-racking it is to be constantly on guard, afraid to say or do the wrong thing for fear someone might find out that we're married in name only and have no intention of remaining husband and wife. We need to change that. Otherwise, waiting another month or so until the annulment is completed will be unbearable. And I can't do it. I just can't," she whispered. "Can you?"

He glanced away and kept his gaze on the fire, which bathed his troubled features with golden light. He remained quiet for so long, she was afraid that silence was going to be his only response.

Finally, when her heart was beginning to race with the fear that he was trying to find the right words to tell her to stop whining about changing the impossible, he replied, "Change how?"

Excited by the mere possibility that he might agree to her plan, she edged forward, knocking the diary to the floor. "By becoming friends. You and I need to become friends."

His head snapped around, and he stared at her. "Friends?"

"Friends," she insisted. "We obviously trust each other to keep the true nature of our marriage a secret. Why can't we also trust each other enough to share anything and everything else we're experiencing, just like we're trying to do now?"

"Friends," he repeated, and his features twisted with disbelief, as if the notion of being friends with her or any other woman was alien to his very nature.

He looked so perplexed, she almost chuckled. It would be hard to resist falling in love with this man, especially when she admitted that her attraction to him, unfortunately, had been growing. Knowing how adamant he was about never marrying, however, made her attraction to him even more ill-fated. "Forget the fact that we're legally married. Just pretend we're . . . we're related, like you and Philip are. You've always been close to one another, haven't you?"

"We have, but—"

"And you've talked and disagreed and even argued . . . and then talked some more, just like good friends do, even though you're also cousins. Am I right?"

"I suppose so."

She leaned back in her seat and smiled. "Then we can do that, too. And before you try to argue the matter, let me point out to you that we've been sitting together and talking for a good half an hour, and I don't believe either one of us has worried about being completely honest with each other . . . about our feelings," she added to avoid lying outright, since she had yet to decide if she could trust him enough to tell him about Eric.

Harrison raked his fingers through his hair and laughed. "If anyone ever found out that I tried to become friends with any woman, especially one as beautiful and intriguing as you are, they'd laugh and assume it was some sort of prank—or have me confined to an asylum."

She dismissed his compliment as nothing more than his usual charm, which had lured other women, like Camille Jenkins and Vienna Biddle, into believing he was smitten with them. "You don't need an asylum. You need a refuge. A place where you can be totally at ease with yourself and with me. Let it be right here in this room. You have to come in here every night you're home to keep Irene or the other members of the staff from become suspicious anyway. Instead of our sitting here, staring at one another until you think it's safe to go to bed in the library alcove, why can't we put that time to better use?"

He cringed. "Anticipating night after night in that freezing bed makes me half inclined to ask if you've thought of a solution to that problem, as well," he replied, indirectly agreeing to her idea.

"In point of fact, I believe you have two options. First, you can return to the city every night where you'll have a warm bed, but you'll also have to contend with Irene, who won't hesitate to berate you for not staying here with me. Or second, you can simply have a warming stove installed in the library."

He laughed. "Because I want to spend hours in the library reading? She'll never believe it."

Annabelle grinned. "Perhaps not, but she would believe that I would like to use the room to read, which I do every morning in the parlor," she suggested before a brilliant idea popped into her head. "Better yet, I think Irene would be thrilled if you told her that we would like to spend our evenings together in the library. We'd have even more privacy for our talks in that room than we have here, and you'd have a warm room to sleep in." She hoped he would agree, since it was slightly awkward to try to have a conversation in this room when there was a large bed only a few feet away from them.

He bent down, picked up the diary that had fallen to the floor, and handed it to her. "I'll speak to Irene about it tomorrow. I have several appointments already set for early this week, but on Wednesday I should be able to take care of buying the stove and having it installed. Just be sure to keep that diary in a safe place so no one can find it and read it," he cautioned.

"It's identical to mine, but it's yours," she said, disappointed that the darker-shaded tome had not been available. "I bought it for you, although it isn't much of a gift, since I had to put it on your account." She handed it back to him. "You needn't worry that anyone will read mine, though. If they do, they'll only find a list of treasures that only have meaning for me. I think you might find it useful to list the treasures you discover every day that God has blessed you with."

He smoothed the cover of the diary with the palm of his hand. "I have no doubt that God exists, but He seems to have forgotten that I do," he whispered. "I sincerely doubt He's blessed me with anything for many years, so while I appreciate your thoughtfulness, I don't think I'll have much, if anything, to write in this diary."

Pain etched his features and despair laced his voice. She knew he had little reason to hope that he could change the direction of his life toward one that was more satisfying . . . which only reinforced her determination to fight her growing feelings for him. "Tonight you do have something to treasure. We've decided to become friends, and one of the greatest blessings in life is friendship."

He held the diary tight in his hand but dropped his gaze. When he looked up at her again, his eyes shifted in color from deep brown to ebony, reflecting an inner struggle she could almost see. "I think I may have a gift for you, too." He cleared his throat. "I need to tell you exactly what you can expect from my lawyer's efforts to legally end our marriage."

She swallowed hard, and her pulse slowed to a miserable thud. "Will there be a delay?" she asked.

"No, I don't expect so, but it seems that getting an annulment isn't a viable option. I had to file for a divorce."

When her heart plummeted to the pit of her stomach and a wave of nausea nearly overwhelmed her, she gripped the arms of her chair. "No annulment? But you promised. You promised!" she cried, devastated by his failure to keep his word. Overwhelmed by the news that she would soon be a twice-divorced woman, she simply could not bear to even think of how quickly and harshly he would judge her if he knew the truth.

"I'm sorry," he whispered.

Somehow she found the wherewithal to listen carefully as he explained why it had been necessary to petition for a divorce instead of an annulment. She could not fault the logic behind his lawyer's advice any more than she could dismiss the stigma they would each carry as a result of a divorce. She sighed. If she ever dared to hope that she could overcome the stigma of being once divorced, that hope would be destroyed forever when she was divorced yet again.

No man would ever be able to overlook the fact she had failed at two marriages or believe the circumstances surrounding each of her divorces.

Which meant she would spend the rest of her life alone. No husband. No children. No family at all.

"Now you know why it's been so important to me that you accept the settlement I offered to you," he explained. "It won't be easy for you once the divorce has been granted and eventually becomes public knowledge. The notoriety alone will no doubt force you to move elsewhere to live, and you'll need funds to do that."

"It won't be easy for you, either," she offered, diverting her troubled thoughts before she slid into a pit of despair she might never escape.

He smiled. "You shouldn't worry about me. I've been labeled a scoundrel, a cad, and a rake. Adding the stigma of being a divorced man is one more I'll have to live with, although I daresay it will be easier to convince a fair number of women that I'm not one to pursue in hopes of marriage. Besides, it's only a matter of time, I suppose, before someone discovers yet another far more serious flaw in my character."

"I can't imagine anything worse," she argued.

"There's only one thing worse than being divorced, which by itself will probably dissuade a fair number of people from associating with me. At least my family fortune will assure that I won't be a complete outcast."

She swallowed the lump in her throat. "What could possibly be worse for any man's reputation beyond being divorced?"

"Marrying a divorced woman," he said immediately. "Society would find that the greater sin, although I'm not certain why a divorced woman is always thought to be one step beyond redemption. Any man who considered marrying her would be twice the fool."

When the blood drained from her face, and she struggled to draw a breath, he leaned forward and took hold of her hand. "I'm sorry. I shouldn't have expressed myself so callously."

She held his hand as if it were a lifeline about to be yanked away, which would surely happen once he knew she had been a divorced woman when he had married her. In fact, given his own words, she now wondered if he would just send her away immediately once he knew the truth, with little regard for her well-being. "There's no reason to be sorry. You only spoke the truth." But Annabelle found she was unable to trust him yet with the secret she had been keeping from him.

He might scoff at the stigma of being divorced and one day overcome it, perhaps, but he would be branded with the stigma of marrying a divorced woman for the rest of his life.

With Eric in the city and Vienna Biddle spreading gossip about the new Mrs. Graymoor, the need to keep her secret had become even greater. And Annabelle found herself facing the same dilemma tonight that had driven her to her room earlier in the day.

Should she stay here or should she go away?

Her first instinct was to leave tonight, sell the wedding ring Eric had given to her, and disappear. But even if she changed her name and moved far away, she would spend every day of the rest of her life doing exactly what she was doing now—living a lie and waiting for someone to uncover the truth.

God couldn't possibly intend for her to carry that burden forever, could He?

Chapter Eighteen

❄

Several days later, Annabelle was relieved to find that Irene was
still sitting on the bench overlooking the river feeding Jonah
when she got there and sat down beside her. "I'm sorry I'm late.
I overslept a bit."

Irene shook her head and tossed a last nut to the mangy squirrel. "Now I know the world's turned topsy-turvy. You overslept,
and Harrison left at first light."

"He did?" Annabelle blurted, then realized her mistake. "He
was gone when I woke up . . . and I . . . I thought perhaps he'd
gotten up early and came out to the cottage to swipe a few of
those molasses cookies before you were up."

"He did, but I caught him and fixed him a proper breakfast
before he left for the city to buy one of those warming stoves and
hire somebody to set it up. If you weren't such a good influence
on him, I'd think he was up to something, which is neither here
nor there. I'm just happy you two are getting along well enough
to want to spend time together in the library."

Pleased that he had acted on her idea, Annabelle tugged her

cape a bit tighter and was glad she had worn a woolen petticoat to keep her legs from freezing.

"Anyway, before I forget, he said to tell you to be ready to leave midmorning. He's coming back to fetch you."

"But I was going to start my volunteer work today, and Philip is coming to pick me up."

"Don't bother yourself worrying about that. He said he's going to stop and tell his cousin not to come," the housekeeper said. She shook the bits of nuts and shells from the man's overcoat she was wearing today and got to her feet.

Annabelle rose to walk back to the cottage with Irene and tried to keep her voice from revealing her disappointment. "Did he say where we were going?" she asked as their footsteps crunched through the icy crust on the snow that still covered the landscape.

"He said it's a surprise, and you should dress warm. Wear one of those woolen petticoats I helped unpack for you," she suggested before she lost her footing and slipped on a slick patch of ice.

Annabelle grabbed the older woman's arm, but the momentum was too great, and they both ended up landing bottoms-up on the ice. Utterly stunned by the jolt of pain that raced up her spine, she had to get enough air back into her lungs before she could speak. "Are you hurt?"

With her face mottled red, Irene took several deep gulps of air before answering. "Other than my pride, nothing's injured," she quipped, and they helped each other back to their feet. "What about you? I hope you didn't hurt yourself. You've got that event tonight at the museum to attend."

Annabelle twisted at her waist, and her back only responded with a twinge. She shook the ice and snow from her cape and smiled. "I'm fine, too. Are you certain you're all right?"

Irene hooked their arms together. "I've had worse spills than that one and didn't get hurt," she insisted as they started walking back to the cottage. "I wish I could say the same for Peggy."

"But Harrison said she wasn't hurt when she fell the other day."

"At the time she said she wasn't, but by the end of the day, she was limping about, claiming her knee was bruised. This morning she was still complaining. I doubt it's much more than a slight hurt, but she'll take to her bed for a few days, like she usually does when she has any sort of excuse, and then she'll be back to her usual complaining self."

Annabelle kept a sharp eye for any other icy patches in the pathway as they neared the cottage. "If she constantly complains, which I've witnessed for myself, it's a wonder you don't . . . I mean, someone with less patience than you have would be inclined to let her go."

"Along with her husband, who complains twice as much as she does. He just has the good sense to wait until you or Harrison aren't around," Irene added. "Whenever I'm tempted to let them both go, I try to remember they do a fair day's work every day and I say a prayer for extra patience instead. Otherwise, my conscience wouldn't let me sleep at night knowing they'd find it almost impossible to keep whatever positions they'd be able to find and hold on to them. Fortunately, having Lotte here is like finding a cloud of fresh air in a smoky kitchen." She opened the kitchen door and followed Annabelle inside.

Grateful for the blast of heat she walked into, Annabelle slipped off her gloves and cape. "Lotte's doing well so far?"

Irene shrugged out of her own coat. "She's young and needs careful training, but she's doing just fine. Now set yourself down while I start breakfast for you. Working with my letters may have to wait a spell. I've got to pack up some of what's left from yesterday's dinner and put it into a basket for Harrison," she said with a grin.

Annabelle groaned. "H-he's taking me on a picnic?"

"He did say for you to dress warm."

"I could add two more woolen petticoats to the one I'm

already wearing and that wouldn't keep me warm enough to enjoy a picnic in the snow," she grumbled and wondered if Harrison belonged in an asylum after all.

❧

If Annabelle insisted on going into the city several mornings every week to volunteer at one of the institutions his family had founded, Harrison was not going to stop her. He had decided, however, that he would be the one to escort her and return to take her home every day and not his cousin, regardless of how inconvenient that would prove to be.

Although he had only completed half of his early-morning mission and had finally purchased a warming stove for the library from Harold McGinley, he still needed to make arrangements to have it installed, since McGinley had taken to his bed yesterday from gout again and could barely walk. He returned to Graymoor Gardens at ten o'clock, told Graham to wait for them in the circular driveway, and hurried into the house expecting to find Annabelle waiting for him in the parlor.

When he found the room empty, he walked back into the foyer. He noted that her green cape was not hanging there as usual and hoped she had gone upstairs to get something she had forgotten. He took the staircase two steps at a time and would have bumped right into Irene on the top landing in the upstairs hallway if he had not dropped back two steps.

Eye to eye with him, she peered over the pile of bedclothes she had gathered up to launder and glared at him. "My first instinct was right. You are up to something. Why aren't you sleeping with your wife instead of that bed in the library alcove? And don't bother to deny it. I just stripped that bed bare down to the mattress because the sheets needed changing."

Caught by surprise, he shot back the first thought that popped into his head. "No one's supposed to go into the library unless I say so."

"That's only when you're at home, which I knew you weren't because I talked to you right before you left this morning."

"You're supposed to be in the kitchen," he argued. "Why isn't Peggy—"

"She's nursing her sore knee, and Lotte's busy storing away the deliveries that came a while ago, which left me to gather up the laundry."

Hoping to escape without answering her question—which was so impertinent that any other member of his staff, either here or in the city, would never have dared to ask it—he looked past her. "Where's Annabelle? Didn't you tell her to be ready for me to take her to the city?"

"Find her yourself," Irene replied and started down the staircase, forcing him to back up against the balustrade.

"The servants' stairs are at the end of the upstairs hall," he quipped.

She stopped right next to him and did not seem to notice that the soiled bedclothes were poking him in the chest. "I must have caught whatever's ailing you, because I can't seem to remember where I belong any more than you do," she snapped and proceeded down the staircase without giving him the opportunity to argue with her any longer.

Thoroughly frustrated and more than annoyed at this point, he charged through every room on the second floor, including the library, which was not as sacrosanct as he had thought, but found no sign of his missing wife. "She must be back in the cottage," he grumbled and took the servants' stairs to the first floor. Since he was still wearing his winter overcoat, he quickly overheated and paused to catch his breath when he reached the basement before he started the long walk through the tunnel that connected the two buildings.

When he heard the faint echo of footsteps coming from the opposite direction, he increased his pace. He slowed down when he finally saw that it was Alan approaching him carrying a load of firewood, instead of Annabelle, and fumed.

"Where's my wife?" he demanded when Alan was within earshot.

Alan hooked his thumb and motioned over his shoulder. "Last I saw Miss Annabelle was about fifteen minutes ago in the kitchen, but that was before I left to get this wood for the parlor."

Harrison walked past the man with long, determined strides and wondered if sealing up this tunnel might be the only way to keep that woman in the main house where she belonged, although he had no idea how to keep Irene in her place, too. When he finally stepped out of the tunnel into the cottage basement, he was muttering under his breath, trying to decide which woman was more troublesome.

"Did you say something, sir?"

Startled, he turned and saw Lotte standing a few feet away, holding an empty crate. "What are you doing down here?" he grumbled, apparently more gruffly than he intended.

Her face instantly flushed bright red. "Irene told me to put the vegetables away over there," she said and used the crate to point to the section of the basement reserved as a root cellar. "Now that I'm finished, I was going to take this crate back down the delivery tunnel."

He cleared his throat and softened his voice to ease her distress as well as his own guilt. "That's fine. I'm looking for Miss Annabelle. Alan said she was in the kitchen when he last saw her."

She shook her head. "She might have been then, but I saw her leave a while ago before he came back. She stopped and talked to me for a bit, but she said she was heading back to the main house. I was real busy, though, so I didn't actually see her leave the basement."

He narrowed his gaze. "You're certain she's not in the cottage?"

"Y-yes sir, but I can check again for you."

When he nodded, she set down her crate and scampered up the stairs. She returned a few minutes later. "She's not there, sir."

He sighed, thanked her, and charged back the same way he had come. Since he had already checked the main house, he knew she was not there. Had she decided to leave him? The only question he had was how she had managed to do that. He had spoken to Philip himself and knew his cousin had not come for her. She might have tried to convince the staff to help her to leave, but he dismissed that idea, too. Even Irene knew that helping Annabelle to leave him was a line she could not cross.

"The delivery. She must have talked one of the Andersons' deliverymen into taking her back to the city." Determined to find her, if only to congratulate her for her fine performance again last night when they had talked together, he chided himself for falling into her trap. "Men simply don't become friends with women," he muttered and stormed from the tunnel, up the basement steps, and through the foyer.

"I should have known it was a ploy. The very moment I told her about the divorce, expecting her to rant and rave, she acted as if she were more concerned about me." He slapped at his thigh in frustration as he left the house. "I should have known. I should have known," he repeated over and over until it became a mantra, which he only stopped muttering long enough to bark at Graham that he wanted to leave for the city and proceed directly to the Andersons'.

Still grumbling his mantra, he yanked the coach door open, peered inside, and stopped dead. "Annabelle?"

She moved her knitting bag and set it down at her feet next to a large wicker basket. "I'm sorry. We must have just missed one another. I was up in my room getting my knitting stick so I could knit on the way into the city when I saw the coach through the window. I hurried down, but you weren't there, so I decided the best thing to do was wait right here. I didn't mean to worry you," she added, apparently noting the frown he wore. "You should have known I wouldn't leave. Not without you."

"Yes, I should have known," he replied. Harrison climbed up into the coach, ready to embark on one adventure he had never anticipated—learning how to be friends with a woman who also happened to be his intriguingly beautiful, unpredictable, and very temporary wife.

Chapter Nineteen

❄

Annabelle was relieved to learn that Harrison had not planned a winter picnic after all, but she still felt a bit apprehensive about encountering Eric when they arrived in the city.

Once Harrison made sure she was safely inside the Refuge, she finally began to relax. Eric was far too interested in his own needs to ever consider showing up here. She left the basket of food with the director of the Refuge, who promised to give it to the elderly widow who monitored the facility after he left at the end of each day, in order to make sure no destitute woman was turned away during the night.

She ventured into the main dormitory and found nearly two dozen women waiting for her, just as the director assured her they would be.

She spent the next few hours visiting with the indigent mothers and their babies while their older children were in another room. Other than caring for their children, she learned that the women's main tasks were to keep their dormitory-style living spaces clean and to operate the kitchen, which relied on donated food, leaving them with several free hours every day.

Surprised to discover that most of them knew how to knit, she also learned they merely lacked the tools necessary and the funds to purchase the wool they could use to make warm socks and other winter essentials for themselves and their children.

The inside of the building was nearly as cold as it was outside, and she was grateful that she had worn all three of her woolen petticoats. She also made a mental note to speak to Harrison about finding a way to secure firewood for the massive fireplace at the far end of this room.

Although burdened by the tales the women had told her, which gave her a frightening firsthand view of how precarious a woman's life could be when she was left alone to raise her children, she left them buoyed by the possibility she could do something more to help them than offer hopeful words.

She made a promise to return the next day and left the women, mindful to be on time to meet Harrison so he would not have to run about looking for her as he had done this morning at home. She stepped outside and a cold wind whipped at her cape, chilling the few bones she had left at that point that had not already frozen. Shifting her weight from one foot to the other to try to generate some warmth, she was scanning the street for any sign of Eric when she spied a sign for a wool shop in the next square. Impulsively, she decided she could probably get to the shop, place an order for some basic wool and knitting needles, and still be back in time to meet him.

Harrison had repeatedly told her to spend as much as she wished, so she did not even have to consider he would object. She kept her hood low enough, however, to cover most of her face to keep anyone from recognizing her as she rushed past the few people who had dared the elements to shop today. She entered the store, and since she was the only customer, Annabelle managed to complete her mission in less than five minutes. She waited at the counter while the shopkeeper, Eleanor Wallace, tallied up the charges. The sum would have strained the wages she had earned for an entire year while she was teaching, but she knew Harrison would dismiss the amount as paltry and instructed the woman to put it on the account in his name.

When the bell over the door announced another customer, Mrs. Wallace paused and looked past Annabelle. "Please look around. I'm almost finished here," she announced before turning her attention back to Annabelle. "I'll see that everything is delivered this afternoon."

"Since it's a surprise, I'd rather pick everything up tomorrow morning. You'll be open by ten o'clock?" she asked.

"Yes, ma'am. I will."

Annabelle smiled. "Then I'll see you tomorrow at ten." She turned to leave but froze when she saw Eric's wife standing just a few yards away from her. Even though they had not been introduced at the Sullivans' ball, there was still a chance that Eric's wife had seen her and someone else had told her Annabelle's name. If she had, she might be tempted to introduce herself now.

While that posed no immediate problem, Annabelle could not take the risk that she would mention to Eric that she had met the new Mrs. Graymoor. She might also describe Annabelle in enough detail that he would be curious about a woman who looked like the secret wife he had divorced.

Fortunately, the woman was so intent on studying an assortment of imported wool that she did not look up to see Annabelle. Once the shopkeeper ushered her new customer into the side room on the opposite side of the shop to show her something else, she also gave Annabelle the chance to slip out of the shop unnoticed if she was very, very careful not to make a sound.

Heart pounding, Annabelle tiptoed as quickly as she could to the door. When she spied the coach sitting directly outside through the small display window, however, she hesitated. The curtains were drawn tight against the cold and wind so she could not see inside. Although she doubted that Eric would have accompanied his wife while she was out shopping, she could not take the chance he had. If he picked the exact moment she decided to step out of the shop to lift the curtain and peer outside, she had no hope at all that he would not recognize her.

When she heard the two women return to the main room of the shop, she was near panic. There was no way she could leave, and there was no place to hide.

Miraculously, the two women walked to the rear of the main display room, so engrossed with their conversation neither woman seemed to realize she was even there. Treading softly, she escaped into the side room closest to her and turned her back as if she were interested in skeins of wool she could barely see through her tears.

She waited five minutes. Then ten more. By the time Eric's wife finally left, twenty minutes had passed and Annabelle's pulse was racing so fast, she was growing faint.

She waited a few more minutes before she turned her head, just in time to see the coach pulling away, and nearly collapsed with relief. Gathering up her courage, she rushed out of the room, convinced that Harrison had already gone inside the Refuge to search for her.

The shopkeeper gasped the moment she saw her. "Mrs. Graymoor! I thought you left a good while ago."

"That's what I'd planned, but I couldn't resist taking a peek at some more wool before I left. I've also reconsidered and I'd like you to deliver everything to the Refuge this afternoon," she gushed and hurried out the door.

Fearful that Eric's coach might turn around and come back in this direction, she picked up her skirts and cape and ran back the entire length of the square. By the time she reached Harrison's coach, she was panting for breath and the cold air had turned her throat raw. She looked up at Graham. "Mr. Graymoor. Did he go inside the Refuge?"

The driver shook his head and pointed at the coach as he started to climb down to help her embark.

She waved him back. "I'll have my husband help me, if I have need," she insisted and opened the coach door by herself. "I'm so sorry I'm late," she said and climbed aboard without giving Harrison a chance to help her.

When she dropped into the seat across from him, he reached over to pull the door closed.

"I'm truly, truly sorry. I was so worried that you'd have to charge around looking for me again or just leave me here to teach me a lesson."

He laughed and tapped at the roof to signal Graham to start them for home. "On the contrary. I've learned my lesson. As I see it, I have two choices when I'm picking you up to go anywhere. I can simply wait for you in the coach, or I can stop at the harness maker today and have him make a special leash you can wear so all I have to do is give it a tug to let you know I'm waiting."

She pursed her lips and put both hands on the seat to keep her balance when the coach rounded a corner. "I should hope you'd choose the former, rather than the latter," she quipped. "I suppose I should be thankful you didn't decide to leave me here so I'd have to hire a hack to take me home again."

"You should have known I wouldn't leave. Not without you," he said, turning her own words against her.

Her heart skipped a beat, and she wondered if becoming friends with this man might be inviting precisely the kind of trouble she did not need. At the moment, she had more trouble than she knew how to handle—trouble that would not go away until Eric Bradley and his wife left the city.

Or she did.

Harrison left after dinner to spend the afternoon with friends, and Annabelle's plans for the afternoon definitely included a nap to calm her frazzled nerves. Before long she'd need to dress for another late evening in the city, where she feared Eric and his wife would also be in attendance.

Instead of napping, however, she had sat at the dining room table with nearly three dozen invitations Harrison had brought back from the city mansion that he expected her to respond to in short notes he would take back with him tomorrow morning to have delivered. After sorting the invitations into two piles, she had spent an hour declining daytime invitations directed to her, just as he told her to do.

She set the pen down and opened and closed her hand to ease the cramps before attempting to write more notes. She stared at the remaining pile of invitations to evening events Harrison said they would agree to attend as a couple and groaned. She wished she could stay here tonight, and the prospect of attending so many affairs in the city made her stomach quiver.

She had been able to avoid an encounter with Eric's wife today, but sooner or later it was almost inevitable that Eric would be at one of these evening affairs, and the only way she could avoid that debacle would be to stay right here at Graymoor Gardens. It would keep her safe from Vienna Biddle, as well.

There didn't seem to be any choice but to accept the invitations, but her mind wrestled with one excuse after another in hopes she could at least stay home tonight. If she said she was tired, Harrison would blame her for getting up so early to walk with Irene and work with her on her lessons. He might even go so far as to forbid her to continue. If she claimed she was not feeling well, he could claim she was overexerting herself by volunteering at the Refuge and take that away from her, too.

She signed her name to the last note she would have to write and sighed. "Short of telling him the truth, I don't have a whisper of a hope to stay home tonight."

"What truth would that be?"

Startled by Harrison's voice, she dropped the pen and splattered ink on the last note she had written. She turned to see him standing in the doorway holding back the baize curtain. "Y-you're back already?"

He entered the room, letting the curtain fall back into place. "Why don't you want to go to the museum with me tonight? I hope it isn't because you're too tired. If that's the case, perhaps you shouldn't get up quite so early or spend the day traveling back and forth from the city, especially when you know we have plans for the evening."

"No. I'm not tired at all," she retorted, annoyed that he had developed an uncanny ability to read her mind. "I've even had enough energy to respond to all these invitations, just like I promised I'd do."

He walked over to her and studied her face so intently, she felt her cheeks warm. "You're not feeling well? Is that it?"

"I'm perfectly fine," she insisted and retrieved the pen she had dropped.

"If you're worried that Vienna might be there tonight, then you shouldn't be. She won't be there. In point of fact, there won't be more than a few dozen people in attendance, if that many."

Grateful that he had introduced the partial truth behind her reluctance to attend the affair at the museum tonight, she moistened her lips. "Are you certain she won't be there? I thought you said this was a very important event at the museum, and from all I could gather at the Sullivan ball, her father is a very important man."

He grinned. "He is, but this event is strictly for the donors who have contributed more than one thousand dollars to the museum this year. After Peale died four years ago—he was the man who started the museum—and his sons took over, many of the donors lost interest and stopped their support. Paul Biddle, Vienna's father, was one of them."

"Why did he stop?"

"Peale's sons weren't as interested in keeping the museum open as much as their father was. They had other interests and still do, one of which is a museum in Baltimore."

"Why didn't you stop your donation?" she asked, surprised that he would be interested in anything like a museum.

He chuckled. "In all truth, I didn't even realize I was still a donor until the invitation arrived, which is usually how I find out that the annual donations my father set up are still in place." He took her hand and helped her to her feet. "Now that that's settled, there's something else we need to discuss. Privately," he said with a wink.

She nodded and walked upstairs with him to the sleeping room they were supposed to be sharing. He raked his fingers through his hair as he crossed the room and plopped down into one of the two chairs that were still sitting where she had put them the day before. "Irene knows that I'm sleeping in the library instead of here with you, and she knows I ordered the warming stove because it's too cold in there for me to get any sleep."

Annabelle's heart skipped a beat, and she sat down across from him. "Are you certain?"

"She told me so herself. This is the first opportunity I've had to speak to you privately about it."

"What did you tell her?" she asked, hoping he had been able to charm the housekeeper into thinking she was wrong.

"I didn't tell her anything. Fortunately, I was searching all over for you and used that as an excuse to escape. I could fend her off like I usually do, but now that you've become so friendly with her, she's bound to mention it to you," he said derisively. "What are you going to tell her?"

"I don't know," she whispered and pressed her fingertips to her forehead to ease the dull ache that had started wrapping around her head. She closed her eyes for a moment and rejected one excuse after another to explain why Harrison was not sleeping in the same bed with her until she found one that Irene was likely to accept.

She opened her eyes and offered him a weak smile. "I think I know a way to make certain Irene won't bring up the matter again."

He sat up a little straighter. "You do?"

She nodded. "How would you feel about being labeled a brute? I promise I won't make you out to be an awful brute. Just a small one, and all I have to do is stretch the truth a bit."

Chapter Twenty

❄

Annabelle survived the event at the museum unscathed, just as Harrison had promised she would. Over the course of the next two days, she even survived another evening affair without seeing Vienna or Eric. But her anticipation grew worse by the hour while she waited for Irene to confront her about the unusual sleeping arrangements she and Harrison shared.

Since the topic had not come up while she sat with Irene outside on the bench feeding the squirrel this morning, she returned to the cottage with the housekeeper ready to bring it up herself once they finished with today's lesson. She sat down at the kitchen table and handed the slate and chalk to Irene. "Before we start on any new letters, you should practice what you've already learned," she prompted.

Irene was forming letters less awkwardly than when she had first begun, but she set the chalk down now before she finished the first two letters. "I can't do it."

Annabelle smiled. "Of course you can. Try again."

"No, I mean I can't do it. I can't hold my tongue a second longer." She took Annabelle's hand. "I don't know why Harrison

has left your bed, but bless your loving heart, you've been keeping your hurt all to yourself. Is there anything I can do to help?"

Now that the moment she had been dreading had arrived,
Annabelle accepted the guilt she deserved for the partial lie she
was about to tell. "He hasn't left my bed. He's just not sleeping
with me all night." She hoped the woman would assume the
blush that warmed her cheeks was due to the suggestive nature
of her words rather than the tale she was going to spin that had
only a bit of truth to it.

Irene's eyes opened wide. "Why not?"

"He's afraid he'll be embarrassed. Do you . . . do you remember
when I first came here, and I had that fading bruise on my eye?"

"I remember. I heard that one of those robbers did that to
you," she replied and narrowed her gaze. "If Harrison took a hand
to you—"

"He did, but perfectly by accident. He didn't mean to hit me,
but . . . but I suppose he's been sleeping alone for so long, he's
not accustomed to sharing his bed," she gushed. "He's rather a
restless sleeper and he struck me with his elbow. It wasn't the
first time he'd accidently jabbed me, but he'd never blackened
my eye before. He's determined to make it the last, which is
why he sleeps in the library, although we're both hoping that it
won't be for long."

She paused for a moment and tightened her hold on Irene's
hand just a bit more. "I hope you understand why he didn't
mention it to you before now or why he didn't explain himself
when you confronted him about it. He's quite embarrassed as
it is, which is why I promised him that I'd explain everything
to you so you wouldn't ask him any more about it. I'm sorry. I
should have told you about it long before now."

Irene shook her head. "I never thought I'd live long enough
to see him embarrassed about anything, but I suppose I'll have
to get used to the idea he's a changed man now that he's married

to you." She touched Annabelle's shoulder. "I won't say another word about it. Now let's get back to my lesson, or we won't have time for you to show me a new recipe today," she said, then erased the slate and handed the chalk to Annabelle.

"How has he changed?" she asked as she shaped the letter *P*.

"You'll see what I'm talking about next Sunday," she replied.

Irene remained mum on the subject, and Annabelle tried to be satisfied that she had finally done what she had promised Harrison she could do.

e

Several hours later, Annabelle had the first real surprise of the day when Harrison dropped her off at the Refuge and told her to hire a hack to go home because he had errands to do that would keep him busy until very late tonight. Her second surprise came only moments later when she found Philip waiting for her outside of the director's office when she walked into the Refuge.

"I heard about the work you're doing here and had to see it for myself," he explained.

"You heard? From whom?" She doubted that anyone beyond the Refuge itself even knew she had been volunteering here— other than Harrison, of course, since this was only her third day here.

"I have developed many reliable sources of information, particularly where you're concerned."

When she frowned, he held up his hand. "Most of it is good."

"But not all," she ventured.

"Sooner or later, the gossipmongers will find someone else to focus on, and Vienna Biddle will find another man to chase."

"I hope I'm alive to see it," she muttered.

He chuckled. "Remind me to tell you a bit more about Miss Biddle later. For now, let's join the women staying here so you can show me the impressive work you've done."

"I haven't done much of anything so far, other than to use Harrison's money to purchase what these women need to help themselves."

He offered her his arm. "It seems we have even more in common than my cousin. That's precisely what I do, although I'm fairly good at attracting donations from men and women who aren't my relatives," he said and opened the dormitory door.

Prepared to spend a few very cold hours here, she walked into the dormitory with him. Although the room was far from being as warm as any of the rooms back at Graymoor Gardens, it was remarkably better than it had been yesterday, and she saw the reason why. In addition to a large stack of firewood along the far wall, there was a blazing fire in the massive fireplace, which warmed the women who were sitting in a circle and chatting while they were knitting.

She looked at Philip in amazement. "Did you arrange for the firewood here?"

"I wish I could say that I did, but it wasn't necessary for me to do anything. My cousin took care of it personally, or so I've been told."

She blinked hard. "Harrison?"

He smiled. "The last I checked, he was my only cousin. In truth, he's shown little interest in the past about supporting anything that might be considered a philanthropic endeavor, but I must say he's changed quite a bit since he married you."

Annabelle frowned. "That's the second time today someone's said that to me."

Certain that Harrison did not bother to tell her what he had done because he saw no need to impress her, she spent the next few hours in a knitting circle with the other women, admiring the work they were doing or showing them how to make a complicated stitch that was new to them. To her surprise, Philip sat right there with all of them, watching them work and occasionally joining in the conversation.

When it was time for her to return home, he escorted her outside and hailed down a hack for her. "When you have time, perhaps I could get your opinion on some ideas I have about improving conditions at several other institutions in the city," he suggested as he helped her into the coach.

Anticipating another afternoon alone, since Harrison was otherwise occupied, she waved for him to get into the coach. "I have time today. Please join me for dinner. I'm certain Irene made more than enough," she offered.

Philip needed no further persuasion and climbed into the coach. Before the wheels creaked and started rolling, she reminded him of his promise to tell her about Vienna Biddle, her voice just a whisper.

He leaned back against the cushion and pointed up to the roof. "It's probably best if we wait until we're back at Graymoor Gardens."

She frowned but decided he was right. "Someday I'm going to live in a world where I don't have to watch every word I say everywhere or anywhere I go with anyone," she insisted as the coach reached a steady but bumpy rhythm.

"That world doesn't exist, at least not here in this city. I'm afraid you'd have to leave to find it, if it even exists."

Annabelle sighed. "Tell me about your ideas."

Philip talked all the way home, through dinner, and most of the afternoon, which they spent in the parlor. The more he talked, the more she learned about his efforts here in Philadelphia as well as New York City and Boston. Deeply moved by his stories of the many people who struggled each day just to survive, she offered one silent prayer after another to thank God she had been spared a similar fate—and to ask for forgiveness for making a single complaint about her situation.

When Lotte returned with a second tray of black almond crescent cookies, Annabelle waited until she set the tray down on the serving table next to Philip before addressing her. "Thank you. Please tell Irene that Mr. Philip will be staying for supper, but we won't need anything else until then," she said, anxious to have the privacy necessary to discuss the one topic that mattered most to her.

"I won't be able to eat a bite of supper if I keep nibbling at these." He snatched up one of the delicate, sugar-crusted treats as the young girl took her leave.

"My mother always made those cookies last, after she finished making the other cookies she was baking for Christmas." With only nine days left until the holiday she loved finally arrived, it would be the first time she celebrated Christmas without her mother. Her heart grew heavy.

"Why is that?" Philip polished off the cookie and reached for another.

"She knew we'd eat every last one before Christmas, and she'd have to bake another batch," she murmured. Before Annabelle got lost in sad, sad thoughts that this Christmas would be far different than any she had had before, she changed the subject entirely. "Now that I've sweetened you up and I don't expect any more interruptions, perhaps you could tell me more about Vienna Biddle, like you promised."

Nodding, he swallowed the last bite and brushed the sugar from his fingers with a napkin he set back onto the table when he'd finished. "Vienna Biddle is twenty-six years old, and she's reached an age where she's considered to be an antique on the marriage market. At one time, she had four brothers who were considerably older than she was, but only two survived to adulthood. The oldest now is Charles. He's been confined to a private asylum for many years, although the family has been able to convince most everyone he's moved to Europe, where he's pursuing a career as an artist. Her other brother, Gerald, left the city rather abruptly about six years ago and disappeared."

"What happened to him?" she asked, half afraid of the answer he would give her.

He shrugged. "Gossipmongers claim he eloped with a serving wench who worked in a tavern along the wharf, but the family insists he joined up with a group of missionaries who set sail for China around the same time. I've never been able to verify either version to learn which is true."

Annabelle's heart, which she had hardened against the young woman, softened. "Poor Vienna. All she has left are her parents, who must be quite elderly by now."

"Actually, her mother died shortly after Gerald left, so it's only Vienna, her widowed father, who is nearly seventy, and a dwindling fortune she's openly declared she's going to replenish by marrying one."

Annabelle dropped her gaze for a moment when she realized the hurt and pain she had seen in Vienna's eyes were not there because she was still in love with Harrison. She was mourning the loss of something even more important to her: his money.

"Harrison isn't the first man she's chased and lost," Philip offered.

Annabelle met his gaze again. "He isn't?"

He hesitated for a moment while he counted up the number on the fingers of one hand. "There were three others before him. Four, if you count poor Trent, but he didn't leave her by choice. He died rather suddenly four years ago, just when he was about to propose, according to Vienna."

"How awful. His family must have been devastated to lose a son so young."

He shook his head. "Trent didn't have any family left. At eighty-seven, most lifelong bachelors don't."

Annabelle gasped. "Eighty-seven?"

"Indeed," Philip replied with a chuckle. "He left his considerable fortune, which Vienna had hoped to inherit, to a number of charities that included a foundation he established, naming me as executor. This did not endear me to her."

"Is that why you return to Philadelphia from time to time?" she asked.

"In part. There was so little left in the foundation at this point, my trip here now was critical. Without additional donations, the foundation would have had to fold."

Annabelle shifted in her seat and wished she had thought to bring her knitting to keep her hands busy. "You've obviously gotten the donations you needed, or you wouldn't have spent the afternoon telling me about your ideas."

He smiled. "I have one substantial donation I received just the other day from my cousin. I was reluctant to leave just yet because I have two very promising prospects that may yield even more, which is just as well, since I've learned that I can't leave Philadelphia at all."

Surprised to learn of Harrison's donation, she was puzzled by Philip's words. "You can't leave? Why not?"

"There hasn't been a ship able to break free of the ice to set sail since early this week. Unlike the roadways in and around the city proper, all the ones north are impassable. They're either covered with ice or buried under snowdrifts, which means I'm a prisoner here, along with anyone else who wants to travel north—at least until the first thaw, which some say may not come until early spring."

Annabelle's heart nearly stopped beating, and she drew several deep breaths of air until she felt it start pulsing again. If Philip could not leave, then neither could Eric. The thought that her former husband would remain here for months was so terrifying she had to fold her hands together and hide them in the folds of her skirts to keep Philip from seeing how badly they were trembling.

Just when she thought there was nothing else that would upset her, Philip did just that. "Since I'm here and we seem to have some time left alone before supper, I should probably tell you about Elizabeth Warren and Alicia Partridge, unless Harrison has told you about them already."

She swallowed hard. "No, he hasn't. Who are they?"

"They're two young women you're likely to encounter who will not be friendly toward you."

"Are they friends of Vienna's?"

He cringed. "Right now, I'd have to say they're more allies than friends of hers, but they have only one thing in common: Harrison was quite attentive to each of them before he turned his attention to Vienna. More important, they each now have a common target, and I'm afraid that would be you."

Before she had the wherewithal to digest the horrifying prospect that there were now three women who wanted to destroy her, thanks to her husband's past exploits, she heard a coach driving up the curved driveway and looked out the window. "Harrison's home early," she murmured.

"Good! I need to tell him that I'll be extending my stay indefinitely," he said, helping himself to another cookie.

While he satisfied his sweet tooth, Annabelle stayed seated right where she was to control her temper before she welcomed her husband home.

When Harrison finally entered the parlor, he took one look at Philip, stopped dead in his tracks, and scowled. "What are you doing here? I thought you were getting ready to leave for Boston."

"He can't leave, which turned out to be fortunate for me,"

she suggested. "He was just telling me about Elizabeth Warren and Alicia Partridge."

He stared at her for a moment before he glared at his cousin, who raised his hands in surrender. "Since you didn't tell her, I only said something because I thought she should know."

"Is there anything else you presumed to tell my wife that you thought she should know?"

"Only about my plans for spending the donation you made to the foundation."

Harrison snorted. "She doesn't need to know about that. Is there anything more you divulged during your visit?"

"Nothing at all. Did you enjoy spending today with your friends at Petty's Island? I'm certain she would love to hear about that, too."

Annabelle rose so quickly she almost lost her balance. "Since the two of you are talking about me as if I'm not here, I'm going to my room, where I plan to have a quiet supper alone so you can feel free to discuss me at your leisure." She looked directly at Philip. "Thank you. I enjoyed spending my day with you, and I hope we can do it again very soon." Then she slowly walked out of the room with as much dignity as she could muster.

She could hear them continue to argue as she walked up the staircase.

"You spent the entire day with my wife?" Harrison charged.

"You spent the entire day with your friends," Philip countered. "If you're that concerned about your wife, perhaps you should spend time with her instead."

She blocked out the rest of their words by humming a tune until she reached her room. Once inside, she closed the door, wondering what she would do if she could end this marriage just as easily as she had blocked out the sound of the two men's banter.

Chapter Twenty-One

❄

Every aspect of the life he had led for the past eight years was changing so fast, Harrison had no idea how to regain control, especially when the past kept rising up to haunt him and further complicate his life.

He climbed up the staircase to the second floor just before midnight, after spending hours alone after Philip had left, to try to find a way back to normal. If he thought it would make a difference, he would pack a travel bag and leave at first light for one of the five properties he had inherited, with the exception of the one in western Pennsylvania he had left only a few weeks ago.

Only two things kept him from acting on his impulse to leave: his responsibility to his late brother, Peter, and his obligation to Irene.

Although he was satisfied he had been able to establish some new rules with Philip during supper where Annabelle was concerned, he doubted he would get any real sleep until he apologized to Annabelle for his behavior this afternoon. Only then could he ask for her help.

When he reached the upstairs hallway, he walked straight

to the library. He was about to open the door when he caught a glimpse of dim light peeking from beneath the bottom of her door. He was surprised Annabelle was still awake at this hour, since she typically rose before dawn, but he was quickly learning that this woman was a bundle of surprises that caught him off guard more often than not.

Hopeful he might be able to apologize before taking to his own bed, he knocked on her door. When she did not answer, he grew worried that she might have fallen asleep without dousing the oil lamp and eased the door open. He slipped into the room hoping to extinguish it and leave without waking her, but he found her sitting at the lady's desk, her back to him.

Apparently she was so engrossed in what she was writing that she had not heard him knock or enter the room, so he shut the door just loud enough to let her know she was no longer alone. When she still acted as if he weren't there, he cleared his throat. "I thought you might have finished responding to all those invitations by now."

"I did," she replied, without bothering to stop or turn to look at him.

He took one step closer to her. "Are you writing down all the treasures of the day in your diary?"

Without responding or lifting her head, she pointed to the table next to the bed where the monogram on her diary caught the glint of the dying embers in the fireplace. Rather than venture another guess, which would probably prove to be wrong again, he decided to be more straightforward and took another step. "What are you writing that's so important you need to do it at midnight?"

He heard her sigh. "A list."

Overtired, overtaxed, and overwhelmed by a totally miserable day that was close to being one of the worst he had ever had, he let out his own sigh. "Answering my question with only two words or less is not merely frustrating. I find it rather rude."

Finally she set down her pen and turned in her seat to face him. "Then you know precisely how I felt when you and Philip were talking about me this afternoon as if I weren't there."

In the ambient light he could not see her features clearly, but judging by her raspy voice, she had either been crying or she was as fatigued as he was. He opened his mouth to argue the point, but he knew he was on shaky ground and abandoned the idea, in part to avoid adding to her distress. "You're right. I'm sorry. If it matters to you, I apologized to Philip, too," he offered, still unaccustomed to apologizing to most anyone for his behavior.

When she nodded her acceptance of his apology, he looked past her to get a better look at what she had been writing, but he was too far away to see anything more than the corner of the paper. "What kind of list are you making?" he asked as he closed the final distance between them.

She turned and folded up the paper. "If you must know, I'm making a list of things I don't want to forget to take with me when I leave," she explained and got to her feet.

When she crossed in front of him and stored the list in her knitting bag, he noted she was wearing that awful wooden knitting stick. "You seem to wear that treasure at your waist more often than not. Perhaps you'll tell me what makes it so important to you." He sat down in one of the two chairs sitting in front of the dying fire and hoped she would not ask him to leave.

She covered the entire piece of wood with her hands and kept it from his view until she sat down across from him and it disappeared in the folds of her skirts. "Did you really come here at this hour of the night to ask about my knitting stick?"

"It's not even on the list of all the things I need to discuss with you, but it's definitely the safest," he admitted. Finding it hard to express his thoughts or feelings to her as openly and honestly as she expected him to do—or oddly enough, as he found himself wanting to do—he instinctively rubbed at the scar that encircled his wrist.

"First tell me why you'd want to keep the pieces of those horrid handcuffs."

He narrowed his gaze and stared at the glowing embers that were slowly being buried under gray ash. "They aren't a sentimental treasure. They're evidence. I turned them over to my lawyer in case we needed to prove that we were coerced into marrying one another."

"The scars on your wrist should be enough to prove that," she pointed out.

He flexed his wrist before he met her gaze again. "In a court of law, more evidence is always better, or so I've been told." He nodded toward the wooden stick hidden by her skirts. "I assume your treasure has a more pleasurable sentiment attached to it than either the handcuffs or my scar."

To his surprise, she removed the knitting stick, in which she stored up to four knitting needles at a time, and handed it to him. The wooden tool was very light and only slightly wider than his thumb. When he laid the wider end, which was wrapped by a band of metal, at the base of his palm, the tapered end, inscribed with the year 1792, extended just beyond his middle finger. Down the center of the tool, hand-carved letters spelled out a woman's name: June Gibbs.

"Was she your mother?" he asked.

Her gaze grew misty. "My father carved that knitting stick for her while they were courting. She gave it to me shortly before she died." Her voice was thick with emotion, and she dropped her gaze. "I was hoping to be able to give it to a daughter of my own someday, but I doubt I'll ever marry or have a family of my own. Not anymore. As far as society is concerned, a divorced woman is . . . how did you put it? 'Beyond redemption.' " Her words were so soft he almost did not hear her.

Beyond redemption.

If he were able to take back any two words he had said over the course of his entire lifetime, those would be the ones he would choose. Deeply troubled by the tears she was trying hard to blink away, he handed her treasure back to her.

Even though he could not name a single man who would risk the social stigma of marrying a divorced woman—even a woman as intriguing as she was—he felt compelled to ease the distress he had caused her. "Forgive me. Just because I'm a total cad for using those words doesn't mean I'm right. Or that you should give up hope that one day you might find a man who would fully understand the circumstances that led to our marriage and divorce and would still want to marry you."

"You may not have been very tactful, but at least you were being honest. Don't you . . . do you ever think about having your own family someday?" she asked as she toyed with the knitting stick, turning it over and over again in her hand.

He swallowed hard. "I think perhaps I did at one time. Very much so."

Her hand stilled. "But not now."

"No," he admitted.

"Is that . . . is that because of the stigma of our pending divorce?"

Anxious to move past the subject of his shattered dreams, along with their current legal difficulties, he answered her as honestly and tactfully as he could. "From my perspective, life is far too unpredictable to consider marriage at all. Having a wife and children is simply risking disaster. I wouldn't want to bring children into this world and leave them orphaned, like my parents did, and have my children raised by someone hired to do the job, like my brother and I were. I'd also prefer not to die with my wife and my children, like my brother did," he admitted, still troubled by memories that had resurfaced so suddenly again today.

After drawing in a deep gulp of air, he continued. "It's easier to avoid all of that by remaining single, and if you doubt what I'm telling you, you might want to ask some of the women at the Refuge if they enjoy the misery they're mired in because their husbands died or abandoned them, leaving them virtually homeless, with broken hearts and fatherless children and no way to support themselves."

When she looked at him, her eyes were glistening with sadness. "You can't isolate yourself from life's troubles. No one can. If you'd take the time to talk to some of the women like I have, you'd learn that they all have one thing in common beyond their reduced circumstances. It's something you've given them because of your support to the Refuge, even though you don't like to discuss it."

He waved his hand to dismiss her words. "If you're referring to the firewood, then I assure you I only had it delivered because you're so adamant about volunteering there. I really had no other option, unless I wanted to take the risk you'd fall ill. That building was uncommonly cold." He got up and added a log to the fire, since the sleeping room was turning chilly.

She leaned forward in her seat. "Your motive isn't as important as your actions," she argued. "Whether you deliberately intended to help those women or not, all they know is that you cared enough to have firewood delivered or that you paid for the knitting tools and yarn they need to help themselves. What they have in common now is that you restored their faith, and you gave them hope. That's what they need to face the future."

He snorted. "For how long? A week? A month? Sooner or later, they're bound to lose hope again or have their faith tested over and over again until it's gone. Wouldn't it be easier all around if they faced that reality? Isn't that all any of us can do?"

Her eyes widened. "Only if we give up and try to live without faith in God, who fills us with hope every time we lose our way."

"As I see it, faith in God just isn't enough, and hope is just a temporary reprieve from heartache . . . which is why I need to talk to you about Irene."

Annabelle stiffened. "What about her?"

He let out a long breath. "I need to talk to her tomorrow morning about a very personal matter. I think she'd find it comforting if you were there with me when I did."

"Why? What's happened?" she asked, and her eyes flashed with alarm.

He retrieved the letter he had received that afternoon from his pocket. "Since you and Irene have become friends, I don't think she'd mind if I shared this letter with you. It was addressed to my father," he said and handed it to her. "Once you've finished reading it, I think you'll understand how difficult it will be tomorrow when we have to tell her that her only child, Ellis, is dead."

Chapter Twenty-Two

❄

Annabelle woke up well before dawn, having slept only a few hours. And the moment she spied the letter Harrison had left with her, she knew the nightmare she thought she'd had during the night was not a nightmare at all.

As surprised as she had been to learn that Irene had had a son, she was doubly surprised to discover they had been estranged from one another for more than twenty years. It was deeply troubling to know they would never see each other again, at least not in this world.

Though Harrison had not been able to shed any light on the reason that Irene and her son had become estranged, Annabelle prayed she would be able to think of a way to help Irene through the tragedy that had befallen her. Before she dressed and left her room, she sat down to reread the letter one last time:

Dear Mr. Graymoor,
I have been asked to notify you that Ellis Cannon succumbed after a brief illness on the 12th of November past at the age of forty-six years, seven months, and twelve days.

On his deathbed, he requested that I contact his mother, Widow Irene Cannon, who was in your employ when he left Philadelphia eleven years ago. I am hopeful she is still a member of your staff, and you can convey his dying wish to her: that she grant him forgiveness for what he did to her and her employer.

Please also extend to her my prayers, as well as my reassurances that he was a recent, but much-loved and respected member of our small community of faith.

I am enclosing a brief note from his widow, Melanie. At her request, this note is to be read only by Ellis's mother, and I trust you will see that it is placed directly into her hands.

With deepest regards,
Reverend Samuel Reagan
Farmington, New Hampshire

She refolded the letter and laid it aside only long enough to dress. Although she was more than curious to know exactly what Ellis had done to both his mother and the Graymoors, she was more hopeful that Irene would reveal what message Melanie's note contained.

Just as he promised last night, Harrison was waiting for her just outside the library, and he was already wearing his heavy winter outerclothes. "Are you absolutely certain this is the best time to tell her?" he asked as he followed her down the main staircase to the front door.

"It's the only time of the day when we can count on her to be totally alone. If she needs more time by herself, which I would expect to be the case after we talk to her, I want to take her back to my room, where none of the other staff will be able to disturb her," she replied and preceded him out the door while he finished a yawn. "You're not accustomed to being awake this early, are you?" she teased.

He closed the door behind them. "I'm accustomed to being awake, but I'd typically be ending an evening out and getting into my bed, not out of it." He let her take the lead as she walked

195

them around the house toward the path that led to the cottage and beyond.

There was not a breath of wind this morning, but the temperature had dropped considerably since yesterday. By the time they reached the path, light flurries of snow were beginning to fall, but she had no second thoughts about coming to see Irene outside and hoped he would not, either.

"I can't imagine where you might go to stay out that late, unless it's at that island place I heard Philip say something about this afternoon. Will we be going there together for an event?" she asked in an attempt to distract them both from thinking about their troubling mission.

He lost his step on a patch of ice and nearly stumbled before he caught himself. "To Petty's Island? That's hardly a place for respectable men, let alone women. I can't say I've ever seen a member of the gentler sex there, even among the workers, and rightly so."

"But you're respectable, and you go there."

"My friends and I go there," he admitted, "but we certainly don't mention it to anyone else. If you want to avoid any more gossip than is already swirling around both of our names, I suggest that you not mention it, either. Especially tonight. This soiree is one of the most important events of the season's festivities, and we absolutely need to attend," he cautioned and looked up at the sky. "I'll have to keep a good eye on the weather. If these flurries build up into a full-fledged storm, we could end up being stranded in the city tonight."

Her heart skipped a beat and latched on to an unexpected opportunity to avoid running into Vienna or Eric or anyone else who posed a threat to her. "I'm not certain I should leave Irene tonight, especially with another snowstorm brewing," she ventured.

"As long as the weather holds, I think she'll probably want you to go. Even so, I need you to go with me tonight, which means that Irene will simply have to do without you until tomorrow."

Surprised and disappointed by his lack of empathetic support, she stiffened her back, but decided not to press the issue right now. Instead, she quickly told him that her chat with Irene about their sleeping arrangements had gone well. "At least you don't have to worry about that anymore," she suggested. She stopped as the path veered off into the woods and shook her cape to knock off the fresh-falling snow that was clinging to it. "We're not far from the bench now."

He stopped and looked around. "I remember the place. I used to go there from time to time myself when I was a boy. It's a good place to think. My brother and I used to sit out here a lot. He taught me how to whittle a bit there, too," he murmured and his gaze grew distant, as if he were reliving the moments he had spent there. "Do you want to go ahead, tell her I'm joining you both today, and come back for me?" he asked.

"I can't see that it will help much. She'll only worry herself while she's waiting," she said.

"Now that the snow is starting, it's getting even more slippery. I don't want you to fall," he explained when he offered her his arm.

She cringed and accepted his offer. "Actually, Irene and I both took a spill the other day, and I'd rather not do it again. Are you certain you don't want to speak to her alone?"

He shook his head. "Since she can't read the note from her daughter-in-law, either, one of us will have to do that for her, too. I suspect she may want you to read it to her instead of me," he replied as he started them down the path.

The closer they got to the bench, the faster her heart began to beat, but the moment she spied her friend sitting there on the bench, her heart started to pound. She did not know what made Irene turn around to face them as they approached her, but she knew that the smile in her eyes would soon give way to tears of grief.

She followed Harrison's lead and was satisfied to be merely an observer as they sat together on the bench with Irene sitting between them. He was both tender and gentle with the older woman when he gave her the news of her son's death. When the shock of his news gave way to a flood of tears, he wrapped his arm around her shoulders, and Annabelle held on to her hand. Even Jonah seemed to sense there was something wrong and scampered off to sit behind a nearby tree and watch from a distance.

When Irene's tears finally subsided, Annabelle handed her a handkerchief. "You're a dear, dear girl," Irene whispered and eased from Harrison's arm to wipe away the tears on her cheeks, as well as a few snowflakes, before they froze. "I suppose I knew in my heart that this day would come, but I was so hoping it wouldn't be for a good long while or before Ellis had righted the wrong he had done," she murmured.

Irene sniffled and wiped away fresh tears. "Although Harrison knows what Ellis did, I want you to know, too." She tugged Annabelle's hand until it rested on her lap with her own. "After his father died, Ellis lived and worked with me here at Graymoor Gardens for Harrison's father. But Ellis was just as restless and dissatisfied with his life as his father had been all the time we were married. One Sunday, he refused to go to services, and we argued about that. Before I knew it, we were arguing about things that he'd let build up for years. He hated being poor. He hated being a servant, but most of all he blamed me for making his father so unhappy that he died young. I left for services without him, but when I got back, hoping we could sit down and talk things out, he was gone. He . . . he'd stolen a horse from the stable and taken some silver and jewelry from the house, which only added shame to my name as well as his own." Another fresh flood of tears erupted when she glanced up at Harrison. "Ellis never ever tried to contact me again, not even to tell me where he'd settled, and he never made any effort to pay for what he had stolen."

"No one in my family holds you responsible for what Ellis did," Harrison reassured her.

"I'm so very sorry," Annabelle crooned. "It must have been very difficult for you after Ellis left the way he did."

Irene swiped away her tears. "I never doubted that the good Lord would watch over my boy, and I never lost hope that I'd see him again one day. Harrison's father, bless his forgiving heart, set it up so I'd never have to leave here, so if and when Ellis wanted to find me or to make amends, he'd know where to look. I know now that that won't happen, but I'm grateful to God that he found his way back to his faith before he passed and had a wife who wanted to contact me."

"Is there anything I can do for you?" Annabelle asked.

"Just sit with me while Harrison reads the note from Ellis's wife." Oblivious to the falling snow, she clasped Annabelle's hand with both of her own and looked up at Harrison. "I'm ready now."

He nodded solemnly and opened the note, but paused to clear his throat before he started reading. " 'Dearest Mother-in-law, I encouraged Ellis to contact you for many years, but he could be a stubborn, prideful man, as I suspect you know all too well, and he was so ashamed of what he had done to you and the Graymoors. Several months before he took ill, he promised that we would come to see you in the spring, for he wanted to see you in person to beg for your forgiveness. Sadly, that is not to be, but I hope you find it a comfort to know that he loved you and that he wanted to reconcile with you and your employer.' "

When Irene started to weep again, Harrison paused to let her cry until she was able to compose herself. At last she nodded for him that she was ready to hear the rest. " 'Ellis was a loving husband to me for the seven years we were married, and he was a good father to our daughters, Kathryn and Susan. Since I have no relatives of my own, I am turning to you for help. I have enough funds to last for the next few months, but we live in a very remote area. There is no way I can support myself and the children here, and I dread the thought that we would become a burden to our friends and neighbors. Since you live in a large city, I am hopeful you will agree to help me find a position there that would allow me to provide for my children, that would also be near you so you might come to know them. If you can open your heart to us, you can reach me through Reverend Reagan. Sincerely, Melanie Cannon.' "

"I've lost my son, but I have two grandchildren," Irene murmured. "Grandchildren!" she repeated and tugged on Annabelle's hand. "That's a blessing I never expected to receive."

"If you like, I can be of help," Harrison said. "What would you like me to do?"

Irene turned and looked up at him. "After what Ellis did, I don't expect you to make a position here for my daughter-in-law, but please let her stay here with her girls for a spell. If my friend Prudence hadn't taken real sick a few months back, I would have been able to arrange for them to stay with her in the city. But she had to let all her boarders go, and the weather's been so harsh for the past month or so, I haven't even been able to visit her. She may have even lost her boardinghouse by now."

She pressed her hand against his coat and snow immediately started falling on her hand. "If you let them all come here, I'll sign a paper that says you can fire me whenever you think I'm too old to work anymore, or you think I'm overstepping my bounds. Just let them come and stay here until Melanie can find work in the city. I'll fix up the garret in the cottage for them, and you won't even know they're here."

"And if I do?" he asked with a hint of amusement in his voice.

"I'll set them in their places, just like I do with you," she replied.

He patted her hand. "Melanie and the girls are welcome to come. Now, why don't we all go back to the cottage where it's warmer. While we're there, Annabelle can write your letter for you, and I promise I'll post it for you first thing once I get back to the city," he said and helped her to her feet.

Annabelle rose but walked behind Harrison and Irene as they returned to the cottage arm in arm and listened to the plans Irene was making. She knew from experience that Irene's preoccupation with the daughter-in-law and granddaughters right now was merely a way for the woman to cope with the tragic loss of her son.

But she also knew that once the shock wore off and the reality of her son's death finally set in, Irene would grieve and grieve deeply, just as Annabelle had done each time she had lost one of her parents. When that happened to Irene, Annabelle vowed to be there for her new friend, ready to listen and to offer what comfort she could, for as long as she needed her.

For now, however, she had a letter to write for Irene, and unless there was a monster snowstorm brewing, she also would have no excuse for not attending the soiree tonight with Harrison.

Chapter Twenty-Three

❄

Irene's grief turned out to be as deep and as overwhelming as the massive snowstorm that developed during the day she learned that her son had died, burying the landscape under five feet of snow.

After being virtually isolated from the outside world for nearly two weeks and celebrating a very somber Christmas out of respect for Irene's mourning, Annabelle was actually looking forward to bidding this past horrific year a final farewell by attending the festivities tonight in the city with Harrison. She'd never really celebrated on the eve of a new year, but Annabelle could not imagine a better time to start the tradition than tonight.

She also hoped that the coming year would mark a new beginning for both of them. They should be receiving word very soon that their divorce had already been granted, which was yet another good reason to celebrate tonight—their marriage would end sometime this month.

As Harrison escorted her into the massive ballroom in the Grand Hotel, she was surprised by the sea of people who filled the room to capacity. At her height, she could not even see if there were any decorations, but the elaborate candle chandeliers added a touch of elegance to the event. Above the din of gay conversation, she could barely detect the strains of music coming from an unseen orchestra. She was relieved when Harrison told her there would not be any dancing tonight and saw for herself there was literally no room for a dance floor tonight.

She leaned toward Harrison, but did not lower her voice for fear he would not be able to hear her. "I'm sorry I had to spend so much time with Irene again before we left today, but it's probably just as well that we're rather late. If we'd gotten here an hour ago like we planned, we'd probably be so far inside this room we'd never be able to leave until half of these people did."

He chuckled and tucked her arm closer to his side. "I'll try to keep a good hold on you, but don't be surprised if we end up getting separated. Like I warned you, you can see that it's a coarser crowd than you're accustomed to and it will only get worse as the night progresses. Do you remember where to meet me if that happens?"

"Downstairs in the foyer by the back pillar at eleven o'clock," she replied, grateful that he had made contingency plans in advance in case they lost one another so they would be able to return to Graymoor Gardens to watch the fireworks display with the staff at midnight. In a crowd this large, she was confident she would not encounter Eric or Vienna. She probably would not even be able to see them if they were only ten feet away.

When Harrison paused and looked around, as if trying to decide where to take her, she glanced around, too, and tried not to gape. Since this was an annual fund-raising event to support a number of the city-sponsored charities, rather than a formal ball, people from all walks of life who had the funds to purchase a ticket were in attendance. At previous events, she had seen ostentatious displays of wealth, which were noticeably absent tonight. She was glad she was not wearing any jewelry other than her opal wedding ring, and she had not worn one of her fancier snoods, either.

Still, she had never seen such garish costumes or scandalously low-cut gowns in one place at the same time as she saw now, and she felt her cheeks actually get hot.

"This way," he urged and led her through the crowd, which parted reluctantly to let them pass. They managed to jostle their way through a thick cloud of heavy perfume that filled the air. She was actually feeling a bit light-headed by the time they worked their way to the group of people he wanted them to join in the far corner of the room.

Grateful that the pale ivory gown she wore had survived the crush of people when they arrived, she held on to his hand and steadied herself before she let go. She took a short breath to test the air, then drew in several deep breaths to clear her lungs before she greeted everyone. She was pleased to already know a few of the people there, but Harrison introduced her to the rest so quickly she never caught half of their names.

While he stepped away to chat with several of the men, Mrs. Wilshire studied her closely from head to toe. "You're almost as pale as that stunning gown you're wearing."

"It's all the perfume. I'm more accustomed to lighter scents," she explained and wondered if anyone could even detect the scent of summer roses she wore again tonight.

The woman standing next to Mrs. Wilshire, whose name Annabelle had already forgotten, smiled as if she and Annabelle were privy to a secret they shared. "Most women seem to be quite sensitive to all sorts of smells and aromas . . . at certain points in their lives."

Darcy French, a young matron dressed in a silk gown made of a hideous shade of chartreuse, nodded as if she, too, shared that secret and stared at Annabelle's stomach. "I hope you don't have to leave early tonight. I was so disappointed at the Sullivans' ball that I didn't have an opportunity to meet you or spend any time with you."

Another new acquaintance, Eliza somebody, who was obviously carrying a child, grinned. "We women do need our rest."

Annabelle blinked hard and finally realized they were all making veiled references to the gossip Vienna Biddle and her friends had spread about Annabelle being with child, and she chided herself for adding fuel to that gossip by leaving the Sullivan ball early, which everyone must have attributed to her alleged delicate condition.

"In point of fact, I need very little rest," she suggested. Gratified by the surprise on each of the women's faces, she proceeded to describe her typical day, which began just before dawn and ended late at night, a routine she hoped would erode the idea she was suffering from some of the typical ailments that assail women who are carrying a child.

She spent even more time, however, describing the volunteer work she had begun at the Refuge, and by the time she finished, two of the women had pledged donations from their husbands.

"Did I hear the word *donations?*" Harrison teased as he returned to her side and took her hand.

"You did indeed," Mrs. Wilshire offered. "Your wife can be quite persuasive, which you know, of course."

He squeezed Annabelle's hand and smiled. "Yes, I do."

"I believe the donations will be enough to purchase cloth for the women at the Refuge who can use it to make clothing. They'll be so grateful," Annabelle informed him, fully aware that the women who had pledged the donations needed little persuasion at all, since they were clearly out to impress her husband with their generosity.

The next hour passed quickly and pleasantly, but Annabelle was both hungry and thirsty when Harrison bid his friends a prosperous new year and left with her in search of refreshments, which had been set out on the far side of the room. Crossing through the crowd, however, proved to be more difficult now, and he kept a tight hold on her hand.

The revelry had increased to such a pitch he had to zigzag to bypass some groups that were extremely addled or others that were too busy celebrating to stop to let them pass by. Although he kept her protected on one side, she felt crushed on the other, and she was glad she had not carried a reticule tonight, because she would have lost hold of it.

She was tempted to ask him if they could simply leave and go back to Graymoor Gardens, but she did not even bother to try. Even if he could hear her, which she doubted, she did not want to leave early for fear someone would notice and add to the gossip already swirling around both of their names.

They were halfway across the room, as best she could judge, when an argument between two men escalated into fisticuffs. Unfortunately, the men were standing right in front of Annabelle and Harrison when they faced off. One man backed into them and broke the hold Harrison had on her hand, and she nearly lost her balance in her effort to distance herself from the combatants.

Within seconds, other men rushed to quell the fight, and she was swept away by the people who pulled back to avoid being hurt. She caught a glimpse of Harrison as he struggled to rescue her, but lost sight of him completely when he was pushed farther away from her in the opposite direction.

With her heart pounding and her feet nearly numb from being stomped on, she edged away, hoping to find her way to the refreshments, where Harrison would hopefully be waiting for her. Even if he weren't, she had no reason to panic, since she knew he would eventually be waiting for her downstairs.

She spent the next half an hour working her way through the crowd and had to stop several times when her gown got snagged and she had to free it from beneath a man's foot. At one point, she simply stopped to catch her breath, but nearly gagged when she inhaled air that was unbelievably heavy with perfume. When she finally was able to breathe normally again, she spied Vienna Biddle and several of her friends chatting together with a group of people standing not five feet in front of her and gasped.

After turning her back to them, she held her place and was about to give up any hope she could escape without being sighted when she spied an extremely tall, very round gentleman, who was probably sixty years old and working his way toward her.

Since he seemed to be headed where she wanted to go, she waited until he was standing in front of her before she smiled up at him. "It seems I've gotten myself lost in this crowd. Would you be so kind as to help me find my way back to my husband?"

Grinning, he offered her his arm. "Ma'am, I'll take you anywhere you'd like to go."

Confident that she could now slip by Vienna and the others, she stepped to the side of him that would keep Vienna from seeing her because of his massive size. In the end, her plan worked perfectly, though she had not counted on passing close enough to Vienna or her friends to be able to hear their conversation.

Once she was safely past them all, her cheeks were burning and her heart was racing. Imagining what gossipmongers were saying was altogether different from actually hearing them. She had never heard anyone refer to her in terms she thought were reserved for sinful women who sold their bodies in the many brothels in the city, and it hurt her. Deeply.

But they inflicted the greatest hurt when they referred to Harrison as a fool because he had allowed her to trick him into getting her pregnant, which forced him to marry her. His final comeuppance, according to Vienna, was the fact that Annabelle had been spotted in the city getting into a hack with another man. Even worse, Annabelle was allegedly using the excuse of volunteering at the Refuge when she was instead meeting with her lover, who was also the father of her unborn child.

By the time her gallant escort led her to the edge of the crowd and left her there to wait for her husband, she was trembling so hard she did not care that she was standing at the entrance to the ballroom instead of the refreshment area. Instinctively, she sought the only refuge she could think of and rushed down the stairs to wait for Harrison in the foyer by the back pillar.

Although the ballroom itself was impossibly crowded, she only passed two couples arriving late to the event on her way downstairs. The foyer itself was empty, and she practically ran to the shadows behind the last pillar. Breathing hard, she leaned back against the cold marble pillar. Even though her heart eventually stopped racing and her breathing returned to normal again, her emotions were still in turmoil.

She was more outraged than she thought humanly possible, yet she was also completely devastated that anyone would talk about her or Harrison so wickedly. After leaning her head back against the pillar, she closed her eyes and prayed that Harrison would come downstairs soon so he could take her home, even though it was probably still half an hour until eleven o'clock.

In the next heartbeat, she heard footsteps approaching and sighed with relief. After quickly fixing her skirts, she stepped out from behind the pillar, but froze the moment she saw that the man who was approaching her was not her husband at all.

He was, however, the husband she thought she had once loved and the very same husband who had set her aside in favor of another.

Chapter Twenty-Four

✳

If there was something more horrendous than a nightmare, Annabelle was not aware of it. But she knew she was looking at it when she saw Eric Bradley walking toward her.

As always, he was impeccably dressed in a tailored set of clothes that fit his slender frame perfectly. The smile he was wearing—that she once thought was so charming—now appeared to be as false as his traitorous heart, assuming he had ever loved her as he once claimed.

Annabelle prayed with all of her might that she could stand up to him and send him away before Harrison came for her. When he stopped an arm's length away from her and folded his hands over his chest, making him look every inch of a bully, she stiffened her back. "What are you doing here?"

"Like so many others, I'm here to celebrate the beginning of the new year at a soiree that has proved to be much more interesting than I ever expected it to be," he replied before he ran his gaze over every inch of her so intensely she felt prickles of shame in every pore of her skin.

"That's not what I meant. How did you know that I'd be here, downstairs in the foyer?" she snapped.

"Quite by accident. A very fortunate accident," he added, "considering the crowd of people upstairs. I've been searching for you ever since I spotted you at the Sullivan ball. When I finally spied you leaving the festivities a few moments ago, I simply followed you. At a respectable distance, I assure you. There's quite enough gossip tonight about the new Mrs. Graymoor as it is." He shook his head. "I must say I'm surprised at how well you've done for yourself. Graymoor is one of the wealthiest men on the eastern seaboard."

She took a step forward, squared her shoulders, and tilted up her chin to let him know he did not intimidate her. "You couldn't possibly be more surprised than I was nine months ago when you handed me divorce papers dated many months earlier and told me you'd already married a woman of more 'substance,' " she said as coldly as she knew how. "If she's here with you tonight, perhaps you can introduce us. I'm quite certain we have much to say to one another."

When he blanched and dropped his arms to his side, she pressed her case, even though her legs were shaking so badly she had to lock her knees to steady herself. "I didn't think you had the courage to tell her about me. It seems that cowardice is but one of your many character flaws I discovered much too late."

He snorted. "For all the gumption you seem to have acquired recently, it's obvious you haven't been completely honest with your new spouse, either. But you needn't bother to introduce me to him. I took the liberty of doing that myself a short while ago."

"You didn't—"

"No, I didn't tell him that I found my way to your bed long before he did, if only to gain access to the funds I needed to pursue someone else. If I had, I might have also asked him if he found it more pleasurable than I did, but I thought I'd save that topic of discussion for later if you're not as cooperative as I expect you to be."

She flinched as if he had slapped her across her face. Because her mother had been so ill, she had spent day and night caring for her during the first week of her marriage, except for the night when Eric consummated their marriage and left for New York City the following morning. His hurtful words now unleashed memories of that very awkward night and his obvious disappointment in her.

Anxious to send him away, she gathered up all the gumption she had left. "If you're worried that I'll tell your wife she married a man who has kept his first marriage and divorce a secret from her, then you can rest assured I have no such intention and will cooperate with you in that regard. As far as I'm concerned, we've never even met."

He nodded. "That suits my ultimate purpose in seeking you out rather well."

She glared at him. "What 'ultimate purpose' could you possibly have? And don't dawdle with any of your fancy legal words. Harrison will be here any moment to take me home."

Eric took a small piece of folded paper from his pocket and put it into her hand. "I've taken a room at a small hotel near here under a different name and written it down for you. We need to talk privately, and when we do, we'll need much more time than we have right now." He moved so close to her she had to take a step back. "Be there at eleven o'clock on Thursday morning."

Shocked that he had any other purpose than making certain she would keep their marriage and divorce a secret, she swallowed hard. "I can't possibly meet you there or anywhere else."

When she tried to hand the paper back to him, he pushed her hand away. "Find a way to be there. If you don't, I assure you that when I meet with your husband and his cousin, Philip, at two o'clock that same afternoon, I'll have much more to discuss with him beyond the donation I'm considering making on my wife's behalf," he snapped and walked off.

Trembling, she stared at his back as he made his way to the bottom of the staircase and scarcely drew a breath until he started to mount the stairs. Once he disappeared from view, she folded the paper he had given to her several times, not even bothering to read it. She tucked the note into the bodice of her gown, but shuddered to think something he had touched was now pressed against her skin.

With her whole world imploding, she stepped back into the shadows behind the pillar and leaned against it for support. Her mind raced with all sorts of questions about Eric's intentions, and she pressed the palms of her hands against the cold marble for support.

Since he had made it clear he had found her less than desirable in the marriage bed, she highly doubted he wanted to be alone with her in a hotel room for some sort of tawdry assignation. But Annabelle quivered from head to toe just thinking about it. The fact that he had married a very well-to-do heiress made her dismiss the notion that he intended to extort her, which was a flawed plan on two points.

First, she had no access to Harrison's fortune, other than using accounts in any number of stores and shops. Second, she could easily reject any demand he might make and threaten to tell his wife the truth.

She pushed away from the pillar and stiffened her back. Meeting Eric at a hotel was well beyond anything she was prepared to do. She was also terrified to think of the gossip that would erupt if anyone saw her going into the hotel without her husband.

She desperately needed to talk to someone about the dilemma she faced, but the only person who might possibly understand her predicament was Harrison. Despite the fact that they had grown to be closer friends over the past two weeks, he was the one person she could not possibly tell at all, since he had no idea she had ever been married before—let alone to Eric Bradley—or that their marriage had ended in divorce.

She stopped abruptly and clapped her hand to her heart. Eric did not know the true nature of her marriage to Harrison, but if he ever found out that she and Harrison were husband and wife in name only and soon to be divorced, he would find a way to use that to his advantage. She was fairly confident he could not possibly know that now, but she vowed to do everything in her power to keep Eric away from Harrison before she knew exactly what he wanted.

Finally, when she was half afraid that Harrison had forgotten all about her, she heard footsteps approaching. She peeked around the pillar, saw his silhouette, and rushed out to meet him. She closed half the distance between them before she could see him clearly, stopped abruptly, and gasped out loud.

He was holding her evening cape in one hand, but he had a bloodied handkerchief pressed to his lips with the other. Blood splattered his shirt and frock coat, and he had a slight bruise already forming on his cheek. "Wh-what happened? What did you do?"

He stopped in front of her and shrugged. "Other than defending my wife's honor, I would guess that I've also managed to give the gossipmongers something new to chew on. I'm sorry I kept you waiting, but I have a blistering ache in my head. Maybe we should continue this discussion later before someone else finds me and decides to take a poke at me."

e

Later turned out to be very late that night.

They were traveling back to Graymoor Gardens when the fireworks had lit the sky over the city of Philadelphia, but neither of them had seen them. They did not engage in any conversation, either, for fear Harrison's lip would start bleeding again.

By the time they finally arrived home, the staff had all taken to their beds. While Harrison went to her room to change out of his bloodied clothes, she hurried out to the cottage. After gathering up some clean cloths and pumping water into a deep bowl, she went outside and filled a pot with snow. She added it to the tray and carried everything back to her room, where she found Harrison sitting in front of the fire he had already rebuilt.

"I doubt the snow I scooped up for you will last very long in here," she offered as she set the tray on top of the serving table he had set between their two chairs.

Bypassing the pot of snow, he dipped one of the cloths into the cold water, folded it into a makeshift compress, and held it against the corner of his mouth and shook his head. "I'd rather not stir up memories of being packed in snow. This should be enough."

She sat down across from him. "The snow will help more, but the cold cloth is better than nothing. Your cheek needs attention, too," she suggested. "Have you bothered at all to look in the mirror?"

"Why should I? I can feel the damage."

"You're still a terrible patient," she quipped, getting up to moisten another cloth with water.

He leaned away when she approached him, but she ignored the glare he shot at her. "You've got dried blood on your chin," she explained. Once he reluctantly removed the cloth he had pressed against his lip, she cupped his chin with her hand. With her other hand, she gently started to wash away the dried blood, but she was unprepared for the warm sensations that traveled up her arm and spread throughout her body.

She could feel his gaze on her, as well, but she dared not glance up at him for fear he would see the effect he was having on her.

When his chin was wiped clean, she pointed to his cheek. "I can't tell if your cheek is merely bruised or if the skin is broken. Do you want me to cleanse that or would you rather do it yourself?" she asked, still deliberately avoiding his gaze.

"You may as well go ahead," he said, but his voice was uncommonly husky.

After rinsing the cloth, she patted his cheek. Satisfied the skin had not been broken, she took a clean cloth, packed it with snow, and put it against his cheek. "Hold this in place while I make another one for your lip."

Surprisingly, he offered no protest except a brief wince, and handed her the cloth he had been using on his lip. His fingers brushed against hers a second time when he took hold of the compress, which triggered yet another swell of sensations.

Annabelle made a second compress with the snow that was quickly melting in the bowl and handed it to him. "The split in your lip isn't very big, so I don't think you need even a single stitch. It should heal up in a matter of days, but you'll fare better if you can get the swelling down quickly," she assured him and returned to her seat.

Grumbling, he planted his other elbow on the other arm of the chair and held the second compress in place, too. "Do I look as ridiculous as I feel?"

She cringed. "I'm afraid you do, but you'll feel much better come morning, and you'll be glad you took the time to take care of yourself tonight."

He snorted. "I'd feel a whole lot better right now if that foul-mouthed idiot had simply apologized for what he said about you, which is all I asked him to do, instead of socking me in the face. He blindsided me, the dolt! I never even had the opportunity to hit him back. He just swung at me and took off with his friends. If the room hadn't been so packed, I would've hit the floor instead of knocking into a few heads before I caught myself. I'd relish the thought that I'd be able to find him again, but I have absolutely no idea who he is or where to look to find him."

"What did he say that made you ask him to apologize?"

He did not reply for several long heartbeats. "Let's just say he spoke unkindly about your virtue," he whispered.

She suspected he had heard the same thing that Vienna had been telling the group of people she was with. Still, she was surprised at his actions, since he had made it clear some weeks ago that he was simply going to ignore the gossip about her.

Rather than confuse the issue at hand by mentioning that, she let out a long breath of air before she looked up at him. "I overheard a bit of nasty gossip tonight about both of us. Perhaps it would be best if we didn't attend any more evening social affairs for a while."

"That may be a good idea. I only have one appointment next Thursday that's rather important, but Philip can still go and make my apologies if I have to cancel that, too," he replied. He paused briefly to adjust the compress on his lip before he quickly explained about meeting Eric Bradley and the man's interest in making a sizable donation to a new charitable endeavor Harrison himself had in mind, although he was not inclined to discuss what that might be.

Now that he had confirmed Eric's claim to have a meeting with Harrison next Thursday, she was hopeful that if he did not appear, she might be able to put off seeing Eric earlier that same morning—until she realized that Eric might interpret that as a ploy on her part and seek Harrison out himself.

"I'd rather not make an appearance socially until I look normal again," he said. "How long do you think that might be?" He placed the compress back on the table, tested out his injured cheek, and winced again.

"No more than a week, I'd guess. But when we go out again socially, there's no need for you to defend my honor every time you hear someone gossiping. If you do, you could end up hurt far worse than you are now. Perhaps it would be better if you ignored any gossip you hear, like you've done in the past."

His gaze softened. "I was wrong to ignore it," he admitted. "As long as you're my wife, it's my duty to defend you and protect your name. You've done nothing to deserve anyone saying anything against you. Absolutely nothing," he insisted, and his dark eyes glistened with tenderness. "I believe I know you well enough now to be confident that you couldn't and wouldn't do anything that would bring shame to yourself or to me."

Annabelle's heart began to race. Apparently the past two weeks they had spent together at Graymoor Gardens had affected him, too. But his softly spoken words added yet another layer to the guilt that already burdened her for keeping her previous marriage and divorce a secret. Even though she knew it would change his opinion of her, she made the decision to tell him the whole truth about her past just as soon as she knew what kind of threat Eric posed to them both.

He leaned forward in his chair and set aside the cloth he had been holding to his lip. "Perhaps if we had met under different circumstances . . ."

Her cheeks warmed, and she lowered her gaze yet again. "Perhaps it's best if we accept the reality that we never would have met at all. We . . . we come from two very different worlds, and we have very, very different views about how we want to live our lives," she whispered. She was surprised by the depth of disappointment that filled her heart, and she held very still until she was able to think clearly again.

When she heard him groan, ever so slightly, she looked up and found that he had leaned back, placed a cold cloth on his forehead, and closed his eyes.

"Would you mind terribly if I didn't sleep in the library tonight?" he asked. "I know you might want to argue that the frigid air in that room might be good for my face, but since that warming stove still hasn't been installed—"

"Of course you can sleep in here," she gushed, concerned that he might have suffered more than a split lip or a minor bruise on his cheek. "Wait just a moment so I can turn down the bedclothes for you," she suggested and got to her feet.

He never opened his eyes, but his smile was still a bit lopsided. "I'm fully dressed and out of sorts, so you needn't bother lining up some logs to make a bundling board. Besides, I'm not certain you'd be able to explain to Irene why the sheets were covered with bits of bark or splinters of wood."

"I'm not very tired. By the time I need some rest, you'll be asleep. Even if you aren't, I believe I know you well enough now that I can trust you," she replied.

But the truth was that Annabelle was quite uncertain she could trust herself not to let him wrap his arms around her, where she would feel safe and protected and loved—if only for one night—before she accepted the fact that he would never, ever be able to love her forever.

Chapter Twenty-Five

❄

Since New Year's Day was on a Sunday this year, Harrison reluctantly left his bed much earlier than usual. If there was ever a day he wanted to sleep late, which he typically did, this would be it. His head was pounding, his cheek was stiff, and the cut in the corner of his mouth had reopened twice while he was getting dressed.

He finally saw Annabelle as they left for services at the country church for the first time in weeks. Inclement weather had kept them at home, and yet another snowstorm was imminent. Since it was entirely possible they could end up being stranded on the way home, all he cared about as he escorted her and the rest of his staff into the church was getting back home as quickly as he could.

When Annabelle noticed the new glass panes in the window and the heat pouring out of the woodstove, she looked up at him with such admiration, he smiled instinctively and winced. He pulled out one of the several handkerchiefs he carried in his pocket today and dabbed at the blood oozing from the cut on his lip before it trickled down his chin.

As he walked with her to the bench where they had sat once before, he could not recall a single moment in his life when anyone had made him feel proud of himself without saying a single word. Granted, he had heard more than a few people praise him for one donation or another, but he always dismissed that praise as nothing more than self-serving platitudes.

Once the service actually began, he had the perfect excuse today not to sing or to join his voice with the others for prayers. But he was surprised to find that it bothered him a bit. When Reverend Bingham stepped into the pulpit to start his sermon, however, he tensed, although he had no reason not to trust the young minister to keep his word.

Reverend Bingham opened his arms and smiled at the congregation. "My dear brothers and sisters in faith, we have much to celebrate on this very special day, have we not?" He paused when the entire congregation responded with a hearty applause and waited for several long moments after silence returned before he continued.

"As we mark the start of another year to serve our beloved Father in heaven, we are indeed blessed to have received an anonymous donation that allows us to celebrate today in more comfort, but I should warn you that this may also encourage me to be a bit long-winded when I preach."

A few people chuckled out loud, but Harrison also detected several deep groans.

The minister motioned for silence. "After reading the passage from Corinthians to you earlier, I am led today to implore each of you to follow God's example and fully embrace the concept of love. Pure, unconditional, infinite love. Beyond faith and beyond hope, love is the greatest of the three virtues and is the very cornerstone of your faith."

He paused to shove his glasses back up to where they belonged. "Embrace His love and then share it, and you will find you have simply made more room in your heart to receive. And as we sing one final hymn together, I encourage all of you to sing with gusto as a commitment to the challenge I have set before you all."

As the congregation erupted into song, Harrison did not even realize he was humming along with them until Annabelle smiled up at him. Not long ago, he would have dismissed today's sermon without giving it a second thought. But when he very carefully offered her a lopsided smile, he knew that the woman standing beside him did not need today's faith message at all.

Although they had only been married one month ago, as of today, he already knew that Annabelle was the embodiment of love as the minister had described it. He also envied the strength of her faith, which was all the more remarkable because she had every reason to doubt it, considering the events of the past few months.

He escorted her to the coach immediately after the services ended to avoid having to answer questions about the injuries on his face. He also did not want to face anyone who suspected he was the anonymous donor, although he feared it was probably very obvious. He did not even pose an argument when she asked to invite Irene to ride back to Graymoor Gardens with them while the remaining staff stayed behind for some refreshments before returning home in the separate wagon they had used to get to services again today.

Once he was seated across from the two women, he tapped on the roof to let Graham know they were ready to depart.

"Was that you I heard singing along with us today?" Irene asked him.

"Hardly. I can barely manage to talk without breaking my lip open, so if you don't mind, I'll keep quiet now, too." He pressed another clean handkerchief to his mouth to emphasize his point.

Sitting beside Irene, Annabelle nodded, but ignored the

warning glare he gave her. "He was humming. I'm so glad you felt up to coming with us today."

Irene sighed. "Coming to services is a great comfort to me. And I'm so grateful you're letting Melanie and the girls come to stay with me," she whispered tearfully.

Although he had already dismissed her offer to void the arrangements that had been made for her to stay at Graymoor Gardens for the rest of her life, he nodded and accepted her gratitude. He handed her the last clean handkerchief he had, and she dabbed at her eyes. "There's a lesson to be learned from all this, and you two should keep it well in mind," she cautioned, but stopped to hold herself steady when the wheels hit a rut in the road and bounced hard before it settled again.

He braced himself for one of Irene's lectures, but he knew better than to try to stop her.

Irene looked from Harrison to Annabelle and back again. "I've never heard you two argue yet, but you will. All married couples have disagreements. When you do, don't let it fester and sulk about it. Talk things out and be honest with one another, even if you have to swallow your pride," she admonished.

He was not surprised by her brashness, and it suddenly occurred to him that she was so ornery with him at times because she thought of him not as her employer but as the son she had adopted after losing her own. And for the second time that day, he found himself looking at a woman whose faith remained strong and enduring, despite the heartache that life that hurled at her.

He just could not decide right now whether he would be better off if the two women of faith sitting across from him were part of his life or not.

*

Less than an hour after returning from services, Harrison decided his life would be considerably less complicated if one of those two women, namely Annabelle, was no longer a part of his life. Since that was clearly not possible where Annabelle was concerned, he planned to keep her here at Graymoor Gardens, well out of view of the elites in the city, until their divorce was final.

While they waited for dinner to be served, he sat across from Annabelle in the parlor and kept his gaze steady. He kept his voice as firm as his determination to convince Annabelle to follow some new rules he had decided would make this next month more bearable for him. "We're living here at Graymoor Gardens for reasons I explained to you when we first arrived in Philadelphia. Since there's merely a month left before we can expect news of our divorce to arrive, I've decided I don't want you going into the city anymore during the day. The severity of the weather, along with my desire to offer no fuel of any sort to those who gossip, is reason enough to remain here. While I find your interest in performing some sort of volunteer work in the city at the Refuge to be admirable, it's absolutely out of the question. Find something else to occupy your time here."

Annabelle stiffed. "Y-you don't want me to volunteer at the Refuge anymore?"

He drew a deep breath. "No, I don't," he replied, a bit more forcefully than he intended.

Her eyes widened in disbelief. "You sound like you're giving me an order and that you expect me simply to obey you without giving me the opportunity to explain how important it is for me to—"

"There's nothing to explain," he argued. "I simply don't want you to be traveling back and forth to the city, and I shouldn't need to remind you that you agreed to abide by my will . . . which means the issue is settled."

"Obviously, I have no choice in the matter, but perhaps I should remind you that while I know I'm obligated to obey your wishes, I don't have to like them any more than I have to like you," she snapped.

She tossed the diary she had bought for him onto his lap, then swept from the room, leaving him with the distinct impression she had dismissed him as easily as he had dismissed her request to volunteer in the city.

Completely frustrated by her petulance, as well as her penchant for constantly challenging him, he was equally baffled by how much he truly wanted to please the woman he was so anxious to divorce. He felt miserable for upsetting her.

When Irene arrived later with his dinner, Harrison braced for another lecture, which she was quick to deliver.

"Didn't you hear a word I said today about settling arguments by talking things out?" she asked as she placed the dinner tray on the table next to him.

He scowled. "Rather than lecturing me, you might try remembering your place in this household once in a while."

"Perhaps I will, once you remember your place as a good husband rather than a peevish one." She turned and left the room.

Fuming, he polished off the dinner she had left for him, but pushed away the plum pudding he knew she had specifically made for dessert because she knew very well that he disliked anything made with plums.

While Irene fumed in the kitchen and Annabelle fussed upstairs in her room, he remained in the parlor all by himself. He might have been able to relax and watch through the wall of windows as the snow built up on the portico, but he was on his guard, waiting for one or both of them to return and continue their disagreements with him.

Determined to maintain his role as the head of this household, if just for appearances' sake, he stared down at the diary Annabelle had given him that was lying on his lap, exactly where she had tossed it. He had not written a word in the diary yet, and he was tempted to drop it into the fire. Instead, he set it on the table next to the tray containing what was left of his supper, leaned back, and closed his eyes.

Less than five minutes later, he heard footsteps. When he opened his eyes, he was surprised to see Lotte coming into the parlor. Gratified for the reprieve, he sat up straight and welcomed her.

"Irene wanted me to see if there was anything else you'd like from the kitchen before she puts everything away. She would have come herself, but . . ."

"But she's still annoyed with me," he quipped and covered the corner of his mouth with his hand as he fumbled for yet another handkerchief.

Blushing, she dropped her gaze. "Yes, sir. I'm afraid she is."

"I don't need anything more tonight, but you should check with Miss Annabelle, too. She's upstairs in her room."

"Ummm . . . she's actually in the kitchen with Irene," she murmured as if she were afraid to tell him, then picked up the tray and left the room.

He sat there fuming for a good twenty minutes. Separately, each of the two women in his life could be troublesome. Together, they could be considered dangerous, and he got to his feet.

He made his way to the basement, determined to end the stalemate and restore peace within his household. He was halfway through the tunnel when he heard someone entering it from the other side and stopped. When Annabelle came into view he held his place and crossed his arms over his chest until she reached him.

She lost her smile the moment she saw him standing there and stopped just out of his reach. "Men who cross their arms over their chests like you're doing appear to be bullies. If that's what you intended, then I don't have anything to say to you."

He dropped his arms to his side. "Are you willing to talk to me now?"

"That depends on whether or not you've reconsidered," she said, just a tad more sweetly.

"Even if this storm abates, I still don't think it's a good idea for you to go into the city with the weather so unpredictable and gossipmongers waiting to judge whatever you do."

Her pale eyes darkened to a deeper shade of green. "And I still think there's no reason for me to miss volunteering at the Refuge. I'm perfectly capable of journeying back and forth without inviting any sort of gossip," she argued.

"I've already told you that it's not you I'm worried about," he countered and ignored the blood he tasted again. "Gossipmongers already have enough to say about you, and I don't think you need to risk adding more."

She moistened her lips. "I don't like being the subject of gossip any more than you do, but I refuse to let gossipmongers control what I do or where I go. While I may agree that you have good reason to want to absent yourself from the city, please don't be so . . . so overprotective where I'm concerned. Or is it your own reputation you're worried about if it becomes known that I'm traveling back and forth unescorted?"

He sighed and raked his fingers through his hair. "Fine. You can go, but on one condition. No, make that two conditions. First, if this storm continues and I think the roadways are too dangerous, you'll wait until I think it's safe for you to go into the city to volunteer. Second, you'll let Graham take you back and forth using my private coach. No more hacks. And no more rides with Philip, since there are some people in the city who don't know he's my cousin."

She grinned. "I agree. And since you seem to be in a much more reasonable frame of mind, you might want to hurry and settle your argument with Irene before she takes to her bed." She drew closer, planted a quick kiss on his cheek, and slipped past him.

Stunned, he held still for just a couple of moments to savor the warm sensation of her lips on his cheek before he started off for the cottage.

One kiss. One spontaneous, very innocent, featherlight kiss.

That's all it took for him to seriously consider that this woman had stolen his heart, and he had only a few weeks left, if that, to get it back. For when he learned they were divorced, he'd have to send her away before he forgot how much heartache that loving this woman would bring.

Chapter Twenty-Six

❄

I can't believe I kissed him. I actually kissed him!

Annabelle climbed into bed after saying her prayers and making an entry in her diary that took a very long time, and she repeated the same phrase to herself that she had been muttering for the past three days. She still had no idea what possessed her to kiss Harrison, but she had had more important worries that burdened her heart—the deep snow that had fallen and threatened to keep her from meeting with Eric tomorrow morning.

She plumped up her pillow and lay down before she pulled the covers up to her chin. In all truth, she really could not fault him for waiting until now to give her permission to travel into the city again. Deep snow drifts had blocked the roads and the staff would have been virtually stranded in the cottage if it had not been for the underground tunnel.

She was very grateful that she would be able to meet Eric tomorrow, find out what he wanted, and convince him to leave her alone. She closed her eyes, hoping she could convince her imagination to rest so she could find some sleep, but bolted upright when she remembered Eric's note. She had not even read it yet to see exactly where she had to meet him.

Grumbling, she climbed out of bed and let the dim light of the low fire guide her as she tiptoed across the shadowed room. Once she retrieved the note she kept hidden in the bottom of her knitting bag, she carried it closer to the fire so she could read it. She unfolded the note. She recognized Eric's handwriting from the many letters he had sent to her the first few months they were married, and read the few words he had written there:

> *Eagle's Nest Hotel off Market Street on Franklin Alley*
> *William Tyler, Room 203*

Her heart flip-flopped in her chest, and she gasped out loud. "That miserable, conniving scoundrel! He took a room under my father's name. He used my father's *name!*" she hissed, and her heart pounded in her chest. Annabelle was so angry she wanted to tear up the note and toss it right into the fire. She thought better of it for only two heartbeats, then threw it into the fire anyway.

She stomped back to her bed and yanked the covers up to her chin. "That cad! That miserable, scheming, conniving . . . monster!" she gritted and held on to the top of the covers as fury surged through her body and left her trembling so hard that the mattress was shaking.

Her fury, however, quickly gave way to bitter disappointment, and she wondered how she had ever thought she loved this horrible excuse for a man at all. Dissolving into tears, she buried her face in her pillow to keep anyone from hearing her. She cried for her kind and sensitive father, who did not deserve to have his name shamed by a man like Eric Bradley, and she cried because her father had left this world so quickly, she never had the chance to say good-bye to him.

She cried for her sweet, trusting mother, who died still thinking that her only child would be safe with a loving husband after she was gone. She cried for herself, too, but for so many reasons, she did not even bother to think beyond the fact that the life she had planned for herself was still unraveling into a never-ending nightmare that got worse with every passing day.

When her tears had been spent, she lay back against her pillow, wiped at her eyes with a corner of the sheet, and pushed the damp tendrils of hair away from her face. Her heart was finally beating normally again, but she was so exhausted, she could not think beyond taking one slow breath at a time. She folded her hands together, closed her eyes, and placed herself in God's care, because without His help, she did not think she would have the strength to get out of bed in the morning, let alone travel to the city.

She did not recite any prayers aloud. She did not even say them silently. Instead, she just lay there, lifted her soul up to God and envisioned that He was abiding deep within her spirit, gently comforting her with His presence and offering words from Sunday's sermon that would sustain her. Faith. Hope. And the greatest of all: love.

She whispered those words aloud, over and over, until her faith was renewed, hope replaced her despair, and love, instead of anger, filled her heart when she thought of the two people God had brought into her life who made her feel safe.

She thought of Irene first, but she fell asleep thinking only of Harrison—the man he had been when they first met, the man he was becoming, and the man she had come to regard with such deep, deep affection that she was just beginning to understand for the first time what it was like to love a man who truly deserved to be loved.

ে

Annabelle arrived at the Refuge the next morning at nine o'clock, and she was relieved that Harrison had decided to stay home for another day or two until his lip was completely healed. Once she was certain Graham had left to drive to the city mansion to deliver Harrison's apologies to his cousin for not being able to meet with Eric today, she made her excuses with Mr. Drummond for not being able to volunteer as long as usual today. Since Graham was not going to return until one o'clock to pick her up, she did not have to worry about him seeing her and left the Refuge shortly before ten.

She had no idea how long it would take her to find the Eagle's Nest Hotel, but the orderly street plan made it easy to find Market Street. Fortunately, the snowfall in the city was half of what it had been on the outskirts, and the walkways had been mostly cleared. She watched her steps carefully to avoid a few patches of ice as she walked, but she reached Market Street without incident. She even managed to finally post the letter she had written for Irene to her daughter-in-law along the way.

The traffic on the road was heavier than she expected, and she made a special effort to keep her deep hood in place to avoid being spotted. She was reluctant to enter a shop to ask which direction to take to get to Franklin Alley and stopped an elderly man out walking his dog instead. Grateful that she only needed to walk east toward the river another two squares in the bitter cold before turning north, she kept her head low as she headed for a meeting that could very well change her life, as well as Harrison's.

She reached the hotel, which was on the other side of the narrow alley, well before ten thirty, but her confidence wavered. This particular neighborhood was as seedy as the aged hotel. She was not looking forward to her meeting with Eric. She wasn't afraid to speak to him alone, but actually walking into a hotel and going up to a room to meet a man who was not her husband was far beyond what she considered to be proper. She backed into the doorway of a closed storefront and pressed her back against the splintered door.

She wrapped her arms around her waist to keep warm and tried to think of an alternative place where they could meet. She doubted that anyone she had met might be at the dilapidated hotel, but she could not take the chance that someone there might recognize her or someone she did know might see her entering or leaving the hotel.

She looked up and down the street and saw a sign for a pawn-shop. She also remembered passing a shop that sold used clothing and smiled. She saved the moral issue of entering the hotel as a problem to be resolved only after she solved the problem of being identified first.

By ten thirty, she had sold her first wedding ring, which she always kept pinned to her chemise so no one would ever find it in her room, and purchased a well-worn gray cape and cracked black leather gloves. She had left the used clothing shop with coins in her reticule and a large package that contained her green cape and matching gloves.

She was walking back to the hotel when she passed a small basement eatery and stopped to walk down the steps to look inside. The interior was too dark to see much, except that there seemed to be very few patrons. She hurried inside as an alternative plan started taking shape in her mind.

Besides boasting much-welcomed warmth, the eatery had several high-backed booths on either side of the kitchen door that offered the privacy she needed, although she would not have a view of the front door. After securing one of the booths for herself, she ordered a sugared cruller and a pot of tea and slipped an extra coin to the serving girl to bring her a pencil and a piece of paper.

By the time the serving girl returned with her morning snack, Annabelle had written a note to Eric to tell him to meet her here, instead of the hotel. She looked up at an old clock on the wall and was confident she could get the note to Eric in time, since there were still twenty minutes left before their planned meeting.

Reluctant to deliver it to his room herself, she caught the servant girl's arm before she left. "Is there any way you can help me? I need to have a note delivered to the Eagle's Nest Hotel."

The girl scrunched up her pocked cheeks. "How soon do you need it delivered?"

"I'm afraid I need it done now," she said and placed several coins on top of her note.

The girl's eyes opened wide, and she scooped up the coins and the note and slipped them into her pocket. "I'll tell my ma I need to leave for a few minutes so I can take it. You want me to wait for a reply?"

Annabelle shook her head. "Just be sure to take it to Room 203 and slip it under the door. That's all you need to do. I have another coin for you when you come back and let me know the note has been delivered," she replied and sighed with relief when the girl gave her a quick nod and disappeared back in the kitchen.

Time passed very slowly, especially since Annabelle checked the clock every two minutes. She tried to eat the cruller, but the fried donut stuck in her throat and she left most of it on the plate. She did finish the pot of tea and was about to order another when Eric suddenly appeared at her table and slid into the seat across from her.

"I see you're still the moral prude I knew you to be. I thought by now Graymoor might have changed that," he quipped.

She ignored his barb and glared at him. "How dare you use my father's name to take a hotel room. How dare you!" she whispered, but made her voice as harsh as she could without worrying that anyone would overhear her.

He grinned, picked up a piece of the cruller from her plate, and devoured it before he answered. "You should be thankful that I was clever enough to come up with the idea several months ago when I started an account in his name to store funds I didn't want my wife to know that I had."

He ate another piece of the cruller, but seemed oblivious to the sugar that stuck to his chin. "Just in case someone you know sees you entering the hotel, you could always claim that you were meeting your father there. No one else here knows that he's dead," he suggested as he brushed the sugar from his fingers and waved the serving girl away when she approached the table to take his order.

"Harrison knows my father is no longer alive," she retorted. "Other than insulting me, there must be a reason you asked to meet with me. What is it?"

He cocked a brow. "You're a bit more direct than I remember."

"I'm not interested in your opinion. What do you want?"

He placed both hands on the table and locked his gaze with hers. "You haven't figured it out by now? Perhaps you're not as bright as I remembered. Obviously, I want money. In return, you have my word that I won't tell your husband or anyone else that he married a divorced woman. Given the reputation he had before he married you, I doubt he'll have much of one left after everyone realizes he was taken for a fool by a simple country girl."

She blinked away her disbelief. "You want money? Why? You're married to an heiress!"

He leaned across the table. "If my wife has a miser's hold on the purse strings, her father has one even tighter on the inheritance she'll receive one day. You may find that amusing, but I assure you I do not. I want my own money, and you're going to see that I get it. Lots of it."

"You're insane," she whispered, horrified again to think she had ever thought she loved this man.

He laughed out loud. "Only a man who was insane would miss an opportunity like this when it falls into his lap." He hardened his voice. "You have a month to think of a way to sweet-talk your husband into giving you a rather substantial lump sum that you will turn over to me. If it takes longer than that, you'll test my patience and the amount will only go higher."

She shook her head. "No, I can't do it. I won't do it. If you continue to press me, I'll go to your wife and tell her the truth. If you think she has a tight hold on her money now, how much tighter do you think she'll hold on to the purse strings then— assuming she doesn't have the courage to divorce you and send you packing?"

He grabbed her arm so hard, she yelped. "Don't threaten me, Annabelle. Don't. Or you may find yourself in a situation you'll like even less than the one you're in," he warned.

Terrified by the pure evil she saw in his eyes, she yanked away her arm, but refused to give him the satisfaction of rubbing it to restore any feeling.

Before she could think of another argument that might dissuade him from attempting to blackmail her, he slid off the bench and got to his feet. "Meet me here two weeks from today. Same time. By then, I'll have been able to assess your husband's holdings and know exactly how much I'll need you to secure for me. I also need to make arrangements to settle somewhere other than Philadelphia or New York City. I always thought western Pennsylvania might be a good place to live, but I have too many bad memories associated with the area. I believe I'll head south, where I've heard the women are much more deferential to their husbands."

Her eyes widened. "You're moving elsewhere? Y-you're leaving your wife and your son?"

He scowled. "Do you really expect me to stay married to that miserly cow when I have a choice in the matter? You are indeed naïve."

"I'm not naïve at all. I was just hoping you still had a shred of decency left," she whispered.

"Instead of worrying about my character or my wife or my son, who will have all the advantages of his mother's money that I'll never have, you'd be well-advised to spend your time thinking of ways to get that money from your husband," he snapped and abruptly left.

Annabelle collapsed against the hard wooden booth. There was absolutely no way she would agree to give Eric a single coin from her own extremely limited funds, let alone Harrison's fortune, and she only had two weeks to think of a way to convince Eric of that reality before they met again. If she failed, she had an additional two weeks before Eric expected her to deliver the money.

The only blessing she could fathom from today's disastrous meeting was that she no longer had to spend every moment at social events fearing he would discover she was living here in Philadelphia with a new identity, because he already had. She also had real hope that by the time his final deadline arrived, she and Harrison would already be divorced, which would effectively thwart Eric's attempt to blackmail her.

All in all, she had one month left to do what she should have done weeks ago. She had to tell Harrison the truth about her past. By then, they might be divorced, but even if they were, she still owed him the truth before she left.

She did not even consider that he would be able to forgive her for not telling him the truth long ago. She would, however, spend the rest of her life wondering if, had she been truthful from the very beginning, he might have been right after all.

Maybe if they had met under different circumstances . . .

Chapter Twenty-Seven

❄

After returning home from yet another evening social event in the city, Annabelle changed and rejoined Harrison in the library instead of her room now that the warming stove had been installed. Only a week had passed since her meeting with Eric, but she had yet to decide what to do to eliminate the threat he posed to her as well as to Harrison.

Seated next to him in front of the warming stove, she kept her hands busy by knitting—a pleasure she had not enjoyed for several days after Eric grabbed her because her arm had been too sore. Miraculously, he had not left a bruise, which was the only good thing that came out of their awful meeting.

"Did you hear any new gossip tonight?" Annabelle asked, curious to see if he wanted to compare the tales they had heard about themselves tonight—and poke fun at it, as they did several nights ago, instead of letting it bother them. She stifled a yawn by tightening her jaw and taking a deep breath so he would not suggest they end the night because she was too tired.

He took a sip of the hot chocolate Irene had made for him

before retiring for the night, wrapped his hands around the pewter mug, and grinned. "I have a few new tidbits to share with you."

She nodded, finished one row of stitching, and started the next.

"The easiest to dismiss is the claim that you're so dissatisfied with the meager allowance I've allotted to you that you pawned your wedding ring," he said and laughed.

She dropped a stitch, and her heart skipped a beat. She had no idea how anyone found out she had gone into the pawnshop, particularly since she had used a different name.

"Since you were wearing your opal ring tonight, that bit of gossip didn't survive for very long," he offered.

She managed to return his smile. Fortunately, she had already exchanged the fancier opal ring for the plainer gold and platinum band she wore at home so he could see for himself that the rumor was blatantly false. "Why . . . why would anyone think I needed funds and doubt your generosity to me?" she asked in a shaky voice, hoping to deflect the topic of their conversation back to him.

He shrugged and dropped his gaze. "Setting aside any and all gossip about you, the only honest answer I can give you is that I haven't been overly generous in the past to anyone or anything, including the charitable institutions my own family established."

She set her knitting onto her lap. "That may be true of the past, but not now. Look at what you've done for the Refuge and the country church and for Lotte. You're also being very generous to allow Irene's son's family to come here to live for a spell. Now that I think about it, you haven't told me much about it, but there's some new charitable endeavor you're planning with Philip, too."

When he looked up at her again, his dark eyes held her captive. "I wouldn't have done any of those things if you hadn't been here."

Her heart started to race. "I don't believe that."

"Why not? I told you before that it was true."

His gaze was so intense and his words were spoken so earnestly, she trembled and picked up her knitting. "What I know is that you said you wanted a warm place to attend services and . . . and you made improvements at the Refuge to ease your conscience if I took sick because it was so cold there," she argued, tossing his own words back at him without mentioning that he had only rehired Lotte to please her. "I had nothing to do with whatever it is that you're planning with Philip, either. That's entirely your doing," she added.

He let out a long breath. "I was going to tell you about it once I was certain it would come to fruition, but I may as well tell you now. I came up with the idea to add a wing to the Refuge to provide workrooms where the women could make goods to sell. They can't stay at the Refuge forever, and it will be easier for them to find a suitable place to live if they have a way to earn the funds they'll need. I'm afraid I never gave any of those women or their children a second thought until you started volunteering there."

She was so excited about his idea and so proud of him for thinking of it that she wasted no thought on the role she had played in drawing his attention to the women's plight. "Do you really think you can make that happen? You have enough money to build the entire wing?"

He set his drink aside. "I could do it on my own, of course, but it's much more important to create a second foundation with a board of directors to draw in citywide support that won't be dependent on any one individual. That's why I need Philip's help. He's much more experienced at that sort of thing than I am."

"Have you gotten any support from anyone else yet?" she asked.

"Not so far," he admitted and covered a yawn. "I have a meeting tomorrow morning in the city with Eric Bradley. Apparently Philip was able to convince him to make a donation last week, but he insists on meeting with me first. I have another meeting in the afternoon with two other people Bradley claims are equally interested, which means I'll be gone most of the day. I suspect Philip will be joining us for supper, although I intend to do my best to dissuade him. He pays too much attention to you to suit me."

Annabelle dismissed Harrison's growing jealousy where Philip was concerned and managed a smile of support. "Are you too tired to share the rest of the gossip you heard tonight?" she asked, changing the topic of their conversation to a safer one.

She was dead wrong about that—and she knew it the moment Harrison told her that rumors she was seeing another man had intensified because she had allegedly been spotted at an eatery in a seedier part of the city with another man. "There's obviously no truth to that rumor, either. In all truth, I find it preposterous that anyone would take it seriously," he said before yawning again. "I'm sorry. I'm dreadfully tired. Did you hear anything new tonight you wanted to share with me before I fall asleep right in this chair?"

The only thing new she had heard tonight was that he trusted her completely, and she had betrayed that trust on so many levels she was filled with shame. If he had not been so tired, she would have confessed to him right now. Instead, she decided to wait until he was fully alert. She shoved her knitting in the knitting bag and got to her feet. "No, I didn't," she admitted. "You should get some rest. You have a busy day tomorrow. I'll close up the house," she suggested.

He stood up next to her and arched his back. "I'll do that before I climb into my very warm bed," he offered. "Will you be riding into the city with me to volunteer tomorrow? If so—"

"I can't. I promised Irene I'd help her sort through some of the trunks in the cottage garret before Alan moves them out. I know it may be some months before she even hears back from her daughter-in-law, but fixing up the garret seems to help her come to terms with losing Ellis."

"Don't spend too much time up in that garret. The warming stove I ordered for up there won't be installed for a few weeks yet," he cautioned, and they left the library together.

Once she returned to her room, she set her knitting bag down and sat down in front of what was left of the fire. The thick logs burning there had been reduced to ashes, and nothing but a few glowing orange embers remained. Her dreams for a happy and satisfying marriage had once been as strong as those logs, but those dreams were now as flimsy as the ashes that remained in the fireplace, and she sighed.

While Alan would clean out those ashes in the morning and set a new fire with yet more logs, she had no hope left anymore that she could ever rebuild her own dream. Especially not with Harrison. His hurts were too deep and his heartache still too real to make it possible for him to love anyone, even Annabelle, who believed in the man of character he had become.

She sat and prayed that God would give her courage to accept the new dream she trusted Him to place within her heart, and the grace to accept it when He did. But she prayed even harder that this new dream would appear before the end of January, when she would be out of Harrison's life forever.

$\backsim$

That afternoon when the rest of the staff had left the kitchen to attend to their chores, Irene walked over to Annabelle and tugged on her chair. "You need a nap today. Harrison sent word he's bringing company home for supper, and you can't risk falling asleep at the table like you almost did during dinner. If I didn't know any better, I'd think you hadn't had a wink of sleep last night. Are you certain you don't have anything you want to talk to me about?"

"Nothing's bothering me," Annabelle insisted for the third time that day. "I'm just tuckered out from being out so late twice this week."

Irene shook her head. "I should never have let you help me all morning with those new recipes you wrote out for me. Now up with you. You need a nap and you're taking one so you don't fall asleep in front of your company later."

Annabelle was so out of sorts from lack of sleep, she giggled. "Philip isn't company. He's family, but I have absolutely no intention of arguing with you about taking a nap. I won't even try. I know better," she quipped as she got to her feet.

"You might try convincing that husband of yours the same thing."

"Convince him to do what? Not argue with you or not to bother trying?" she teased, though she dreaded the thought of walking through that long tunnel to get back to the main house.

"Both," Irene insisted. "Now scoot. I've got a menu already in mind for supper and I've got lots of work to do, including putting an iron to that pretty green gown you're wearing tonight."

Annabelle cocked a brow. "I'm wearing the green one?"

"It matches the color of your eyes. Besides, Harrison asked me this morning to make sure you wore it," Irene explained. "I'll send Lotte up with your gown later when it's time for you to get ready," she promised and gave her a nudge which nearly knocked Annabelle over before she headed for the basement.

᷐

Annabelle did not know how she managed to stay on her feet long enough to get back to the house and up to her room. She did not even remember falling asleep in her bed, but she felt utterly refreshed when she walked into the dining room just before she expected Harrison and Philip to arrive. She found Irene standing by the table.

"You look beautiful," the housekeeper whispered.

Annabelle's cheeks warmed. "Thank you for ironing my gown."

"I owe you more than that for all your help today," her friend countered and waved her hand to direct Annabelle's attention to the table. "I just stopped in to make sure Peggy and Lotte set the table properly. What do you think of it?"

Annabelle looked at the table and blinked hard. They always dined at home rather informally, even with Philip as their guest. Tonight, however, Irene had the table set with sparkling china dishes and heavy silver flatware that rested on a damask tablecloth as white as the snow outside. The candles on the two candelabras in the center of the table had not been lit yet, and one more sat on the sideboard, which they had never used before.

Although she preferred a more casual table, this one was stunning, and she told Irene so. "I have only one minor complaint," she ventured. "There are four places set on the table. We only need three."

Irene looked at her down the length of her nose. "I told you company was coming tonight. We need all four."

Surprised that Harrison would be entertaining company here, since they had moved out to the country estate to avoid it, she latched on to a happy thought. "Is Philip bringing someone special with him?" she asked, hopeful he had met someone he liked well enough to have Harrison invite her to supper, too.

Irene sighed. "He is, but it's apparently not the 'someone special' you or I might like him to bring. He's much too busy to think about courting, although he does act a bit moonstruck whenever he's around you."

Annabelle's heart skipped a beat. She found Irene's comment about Philip as odd as Harrison's jealousy of his cousin, but she was more interested in knowing who their guest would be tonight. "I don't suppose you know who might be coming, do you?"

"I most certainly do. Not that Harrison bothered to tell me.

The young man who delivered Harrison's note told me. I don't actually know the man who's coming, but he must be important or Harrison wouldn't have invited him to come to supper all the way out here. Maybe you know him. His name is Bradley. Eric Bradley."

Chapter Twenty-Eight

❄

Annabelle grew up picturing Hades as a fire-filled pit in the netherworld filled with a cacophony of horrible screams, groans, and voices pleading for mercy. But tonight she got a glimpse of a Hades that was right here in her own house.

With Harrison sitting at one end of the dining room table and Philip at the other, she sat in the middle, directly across from Eric. She kept a smile on her lips as she listened to polite conversation between two decent and honorable men on either side of her and Eric, but she had to plant her feet on the floor so she would not jump up and scream.

Harrison and Philip had had no idea that the third man who was at the table was the devil incarnate. Or that she knew it and could not warn them without causing a terrible scene that would spell disaster all around. She had burned the note he had slipped to her and so had no proof of Eric's evil intentions—intentions he would no doubt deny.

Irene finally arrived with the last of several desserts that she set on the sideboard while Peggy and Lotte cleared the last of the supper dishes from the table. Annabelle could barely stand the thought of trying to eat anything, even dessert. She had nervous cramps in her stomach, and her throat was raw from swallowing bile. She also had little feeling in her lips, since she wore a frozen smile throughout most of supper.

Irene glimpsed at Annabelle's supper plate before Peggy took it away and instantly frowned. "You barely touched your supper. If you're not feeling well, I can stay and serve the desserts for you, or these gentlemen can serve themselves," she whispered.

Unfortunately, Harrison heard her and interrupted his conversation, which drew the other men's attention to Annabelle, as well. He looked at her with genuine concern, which only added to her guilt. "You've been uncommonly quiet all through supper, and you look a bit peaked. Aren't you feeling well?"

She forced her lips into a broader smile and got to her feet. "I feel perfectly fine. I'm just a bit overwhelmed. Tonight is really the first time we've entertained guests outside of family," she explained. She joined Irene at the sideboard, but deliberately avoided making eye contact with her for fear the woman would take one look into her eyes and know that Annabelle was not being honest.

"Why don't you tell everyone what I fixed for dessert, and I'll dish out whatever they want," Irene suggested in a tone that defied any argument.

Grateful for the opportunity to put her back to Eric, Annabelle gave her full attention to the top of the sideboard. "There's Irene's specialty, apple pie. She also made two kinds of cookies, molasses and almond crescent, that are quite delicious." She took several steps toward the final dessert and smiled. "She's also used one of my mother's other recipes to make a sweet custard, which is a particular favorite of mine," she announced, unable to resist the urge to say something to needle Eric, since he had favored the sweet custard she had once made for him, without Harrison or Philip realizing what she was doing.

When she turned around to face the men again, she met Eric's gaze and saw a brief flash of surprise in his eyes that disappeared when she stared long and hard back at him. "What would you like for dessert, Mr. Bradley?"

He grinned at her. "I've never been able to pass up apple pie, but I wouldn't mind a dish of custard, as well. I had some exceptional sweet custard a while back when I was traveling, which, sad to say, was the only highlight of a rather miserable experience," he said, chuckling as he looked from one end of the table to the other. "I'm certain you gentlemen have each endured journeys that were less pleasurable than you had hoped," he added. "It's been my experience, however, that those are the trips that often end up yielding rewards you never anticipated at the time. I can only hope this will be true of this trip to Philadelphia with my wife. She's been quite upset that we've gotten stranded here."

Stung, Annabelle silently fumed at his audacity as Philip replied, "I would have to agree with you. In all truth, I've learned over the years not to judge my efforts during a journey too quickly. Inevitably, some good always comes of honest effort."

Harrison nodded, but caught Annabelle's gaze and held it when he smiled at her. "I once thought my last trip might end up a total failure, but as you both know, my life was changed altogether once I met and married Annabelle."

Although she might have believed he meant his words as a double entendre only the two of them would understand, his gaze was too steady and his smile too dazzling to be anything but sincere. Although she accepted his compliment as yet another example of his ability to charm most everyone he met, it eased the sting of Eric's veiled reference to her failure as a wife and his pending plans to extort even more from Harrison than the meager inheritance he had taken from her.

Dropping her gaze, Annabelle waited until Irene had put Eric's dessert on the table in front of him before facing Philip.

Dear, sweet Philip. He was so earnest and kind, she doubted he had any notion that men like Eric Bradley even existed in the selfless world he had made for himself.

Still, she did notice that he looked at her rather intently several times tonight when he thought she was not looking, but dismissed Harrison and Irene's idea that he had become smitten with her. "What would you like tonight?"

"Those almond crescent cookies, and don't be stingy, Irene," he teased and winked at the housekeeper.

In return, Irene piled cookies onto his plate so high that Annabelle had to tread lightly to make sure none of the cookies slipped off the plate before she set it down in front of him. "If you'd like more, there's plenty."

"I think I'd like a small sampling of everything, especially since you didn't make anything with plums in it for a change," Harrison teased as Irene walked past the back of his chair.

After Irene cut a slice of pie and stacked three of each kind of cookie onto his plate, she set it in front of him before she took her leave. In the meantime, Annabelle filled a small cup with custard, placed it next to his dessert plate, and took a step back. "With your permission, I'd like to leave the three of you now, too. I know you have important business to discuss, but since I have little to offer in this regard—"

"On the contrary," Eric argued. "Philip and your husband have an opportunity at the Refuge that my wife and I are most interested in pursuing. They've both mentioned the work you're doing at the Refuge for those pitiful women and their children. When I told my wife about it, she was curious to know more. I'm afraid I promised her that I'd ask if you'd be kind enough to show me your efforts firsthand before we make any commitment to the new addition at the Refuge." He looked at Harrison and Philip. "Perhaps you two gentlemen would be able to join us."

Philip shook his head. "If you want to know anything about

the Refuge as it stands now, Annabelle is the best one to show you. I'd be glad to join you afterward, though, to show you where we would like to add the workshop."

Harrison cleared his throat. "Since I usually escort my wife to the Refuge, I may as well stay and join you when she shows you around the facility. Is there a day next week that suits you best?" he asked Eric.

Before he could answer, Philip held up his hand. "The only day next week I have any time free is on Thursday. If that doesn't suit everyone else, I could try to change one of my other appointments."

"Any day next week suits me," Harrison offered and looked to Eric.

When Eric's gaze hardened briefly, Annabelle caught her breath and held it for several long heartbeats before exhaling. She and Eric were scheduled to meet again next Thursday, but she would be ecstatic if he had to postpone their rendezvous, particularly since she had not thought of a different location where they could meet. Besides, if he had to push their meeting back, he might also extend his final deadline, too.

"Although I have another meeting planned for next Thursday morning that's rather important, I'm fairly certain I can reschedule it for the afternoon. Let's plan on Thursday morning at ten o'clock for now. I'll let you both know if I have a problem and need to reschedule our meeting until the following week."

Disappointed to get only a few hours' reprieve, Annabelle also decided she would find some excuse to make it impossible for her to see him next Thursday afternoon. "If that's settled, I should like to bid you all a good night." She got Harrison's nod of approval and left the dining room before Eric found another excuse to keep her there.

She mounted the staircase and went straight to her room, only to find Irene waiting there for her. "You might be able to fool every one of those three men downstairs, but you can't fool me any longer. Something's been wrong for nearly a week now, and I'm going to stay right here until you tell me what it is."

⌒

Harrison went straight to Annabelle's room before the coach carrying his guests back to the city had reached the end of the circular driveway in front of the house.

Even though she had left the table a good four hours ago and there was not a sliver of light coming from beneath her door, he was troubled enough by events tonight to knock at her door anyway. When the door eased open, Irene nudged him back when she stepped out of the room into the hall and closed the door behind her. She held one finger to her lips and motioned for him to follow, and she led him into the library.

Once she closed the door behind them, she gave him the most disappointing look he had ever seen her wear when she was about to give him a lecture.

"What's wrong? Is Annabelle truly ill?" he asked.

She sighed and shook her head. "If you consider a broken heart to be a sign of illness, then I'd have to say yes. She's ill, which is why I sat with her until she finally fell asleep about fifteen minutes ago."

He furrowed his brow. "A broken heart?"

"That's my diagnosis, although she didn't admit to it," Irene replied. "I don't know exactly what's going on between the two of you, and Annabelle is too loyal to you to tell me much of any-thing. My guess is that the gossip that's apparently churning in the city about the two of you is simply too hard for her to bear on top of knowing that you aren't happy with her."

"I never said I wasn't happy—"

"For a man supposed to be a charmer, I thought you'd know that it doesn't matter what you say. It's what you actually do that matters," she argued. "I'm not the one to judge what you've done to make her so upset tonight, but anyone with a pair of eyes in his head should have been able to see that she hasn't been herself for a good while. I can't tell you what you need to do to let her know how much you love her, but you need to do it now. You might try spending the night with her instead of skulking in here to sleep every night on the pretext that you're so restless when you sleep you're afraid to hurt her again. That's nonsense. You know it, and I know it. And if you have any plan to keep her out here permanently while you go back to the city mansion to enjoy the life you led when you were single, don't count on me to help you win her back when you finally come to your senses—because it'll be too late. Once you've set a woman outside of your life, she won't ever trust you not to do it again." And with that she turned and walked out of the room.

Totally confused, he stared at the door she had closed behind her for a very long time. He was more than annoyed that Annabelle had spoken so frankly to Irene about their marriage, although she had not broken the illusion that she had married him because she loved him. After the long talks they had shared together at night, he found it hard to believe he had missed how unhappy she was and simply assumed she found entertaining to be overwhelming.

Rather than spend the entire night here in the library, which would only incur Irene's wrath in the morning, he went back to Annabelle's room, pulled a chair next to her bed, and sat down. The few embers still glowing in the fireplace did not provide enough light to see more than the silhouette of her face, but he could see every one of her features with his mind's eye.

From her pale green eyes to her oval face to her long blond hair, she was a flawless beauty. But it was her giving heart and her strong faith in God—as well as her ability to bring out the best in him—that led him to nearly the same conclusion that Irene had flung at him.

He did not love Annabelle as Irene had claimed, but he was definitely on the verge of falling deeply in love with her.

And, torn between loving her and the searing pain he knew would come if he ever lost her or the children they might have together, he silenced the yearning in his heart and soul for this woman and made a vow to separate himself from her before it was too late.

To distract himself from questioning his decision or from worrying about what he would do about Irene when she learned he had actually divorced Annabelle, he kept his mind occupied by thinking about Eric Bradley . . . and tried to understand why the more time he spent with the man, the more he disliked him.

~

Annabelle stirred awake just after dawn, but gave a start when she rolled over and saw Harrison sleeping in the chair next to her bed. She did not know how long he had been there, but he must have been there all night if Irene had spoken to him after Philip and Eric had left last night as she had threatened to do.

Since she had promised Irene to sleep late today instead of meeting her at the bench or in the kitchen before breakfast for her lessons, she had no excuse to give him for slipping out of her room without speaking to him. She had no place to hide if he woke up and found her missing, either, so she glumly accepted the fact that she would have to explain herself to him as soon as he woke up.

She lifted herself up and leaned on her elbow to take advantage of this unusual opportunity to study him unobserved, but he opened his eyes just when she got comfortable in the new position, and she froze in place.

"I'd bid you a good morning, but I'd rather wait to hear your explanation for why you told Irene you were unhappy in our marriage before I jump to any conclusions about the day," he said as he stood up and arched his back to stretch his cramped muscles.

She swallowed hard. "You know how intuitive Irene can be. She senses something isn't quite right between us, and I needed to tell her something that would satisfy her, at least for now. And to be precise, I didn't tell her I was unhappy," she added. "I said you were."

He grew still, furrowed his brow, and stared down at her. "And that makes a difference?"

Before her arm turned numb from supporting her, she sat up and arranged the bedclothes to cover herself as best she could. "It makes all the difference, and before you start lecturing me about not revealing anything about our relationship to her, you might want to think about something else first."

He snorted and rotated his head in a circle, as if he was trying to ease a crick in his neck. "I spent most of the night in that awful chair wondering if there was anything you could say to me that would justify what she says you told her, but I still have no idea why you did. Enlighten me."

She drew in a deep breath. "It's the middle of January. If your lawyer is correct, you should be getting word in a matter of weeks that we're divorced. I know you're planning to keep our divorce a secret for some time before you announce it, but did it ever occur to you that unless Irene has some sense that we're not getting along now, she'll try her best to keep me from leaving in less than a month?"

He snorted again and dropped back into his seat. "I should have known better than to move out here. She's a troublesome, meddlesome woman who—"

"Who loves you very much," she offered. "She only wants what's best for you . . . or what she thinks is best for you." She twisted the end of the covers with her hands. "I'm sorry. I know I should have spoken to you first before I told her anything, but when I got back to my room last night, she was waiting for me and demanded to know what was wrong last night. I had to say something."

He blew out a long breath, cradled the back of his neck with his hands, and leaned back to stare at the ceiling. "You don't need to apologize. You're right. I've been so preoccupied with convincing her we were happily married just to keep her from suspecting anything was wrong that I didn't stop to think how I was going to explain to her why we were happy one day and you were leaving the next," he admitted and sighed. "I know that as far as Irene is concerned, I'll take full blame for ending our marriage, but you made matters worse by telling her I was breaking your heart. Was that really necessary?"

She clapped her hand to her heart, but dropped it when she realized he might assume she was trying to hold the pieces of her heart together. "I never said any such thing!"

"Maybe you didn't actually put it into so many words, but that's what she claims you meant," he countered.

She huffed. "I don't see how it hurts if she thinks I'm heart-broken . . . or would you prefer for her to think I've feigned my affection for you and only married you for your fortune like everyone else in the city believes?"

He dropped his gaze and rubbed the scars on his wrist. "I'm sorry. I had no idea that this marriage of ours would end up being so complicated or so difficult for you to endure, even temporarily."

"You couldn't know. Neither could I," she murmured. "It really won't be that much longer until your lawyer gets word that your petition for divorce has been granted, will it?"

He shook his head. "I don't expect it to be, but I'll see my lawyer tomorrow. Perhaps he can give me a better idea of how much longer it will take." He got to his feet. "In the meantime, we'll just have to make certain we talk things through each night like we've been doing. I only have one other concern I wanted to discuss with you."

She nodded. "Of course. What is it?"

"Eric Bradley," he said and paused to clench and unclench his jaw. "I may not like the way my own cousin looks at you, but I intensely dislike the way Bradley was looking at you last night. I'm a fairly good judge of character, and I simply don't trust the man. I don't ever want you to be alone with him for any reason," he said firmly, then cocked his head and looked at her closely. "Now that I've had a chance to think about it, I suspect you weren't yourself last night at supper because he made you feel uncomfortable. Am I wrong?"

"No, I . . . I don't like him, either," she admitted. She had to figure out a way to send Eric Bradley and his malicious threats out of her life, as well as Harrison's. Permanently.

Chapter Twenty-Nine

❄

As the following Thursday unfolded, the unexpected became the norm before Annabelle even left Graymoor Gardens.

Peggy, Alan, and Lotte were all sick in bed with a stomach ailment that had started during the night, and Irene was so busy running back and forth between their rooms to clean up every time they retched or to change soiled bedclothes, she had had no time to cook breakfast, let alone take her lessons.

Annabelle actually prepared the morning meal, which she and Harrison ate in the kitchen. After fixing a plate for Irene and cleaning up a bit, she hurried back to the main house to grab her cape. They had less than an hour to get to the city for their meeting with Eric, and she hoped Harrison was not annoyed with her for taking so long.

He was pacing the length of the foyer, dressed to leave, when she arrived. She offered him an apology as she retrieved her cape.

"You don't need to apologize or rush into your cape. I'll be going into the city alone this morning."

Stunned by his unexpected announcement, she held the cape in front of her. "I'm not going?"

"While I was waiting for you, I received a note from my lawyer. He says it's absolutely urgent that we meet as soon as possible, which can only mean he must have news about our divorce," he said, obviously aware there was not a member of the staff around to overhear him. "I sent a note back to him with his messenger and assured him I'd be able to meet with him this morning at nine o'clock. I expect to be there a good while. Clearly, this is far more important than our meeting with Bradley. Since I won't be able to be there at all, I won't have you seeing him alone." He started to cross his arms over his chest, but dropped them before she could offer a frown of disapproval.

She caught her breath and held it for a moment. From the drawn expression on Harrison's face, she could not tell if he was more anxious to learn if they were finally divorced or worried that she might not defer to his wishes. "I won't be meeting with Mr. Bradley alone. Philip will be there, and he can bring me back home in a private coach from your city home." She slipped into her cape without his help.

She prayed her argument was convincing enough. If she could see Eric this morning and get him to tell her the amount of money he wanted her to give him, she would not have to see him in the afternoon. If Harrison's divorce petition had already been granted, she would never have to see him again, since his plan would be thwarted long before the two-week deadline when he expected to receive his money.

When Harrison scowled at her, she offered him a smile and took his arm. "A donation from the Bradleys to help expand the Refuge is important. I don't like Mr. Bradley any more than you do, but I can tolerate him for an hour or two. Besides, Philip is always, always on time and more often than not, he arrives for his appointments early. He won't let anything happen to me."

He stiffened and narrowed his gaze. "Perhaps I should just

send a messenger to Bradley and my cousin and tell them to meet us at the Refuge this afternoon."

"Even if Philip can be there later, Mr. Bradley has another appointment, which he moved back so he could meet with us this morning, remember?"

His gaze hardened. "You'll be sure to stay with Philip every moment Bradley is there and come directly home after he leaves?"

"I will," she promised, pained by her deliberate lie. Oh, how she needed to rectify her sin of omission and explain everything to Harrison.

She turned and prepared to leave this house as Mrs. Harrison Graymoor, the former Mrs. Eric Bradley, ready to become the twice-divorced Annabelle Tyler.

~

After spending nearly an hour with the women in their knitting circle and explaining that they would be having a very important visitor today, Annabelle excused herself to wait for Philip and Eric in the front foyer fifteen minutes before ten o'clock.

Instead of Philip, Eric unexpectedly arrived first, and he looked about as he approached her. "I'm surprised you don't have your husband and his cousin standing guard over you. After dining with all of you, I can't decide which of the two of them is more devoted to you, a point I find very interesting indeed."

"Harrison won't be coming today, but I expect his cousin to arrive any moment," she replied. "Say whatever it is you need to say quickly."

He stopped in front of her and snickered. "I don't have anything to say to you," he argued, took a slip of paper from his pocket, and handed it to her. "I've written down the amount that I want and the name of the bank where I have the account where I expect you to deposit the funds. Added to the funds I've managed to squeeze out of my wife, I'll be quite satisfied to leave you both behind as unpleasant but highly profitable memories. You'll be happy to know I've decided that it won't be necessary for us to meet again, but the deadline still stands. If the money hasn't been deposited by noon two weeks from today, I'll have my own meeting with your husband."

Instead of looking at the paper, she folded it over and over until it was slim enough to slide into the knitting stick she wore at her waist. Whatever amount he demanded did not really matter, since she had no intention of paying him. "Would that account be in your name or my father's?" she snapped, keeping one eye on the door to make certain she saw Philip the moment he arrived.

He removed his winter overcoat and hung it on the peg next to her cape, and she shuddered with the memory of seeing their outer garments hanging side by side in the small cabin they had shared with her mother for the short week they lived together.

"If you must know, Eric Bradley will no longer exist once you've made your deposit. William Tyler, on the other hand, will be alive again and ultimately living in a place where there is never any snow," he said as he shook the snow from his boots.

If she did not have a conscience or a faith that kept her from acting on her first impulse, she would have taken out one of her knitting needles and plunged it straight into his scheming heart. Instead, she refused to give him the satisfaction that she was angered by the fact he was going to live out the rest of his life using her father's name. "What you call yourself or where you live matters nothing to me," she retorted. "If all you wanted to do today was to meet with me to give me your instructions, then I would prefer if you left now. I'll make your apologies to Philip for you."

He laughed. "And miss watching that foolish man nearly swoon every time he looks at you? I'm rather looking forward to the amusement, although I daresay your husband was not pleased, if you cared to notice."

When she scowled at him, he ignored her, looked around at the gray stone walls in the foyer, and shuddered. "There's time yet before I admit that my wife and I won't be making a donation to this awful place. Why anyone would waste good money on the hapless souls who end up here is a mystery."

Fuming, Annabelle was tempted to blister his ears and tell him exactly what she thought of him, but Philip chose that precise moment to arrive.

"I see you're both already here waiting for me," he said and quickly removed and stored away his outerwear. After shaking hands with Bradley and offering his own apologies for Harrison's absence, he offered his arm to Annabelle.

She was grateful for his presence, if only to keep her from doing or saying anything that would have her on her knees tonight asking for forgiveness.

An hour later, when Eric abruptly ended the tour and left, offering the excuse that he needed to return home because his son was feeling poorly today, she was so relieved that she found it hard not to grin.

Philip, on the other hand, was clearly dejected. "I don't think we'll be seeing Mr. Bradley again," he said as he helped Annabelle slip into her cape. "I was certain he would be making a donation."

She tied the top of her cape closed before donning her gloves and retrieving the knitting bag she had stored on the floor below her outerwear while he put his overcoat on. "I suspect you're right, but you shouldn't be too disappointed. Didn't you say you have two other prospects you'll be seeing this afternoon?"

He nodded. "I sincerely hope they're more interested than Bradley turned out to be." The smile he offered her looked half-hearted. "I suppose that just means I'll have to try harder when I meet with them," he said, slipped his hand inside of his coat, and checked his pocket watch. "I still have a good three hours left before my first appointment. Would you care to join me for a bit of dinner before I get you back home?"

Determined not to break the rest of her promise to Harrison, she shook her head. "I really shouldn't. Except for Irene and Graham, the rest of the staff took sick during the night and it's been a terrible strain on Irene. I'd like to get back to help her. I suspect I'll have a battle on my hands, but I hope I can convince her to rest a bit while I make dinner."

The disappointment that dulled his eyes quickly disappeared. "I have a better idea. Let's go back to the city mansion instead. We can eat there, and I'll have Mrs. Farley tell the cook to pack up enough dinner for everyone else back home. That way, both you and Irene will be able to rest awhile this afternoon."

She paused to consider his offer. She did not think Harrison would have any objection, since she and Philip would be dining at his city home where they would be surrounded by his staff. "I accept, on one condition. I'd like to ask Mrs. Farley to have the cook make some good broth for Irene's patients. They probably won't be able to eat regular food for a day or two."

"Done," he pronounced, then led her outside to the coach that was waiting for him and helped her inside. Once he joined her, he offered her another unexpected opportunity. "I know you spend most of your time in the city at the Refuge. If there's anything you'd like to stop and purchase before we go home, we can do that."

She smiled, as grateful for his offer as she was relieved that she still had the coins from selling her first wedding ring in the bottom of her knitting bag. If Harrison did learn this morning that they were now divorced, she did not know if she would have another opportunity to buy something she had been thinking about for a while, although she had yet to decide exactly what that would be.

"If you're certain it won't be a bother, there is one stop I think I'd like to make. I've heard there's an emporium of sorts in the city where a number of merchants have their shops, all in the same building."

"That would be the Philadelphia Arcade. At last count, I believe there were eighty or ninety tenants. It's not far from here at all. I'll take you there."

True to his word, Philip escorted her into the massive marble-faced building less than ten minutes later. Overwhelmed by the sheer number of shops and their offerings, she feared she would never find what she was looking for in less than a full day.

Until she saw something that caught her eye in one shop that drew her inside, with Philip by her side.

She inspected a small square mirror framed in rich brown leather that was rather heavy, considering it was no bigger than the palm of her hand. She decided at once that it would make the perfect gift, but held her breath until the shopkeeper told her the price. Relieved that she had enough coins, she waited patiently at the counter with Philip while the shopkeeper wrapped up her purchase.

"While the mirror is quite unusual, it's a bit masculine in style. I'm surprised you didn't choose something more delicate, like this oval one." Philip pointed to a small mirror framed in white leather strips woven in a more feminine design.

Reluctant to tell him that the mirror was not for her, she shrugged. "I'm afraid I'm accustomed to more sturdy and durable things," she replied and hoped she would find the words to explain her gift in writing when she wrote the note she would attach to it before she left it for Harrison to find after she had gone.

And if Harrison was right this morning and his lawyer had summoned him to inform him that their divorce had been granted, she would be leaving within days. If so, she had to tell Harrison the truth about her relationship to Eric Bradley. Tonight.

Chapter Thirty

❄

Harrison had been anticipating the summons to his lawyer's office for weeks, but he had still been caught off guard when Marshall's messenger had arrived unexpectedly this morning.

He reached Marshall's office precisely at nine o'clock, which was the time he had specified in his response, but his lawyer was in a meeting with another client for nearly an hour before Harrison finally was able to see him. "Please tell me you have good news for me about the divorce," he said as he took a seat in front of the man's desk.

Marshall shook his head as he cleared all but two of the files that littered his desk, then placed them directly in front of Harrison. "I don't remember handling more than a handful of other divorces since I opened my practice nearly forty years ago, but I've never regarded the end of any marriage as 'good news.' " He opened one of the files and pulled out two long sheaves of papers, which he handed to Harrison.

"As of the seventh of January, you were legally divorced from your wife. Although I have the original court decree from Indiana, you have a copy in your hands, as well as one I prepared for

Annabelle. You should keep yours in a safe place, where no one is likely to find it."

Harrison folded the papers together and set them on the desk in front of him, but he was surprised that he was not as excited as he expected he would be now that the nightmare that had begun almost two months ago was nearly over. All that remained to be done was to get Annabelle settled safely somewhere other than in Philadelphia, and he would finally be free to resume the life he had before he left on that fateful holiday in the fall. "Did Fennimore mention if he had any particular problems?"

His lawyer chuckled. "The poor man must have been traveling day and night to get this done so quickly. He was so tired when he arrived here late yesterday that I doubt the man could remember more than his own name. He did turn over another document that I'll hold for safekeeping unless you want to take it home. It's a deed to one hundred acres of land in Indiana you now own."

"You have all of my other important documents. You may as well keep it here. And see that Fennimore is well rewarded," he added before he checked his pocket watch. "It's just after ten thirty. Unless there's something else we need to discuss today, I can still keep another appointment if I leave now," he suggested, anxious to get to the Refuge while Bradley was still there.

"Don't rush off. There's something rather important I need to share with you," Marshall insisted. "Before I do, you should know that I've drawn the funds for Annabelle's settlement. Do you want to give it to her, or would you rather send her to my office to collect it?"

"I'll take it with me," he replied, and his lawyer set an envelope on top of the divorce papers Harrison was going to take with him. Curious to know what else the lawyer had to say, he left everything sitting on the desk and nodded. "Whatever it is you need to say, be brief. I really do need to leave for my other appointment."

Marshall leaned forward in his chair and rested both palms on the top of his desk. "When you first came to me to ask me to arrange for your divorce, you told me to do whatever I thought necessary to make that happen. Do you recall saying that?"

"Not really, but I have no reason to think that I didn't. We both know you always have full rein to act on my behalf." He cocked his head. "Why?

"I hired an investigator to look into your wife's background, and I have a copy of his report I want you to read."

Harrison shook his head as if he had misheard the lawyer. "You did what?"

"I hired an investigator to look into your wife's background," Marshall repeated a bit more firmly. "You may have been quite satisfied that you knew all there was to know about the woman you were forced to marry, but I'm your lawyer. You pay me well to protect your interests, and I felt it was necessary to have her investigated."

"You were hired to protect my business and financial interests, not my personal affairs," Harrison spat, furious with the man's audacity.

Marshall matched his client's hard glare with his own. "In this case, I don't see how you could separate one interest from the other. Did it ever occur to you that Annabelle might have played a less-than-innocent role in that robbery and your subsequent forced marriage, or that the real profit would not have come from the robbery itself but from a divorce settlement she planned to share with the other conspirators? You may have dismissed that possibility, assuming you even thought of it in the first place, but I didn't have that luxury."

Harrison pointed to the file containing the investigator's report and shook his finger at it. "If you don't remember, then let me remind you that Annabelle was extremely reluctant to even sign the settlement agreement, let alone accept it, which she still asserts she won't do. She could never be part of any scheme or conspiracy to do anything wrong. It's simply not in her nature. If that's what your investigator claims in his report, then you need to burn it, because it's more than worthless. It's a slanderous attack on her character that I have no intention of reading," he hissed, prepared to fire this lawyer and hire a new one before he left the city today.

Marshall lifted both hands in mock surrender. "That's not what the report contains at all, but it could have. If I may be bold enough to remind you, you've misjudged more than one woman in the past, including Vienna Biddle, who has used your rejection as an excuse to malign you as well as Annabelle. I could also mention Jane—"

"I wasn't married to her or any of those other women," Harrison retorted, reluctant to discuss the few but costly mistakes he had made with other women. "I know Annabelle better than I've ever known any woman. I've lived with her for nearly two months now, and I know her heart better than I know my own. She's absolutely incapable of guile."

"On one level, perhaps she is. But it's often difficult for a man to accept there are any flaws in a woman as lovely as Annabelle, especially when he doesn't even realize that he truly loves her. Or that the woman he was forced to marry might have come to hold him in high regard or even fallen in love with him, as incredible as that might seem to be."

Harrison dismissed his lawyer's words. His affection for Annabelle might have grown, but that was the extent of it. He also rejected the possibility that Annabelle had any feelings for him beyond a genuine concern for his character.

He had detected a few glances from her that spoke of an affection that went beyond the friendship they now shared. But he was certain they were nothing more than an effort to keep others from guessing the true nature of their relationship. "You're either daft or addled, and I don't like the fact that you said Annabelle might be capable of guile on any level. She's told me all about her past. I know she was trained and has worked as a teacher, but gave up her position after her father died. I know she cared for her ailing mother until she died, too, and she was coming here to Philadelphia in search of a new position. But she'll never be able to teach again—not with being divorced. So as you can see, there's nothing you can tell me that I don't already know. Nothing. Destroy the report," he insisted. He got to his feet and snatched up the papers, as well as her settlement.

His lawyer stood up to face him eye to eye. "Life won't be easier for either of you if anyone else finds out what this report contains, but I can assure you that the investigator has been paid rather handsomely to hold his counsel. I'm sorry. I didn't know how close you and Annabelle had become. I just assumed that she hadn't told you about her previous divorce."

Harrison flinched, as if he had been punched square in the gut. His heart pounded hard with denial, and his hands tightened on the papers he was holding. In fact, he was actually weak in the knees for the first time in his life, and he eased back down into his seat.

"You didn't know," his lawyer murmured and sat down, as well.

Harrison shook his head, but his thoughts were so jumbled he could not trust himself to say anything beyond one word: "No."

With a deep sigh, Marshall opened the report. "I assume you'll want to take this with you and read it carefully, but I can tell you what it contains about her previous marriage and divorce, if you like."

Harrison felt as if he had been plunged into madness, but managed a nod.

"Annabelle married for the first time on May 28, 1829.

Apparently her husband only remained with her for one week before returning to New York City, where he practiced law and presented himself as a single man. Without her knowledge, apparently, he quietly obtained a divorce some time later, also in Indiana oddly enough, and subsequently remarried. It appears he returned to western Pennsylvania to inform her he had divorced her some months ago, which is what likely prompted her to leave the area around the same time that you left your country estate near there. You know the rest," he murmured.

Stunned, Harrison had only one question to ask before he left and confronted her with the secret she had kept from him. "Was Tyler her maiden name or her married name?" he asked, if only to know if she had lied about that, too.

"That was her maiden name, I believe," the lawyer replied. He opened the report and skimmed through to the third page before he stopped and nodded. "Yes, Tyler was her maiden name, which she apparently took to using again after her divorce. Her married name was . . . here it is. Bradley. If you're even interested, her husband's name was Eric. Eric Bradley," he noted and furrowed his brow. "That's interesting. It just occurs to me now that I met a man with the same name only last week when I went to a dinner affair at the Wilshires'," he noted and closed the report. "It's not an uncommon name, I suppose. Just an odd coincidence."

"It's more than odd, and I don't believe in coincidences," Harrison said, sure that his instincts about Bradley had been right.

"If you like, I can have the investigator look into it."

"Don't bother. I'll take care of it. Just hold on to that report. I'll read it another time," he insisted and left without saying another word.

However improbable it might be, he instinctively knew that the Eric Bradley he had met and had entertained in his own home was the same Eric Bradley who had married Annabelle, then set her aside. He was also the very same man who was at the Refuge with her right now, and he abruptly took his leave, determined to confront the two of them while they were still together.

He was outside before he remembered that his driver had taken his coach for a few minor repairs. By the time he hailed down a hack and arrived at the Refuge, it was after noon and everyone he expected to find there had already gone.

Fully frustrated, he left, but he had no desire to go back to Graymoor Gardens and confront Annabelle until he was confident he was able to come to grips with what he had learned about her past. Returning to his city home made little sense, because he did not want to see anyone, including Philip, until he had better control of his emotions.

He hailed yet another hack and went to the deserted docks that lined the Delaware River. He knew he would not likely encounter anyone here, let alone someone he knew. He paid the driver to wait for him and started walking along the docks, where he found a most unusual sight. The current in the river was frozen absolutely still, and half a dozen ships were locked midriver in ice while over a hundred others were waiting for the spring thaw to leave the port.

Overhead, thick gray skies obscured the sun, and the wind along the river whipped at his body and numbed his face. Other than the pain of her deception, however, he felt nothing and walked slowly past the docks without seeing another human being.

On one hand, he felt bitterly betrayed. Annabelle had lured him into a friendship that was based on trust and honesty, yet she had not trusted him with the truth that she had been married and divorced before they even met. Not that it made any real difference now that they were divorced from each other.

Still, he had shared thoughts and feelings with her that he had never shared with anyone before, and it hurt him deeply to think she had not been able to do the same. Her betrayal also reinforced his vow never to become close with anyone, if only to avoid the hurt he was experiencing now.

He stopped for a moment to stare at a lone bird perched atop a mast on one of the ice-locked ships, as if it had been exiled from the rest of the flock and had nowhere else to go. He could not find fault with Annabelle for not telling him the truth any more than he could even try to comprehend the pain she must be enduring after not one husband, but two had rejected her.

He had no doubt that she had been subjected to gossip in her hometown after Bradley divorced her, which made the gossip that was swirling around her name now even worse for her to tolerate. If anyone here ever found out she had been divorced a second time, she would be a pariah, exiled as surely as that lonely bird had been. He had no knowledge of what had happened during their weeklong marriage that had led Bradley to divorce her, but he was positive she had done nothing to deserve his rejection.

Shivering, he turned and walked briskly back to the hack. As sympathetic as he might be to Annabelle's situation, he was furious with Eric Bradley. Setting aside the man's treatment of Annabelle, his audacity was appalling. It suddenly occurred to Harrison that Bradley's interest in visiting the Refuge or making a donation to the facility may have been nothing more than a ploy to keep in contact with Annabelle.

If that was true, he wondered why. The only possible reason he could think of was that Bradley might be worried about his own reputation if Annabelle told anyone of their previous relationship and his status as a once-divorced man.

Fearful that Bradley might have bullied Annabelle in some way, he took little comfort knowing that his instincts about the man had been proven right and hurried his steps. If Bradley had threatened her in any way, Harrison would make him wish he had never come to Philadelphia at all and send him packing back to New York City, where he belonged.

When he finally reached the hack, he was panting and his throat was raw as he hailed the driver's attention. "Can you take me to Graymoor Gardens?"

"Yes, sir. I know the way."

"Make it in half the usual time, and I'll double your fare," he offered and climbed into the coach. Without bothering to stop and try to understand why he cared what happened to Annabelle at all, he had one decision to make before he reached Graymoor Gardens: Should he tell Annabelle about their divorce before or after he told her about the investigator's report?

Chapter Thirty-One

❄

She had run out of time.

Annabelle finally faced the truth the moment she walked back into the house at Graymoor Gardens. She had no reason to doubt that Harrison would return home and inform her that his petition for divorce had been granted. Even though some might argue she had no reason to tell Harrison the truth about her former marriage and divorce at this point, she still felt a moral obligation to tell him. Even if he had been wrong and his lawyer had summoned him into the city for another purpose, the burden of guilt she bore for keeping the truth from him was too heavy to endure any longer.

She carried the food and broth she had brought back with her out to the cottage, only to find the kitchen silent and deserted. She assumed Irene was taking a much-needed nap and stored away the foodstuffs before returning to the main house.

Since she expected Harrison to return home soon, she went up to her room. Once she had quickly stored away the gift she had bought for him as well as her knitting bag, after removing Eric's note, she returned to the door and left it ajar. She glanced at the chairs in front of the fire where they had sat together in the evenings before the warming stove had been installed in the library and moved them a little farther apart before adding a few logs to the fire to keep it burning for the rest of the afternoon.

She was satisfied with the arrangement of the room, but Annabelle grew uneasy now that the moment she dreaded had finally arrived. She was too nervous to knit while she waited for him, so instead she sat down at the writing desk and looked over the list of things to remember when she left. She blinked back tears, for she did not know what had inspired her to include her heart on that list. She quickly crossed it off and braced herself instead to see rejection and scorn in his eyes whenever he looked at her.

She had just put the list back into the drawer when she heard heavy footsteps coming up the staircase. She bowed her head to say a quick prayer for courage before she slipped Eric's note into her pocket and waited for Harrison.

Her heart was beating so fast at this point, she was afraid he would be able to hear it. Her hands were shaking so hard she had to fold them together to keep them still, and she swallowed to clear the lump that had lodged in her throat.

Although the door was half open, he paused to knock on the doorframe. "May I come in?"

"Please," she murmured, not missing the aura of sadness that surrounded him as he joined her. "Did the lawyer have the news you expected?"

"He had rather unexpected news, which I can tell you about later," he replied before sitting down and staring into the fire.

She dropped her gaze, but rejected the idea that she had been given a reprieve. "I'm sorry. I know how convinced you were he would give you the news that your petition for divorce had been granted."

He sighed but did not meet her gaze. "How did your meeting

go with Eric Bradley?" he asked, and his voice sounded as weary as he looked.

Annabelle found the gumption that Irene claimed she had and drew a deep breath. "He left rather abruptly. I'm sorry, but Philip seems to think that Eric won't be making a donation after all."

He looked at her and furrowed his brow. "Eric?"

"There's much I need to tell you, that I should have told you weeks ago, but . . . but I never had the courage. At one time, Eric and I were married. Very briefly," she added as she saw his eyes darken. Speaking slowly, she carefully explained Eric's whirlwind courtship and their extremely short marriage. She tried her best not to sound bitter when she told him how Eric had secretly divorced her and taken the money that would have been her inheritance and used it to court the heiress he eventually married, but her shame was too deep and her voice was too shallow to her own ears to tell if she succeeded.

"I know I should have told you the truth weeks ago," she offered, "but I . . . I didn't know how. Then, when I saw Eric and realized he was going to be staying in the city for some time, I was petrified that he would see me, too. I never meant for my past to hurt anyone other than myself, especially you." She paused to blink back tears. "You once told me that the only thing worse for your reputation after you were divorced would be to marry a divorced woman. I can't bear to think of the damage I'll have done to your reputation if anyone were to find out that you actually did. I don't expect you to forgive me, but I would hope one day you'll understand why I waited so long to be honest with you."

When she finally had the courage to look into his eyes again, he was studying her, as if he could not quite believe what she had told him. "If you doubt what I'm telling you, I still have my first marriage certificate and my divorce papers," she offered, rather surprised that his gaze had not been condemning. "Do you . . . do you want to see them?"

He shook his head. "No, I believe you, but after all you said in the past about being honest with each other and trusting each other, you were neither. At this point, I'm not particularly interested in knowing why you held this back from me, but I have to admit that I'm curious as to why you're telling me now."

Stung by his well-deserved criticism, she trembled. "I'm afraid I . . . I had no other choice," she managed, but lost her courage as well as her voice.

He cocked a brow. "Why not?"

She drew a long breath and pressed her hands together so hard the bones in her fingers ached. "Do you remember the gossip we both heard about my being seen with another man in the city?"

He simply stared at her.

"It wasn't exactly gossip that was based on a misunderstanding. It was true. I left the Refuge and met with Eric two weeks ago, but it wasn't because I wanted to see him. He was at the soiree on New Year's Eve, and he followed me downstairs right before you did. He demanded that I meet with him two weeks later at a hotel where he'd taken a room under another name."

"For what purpose?" he gritted.

She felt her cheeks grow so hot, she thought they might have caught on fire. "Eric has no interest in me in that way, but I . . . I still couldn't make myself actually walk into that hotel to meet one man when I was married to another, even if I was his wife in name only. I changed into some used clothing I bought at a shop nearby and sent him a note telling him to meet me at a basement eatery where I didn't think anyone would see us. Obviously, I wasn't as clever as I thought I was. Someone must have seen us."

Harrison snorted. "Obviously. What did he want?"

She took out the paper he had given to her today and handed it to him, which he held in a clenched fist without reading. "Before I met with him, I had no idea. He'd already admitted that his wife did not know she had married a divorced man, and he was just as concerned about hiding the truth from her as I was from you. He'd also made it perfectly clear he had no interest in me, and I foolishly assumed he had access to his wife's abundant funds—so I dismissed the idea that he might want any money from me. I was wrong."

"How so?"

"When I finally met with him, he told me that his wife doesn't allow him much, if any, access to her fortune. He plans to take the money he expects to receive from me and leave her, just as he left me. If I fail to pay him, he's threatened to confront you and tell you that you married a divorced woman. He didn't have a sum in mind, but I had to agree to meet again today so he could tell me how much he wanted. He had no idea of our *arrangement*, and I certainly couldn't tell him, so I just went along with him."

Harrison leaned forward in his chair. His gaze was riveting, and he did not look away from her to open the note. "Why didn't you tell me? I could have done something to stop him."

"I thought you'd get word that we were divorced before I had to meet him again. When you and Philip made arrangements for me to give Eric a tour of the Refuge today, I hoped to postpone the meeting beyond this afternoon and gain even more time. Instead, Eric arrived even earlier than Philip, gave me that note, and told me to deposit the funds in a bank where he'd established an account some time ago under the same alias that he used to take a room in that hotel. He's expecting the funds to be there by the second of February."

Harrison opened the note and read it, but his gaze was so shuttered she could not tell whether or not he was shocked by the amount. "Is William Tyler any relation to you?" he whispered.

Her eyes welled with tears she had to blink away. "He was my father."

His jaw tightened. "What did Bradley say he would do if the funds weren't there by the date he put on the note?"

"He said he would meet with you later that day. I was so hopeful that your lawyer had good news for you today about our divorce, which would undermine his blackmail attempt entirely, but now . . ."

"Now it's time for me to step in," he said and got to his feet. "I'm disappointed that you didn't come to me earlier about this, but rest assured. Eric Bradley won't be bothering either one of us again."

When he started to walk away, she followed him. "What are you going to do?"

He stopped and turned to face her. "If you must know, I'm going back into the city to confront him. If he fails to see that his effort to extort money from me is not in his best interests, I'll speak directly to his wife."

She rushed over to him and grabbed his arm. "No. Please. You can't tell her."

He snorted. "Why not?"

"Because it's not her fault that she married such a horrid man. She doesn't deserve to be hurt or to have her name associated with scandal. She has an infant son. He'll be hurt, as well. I don't care whether you confront Eric or not, but you can't tell her. Please."

He held her gaze for a very long time before he looked away. "I'll wait for now. If I can think of a way to stop Bradley without telling his wife that she's married to a lying, scheming louse, then I won't."

She swallowed hard and dropped her hand. "Thank you."

He did not answer her and started for the door.

"Did your lawyer have any news at all about how much longer it will take before you get word that we're divorced?"

He stopped but did not turn around to face her. "I should be able to tell you in just a matter of days that we're divorced, and I'll make arrangements for you to leave." He then walked out of her room.

She stood in the middle of the room and stayed there until she heard him enter the library and close the door behind him. She was still standing there long after the echo of his footsteps had faded away, unable to do more than take one shaky breath at a time.

When she had imagined his reaction to being told about her previous marriage and divorce, she had expected him to be angry or to raise his voice to her, which is exactly what Eric would have done. Harrison's disappointment in her, however, hurt much more than even his scorn would have, and she could not help but compare the two very different men who had married her.

Both men were quite good-looking, but Eric's looks were also a source of vanity she had never seen Harrison exhibit. Eric was self-centered and motivated by greed. To be fair, Harrison was also quite self-absorbed when she first met him, but he had changed. He was becoming much more generous with both his time and his wealth, and using it less for his own interests and more to help others.

Eric's character was so deplorable she gave up trying to think of one redeeming quality he possessed. Harrison was a man who was trustworthy, dependable, and kind to a fault.

Not that long ago, when Eric had first proposed to her, she thought she was truly in love with him. She realized now that what she had felt for Eric was not love, but merely a foolish infatuation that had blinded her to his faults. And if she were completely honest with herself, she had to admit that when her mother became so very ill, she leaped at the chance to marry Eric to secure her future because she did not trust God enough to do that for her.

She eased her door closed before she let her tears fall free and climbed into bed. Pain unlike any she had ever known filled every corner of her heart and soul. Once she pulled the bedcovers around her, she buried her face in her pillow and cried until she had no more strength . . . and then she cried some more for being such a fool.

She had been humiliated and distraught when Eric divorced her, but she was beyond devastated now. Not simply because Harrison had helped her to discover the miracle of true and abiding love. But because she knew she had just lost any hope that one day he might have loved her, too.

When her tears were spent and her body was nearly numb with exhaustion, she used what little strength she had left to sit up and make an entry in her diary before she was too mired in self-pity to remember to record today's treasure in her diary:

Today I was blessed to realize that I have fallen in love with a good and decent man. And though I have lost him forever, I will treasure the precious days we shared together.

She stared at the entry until her tears began to fall again. Sighing, she closed her diary and prayed she might one day remember the joy of loving him instead of feeling only the pain of knowing he would never forgive her or be able to love her in return.

Chapter Thirty-Two

❄

Early Monday morning, Annabelle followed Irene up the narrow staircase to the cottage garret with a heavy heart.

She had not seen or talked to Harrison for four days, ever since she had confessed to the secret she had been keeping from him, and she was beginning to wonder if he was planning to avoid her altogether and simply send his lawyer with the news of their divorce instead of bringing it to her himself.

When she reached the last step, Irene was literally beaming with the biggest smile she had worn since learning of Ellis's death. "Well, what do you think?"

She glanced around and caught a bit of Irene's excitement. "I think you've done amazing work up here," she said. Although the garret had been transformed into a suitable room, it was still very cold. But bright sunshine streamed through the freshly washed windows at either end of the long, narrow room and reflected on the worn, but polished, floorboards.

Because of the sloped eaves, most people, including Irene, would only be able to stand up in the very center of the room, but Annabelle's short stature proved to be an advantage as she walked around. She passed by a pair of child-sized chairs and an old rocking chair Alan had repaired that had been grouped together on top of a serviceable rug braided with remnants of outdated clothing Irene had found in some old trunks that looked as if they had been worn before Annabelle was born.

When she stopped next to a bed tucked under one of the eaves, Irene walked toward her.

"That's a trundle bed, so I'm hoping it'll serve for Melanie and the girls."

"I don't recall Melanie mentioning in her letter how old the girls were, but since she and Ellis were only married for seven years, they can't be much older than five or six. They should fit," Annabelle replied.

Irene pointed to a far corner. "I've got a cradle over there, just in case the youngest one is still a babe, and there are the two trunks I cleared out for whatever they bring with them. The warming stove, which should arrive in another week or so, should keep them cozy."

Shivering, Annabelle walked over to Irene, put her arm around her, and hugged her close. "You've thought of everything. Melanie and the girls should be very pleased. They're very blessed to have a place here with you instead of a boardinghouse where they wouldn't have anyone to care about them like you will." She tried not to dwell on the reality that she would soon have to say good-bye to the only friend she had left in the world.

"You're cold. I told you to put on a sweater before you came up here. Let's get you back to the kitchen, where I can fix you something to warm you up again," Irene insisted and led her back to the staircase. "Those steps are mighty steep. You go first. That way if I stumble a bit, you can catch me."

"Who's going to catch me if I lose my balance?" Annabelle teased and started down the staircase.

"I don't know, but it won't be that husband of yours. He's as rare to see these days as a smile upon your own face." Irene put one hand on Annabelle's shoulder for support and followed her down the steps.

Annabelle knew she owed Irene an explanation for keeping to her room and completely avoiding her these past few days while she decided when and how she would leave Graymoor Gardens on her own terms instead of Harrison's. She also desperately needed Irene's help to carry out the plans she had made to leave, but she could not afford to have their conversation overheard.

By the time she reached the sun-drenched kitchen, where dinner was bubbling on the cookstove, she knew there was one place that afforded the privacy she needed. And since the clouds had finally decided to let the sun make an appearance today, this was the one day that would make it bearably pleasant.

Irene's feet had scarcely touched the kitchen floor before Annabelle set her plan into motion. She looked at Irene and grinned. "I have an idea."

Irene narrowed one eye. "What might that be?"

"Let's go on a picnic."

"Did you say a *picnic*?" Irene asked and shook her head as if she were trying to clear out her ears.

"There's nothing wrong with your hearing," Annabelle teased. "I'm going back to the main house to get my cape and a couple of blankets. While I'm there, I'll tell Peggy and Lotte that we won't be joining everyone else for dinner. In the meantime, you need to pack up some dinner for us and dress warm. Just be ready to leave by the time I get back. If you take too long, we'll lose the warmest sun of the day," she cautioned and hurried down the basement steps.

Irene called after her, "What if Harrison shows up for dinner? What's he going to think if he finds out we've gone off for a picnic in the middle of winter?"

Annabelle chuckled, but she did not slow her steps. "Do you care?"

"Not a whit, but—"

"Neither do I. Now hurry!"

e

The air was still and the sun was uncommonly warm while they ate their picnic dinner on the bench where they had sat together so many times before.

Now that they were finished, Irene packed what was left of their dinner back into the wicker basket resting between them, but hesitated before she closed the lid. "Are you sure you don't want to eat that last chicken leg?"

Annabelle groaned and patted her stomach. "I don't think I have room left. I've already had three helpings of everything. Dinner was truly delicious. Thank you."

Irene took a sack of nuts out of the basket and smiled. "It's about time you started eating normal again. You've barely touched your food lately," she complained. After laying the bag of nuts in her lap, she set the basket on the ground and looked from one direction to the next. "I haven't seen Jonah for a few days, either. I hope nothing's happened to the poor thing. I'm afraid I may never see that mangy squirrel again."

"Maybe you'll see him tomorrow morning. It's rather late in the day now." Annabelle took a deep breath for the courage she needed to keep to her plan for today. "I've wanted to talk to you about something for some time now, but it's very difficult," she began. "Did you . . . did you ever have something so very private and painful that you couldn't talk about it to anyone but God? Not even to your closest and dearest friend?"

Irene bowed her head and held very, very still. When she finally looked up at Annabelle, her eyes were glistening with tears.

"Harrison's left you, hasn't he." It was a simple statement of fact rather than a question that needed to be answered.

Annabelle blinked back tears of her own. She did not know how Irene was able to know the things she did, but before she could say anything that could possibly ease the woman's distress, Irene edged closer to her, took her hand, and pressed it to her heart. "I know there's nothing I can say or do to set things right between the two of you. I tried my best, but I guess it just wasn't good enough," she whispered. "You must know that I treasure you as much as I'd treasure my own daughter, if I had one. I'm so, so sorry Harrison doesn't see you for the precious woman you are."

Annabelle's heart swelled, and she struggled to find her voice. "I love you, too, and I . . . I shall miss you terribly . . . but there's something I need you to promise me," she said, grateful that Irene did not press her for any details of why her marriage to Harrison was ending.

Irene's teary gaze brightened. "Anything. Absolutely anything. You have my word."

"You must promise me that whatever happens, either before I leave or after, you won't say anything to Harrison about me or nag him to tell you why we're no longer going to be together or try to bully him into changing his mind."

Irene snorted and dropped their joined hands. "I promise, but I'm not really a bully, am I?"

Annabelle gave her a skeptical look.

Irene huffed. "Maybe I am, but only with Harrison. He needs a nudge now and again to keep him on the right path. I'd like to give him a good tongue-lashing right about now, and I'd do exactly that if I hadn't promised you otherwise."

"I do need your help before . . . before I leave," Annabelle prompted, and she was relieved when the woman's frown turned up into half a smile. "I don't know how soon that will be, but it's likely just a matter of days. I have a number of things I'd like to do, and I'm not even certain I can get them done in time. I'd rather not let Harrison know, which means I can't let Graham drive me into the city or send for a hack. Can you think of any way I can get in and out of the city this afternoon without anyone here knowing it?"

Irene furrowed her brow for a moment before she brightened. "I might have a way, as long as you're not fussy about how we do it, but it wouldn't be until tomorrow."

"We?"

"I'm not letting you go off alone. I'm going with you," the housekeeper argued.

"I don't think that's wise," Annabelle countered. "I don't want you to get into any trouble on my account if Harrison ever found out you helped me, let alone went with me."

"Why? What's he going to do about it? He can't fire me, remember? The only time I think we could both slip away would be tomorrow. Can you go then, or will that be too late for what you need to do?"

"I was hoping to go to the Refuge tomorrow for the last time, and I don't think I can wait until Wednesday." More than annoyed with herself for wasting the past few days in self-pity, she sighed. "Are you certain we can't go today?"

"Not the way I think is best. The only delivery I'm expecting this week is coming tomorrow."

Annabelle furrowed her brow. "What does a delivery have to do with my plans?"

"Everything," Irene argued. "When they head back to the city, we could go back with them. I've done so a few times before, so nobody here will think it all that unusual. If we work it right, they won't even suspect you went with me if I can figure out a way to get Lotte's cape for you to wear. She's not much taller than you are. As long as you keep the hood up and your head down, nobody will be any the wiser."

"I think it might work, but I won't need Lotte's cape, and we can't risk having her notice that it's gone. I've got an old cape I can wear. Can you tell me about that boardinghouse in the city that your friend operates?"

"I'll do better than that. I can't promise she's up to taking boarders, but I'll take you there tomorrow and we'll find out." Irene got to her feet and urged Annabelle to do the same, emptied the sack of nuts on the ground, and picked up the basket. "I know it's only been a week or so since you posted that letter to Melanie, but do you think we could make a stop in the city while we're there to see if she's written back to me yet?"

"Just in case I have to leave sooner than I expect, I think I'd better go to the Refuge this afternoon. I'll check for you before I come home. Please tell Graham to get the coach ready for me as quickly as he can," Annabelle replied and urged her companion to walk just a little faster.

$\mathcal{C}$

After a quick change of clothes and an equally quick ride into the city, Annabelle arrived at the Refuge in midafternoon. She left an hour later with her emotions in turmoil. While she was pleased that she was able to say farewell to most of the women and to explain in person that she would not be returning, she was troubled to leave them knowing that no one else was prepared to replace her.

Graham stopped at the post office on the way home. Rather than take the risk of seeing anyone she knew, especially Harrison, she waited in the coach while he went inside to see if there was a letter from Melanie for Irene. He had only been gone for a few moments when there was a knock at the coach door before it swung open.

Startled, she clapped her hand to her heart. "Philip!"

"I'm sorry. I didn't mean to startle you. I was just posting a letter to my sister in Boston when I ran into Graham, so I thought I'd keep you company while you're waiting for him," he offered and climbed aboard, bringing a burst of cold wind with him.

He sat down across from her and quickly shut the door. "Forgive me if I'm being too bold, but I need to talk to you. I gave up trying to talk to my cousin. He's as prickly as a cactus and twice as secretive. You haven't been back to the Refuge since last week, and in all truth, I was prepared to ride out to Graymoor Gardens tomorrow to see if you were all right. I don't know what's going on between the two of you, and it's not my intention to interfere—unless you think it might help."

She had to struggle, but she managed to hold back the tears that welled up. "I'm sorry. I . . . I really can't talk to you about it. You should speak to Harrison, but please don't push him for answers now. I'm sure he'll explain everything to you . . . when he's ready."

"Are you certain there's nothing I can do?"

When she nodded, he let out a long sigh. "I love my cousin like a brother, but sometimes he can be such a stupid fool," he grumbled. Then he gazed at her with great tenderness. "I'm sorry. I was hoping I could help, but I'll do as you ask and hold my counsel. For now."

Although she did not dare confide in him, she was relieved that he had agreed not to speak to Harrison. She did, however, take advantage of this unexpected opportunity to speak to him privately before she left. "I don't know if I've ever told you this before, but I'm very grateful to you for making me feel so welcome here and for helping me to start volunteering at the Refuge."

He smiled and waved away her words. "There's no thanks necessary. You're family. We take care of one another. Despite my impatience with my cousin, I'm certain he isn't foolish enough to let whatever argument you two have had last much longer."

Unable to tell him this could very well be the last time they saw each other or that she would not be a member of his family for much longer, she was relieved when Graham returned to inform her that there was no letter waiting for Irene.

Philip took the driver's return as a signal for him to leave, and he disembarked. Before he closed the door, however, he offered her a smile. "You know where to find me if you need anything. Anything at all."

She smiled. "I do. Thank you," she said, managing to hold back her tears until he closed the door. Once they started to fall, she could not stop them, and she finally gave up trying and cried most of the way back to Graymoor Gardens.

By the time the coach drove up the curved driveway in front of the house, her tears were spent and her cheeks were dry, but her eyes felt thick and scratchy, and she was surprised by how drained and exhausted she felt. To be fair to herself, coming face-to-face with the prospect of losing her friendship with both Irene and Philip in the same day had been hard, and she prayed they would be true to their word and let her leave without confronting Harrison.

She disembarked as soon as the coach stopped and hurried into the house, praying she could get back to her room and put a cold compress on her face before anyone saw her. Her heart was racing as she rushed up the staircase. When she finally reached the safety of her room, she ran inside, shut the door, and closed her eyes as she leaned back against it.

"I was beginning to wonder if you were coming back."

Startled, she opened her eyes. Harrison stood in front of the fireplace, and there were a number of papers and envelopes sitting on the serving table. But instead of the two chairs where they usually sat together, there was only one.

"Please sit down," he said. "We need to talk about what we must do, now that I'm able to tell you we're legally divorced."

Chapter Thirty-Three

❋

Harrison watched Annabelle come toward him as if she were walking to the gallows and he was her executioner.

He had been angry and deeply disappointed in her for not telling him about her previous marriage and divorce before he learned it from his lawyer. Yet Annabelle had defused that anger and eased his disappointment by being more worried about the consequences he would face as a result of marrying a divorced woman than worrying about being twice divorced herself.

He had been twice as angry to learn of Bradley's blackmail attempt and wanted nothing less than the man's destruction, but again, she had tamed his anger by expressing concern for Bradley's wife and young son, who could be hurt by anything he chose to do to punish the scoundrel.

If he thought being apart from her for four days would make it easier to face her now, however, he was proved wrong again the moment she entered the room.

His heart lurched and his arms ached for want of holding her, and the closer she got to him as she crossed the room, the more he knew it might take a lifetime to forget this beautiful, amazingly gentle and selfless woman. He did not know why he had not told her four days ago that their marriage was over, but he embraced the pain of saying good-bye to her now as the only real choice he had. Not if he had any hope of keeping even more heartache at bay as his parents and brother had suffered.

When she sat down on the edge of her seat, he noted her red-streaked eyes and drew in a deep breath. Instead of worrying about whether or not Bradley was responsible for her obvious distress, he asked her directly. "You didn't encounter Bradley while you were in the city, did you?"

She kept her gaze focused on the documents sitting on the serving table and shook her head. "No, I only went to the Refuge to say good-bye to everyone, and we both know it's highly unlikely he would show up there," she replied. "Have you decided what to do about his threat? Since you've gotten word that we're now divorced, I wonder if you have to do anything at all."

Satisfied that Bradley was not the reason she had been crying, he took a step away from the fire, which was making him uncomfortably warm, but remained well behind the serving table to keep his distance from her, too. "I still have until the deadline next week to decide what to do about his threat, but I can't simply ignore it any more than I can tell Bradley outright that I won't be paying him a single coin because you and I are now divorced. The last thing I want is to have that news spread around the city less than three months after notice of our marriage appeared in the newspapers, and he'll do just that, just for spite," he said firmly and squared his shoulders. "I'll be the one to decide when and how I announce our divorce, not him."

She met his gaze and held it. "Please keep your promise not to involve his wife."

He nodded, albeit reluctantly, and somehow found the strength to glance away from her amazing green eyes to look down at the serving table. "My lawyer has prepared a number of documents that are yours to keep. In addition to a copy of the official court decree ending our marriage, which is dated for the seventh of January, you'll find a copy of the settlement agreement you signed."

She moistened her lips, but made no effort to take the documents. "There are also two envelopes lying there. What are they for?"

"The thickest contains the first settlement payment, which is yours now that the divorce has been granted. You'll need funds to establish yourself elsewhere," he added, hoping to erase her frown.

"How soon would you like me to leave?" Her words were so soft he barely heard her.

"I'd like you to be out of the city by next Thursday, which is Bradley's deadline. Whatever I decide to do, I'd feel better about doing it if I knew you were far away from that man so he can't take out his frustration on you. In the meantime, you'll stay here, but I don't think it would be wise to leave the estate. I'll be staying here again until you leave, too, so if there's anything you want or need, just tell me. I can have the items ordered and delivered here, or I can have the dressmaker or whomever brought to you here. Either way, be sure to put your purchases on my account and save your funds for later when you truly need them."

Her head snapped up, and her eyes were wide with disbelief. "I can't even leave here before then? Not even to shop?"

He stiffened his back. "I won't risk having you encounter Bradley, not even by chance. If you're at the estate with me and he has the gall to show up here again, I'll be here to protect you."

She huffed. "I didn't need you to protect me when I met with him twice before. He wouldn't dare do anything to me now. Not before he has the money he's demanding, and by the time he finds out that he won't be getting any money at all, I'll be gone for good."

"I wish I could be as confident as you are, but I'm not," he said gently. "I don't trust Bradley, and you shouldn't, either."

"After how he betrayed me, I don't think I need to be reminded of how untrustworthy he is. He has no character at all, but he's not stupid."

"Perhaps not, but he is desperate. And desperate men often do stupid things," Harrison countered and held tight rein to his temper before he lost it. "I don't know why staying here for the next week or so should be such a problem. You tolerated much worse when we were left stranded by those robbers and then spent a rather miserable week at that inn."

She got to her feet and sighed. "The problem is simply this: I didn't have any other choice then. I do now, and since we're no longer married, I would hope you would respect the fact that I'm free to make my own choices, even if that means you don't like them."

Totally frustrated, Harrison raked his fingers through his hair, but he refused to let this mite of a woman get her way and put herself at risk. "After next Thursday, you can make all the choices you want. Until then, I'll decide what you can do," he said and snatched up the envelope containing her funds. "You can have this when you leave."

Her eyes widened with horror. "You're keeping my funds?"

"I'm keeping you safe," he argued and handed her the second envelope. "There are two tickets inside for you. Traveling anywhere north right now is nearly impossible, so next Thursday morning, Graham will take you to Havre de Grace in Maryland by coach. From there, you can sail south to Charleston using one of the tickets or to Richmond using the other. I'll leave it up to you to choose where you'd like to go, and that's the only choice you need to consider right now," he said firmly. "Come spring, when travel is easier, you can settle wherever you like, as long as it isn't in Philadelphia."

She paled, but stiffened her back and tilted up her chin. "I'm not moving south. Not now. Not ever. And if you try to make me go there, you'll . . . you'll have to find those handcuffs you treasure so much, put them back together, and secure me to the coach to make me go." She tossed the envelope onto the table and snatched up the documents, as if he might take those away from her, too. "These are mine," Annabelle snapped. "It seems as though I may have started a collection, although I doubt I'll ever want to add to it. Marrying one man I couldn't trust and another who doesn't trust me enough to find my own place to live is quite enough."

"You don't have to be so willful," he argued. "What's wrong with moving south for a spell?"

She did not look back but answered him on her way to the door. "That's where Eric wants to settle. I'd rather be handcuffed to that coach again for the rest of my life than take the chance of ever seeing him again. And you needn't worry that I'll choose to stay in Philadelphia. I don't want to see you, either," she replied and walked toward the door.

"Where are you going? We aren't done talking," he argued, anxious to make her understand he had no reason to suspect that she would have any reason not to want to settle south, at least temporarily.

"Since you've proven yourself to be completely unreasonable, I'm finished talking. And if you must know, I'm going to find a lock for my door," she snapped and disappeared into the hallway.

He stared at the doorway but did not even consider going after her. Although he had avoided seeing Irene when he arrived, he had no desire to see her now, especially with Annabelle charging around the house looking for a lock for her door. He picked up the envelope with the tickets, went straight to the library, where he knew no one would bother him, and slammed the door behind him.

After tossing both envelopes onto the desk, where they landed next to the diary she had given him, he paced from one end of the room to the other. Instead of stopping to pick up some of the funds that had fallen out of the envelope, he tried to understand why his talk with Annabelle had exploded into a disaster he had no idea how to mend.

Keeping her isolated out here until he settled things with Bradley made as much sense to him as making arrangements to send her away. He obviously had much more experience at escaping from difficulties than she did, and he was truly surprised she did not realize that she should be grateful for his help, instead of rejecting it outright as merely an effort to control her.

Recalling the horrified look on her face when he took back her settlement funds, he braced to a halt. "That was a stupid thing to do. Stupid," he grumbled. He was half afraid to admit he had been desperate enough at that point to do most anything to make her listen to reason—a realization that doubled his determination to keep her away from Bradley.

He kicked at the floor and started pacing again. Sending her south was no longer an option, and he could have told her that if she had not stormed out without giving him a chance to explain that he never would have sent her south if he had known Bradley intended to settle there someday.

Eventually he reached the only conclusion that made sense to him: Find Annabelle, apologize, and ask her to talk to him to settle their differences. Before he left, he stopped long enough to put all of the money that had fallen to the floor back into the envelope. When he entered the hallway, however, he saw Alan walking toward him carrying a wooden work tray containing his tools.

"I was hoping to see you, sir. Before I put these locks on either side of the sleeping room door, I wanted to make sure you don't have any objection. The one for the outside only has one key."

Harrison let out a long sigh and knew he would have to offer her a very, very good apology. "Put them on, for now. Is Miss Annabelle downstairs?"

"The last time I saw her, she was in the kitchen with Irene. Do you want me to tell her you want to see her when I get back there?"

"Don't bother. I'll speak to her later during supper."

"I'll make sure Peggy sets the table up here for two, then," he offered and continued down the hall.

Harrison took the servants' stairs to the first floor. Whether he liked it or not, he would have to go out to the cottage to see Annabelle and convince her to sit down and talk to him. Having Irene there might even help, since she could remind Annabelle of the advice she had given both of them about never parting with harsh words left between them.

He took the basement steps two at a time and hurried into the tunnel. He and Annabelle might not be married anymore, but they were both going to be living in this house for the next week or so. He did not need a senseless argument between them to make it any harder, and neither did she.

He practically ran the entire length of the tunnel and stopped at the bottom of the basement steps in the cottage to catch his breath before he started up the stairs. As it turned out, Annabelle was not in the kitchen, but Irene was there standing at the table slicing up some apples. "I thought Annabelle was here. Can you tell me where she went?"

She did not respond to his question. She did not even look up to acknowledge the fact that he was in the room, but he repeated his question anyway, then braced for a lecture that would probably be blistering.

When she finished slicing up the apple in her hand, Irene set down her knife and looked up at him. Instead of launching into a full-blown reprimand, she gazed at him with disappointment and disillusionment, which was much more disconcerting than any words she might have used.

"Please," he murmured. "I need to speak to her. Can you tell me where she is?" he asked, growing concerned that Annabelle had decided to run off.

"I promised not to say anything to you about what you did to a certain someone you've tossed away like a piece of strudel filled with plums," she said, completely ignoring his question.

Stung, he wondered if she would ever understand why he had divorced Annabelle. Since he had no intention of ever telling her their marriage had been nothing more than a façade, he held silent.

She narrowed her gaze. "If I could say something to you to answer your question, I'd simply say that the certain someone you're looking for is upstairs in the garret that I've fixed up for my son's family, and she's measuring the windows for the curtains she wants to make. I hope that while you're keeping that someone here as a prisoner, you won't try to stop me from going into the city tomorrow. I need to buy the fabric for the curtains, and I intend to stay for a while to visit with an old friend."

His frustration mounted with the woman's refusal to even say Annabelle's name. "As long as you go alone, you're free to go. I'm not planning to leave the house tomorrow. Use my coach," he suggested, hoping to redeem himself a bit.

She furrowed her brow for a moment, as if she was trying to decide whether or not to accept his offer. "Thank you. That's a good idea," she replied and started slicing another apple.

"Do you think it's a good idea if I go up to the garret and try to speak to Annabelle?"

This time, she glared at him. "I think you should leave a certain someone completely alone for a few days, whether those locks are on the sleeping room door or not. If I was free to remind you, which I'm not, you might consider it as just the beginning of the penance you'll have to do for the rest of your life, assuming you don't come to your senses," she snapped and resumed her task.

Although he did not usually follow Irene's advice, he took it now. "You can tell that certain someone that the locks aren't necessary. When she's ready to talk to me again, I'll listen," he promised and left to return to the main house.

As his footsteps echoed in the tunnel, memories of living here with Annabelle flashed through his mind. He once thought it was difficult to live here with two troublesome women; now he simply wondered how long it would take to get used to living here again with only one.

Chapter Thirty-Four

❄

Annabelle knew Irene could be very clever, but she was still impressed when the woman actually managed to secure Harrison's private coach to take her into the city the next morning. She also had Annabelle hiding inside, along with the canvas sack she filled, before the coach pulled away.

When they arrived in the city, slipping out of the coach without the driver seeing Annabelle proved to be a challenge. She managed to get herself, as well as her heavy bag, into the used clothing store she had visited once before without being spotted while Irene walked to a shop a few doors down on the opposite side of the street.

Relieved to find she had the shop to herself, she had no trouble trading all of her evening gowns and matching snoods for more suitable and durable day gowns. She had to agree to take half of what the shopkeeper originally offered and less half again to convince the woman to hold the evening gowns back for a month before putting them up for sale, but she was still more than satisfied.

With her new garments stuffed into the canvas bag and her

heart racing in anticipation, she looked through the shop window and kept her eye on the coach, which was parked right outside the door. Once Irene returned with a bulky package, which Graham stored inside for her, she climbed in. Annabelle waited until he walked around the other side of the coach before she clambered in while he got back up to his seat.

Panting from the exertion of getting that heavy bag into the coach, she held the door closed with one hand to keep it from flying open. It wasn't until the coach started moving again that her heart began to beat normally. "We did it!" she whispered, but Irene put her finger to her lips to warn her that even whispering to each other could spell disaster.

When the coach stopped the next time, Irene let herself out again but stayed to talk to Graham while Annabelle slipped out and hid behind the rear of the coach. She was pleasantly surprised to see that they had arrived in a very modest but clean working-class neighborhood that appeared rather deserted at midmorning. Annabelle was anxious to see the boardinghouse where she hoped to live just long enough to find a position listed in the newspaper that would take her far away from here.

Many of the redbrick homes that lined the narrow street were joined together, but there were a few free-standing houses. She assumed that most of the men and women who lived here were already at work, but smoke pouring out of some of the chimneys proved there were some people at home, and she longed to get out of sight. She did not know which home was Widow Plum's boardinghouse, but she prayed the woman had recovered enough to take in boarders again. She also trusted Irene to recommend a place where Annabelle would be safe and no one would recognize her as the wife of Harrison Graymoor.

"Former wife," she whispered and glanced down at the gold and platinum band on her finger she still wore to keep the staff from asking questions. She had had no reservations selling the wedding ring Eric had slipped onto her finger, but she had no intention of keeping this ring or the more expensive opal one—let alone selling them. Since she had no other funds to use to pay whatever it was going to cost to live in this boardinghouse, she resigned herself to taking some of the money from her divorce settlement and was frustrated that Harrison had taken it away from her.

When she finally heard Irene tell Graham to return for her in four hours, she was surprised to learn they would be here for that long. Irene walked with her to the door of the closest freestanding house.

"I have a very important errand of my own to tend to," Irene offered. "I should be back in an hour. Two at the most."

"Aren't you even going to come inside to introduce me?"

Irene patted her arm. "You'll do fine on your own. Just tell Prudence you're my niece. She's expecting you," she said and started walking away.

"You don't have a niece, do you?" Annabelle argued as loud as she dared without drawing undue attention to either one of them.

Irene chuckled. "No, but she doesn't know that. I'll explain everything to her once you're out of the city." She then hurried off.

Although Annabelle was tempted to run after her friend, she was more worried about getting out of sight. She noticed a small sign that read *Widow Plum's Boarding House* next to the door. The widow's name reminded her of how much Harrison disliked the taste of plums, and she knocked quickly to keep from stirring up any more bittersweet memories. Almost immediately she heard distant footsteps shuffling inside, and she waited for Widow Plum to answer the door instead of knocking again.

The door creaked open, revealing a rather tall, elderly woman with snow-white hair hanging down her back, country style, leaning heavily on an old gnarled branch she was using for a cane. She greeted Annabelle with a warm smile that revealed a missing front tooth and urged her inside. "I'm not taking guests at the moment, but do come in out of this dreadful cold. I've got water heating on the stove. I hope you'll stay and at least share a pot of tea with me."

Deeply disappointed that she would not be able to take a room here, Annabelle stepped into the front parlor, where sheets covered all of the furniture, and closed the door behind her. "I'm sorry to bother you, but Aunt Irene told me I might find accommodations here. She actually brought me here, but she had to leave on an errand. She should be back in a bit."

"Oh! You must be Annabelle. I've been expecting you," the woman gushed as she led her through the parlor. "I may not be taking boarders, but I always have room for someone as special as you are," she insisted as they walked into a small dining room where the furniture had likewise been covered.

"Don't mind all this," the widow said between labored breaths. "I've been feeling so poorly these past few months that I haven't been up to doing much housekeeping. Fortunately, my boarders were able to find other accommodations." She tapped a door open with the tip of her cane and led Annabelle into a very warm kitchen.

The room was larger than Annabelle expected, but she stared at the narrow cot hugging the back wall where Widow Plum apparently had been sleeping. "I'm here by myself, so I haven't bothered to waste precious firewood trying to keep any of the other rooms warm. Now that you're here and I'm feeling up to taking the stairs once or twice a day, maybe I can sleep in my own bed tonight."

Annabelle's cheeks grew hot. "I'm sorry. I didn't mean to stare."

When the woman laughed, her clouded blue eyes almost twinkled. "I don't blame you for being more than a little curious about that old cot," she said and pulled a chair out from beneath a scarred wooden worktable. Once she plopped down, she rested her cane across her lap and sighed. "I'd tell you not to bother getting old, but you probably wouldn't listen," she teased before a coughing spell interrupted her.

When she finally caught her breath, she smiled at Annabelle. "I guess I'm not as recovered as I thought. A cup of tea right about now would really help, and the water should be hot enough by now. If I could bother you to get some tea out of a canister in that corner cupboard over there and add it to the teapot sitting next to the stove, I'd be grateful. I'll get another cup and saucer ready for you."

"I'll take care of that," Annabelle suggested. She slipped out of her cape and gloves and stored them on a peg by the back door. Following the woman's directions, it did not take more than a few minutes to get a strong cup of tea ready for them, and she sat down to join her hostess at the table.

"You're as dear as I thought you'd be," Widow Plum crooned. "Then again, anyone related to Irene couldn't be anything else. I know you're only able to stay with me for a few weeks, but that suits me fine, too," she said, then added four generous helpings of sugar to her tea and a dollop of cream.

Annabelle took a sip of tea, which she preferred without either sugar or cream. "I would very much like to stay, but I really should ask you how much you charge for a room. I don't need a very large one." She couldn't help finding it a bit odd to be worrying about money again after having given it no thought for the past few months.

The widow set her teacup down. "I can't charge you anything at all. Since I can't pay you much for helping me set this old place back to rights again until I'm able to take in boarders again, your room and board are included. Didn't Irene tell you that?"

"No. No, she didn't," Annabelle replied.

"If you save up your earnings instead of spending it, you should have enough to tide you over a short while. Hopefully you'll be able to find a more permanent position before your funds run out. I'll be glad to let you stay here without charge if it takes a bit longer than you expect."

Annabelle dropped her gaze. "You're very generous."

"I can hardly be anything less. Not when people like Mr. Graymoor have been so good to me."

Annabelle's heart skipped a beat and her head snapped up. "Did you say Mr. Graymoor? Do you know him?"

"Only through Irene. I've never actually met the man, but you can rest assured that I was flabbergasted when he sent his driver to see me and gave me enough funds to make sure I could see a doctor and keep the boardinghouse, too. Without his help, I would have lost it for sure. I even sent him a note to thank him and to reassure him that I would repay him once I was up to taking in boarders again, but he wrote back to tell me the only way I could repay him would be to help someone else when they needed it. It may as well be you."

Stunned to learn what Harrison had done for the widow, Annabelle wondered how generous he would be if he ever found out this woman was helping her.

They spent the next hour talking about Annabelle's duties before Widow Plum gave her a tour of the house. Another hour passed before they returned to the kitchen, in part because the elderly woman had to walk so slowly. At this point, Annabelle was growing anxious for Irene to return.

When she finally heard a knock at the front door, she leaped to her feet. "That must be my aunt. I'll let her in," she insisted and rushed out of the kitchen, through the dining room, and into the parlor.

"I was getting worried about you," she said once she opened the door, but she took one look at the man standing behind Irene and lost every thought in her head.

Irene stepped into the house but left the man standing outside. "Quick. Grab your cape. You have to leave right now. I'll stay here with Prudence. If you don't get back before Graham returns with the coach, I'll have to leave, and you'll have to find your own way back to Graymoor Gardens. Now scoot!"

Too shocked to do more than follow Irene's order, she was terrified that Harrison might have gone into her room and discovered her missing. She raced back to the kitchen and grabbed her cape, not bothering to pick up the gloves that had fallen out of the pocket while she rushed back to the front door.

Philip was still waiting for her on the steps, and he had her inside a rented hack before she had her wits about her. She collapsed into her seat as the coach started off.

Poor Philip. Even in the dimness that enveloped both of them, he appeared to be very worried about her. Upset at Irene for involving him, she sighed. The last thing she wanted was to come between the two men, and she hoped Harrison would find a way to reconcile with his cousin.

"Before you leap to conclusions or get annoyed with Irene for coming to speak to me about your situation, let me reassure you that she's very loyal to you as well as to my cousin. Don't worry. I'm sure he has no idea you left Graymoor Gardens and came into the city."

She resisted the urge to pull back the curtain on the window next to her to see if Harrison was following them or to tell Philip how disappointed she was that Irene had brought him to the boardinghouse. "H-how can you be so certain?"

"If my cousin had any idea you were gone, he'd be turning this city upside down to find you. He'd create such a ruckus in the process, we both would have heard him by now," he teased.

"Perhaps," she admitted.

"He'd make an even bigger ruckus if he found out you were sitting here all alone with me."

She narrowed her gaze, but she still could not see his features clear enough to suit her. "You're his cousin. Why would he care?"

He reached over and took her hand. "Because my cousin knows that I have very deep feelings for you. My first loyalty is to Harrison, but now that Irene has told me he's foolishly set you aside, I no longer feel compelled to deny my feelings. I care for you, Annabelle, and I don't want you to leave Philadelphia. Not alone."

Horrified that Irene had betrayed her trust and confided in him, she was more alarmed by his tenderly spoken words and eased her hand free. She was also very confused by his declaration and shook her head. "I don't understand what you mean."

He took her hand again and held it clasped between his own. "I know it's too soon for you right now, but I want you to know that I'm prepared to wait as long as it takes."

Even more confused, she asked, "Wait for what?"

He cleared his throat. "Even if you don't have feelings for me now, I can only hope and pray that one day, when you're no longer bound to my cousin, that you'll consider . . . that you might agree to become my wife."

She yanked her hand away. "Y-you want me to marry you?"

"Someday. When you're free," he explained. "Over the past year or so, I helped to raise enough funds to build a very different kind of facility for orphaned children that will be built about twenty miles from Boston in a very rural area. Right before I left to come here, the directors asked me to operate the facility, although I'd still need to leave to raise donations now and then. At the time, I wasn't interested, but I don't have to give them my final answer until March," he said. "Come with me. There's so much good we could do together. You could teach at the orphanage, at least for a while, and perhaps with time, you might find your feelings for me—"

"I already have very strong feelings for you, Philip, but . . . but not in the way you might hope. I . . . I care for you as I would for a brother, not as . . ." Her voice trailed off, and she dropped her gaze, deeply troubled that she had not been able to see that his feelings for her went beyond friendship, which is exactly what both Irene and Harrison had been able to see, not to mention Eric. "If I misled you in any way, please forgive me."

He let out a long breath and held silent for a very long time as the coach creaked up and down the city streets. The silence grew until it was nearly unbearable, but finally, he let out another long sigh. "No, you never misled me," he reassured her and shook his head. "Irene was right. She told me I'd be making a mistake to propose to you. I should have known better than to hope a woman like you could ever love someone like me. If I've offended you in any way, I hope you can forgive me."

Moved to tears, Annabelle took his hand. "You're an amazingly kind and generous man. I'm honored by your proposal, but you deserve someone far better than I am to be your wife. Be patient, Philip. You'll find her one day. I know you will," she promised.

"And what about you, dear Annabelle? What's going to happen to you?"

"I don't know," she whispered. "I really don't know, but I have to believe in God's plan for me and trust Him to provide for me."

He edged forward in his seat and stared at her long and hard before he sat back again. "You still love Harrison. Despite the fact that he is setting you aside, you still love him." His voice was filled with disbelief.

Annabelle wanted to deny what he said, but she didn't have the courage to lie to him or to anyone else anymore. Instead, she simply let his words hang in the air between them as the coach carried them through the city streets she would soon leave behind, along with her heart.

But she would not leave until she had a long, hard talk with Irene to find out why she had broken the trust Annabelle had placed with her and told Philip that her marriage to Harrison was over.

"I'll take you back to the boardinghouse now," he offered.

"No. I need to go back to Graymoor Gardens."

"I think it might be best if you didn't go back there at all, and Irene agrees with me. If you're worried about collecting your things, she said to tell you she'll bring them to the boardinghouse."

"Please. I just need to go back home," she insisted. "Will you help me and take me there, or will I have to get there on my own?"

Chapter Thirty-Five

❄

Philip grumbled and groused all the way back to the countryside, and he continued to complain as he helped her out of the coach. "It doesn't make any sense to leave you here. It's a good mile walk to the main house," he whispered, keeping one eye on the driver.

"If you leave me off any closer, someone at the house might see the coach, even if Harrison doesn't. Besides, I like to walk. And don't forget to go back to the boardinghouse to see if Irene's still there so you can tell her where I am. Ask her to bring my gloves, too." At midafternoon, the sun had disappeared behind a gray blanket of clouds, and the wind was growing stronger by the minute. She really wished she had picked up her gloves so she could wear them now.

When she turned to leave, Philip grabbed her hand. "It's not too late to change your mind and come with me."

She slid her hand free and cupped his cheek. "You're a dear, dear man. Please don't settle for anything less than a woman who can love you with her whole heart," she whispered, then turned and walked away, directly into the wind.

She trudged back to the house along the rutted roadway

through melting ice and snow that was starting to refreeze. The bottom of her cape and skirts were caked with mud and snow, and her feet were numb long before she reached the circular driveway. Her hands fared no better, and she had to squint to protect her eyes from the biting wind. She did not have to stretch her imagination very far to envision her nose and cheeks as cherry red, but she did try to press her lips together to keep them from freezing.

Still, by the time she neared the house, she had a good sense of what she had to do and how she had to do it in order to leave and return to the boardinghouse with a clear conscience. She let herself in the front door of the house.

Annabelle lost any hope she might get up to her room without being noticed when Harrison appeared at the top of the stairs before she even reached the middle steps.

"You've been outside?"

She hesitated for half a heartbeat before she continued climbing up the staircase. "I w-went for a w-walk," she offered, and she was disappointed when he did not step aside to let her pass at the top of the stairs.

When he studied her from head to toe and frowned, she clenched her teeth to keep them from chattering.

"Unless you plan to spend a few days in bed to recover from being so chilled, you might want to consider dressing more appropriately for the cold. I haven't seen that dreadful cape before, but it's not heavy enough for this weather, and you're not even wearing your gloves."

She glanced down at her cape and cringed. She had completely forgotten she was wearing the one she had bought at the used clothing shop. "I-I'm afraid I m-managed to lose m-my gloves."

He stepped aside rather abruptly. "I was hoping you'd agree to sit down and talk to me, but you're in no condition to do that now. You need to warm up first. While you change into dry clothes, I'll get Lotte to fix something hot for you to drink. May I join you in your room later so we can talk?"

She barely managed to nod before he turned and headed for the servants' staircase. Although she was tingling all over as her body started to thaw, she managed to get to her room and change fairly quickly. She shoved the cape under the bed, hoping he would forget all about it if he did not see it again, and moved his chair back to where it belonged. She even had a few minutes to sit down in front of the fire to gather her thoughts.

When he returned a few minutes later carrying a tray with two mugs on it, she was not surprised he had brought it instead of Lotte. He set the tray onto the serving table that still separated the two chairs and handed her a mug. "The cider shouldn't be too hot to drink at this point."

She took a tentative sip before she risked a longer one, but the brush of his hand sent warm sensations coursing through her body long before she felt the effects of the cider.

He put an envelope on top of the serving table as he sat down, but left the second mug on the tray untouched. "Before I say anything else, I need to apologize. I had no right to treat you so . . . so poorly," he admitted, and his gaze was truly as sincere as his words. "The settlement funds are rightfully yours to keep and to spend however and whenever you wish."

Heartened by his apology, she offered him one of her own. "I'm sorry I acted so poorly myself. Putting a lock on my door was childish."

He smiled and relaxed back in his chair. "Now that we have our mutual apologies out of the way, I hope we can talk to one another like we used to do. I'd like you to consider something."

She took a cinnamon stick from the serving tray and stirred her cider without giving him any indication she was willing to consider anything at all.

When she did not object, he continued. "Eric Bradley is still a threat to both of us, and he'll remain a threat until I talk to him next week. In the meantime, I'd feel much better if you stayed here with me where I know you'll be safe. He wouldn't even be a threat to you if you hadn't been married to me, and I'd never forgive myself if anything happened to you."

She met his gaze and her heart began to race. Since they were quite alone, there was no need for Harrison to feign any affection for her now, and the love she saw in his eyes was as real as the love she had hidden from him, too. Her heart swelled with both joy and hope. "He would not be a threat to you at all if you weren't my husband and had the wealth that you do. I'd never forgive myself if anything happened to you, either," she said.

For several very long, very precious heartbeats, she could actually feel the miracle of truly loving a man and being fully loved in return. Love that brought out the best of each of them and promised a lifetime of happiness. Love that would sustain them and keep them strong in faith as well as hope. Love that was such a blessing to be treasured, she did not need to record it in her diary because it was indelibly imprinted on her heart.

Just when she thought she might have been given the greatest blessing of her life, he dropped his gaze and her heart trembled. He had been without love for so long and had been so desperately hurt by losing everyone he had ever loved, he obviously refused to risk having that happen all over again by keeping her in his life. She struggled against the deep sadness that overpowered her, but she was surprised when he finally looked up at her again.

His gaze was steady, but his dark eyes were shadowed by the same incredible sadness she felt. "Will it be too difficult for you to wait to leave until next week when I see Bradley? You could use that time to decide where you'd like to settle temporarily so I could purchase the travel passage for you."

Now that she knew their love for one another was ill-fated,

leaving immediately couldn't be soon enough. "I could send Eric a note and tell him I'll be depositing the funds this Thursday into his account, but I could tell him I need to see him at his hotel first. He wouldn't dare risk turning me down, and I wouldn't have to wait until next week to start my new life. Neither would you."

He held silent and seemed to mull over her idea. "Although I've already set a number of things into motion, I don't know if I can be ready that soon. But I can try," he promised, picked up his mug of cider, and took a long draught. "Do you remember the name of the hotel where he took a room?"

She doubted she would ever forget it and told him, along with the room number. "He's registered under the same name that's on the account. My father's name." She set her mug back onto the serving tray before he noticed it was shaking.

"If this is going to work, I need to go into the city this afternoon. If I can accomplish what I need to do, which I rather hope will be the case, I'll be home tonight. If not, I'll be back before dinner tomorrow," he said and got to his feet.

Surprised, she stood up, too. "You're leaving me here? Alone?"

"Only for an hour or two. I'll stop and ask Philip to stay here while I'm gone, just in case I can't make it back here tonight," he explained, but she could see he was not very happy about it.

Given her talk with Philip, neither was she. "Asking him to come all the way out here to stay with me really isn't necessary, is it? If you're right about getting everything done this afternoon, it's only going to be a matter of a few hours before you're back. I can stay in the house and tell the staff not to let anyone in who might come to call. Even if there is a problem, Alan will be here if I need his help."

He clenched and unclenched his jaw. "You're right. But if it takes longer than I hope, I'll return tonight anyway. I can always leave again tomorrow at first light for the city, which might be better all around. You could even go with me. After I finish up what I have to do, I could take you to shop for whatever you want or need to take with you when you leave."

She moistened her lips. "I can't go with you tomorrow. I . . . I have other plans."

"Such as . . ."

"I may be leaving a lot sooner than either of us thought, and I want to make the curtains for the room up in the cottage garret," she explained, choosing her words very carefully to avoid an outright lie.

"Then plan on my return here tonight. I may be very late. If I do need to go to the city again in the morning, you may have to wait until late tomorrow afternoon to learn if everything is set for this Thursday."

"That's fine," she whispered. She dropped her gaze so he would not see the truth shining in her eyes and discover she planned to be gone long before then and walked over to the writing desk to pen her note to Eric.

℮

Irene had left the clothing Annabelle had bargained for at the boardinghouse, but she did return with the fabric for the curtains, as well as the gloves Annabelle had left behind.

Unfortunately, she also brought a bit of an attitude back with her, and she continued to banter with Annabelle almost exactly the way she typically argued with Harrison. "I did *not* break my word," she repeated while Annabelle paced from one end of her room to the other, and she counted off the rest of her argument with her fingers. "I spoke to Harrison, but I did not lecture him or nag him or bully him. I'll admit that I did speak to Philip, but I never made any promises to you that I wouldn't."

Frustrated to the limits of her patience, Annabelle rocked back on her heels and stared at the housekeeper, who was standing next to the bed, trying to scrape off mud from the hem of the old cape Annabelle had worn today. "I didn't think I had to ask you to hold your counsel where Philip was concerned. I thought you were friend enough to understand that whenever I confided in you, you would keep it between us," she added, hoping something she might say would make a dent in the armor of righteousness the woman was wearing.

Irene never lost her rhythm and continued to work at the hem. "I didn't actually tell Philip all that much."

"In addition to telling him that I had to leave Harrison, which is so terribly, terribly private, you told him where I'd be living until I find a position and get out of Philadelphia!"

"No, I told him where to find you today. I never told him you'd be living there," she argued without addressing Annabelle's biggest complaint. "Did you?"

Annabelle pursed her lips. "Of course not, but—"

"I didn't tell him to propose to you, either. That was all his idea, so don't try to blame that bit of ridiculousness on me," Irene quipped.

"He told me that," Annabelle admitted and sat down on the edge of the bed directly across from Irene. "And it wasn't ridiculous at all. It was sweet. He's a very nice man."

Irene sniffed. "Apparently not sweet enough or nice enough to make you want to marry him someday when you're free again. You could do worse. It won't be easy for you, you know. Most men won't want to be bothered with you once they find out you're soiled goods."

"Irene!" she cried, horrified to have anyone refer to her as "soiled goods," let alone someone she thought was her friend.

"I didn't say *I* would. I said *they* would," the woman argued and shook her brush at Annabelle. "That's not the worst thing folks will think once they find out you couldn't even convince the man who loved you enough to marry you in the first place to stay married to you for longer than a few months."

"Irene!"

The housekeeper ignored Annabelle's outburst, set down her brush and shook out the cape. "There. The cape is almost as good as new again. All it took was a little hard work." Once she had the cape neatly folded, she set it back on top of the bed and looked directly at Annabelle. "You had the chance today to put all of this behind you, and I'm not talking about accepting Philip's marriage proposal. You could have stayed with Prudence at the boardinghouse, but you didn't. You came back here. Now are you going to stay and drop that pride you're wearing like a badge of honor long enough to tell Harrison that you love him and you're not leaving until he realizes he loves you, too?"

"I do love him," Annabelle admitted, "and I . . . I know he loves me, too, but it's . . . it's terribly complicated. I tried talking to Harrison today, but . . . please. Don't make this any harder for me or for him than it already is."

Irene walked around the bed and sat down next to Annabelle. She put her arm around her, held her close, and rocked her from side to side as Annabelle let the tears fall. "Sh-h-h. Don't cry. It's not your fault. Poor Harrison. He's so afraid of loving you, he can't let you stay. I know. I know," she crooned. "Don't worry. He'll discover all by himself that he can't live without you, but I'm afraid he'll be quite an old man by that time." She chuckled through her own tears. "If I have anything to say about it, I plan to be here to see it, even though I might be a hundred by then. Can I say something to him then about what an idiot he was to let you go?" she teased.

Annabelle sniffled. "You can tell him when you're a hundred and ten. But don't call him an idiot. Just tell him that I never loved anyone before in my entire life like I came to love him and never did again and that . . . that I spent the rest of my life still loving him. Can you do that for me?" she asked, grateful the friend she needed Irene to be was back again.

"I surely can," Irene pronounced. "Now let's talk about how soon you want me to get you back to that boardinghouse."

Chapter Thirty-Six

❄

Now that Bradley was about to be ensnared in the trap that had been set for him, all Harrison had to do was hope that the man was as desperate as he thought he was, if not equally stupid.

While he waited for Bradley to return to his hotel room on Thursday after arranging for the man to be sent out on a fool's errand an hour ago, he reviewed a mental checklist to make certain he had not forgotten anything. He sat in the one rickety chair in the room he had placed at an angle so Bradley would not see him until after he entered the room and closed the door. Within easy arm's reach, the documents Harrison had brought with him after rushing about this morning were neatly arranged in a specific order on top of the scarred dresser in the corner. Most importantly, Annabelle was safe at home at Graymoor Gardens, so he did not have to worry about her at all. The only thing he might regret later was involving Philip, although he had no one else he could trust as much as his cousin, who had no idea what Harrison was really doing today.

He was satisfied that the scheme he had reviewed with his lawyer before coming here was legal, albeit in the loosest interpretation of the law and ethically questionable. Before he wasted a single worry about what he would do if Bradley failed to show up, he heard footsteps approaching the door.

He concentrated on Annabelle's image to ease the tension wrapped tight around his chest. The moment he saw the door-knob begin to turn, he held his breath, and he did not exhale until Bradley had entered the room.

Once Bradley shut the door and finally saw that Harrison was sitting in his room, the man's eyeballs nearly popped out of his head. One of his cheeks began to twitch, and he took a step back.

"I know you were expecting my wife, but she's been detained rather indefinitely," Harrison offered and stood up. He nudged the chair with his foot to slide it across the planked floor. "Have a seat. I have a number of documents you need to read. Until you do, I'm afraid you're not free to leave. If you try, once you open the door, you'll see that there's someone now waiting at the top of the staircase down the hall who will convince you otherwise."

Reluctantly, Bradley sat down and offered no protest when Harrison told him to pick up the first document and read it. The man's hands were shaking so hard, Harrison wondered if any of the words were less than a total blur, but he appeared to read the document before he set it back into place. "All it states is that Annabelle's father, William Tyler, died a number of years ago. How could that possibly be of any interest to me?" he snapped.

Harrison folded his arms over his chest and fully intended to be perceived as a bully if that's what it took to guarantee this man's cooperation. "Pick up the second document and read it."

Bradley was sputtering by the time he finished reading the document and tossed it back onto the dresser without bother-ing to fold it. "Y-you actually got a sworn statement from the desk clerk to prove I used a dead man's name to register for this room? If this is some attempt to intimidate me or to convince me that I'll have to face charges for impersonating a dead man, then you've made a serious mistake. I'll have you know—"

"The mistake you made was to threaten my wife and to blackmail her," Harrison hissed and closed the distance between them. "That was a very, very serious mistake on your part."

Bradley's gaze hardened, but when he attempted to stand up, Harrison glared at him—hard—until he reluctantly sat down again. "You were more than just wrong to threaten Annabelle. You were very, very stupid, and I have little tolerance for stupid men, particularly when they interfere in my life in any way." He handed him the next document. "You can read this later. I don't need to take it with me. I have the original, along with ones for all the others. This document simply confirms that you opened a bank account at Hunterdon Bank some time ago under the name of William Tyler. It was signed by the bank president, who remembers you rather well, considering you were there just last week to make another deposit, as well as this morning," he said before he handed him the fourth document. "There's not much to read here. It's just a document stating that as of ten o'clock this morning, the funds in William Tyler's account increased by one thousand dollars, which is, oddly enough, the amount of the donation you told me you were going to make to the Refuge before you changed your mind."

"That's my wife's money," Bradley argued.

"Not anymore," Harrison said. "According to this next document, which declares that any and all residue remaining in the estate of William Tyler belongs to his sole surviving heir, Annabelle. The bank president was most accommodating in that regard, as well. After he closed that account, he transferred the funds immediately to an account I've established there in Annabelle's name. I won't bother you with the details of how I convinced him to cooperate, unless you insist," he added.

Bradley leaped to his feet, and his face was blister red. "That's my money. It's mine. You can't take it from me!"

"If you truly believe that, you can always hire a lawyer and sue me," Harrison offered calmly. "I'm quite certain your wife will not find it very entertaining to sit in court and listen to you explain why you've taken money from her and put it into an account under another man's name—a man who just happens to have been your former father-in-law. Annabelle has all the documents I need to prove exactly when you married her and when you divorced her, as well," he said coldly.

"If you honestly believe that your wife will be inclined to be understanding when she learns that she married a divorced man who claimed he had never been married before," he continued, "then you might want to consider what she'll think when she sees a note in your own handwriting demanding that the sum of ten thousand dollars be deposited in that very same account." Harrison pulled Bradley's note, which Annabelle had given to him, out of his pocket and held it up for Bradley to see before quickly storing it away again.

"But you can't—"

Harrison took a step closer until he was practically nose to nose with the man. He enjoyed looking down at him. "I can and I will. And if you ever so much as look in my wife's direction or tell anyone that you were once married to her, I will take every one of those documents straight to your wife. I believe I can easily convince her she should handle the matter instead of going to the authorities. For your son's sake, as well as the scandal that would ensue if she chose to divorce you, she may decide to remain married to you, but I suspect you'll never find your way into her good graces again. At the very least, you'll never get another coin from her for the rest of your life, which will hopefully be as miserable as she can possibly make it for you."

Clearly defeated, Bradley shook his head. "I can't believe you'd do all this for Annabelle. For *Annabelle?*"

"I'd do all this and more. And now I'll leave you to see what's in the final envelope," he replied and let himself out of the room. He joined Philip at the end of the hall and they descended the staircase together.

"Well? Were you able to convince Bradley to make the donation after all?" Philip asked innocently.

"I'm afraid not. It appears that Bradley has far less at his disposal than he led us to believe, but don't fret. Since you've won the wager we made, I'll make the one-thousand-dollar donation myself. I'll see you again late next week."

Anxious to get back to Annabelle to tell her that Bradley no longer posed a threat to either one of them, he walked outside and around the corner to where Graham was waiting with the coach to take him back to Graymoor Gardens. When he finally arrived home, he did not find her waiting for him in the parlor and took the main stairs two at a time. Pleased to find her door unlocked on the outside, he knocked softly. When she didn't answer, he knocked harder.

He called out her name and took half a step inside, but he could still see that she was not there. In fact, the room itself felt empty, as if she had never been there at all. With his heart pounding, he walked into the room, saw the note lying in the middle of her bed next to two small packages and the envelope containing her settlements funds, and his chest tightened with dread.

He did not have to count the settlement money inside of the envelope to know it was all there, so he picked up the smallest package instead. He knew by feel alone that it contained the two wedding rings he had bought for her.

Unprepared to see them quite yet or to think about what he planned to do with them, he set the package back onto the bed. When he opened the second package, he found himself staring into a mirror, looking at the face of a man who had lost the only woman who had ever laid claim to his heart before he had the opportunity to create one final memory when he bid her farewell.

He set the leather-framed mirror back on the top of the bed and opened the note that had been attached to the mirror:

My dearest Harrison,

While I am no longer a part of your life, I am leaving this small gift with you. If you ever doubt again that you are a man of great character, all you have to do is look into this mirror. When you do, you will see the man that I saw every time we sat and talked together—a man who has a giving heart and a caring spirit, who now shares his wealth with little encouragement from others and a man who is capable of being a valued friend.

I pray that you will remember me with great affection, for that is how I will always remember you, and place your trust in God who will love us and comfort us both during the difficult days ahead.

Annabelle

Grief-stricken, he closed his eyes and whispered her name, just once, before he accepted the reality that he would never see her again. He did not regret a single moment he had spent with her, but the pain of knowing those moments were gone forever was so great that he vowed to never make the mistake of falling in love again.

Never. Never. Never.

Chapter Thirty-Seven

❄

Learning to live with Annabelle had been hard enough, but living without her was proving more difficult with each passing hour.

Desperate to ease the gnawing pain that intensified with the dawn of each new day, Harrison threw himself with reckless fervor back into the life he had led before he met her—only to find that he found no pleasure in the entertainments he had always enjoyed with likeminded friends on Petty's Island.

He finally returned to Graymoor Gardens at midmorning a week later to embrace the pain completely, once and for all, in an attempt to finally end it. But he was more exhausted, broken in spirit, and heartsick than he had been before he had left.

Avoiding Irene entirely, he locked himself in Annabelle's room and gave Lotte instructions to leave his meals on a tray outside of the door. Surrounded by crushing memories, he sat in front of the fire and stared at Annabelle's empty chair. While their frank and open talks were often not easy for him, at least at first, he had learned what it was like to have a friend whose opinion he valued and whose character inspired him to improve his own.

It was the memory of Annabelle, simply Annabelle, however,

that haunted him the most. He could still envision her pale green eyes, alive with excitement as she shared her enthusiasm for the volunteer work she had done, or shadowed to a darker green by the scandal that wound around his name, rather than her own. He could hear her voice, encouraging him to share his talents and wealth with others, yet rejecting the settlement funds she rightly deserved.

But most of all, it was the deep and abiding faith that held her steady, even when he set her aside because he could not take the risk of loving her and keeping her in his life.

Although he had not been able to pray for years and had little interest in his faith until Annabelle walked into his life, it was nearing midnight when he was inexplicably drawn to the Bible she often read that was lying on the writing desk.

He picked it up and saw that she had left it open to the passage from Corinthians that she loved. He carried the Bible back with him and sat in front of the fire to read it, over and over, until it was as familiar to him as her beautiful face.

"Faith. Hope. And love," he murmured and flipped through the pages of the Bible. In the simplicity of those three little words, would he find the core of the faith that sustained Annabelle and actually claim it for himself?

When his fingers touched a page thicker than the others, he paused and worked his way back until he found it again near the center of the book. He had not seen this page before or realized that this particular Bible contained a record of his family that dated back to his great-great-grandfather, who settled in Philadelphia over one hundred fifty years ago. Marriages, births, and deaths were all listed in a variety of handwritings, and they testified to generation after generation of Graymoors who had made this city their home and claimed this faith as their own, as well.

Using the tips of his fingers, he traced the names of his parents, the older brother he could not remember, and his older brother

Peter, along with Peter's wife and two sons. Harrison's name and the date of his birth, however, stood alone, real testimony that the Graymoor family name would end with him.

He knew he had not updated the record to include the date of Peter's death, along with his wife and sons, and he dismissed the possibility that Irene was responsible. Even though she was just learning how to write, she would never have made those entries without his permission. Not in his family Bible. That left Annabelle as the obvious suspect, and he narrowed his gaze to study the record again.

She had not listed her name or the date of their marriage, which made sense, and he wondered if she had, would he have had the courage to make an entry noting the date of their divorce?

Deeply troubled, he juxtaposed the pain of living without her with the incredible risk he would take to love her and keep her as part of his life, inviting the pain that he knew only too well could follow. Either way, he would be hurt, and he could not decide which path to take or which hurt would be greater.

Desperate to find an answer to the dilemma he faced, he paged through the Bible until he found the passage in Corinthians again. He pressed his hand to the page, closed his eyes, and opened his heart to receive the love of God he had rejected for so long.

He whispered the passage he had memorized by now, word by word, over and over again. Finally, when his voice was hoarse and his spirit had been broken and bowed down to the will of God, his very soul filled with faith, with hope, and with a love so overpowering that he literally dropped down to his knees. And there he found the courage to do what he thought he had forgotten how to do: He prayed.

$e\!\sim$

After living at the boardinghouse for a week and swinging from despair one hour to hope the next, Annabelle finally came to accept that Harrison was not going to change his mind and keep her as part of his life.

After spending that same week working at the boardinghouse, she also knew she definitely did not want a similar position again anywhere else, regardless of how much it paid. It was nearly eleven o'clock again tonight before she had a new but late-arriving boarder settled into a room, and she collapsed into her own bed, which was actually the cot Widow Plum had once kept in the kitchen.

The elderly woman was extremely kind and the only saving grace to working here. Otherwise, Annabelle found the position so physically demanding that she ached from head to toe. Her hands were raw from scrubbing every room. Her back was sore from moving furniture and carrying loads of laundry up and down three floors on the only staircase in the house. Her entire body was stiff from overwork, but it was her broken heart that caused her real pain.

Unable to find a position on the cot that did not hurt some part of her body, she got up. Even though she was so exhausted she doubted she could get her eyes to focus properly, she lit the oil lamp and spread the newspaper out on the cot to see if there was a position posted today that had not appeared before.

She did not know how it happened, but the next thing Annabelle knew, it was dawn. She woke up with a start when she saw the newspaper spread out beneath her, but with little time before she had to help start breakfast, she did not bother to read the first page at all.

Instead, she opened the four-page paper searching for the section where she would find the notices for positions printed among other advertisements for various shops, available houses or land listed for sale, and the notice Widow Plum had posted three days ago announcing that her boardinghouse was now accepting new clients.

She caught a glimpse of something on the inside page that grabbed her attention, and she clapped her hand to her mouth to keep from squealing out loud while she read it:

> *Mr. and Mrs. Eric Bradley and their infant son, Daniel, recent esteemed visitors to our city, have departed for an extended holiday in Richmond, Virginia, where the weather is far more hospitable than we all are struggling to endure here. They expect to return in the spring to their home in New York City.*

"Harrison did it! He actually got Eric out of the city!" she whispered, and her heart lurched in her chest for want of being with him again.

Hopeful that God's plan for her life might become clearer to her today if she found at least one notice for a position far away from here, she quickly scanned the notices and squealed out loud this time when she saw a position she actually found appealing:

> *Widower moving west in March requires a mature woman of faith for housekeeping responsibilities and the care of four young children during journey and thereafter. Respond to this newspaper by 18 February and include references. M. L. Lerner*

"I could handle this position. I know I could." She quickly refolded the paper and stored it under her pillow. Even the prospect of providing references should not present a problem, assuming Irene and Widow Plum would be willing to vouch for her character as well as her willingness to work hard. She dismissed the idea of getting any kind of references for the work she had done at the Refuge as too risky for a host of reasons, and sighed. She had not even thought of doing volunteer work since she arrived here. She had not even picked up her knitting, for that matter, for the same reason: She had absolutely no free time.

Heartened by the fact she had finally found a notice for a

position that appealed to her, she closed her eyes to whisper a prayer of thanksgiving. She quickly said another to ask God to heal her broken heart and give her the strength and courage to follow the path He had set before her—a path that seemed to be leading her away from the man she still loved so deeply.

She arrived downstairs a little later than usual but she still managed to get to the kitchen before Widow Plum. Shivering, she added some wood to the cookstove to heat the room as well as to get it ready to use to make breakfast. She was pumping water into a pot to parboil some potatoes to fry before she remembered to whisper a prayer that Irene would come for another visit soon and bring the diary Annabelle had forgotten to pack.

Although she still could not fathom why she had not remembered to bring her diary, of all things, her heart was a little lighter knowing Irene would keep it safe until she was able to bring it to her. She took out a bowl and a sharp knife and set them onto the table before she lugged over a large sack of potatoes that needed peeling.

She had barely started her work when she heard a knock at the front door and hurried to answer it. "It's barely six o'clock. If boarders would take the time to read the notice in the newspaper more carefully, they'd know not to arrive before ten o'clock in the morning," she grumbled and opened the door.

"Wearing a face like that will send boarders in the other direction," Irene teased before stepping into the house.

Stupefied, Annabelle could scarcely believe her eyes. "What are you doing here again so soon and so early?"

"Coming to see you—and don't ask me how I got out of there so early. I don't quite believe it myself. I can only stay for a few minutes so I can get back home with Mr. Anderson's deliveryman before anyone finds out I'm gone. By the way, I finally found Jonah yesterday. Or I should say, he found me again. He's keeping company with another squirrel. Now I've got two critters to feed."

"Did you find my diary?" Annabelle asked as they passed through the dining room into the kitchen.

"I haven't been able to look for it. Harrison was back by the time I got home last night, and he'd already locked himself up in your room and told Lotte to leave his meals on a tray outside the door. Even if he decides to leave the room, he'll probably lock it up, and he's got the only key."

Alarmed, Annabelle helped Irene out of her coat. "He's in the same room as my diary?"

Irene waved away her distress. "That diary can't be in plain sight. Otherwise, you would have seen it, which means you wouldn't have forgotten it in the first place. In the second place, Peggy was the one who cleaned the room right after you left, and she didn't find it either, which means the diary is probably on the floor underneath your bed."

"How can you be so sure?"

"Because that's the only place it could be, and she doesn't usually clean underneath the beds. She complains it's too much trouble," she explained.

Unconvinced, Annabelle pressed her friend further. "Can't you get Alan to take the lock off the door so you can get inside?"

Frowning, Irene plopped herself down at the table, picked up the knife, and resumed the task Annabelle had just begun. "Not with Harrison in there. Besides, Alan's afraid of his own shadow. He wouldn't do anything unless Harrison told him he could. But don't worry. I have a plan."

"You usually do. Should I ask what that plan might be, or am I better off not knowing that, too?" she teased and took the flour and other ingredients out of the larder to start making up the dough for the biscuits Widow Plum wanted to serve with breakfast.

"As soon as I know exactly what it is, I'll let you know," Irene replied and her cheeks turned pink. "I'm not sure how I'll manage to do it yet, but I intend to take that lock off myself if I have to, get the diary out of your room, and put the lock back on again without anyone being the wiser." She set the potato she had peeled into the bowl and grabbed another one.

"As simple as that," Annabelle murmured and drew a deep breath. "How is Harrison doing? Really?"

"It's hard to tell, because I've only seen him once since you left. I think he blames me for helping you leave, even though he can't prove a thing, but I'm keeping my promise. I haven't uttered your name once. How are you faring? Anything interesting in the newspaper yet?"

Although Annabelle was dismayed to hear that Harrison was not faring well, she was so excited about what she had read in the newspaper this morning that she had to remeasure the flour she was doling into a bowl twice. She had the news about Eric leaving the city on the tip of her tongue before she realized Irene did not know anything about Eric at all. "I did find something today," she replied and quickly shared the details about the position. "I'll need references, of course, and I was hoping you would give me one. I know you're not up to writing words and sentences yet, but if you tell me what you want to say, I could write it down for you and have you sign it."

Irene's gaze grew troubled. "Are you sure this is what you want? It's only been a week. Harrison could still change his mind."

Annabelle blinked back tears. "Leaving is what's best for both of us. It's what he wants."

Sighing, Irene nodded. "Why don't you just write what you want and let me sign it. How soon did you say you had to reply to the notice?"

"By the eighteenth of February."

"Then we've only got nine or ten days. Write up that reference. I'll try to get back in a day or two to sign it." She put a third peeled potato into the bowl and grabbed her coat. "I'm sorry I have to leave so soon, but I have another errand I have to run. I'll see myself out," she said.

She planted a kiss on Annabelle's cheek before she walked out of the kitchen and well before Annabelle even had the chance to ask her what kind of errand she could possibly have at this early hour.

When Philip had not been waiting for her in the city earlier today, as they had originally planned, Irene returned to Graymoor Gardens and the news that Reverend Bingham had invited everyone to come to church on Saturday to see him married to one of Edward Cranshaw's daughters, Eliza.

Once she had supper started later in the afternoon, she put Lotte in charge of the kitchen and donned her coat. "I need a bit of fresh air. If anyone asks, tell them I needed to be alone for a while," she explained.

She walked along the pathway into the woods with a confidence that was rewarded when she found Philip sitting on the bench waiting for her.

He stood up the moment she approached. "I'm glad we had set up a second plan to meet here just in the case the first fell through. I'm sorry, but I just couldn't be there this morning to talk to you like I hoped I would."

"You're here now. That's all that counts," she said, and he sat down beside her once she had taken her seat. "We've got a bigger problem than I thought and little time to fix it," she offered. "Are you certain you're up to helping me set things right between Harrison and Annabelle?"

He let out a long sigh. "I've had time to think about what Annabelle said, and I can see now that she's right. We have no future together, but I still care about her enough to want to help her and my cousin to resolve their differences."

"That may take some doing," she said. "Harrison locked himself into her room yesterday and won't come out, and Annabelle found a notice for a position in the newspaper today. I had to agree to give her a reference, and I think Prudence will give her one, too."

He nodded. "Yes, I saw the notice. If I recall correctly, she has about ten days to reply to the notice. With references, she probably stands a good chance of securing the position."

"Which means we have little time to get Harrison to come to his senses."

"That won't be easy, since we both promised Annabelle we wouldn't say anything to Harrison to make him change his mind."

"That's true," Irene admitted. "I only have one promise I really can't break, but I wouldn't mind breaking the others. But I know I didn't promise her I wouldn't *do* anything. Did you?"

He furrowed his brow. "No, but—"

"Good," she pronounced with a slap to her thigh. "Harrison needs a nudge or two. I've got a couple of my own in mind, but I think you can do me one better, assuming it won't be a problem if Harrison gets really, really angry with you."

He chuckled. "I'm accustomed to it. Just tell me what you want me to do."

And she did. In great detail.

By the time she returned to the cottage, supper was ready to be served, but she decided to let Lotte leave Harrison's supper tray outside of his door and wait until morning to implement the plan she had worked out with Philip.

If all went well, Harrison and Annabelle would be back here together within a few days. Hopefully, they'd be so happy that they both would forgive her for manipulating their reunion. If not, she would simply have to find another way to bring those two young people to their senses.

Chapter Thirty-Eight

The pounding at his door woke Harrison up the next morning, but it was Irene's loud voice that startled him out of bed where the scent of summer roses that Annabelle favored still clung to her pillow and had soothed him to sleep only a few hours ago.

"Unlock this door, Harrison. That room you've been hiding in needs to be cleaned. I'm coming in to clean it, whether you like it or not. Don't make me stand here all day pounding on this door," she demanded and emphasized her words with a few solid hits at the door that sounded like she was using a mallet instead of her fist.

Too tired to argue with her, he picked up the Bible he had read during the night whenever he stumbled in his awkward attempts to pray and walked unsteadily to the door. He fumbled to slide the bolt free, opened the door, and stepped aside.

"I'm glad to see you haven't lost all your common sense. You'll only be in my way, so I've set a breakfast tray in the library for you. If I'm not finished by the time you're done eating, you can hide in there until I am." She entered the room carrying a scrub brush in one hand and a pail of water in the other.

When she looked up at him, she braced to a halt, sending water sloshing over the brim of the pail. "You look terrible," she said gently, but her eyes widened when she saw the book he was holding in his hands. "You're reading the Bible?"

"Just taking it back to the library," he offered, reluctant to tell her the truth when he had not quite come to terms with it himself. "I was paging through it when I found a page with my family history that I'd never seen before. Did you give Annabelle the dates to enter for Peter and his family?"

She nodded. "She said she thought it might be too upsetting for you to do. I asked her why she didn't add her name next to yours and the date you were married, but she said that it would be up to you to make that entry. I don't suppose it matters now that you don't want her anymore."

He blew out a long breath, unwilling to let Irene know that he was beginning to think he may have been wrong to do that. "I'll be in the library. Just knock when you're done cleaning up in here so I can come back, but leave the bedclothes. They don't need to be changed."

Once he sequestered himself in the library, he bypassed the tray of breakfast food Irene had set on top of the desk and put the Bible back onto the shelf where it belonged. His hand lingered on the spine of the book for a moment before he sat down at the desk. He polished off breakfast without really tasting anything.

When he noted his muted image staring back at him from the silver coffeepot in the center of the tray, he frowned. The stubble that covered his cheeks reminded him that he had not bothered to shave for days. His eyes were bloodshot from lack of sleep, and his hair was a knotted mess. "Irene's right. I do look terrible," he said, feeling a bit embarrassed that she had seen him so disheveled. He was grateful she could not see the turmoil that still plagued his spirit and troubled his soul any more than he could, but he felt it as clearly as he would have felt an infection raging through his body.

He glanced across the room and stared at the Bible he had placed on the shelf. Eventually, when his mind was on the verge of completely shutting down, he knew beyond all doubt that the only cure for the disease that had assaulted his spirit for years lay within the pages of that Bible . . . and his own willingness to open his heart wide enough to embrace the healing grace God offered to him.

Unfortunately, he was so tired at that point that he knew he would not be able to make his eyes focus on a single printed word until he got some sleep. He picked up the breakfast tray, set it on the floor outside of his door, and turned to go back into the library when Irene called out to him.

"You can go back into that room again."

He watched her walking toward him and was dismayed to see that she was carrying a basket filled with the linens she had removed from the bed. "I asked you not to change the bedclothes. They weren't soiled."

She waited until she was standing right in front of him before she replied. "No, they weren't, but it doesn't do you much good to sleep on these. They smell like summer roses," she said, motioning with the basket in her arms. "They'll only remind you of Annabelle. I'm certain that's the last thing you want to do, although anyone who loved her can still feel her presence everywhere in this house." She hoisted the basket from one hip to the other. "If that bothers you, you can always leave and move back to the city. The rest of us have to stay here and live with the fact that she's gone," she whispered and walked away.

Before the echo of her words had faded, he was back in Annabelle's room with the two things that kept him from returning to the city: his family Bible and the diary Annabelle had given him that he intended to start keeping very soon.

Early the next day, Harrison had just finished saying morning prayers, a ritual he wanted to make routine, when Irene knocked at his door.

"Get out of bed, get dressed, and eat some breakfast. I'm leaving it on a tray outside of your door. And don't dawdle. We're all leaving for church in an hour, and I'm not going to arrive late because you couldn't get ready in time."

He furrowed his brow. Unless he had completely lost track of the days, which was entirely possible, today was Saturday, and he had no idea why everyone would be getting ready for services that would not be held until tomorrow. He walked over to the door and opened it, just in time to see Irene reach the main staircase.

"It's Saturday. Why is everyone going to church?" he asked, not quite certain he could attend services in the church where he would be surrounded by more memories of Annabelle.

She looked down the hall at him and smiled. "Reverend Bingham sent word the day before yesterday that he's getting married today. Apparently, he's invited the entire congregation."

Absolutely certain the last thing he needed was to witness a couple exchanging their marriage vows, he squared his shoulders. "I'm not going to the church, but you can give Reverend Bingham my best regards," he said firmly.

To his surprise, Irene smiled at him. "I'll tell him, but I think I'll let him find out for himself that you don't have much respect for the institution of marriage. In all truth, I didn't really expect you'd want to go, so I invited Philip to represent you. I don't know how long we'll be, but I'll leave some dinner in the kitchen for you," she said sweetly before she walked away.

He was annoyed by her new ability to give him a lecture with words dripping with sweetness, but he was completely irritated that she had taken the liberty of inviting Philip to attend in his place. Too busy to waste time on such distractions, he shut his door and returned to the spiritual battle he thought he was beginning to win.

Several hours later, he got up from his knees and sat down in front of the fire. When he finally set the Bible aside, he felt completely at peace. He had never questioned the existence of God, but now that he had welcomed Him into his life and asked His forgiveness for going so far astray from the Word, Harrison was nearly ready to tackle an equally difficult task: asking Annabelle to forgive him, too.

Although he was not ready yet to ask her if she would be willing to consider becoming a permanent part of his life, he prayed he would soon be blessed with the courage to take that risk and fully believe God would help him keep his faith strong when life's troubles tested it. The best way he could think of to focus on the blessings he had already received would be to start recording them in his diary.

Before he started writing, however, he stopped long enough to walk out to the kitchen to get his dinner without worrying about seeing anyone else. He finished up a platter of sliced ham and corn relish that Irene had set out for him, but looked at the three desserts lined up on the other end of the table and wrinkled his nose. He did not know whether it was the plum pudding, the plum strudel, or the butter cookies topped with plum jam that was the most unappealing, but he bypassed them all.

Still hankering for something sweet, he gave up and started down the basement steps when he was struck by an idea. He bounded back up the steps and went outside without bothering with a coat. He had to search the woods for a good while before he found the size branch he wanted. Once he did, he went straight to the toolshed to get the proper tools before he hurried back to the cottage.

Once he was back in Annabelle's room, he locked the door behind him. He had not whittled a stick since he was a boy, but once he sat down and gave it a try, he was surprised at how quickly he remembered the techniques his older brother had taught him. He did not know how serviceable the implement he was making would be, any more than he knew if he would actually finish it. Still, the task was a way to keep focused on doing something with his hands, and he found the work cathartic.

It was late afternoon when he finished. His fingers only bore a couple of small cuts and nicks he barely felt, and he was not displeased with his efforts, in spite of the fact the final product was extremely crude.

He slipped the knitting stick into his pocket to keep a reminder of Annabelle close to him, but he did not bother to clean up the wood shavings on the floor. Instead, he walked straight to the lady's writing desk and picked up the diary he had brought with him from the library. As he walked over to his chair, he thumbed through the pages, wondering how long it would take to fill this diary, but stopped abruptly. The pages were not empty at all. Nearly all of them were filled with entries, and after he read just a few, he realized the handwriting belonged to Annabelle, who had made a daily record of the blessings she called her treasures.

Ashamed that he had invaded her most private thoughts, even inadvertently, he pressed the leather covers together and held it tight in his fist. Too late, he remembered that his diary was identical to hers, but he did not have to think very hard to know that it was Irene who must have switched the diaries. The only question he really had was how or why Annabelle had left her diary behind at all when it was so very important to her.

He put the diary back onto the writing desk and returned to sit by the fire. He deeply regretted reading several of the entries, but he was overwhelmed that his name appeared on nearly every one of them. If she once thought that he was a blessing to her, would she be able to think that again, in spite of what he had done to her? If he had the courage to ask her to come back to him, would she? Or would she send him away, unable to forgive him now and forever?

He took the knitting stick he had made out of his pocket and turned it over and over in his hands. He was lost in his own thoughts and torn with indecision when loud but familiar voices and pounding footsteps coming down the hall toward his room interrupted him.

"I told you to stay downstairs," Irene cried.

"I'm going to see my cousin, whether he wants to see me or not. I haven't done anything to be ashamed of, which is not something he can claim," Philip argued. "Annabelle shouldn't have to spend the rest of her life alone because he's a complete dolt."

"Are you daft? He'll strangle you with his own hands if he ever finds out you proposed to Annabelle," she argued. "You don't even know how long it will be before she's free to remarry."

"That's what I intend to find out. Right now."

Harrison charged to the door, had the bolt free before he felt the next heartbeat, and swung the door open so hard it hit the wall and would have bounced back to hit him if he had not caught it with his hand. He glared at his cousin, who was just within arm's reach, and he had to clench his fists to keep from slugging him right in the nose. "You proposed? You actually proposed? To my wife?" he snarled.

While Irene had the sense to back away, Philip took one step closer and glared back at him. "Why do you care? You obviously don't want her. At least I can sleep at night knowing I made an effort to find her and make sure she was all right after you decided to set her aside instead of hiding in my room like you have."

"I'm not hiding," Harrison gritted. He squared his shoulders. "Where is she?"

"If you really want to find her, you'll plumb have to do it without my help," Philip argued. "I just plumb promised her that I wouldn't tell you. Besides, I'm not going to let you spoil my chances of changing her mind any more than I'm going to give up asking her again and again until she plumb gives up and says yes."

Harrison looked past his cousin to Irene, who wore a guilt-ridden expression. "I can't tell you either, I plumb promised I wouldn't tell you, either, and you're plumb crazy if you think I'm going to break that promise. I already broke too many others."

Frustrated to the point of complete exasperation, he threw up his hands. "Stop being so fixated on the word *plum*! Just tell me where she is, and I promise you, she'll forgive you for breaking your promise, assuming she can forgive me for what I've done. But I can't even talk to her unless you tell me where she is."

Irene grinned. "You're a plumb smart man. If you truly want her badly enough, you'll figure it out," she replied and tugged on Philip's arm. "Come downstairs with me. I'll fix you up with some nice warm plum pudding. I learned how to make it just last week when I was visiting my friend in the city," she murmured, placing uncommon emphasis on the word *friend*.

Harrison slammed the door but only took a few steps before it hit him. "Widow Plum! She's staying with Widow Plum!" He grabbed the one thing he needed to take with him before he charged back into the hall.

Both Irene and Philip had disappeared from the second floor, but she was waiting for him when he reached the bottom of the stairs in the foyer. "Where do you think you're going?"

He grinned. "I've got a sudden hankering for plums."

She handed him his coat. "It's about time you figured it out. Graham is out front with the coach. Don't you dare come back without her."

"I don't intend to," he replied, filled with faith enough to believe he could convince her to stay.

Chapter Thirty-Nine

✻

Grateful that the boarders would not be returning for supper for another two hours, Annabelle left Widow Plum, who was dusting the furniture in the parlor, to change the bed linens in two of the sleeping rooms on the second floor. She climbed up the steep wooden staircase with a heavy heart and weary footsteps.

Unfortunately, the fog of despair that was clouding her faith today made it almost impossible for her to think about anything other than the pain of any future without Harrison. After setting the fresh bed linens on top of a trunk at the foot of the bed, she folded up the faded quilt, set it onto the trunk as well, stripped the soiled bedclothes, and laid them in a pile on the floor. *I wish I could change my life this easily*, she thought as she tucked in fresh sheets around the edge of the mattress.

Satisfied with her work, she picked up the soiled sheets, unaware that she was dragging one on the floor until she tripped and fell to her knees. Although her one knee landed on top of the bundled sheets, her other knee cracked hard enough on the bare floorboards to bring tears to her eyes. The impact opened the floodgates she had been guarding all day, and once she started to cry, she simply could not stop and she had to bury her face in the sheets she was carrying to silence the sobs that made her body tremble and her spirit flood with grief.

When the spring that provided her tears finally drained, she wiped her face and got back to her feet. Exhausted, she also felt oddly refreshed, but she knew her tears would be replenished long before she would be able to hold them back again. She limped for a few steps to test out her knee and sighed with relief. The last thing she needed was to injure herself now when she had to convince someone to hire her.

She had just stripped the soiled bedclothes from the bed in the room across the hall when she heard Widow Plum call out her name. "Annabelle, dear. You have a caller."

"I'll be right there," she said, excited that Irene had returned so soon for a visit. She was also pleased that she had already written out the reference for Irene to sign and quickly finished restoring the bed to order.

Though her vision was nearly blocked, Annabelle was determined to carry both sets of soiled bedclothes downstairs. She held on to the banister with one hand as she shifted the bundle of sheets so she would not trip down the steps.

Descending carefully, she peeked above the mound of linens and her heart practically stopped. Harrison was standing at the bottom of the stairs. She tightened her hold on the banister when he took the first step without taking his eyes off of her.

"You forgot something, so I thought I should bring it to you," he said quietly.

She swallowed hard. With the sheets blocking all but his face, she could not see what he was carrying in his hand. She trembled to think he had found her diary, but the possibility that he had read it made her knees weak. "You can give the diary to Widow Plum to hold for me," she whispered, hoping he would leave before she lost her dignity and begged him to stay.

He took another step. "Widow Plum is in the kitchen, and your diary is safe back at Graymoor Gardens. This is something else entirely."

She could not imagine she had left anything else behind, but before she could tell him that, he was one step higher on the staircase and close enough now that she could see that his eyes were gazing at her with the same deep affection she had hidden from him for so long.

Her heart began to race when he took the next three steps, stopping when his face was level with hers. After he gently removed the sheets from her hands and tossed them over the banister, he placed a wooden object into her hand, and from the cuts on the tips of his fingers, she knew he had made it for her.

Through tear-filled eyes, she glanced down and saw a very crudely made knitting stick that made her heart swell the moment she saw her first name engraved down the center. Her fingers were trembling so hard, she had a difficult time turning the knitting stick over. On the back, she saw her name engraved above the year 1832.

She struggled to find her voice. "Is this . . . is this a courtship gift?" she asked, overwhelmed by the possibility that he might want her to be a part of his life.

His dark eyes glistened when he captured her gaze and held it captive. "Only if our courtship is short. Very, very short," he said. "I love you, Annabelle. I was so very, very wrong to think I could ever live without you. I want you to know that I've made my peace with God, and I know now that He never stopped loving me or watching over me, even when I turned my back on Him. And I also trust that He will love us and comfort us, no matter what troubles life has in store for us." Harrison took one more step.

"Marry me, Annabelle. Today. Tomorrow. Or as soon as you're ready to forgive me. However long it takes, I'll wait for you to—"

"Today. Today will be perfect," she whispered and stepped

into his open arms where she belonged, her spirit soaring straight to the heavens. She wrapped her arms around the most treasured blessing He had ever given to her and held on to him with all of her might, her tears falling freely as she felt his heart beat against her own for the very first time.

Acknowledgments

❄

I have been blessed again to receive great support during the writing of *Hidden Affections*, and I have many people to thank. As always, my editor, Sarah Long, helped me to fine-tune the story idea as well as the manuscript. Thank you, Sarah, for your generous spirit and your valuable insight. Linda Kruger, my faithful, faith-filled agent, gave me the idea to have a heroine and hero handcuffed together in my next book. I hope I haven't disappointed you, Linda. My sister, Carol Beth, once again allowed me to spend the summer writing in her home on Anna Maria Island in Florida. I love you, sister dear! And to the lovely ladies at Shell Point, you made my summer very special once again.

Author Note

❄

Hidden Affections takes place in and around Philadelphia, Pennsylvania, during the winter of 1831–1832. I have tried to stay true to the area as it existed in the early nineteenth century, but I have used my "literary license" to create the background for my story.

The city and port of Philadelphia, for example, actually were frozen during the winter of 1841–1842, from early November until the middle of May. Outbreaks of yellow fever and cholera epidemics, unfortunately, occurred periodically, but I moved them around to keep them in the background of the story. Petty's Island actually exists, although the rowdy behavior that took place there is dated a bit later.

The fictional country estate of Graymoor Gardens is loosely based on an actual house, The Solitude, which was built by William Penn's grandson in 1784. The tunnel at The Solitude still exists and is historically significant because it is a rare example of perhaps the first tunnel in the United States that was built to be used by servants. The Solitude is still standing on the grounds of the Philadelphia Zoo, and groups of visitors can arrange for a tour. Readers who are interested in The Solitude can take a virtual tour by visiting the Philadelphia Zoo website: *http://www. philadelphiazoo.org/zoo/Visit-The-Zoo/The-Solitude-House.htm*.

Readers who are interested in the history of Philadelphia can find lots of fascinating information in two books that I used for my research: *Philadelphia: A 300-Year History* by the Barra Foundation (1982) and *Imagining Philadelphia: Travelers' Views of the City from 1800 to the Present* by Philip Stevick (1996).

Several Web sites also provided historical information that was quite helpful. I am grateful to Yossie Silverman (*www.black-steel.com*) and Stan Willis (*www.handcuffs.US.com*) for their help in understanding what Darby handcuffs looked like and how they worked. My colleague, Mrs. Christine Wilson, shared her knowledge of knitting with me, but I found an actual knitting stick that women used long ago so they could knit while "on the go" at *www.needled.wordpress.com/2010/01/21/sticks*. I encourage readers to visit to see Jane Brown's knitting stick, which is dated for 1825, and also ask for their forgiveness for any mistakes I may have made while creating *Hidden Affections*.

Delia Parr

More Heartwarming Romance from Delia Parr

When Jackson Smith, a young and handsome widower, offers his housekeeper something quite out of the ordinary, can Ellie look beyond mere necessity and risk opening her heart?

Hearts Awakening

Using an assumed name, Ruth Livingston seeks solace and safety in a small East Coast town, where she meets the mysterious Jake Spencer. But is their growing affection for each other enough to overcome the secrets that separate them?

Love's First Bloom